The Downward Path

The Perizidon Series

Book Two

Matthew D. Moore

ISBN (hardcover): 979-8-9898754-2-9
ISBN (e-book): 979-8-9898754-3-6
Library of Congress Control Number: 2025922930

First hardcover edition November 2025
First e-book edition November 2025

Editing by Shannon Cave (reedsy.com)
Cover Art by Lisa Dunaway
Map by Catherine Pallotta

Printed and Published by MD Moore through IngramSpark
Indianapolis, IN USA

To Christine, for everything you do for me and the family;

To Jonathan and Rachel, for taking pieces of me and making them better parts of your unique and wonderful selves;

To Shane, who creates and writes about better characters than I do on a daily basis;

To Lisa, Matt, Rob, and others for greatly appreciated reviews and feedback on the manuscript;

To Kim, for keeping me sane and not throwing pens at me even when I deserve it;

And to my sister, Deborah, who is just crazy awesome.

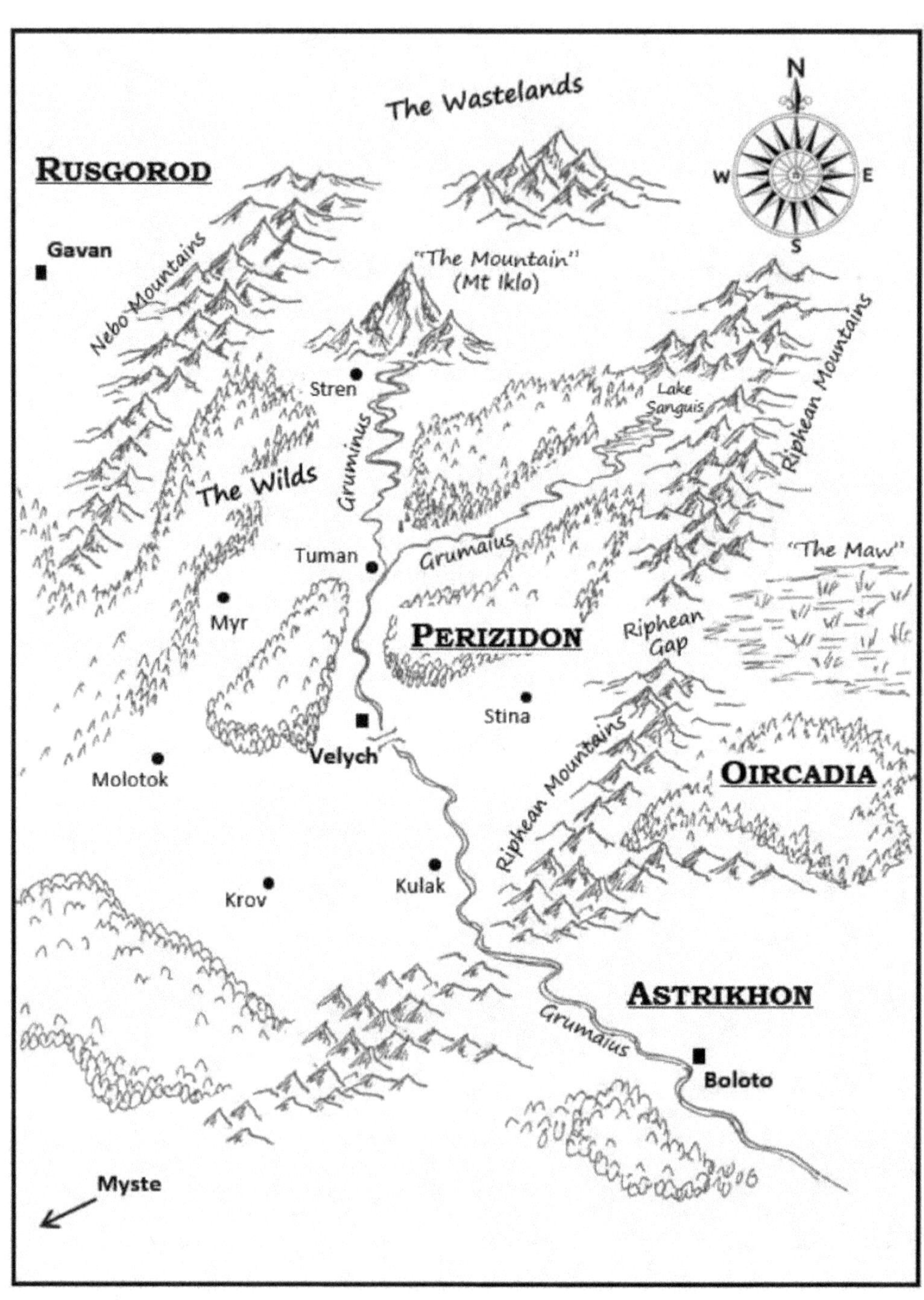

The Wastelands
RUSGOROD
Gavan
Nebo Mountains
"The Mountain"
(Mt Iklo)
N
W
E
S
Stren
Gruminus
Lake Sanguis
Ripheam Mountains
The Wilds
Tuman
Grumaius
"The Maw"
Myr
PERIZIDON
Riphean Gap
Stina
Velych
Molotok
Riphean Mountains
OIRCADIA
Kulak
Krov
ASTRIKHON
Grumaius
Boloto
Myste

PROLOGUE

The Inquisitor: A Backstory

The Most Reverend Basil Melnik, Archbishop of Myste, rubbed his eyes and attempted to focus his thoughts on the problem at hand. His flock was becoming more upset with the inquisitor's apparent inaction with every passing day, and he was beginning to regret his decision to request help from the Holy See. What he thought would be a perfunctory review of a murder case had turned into a full-scale investigation.

The people are right to be annoyed with the delay. That demanding woman and her "methods of observation" will be the death of me! Can she not see the truth as it has been laid out in front of her?

He sighed heavily, crossed himself, and got up from the kneeling position at the side of his bed. The inquisitor nominally reported to him, although things grew murky with church hierarchy where the inquisition was concerned. While he didn't want to outright order her to wrap things up, he had to know if she was close to rendering a verdict. And he had just decided that he needed to know tonight.

If she is no closer to a decision, I must impress upon her that time is running out. But she knows this already, so why does she dither?

Basil left his sleeping quarters, proceeding at a quick pace through the rectory and then outside. It was after Compline, and most souls would be in bed soon. However, he knew that the inquisitor would still be working in the abbey's library where she had spent the past several days conducting interviews. It was only a short distance away, and the cool night air invigorated him as he walked and thought about who he was going to see.

It's not as though she's been insulting or overly physical with anyone. But I know most people feel unsettled around her, if only because of those grey eyes of hers. It's like they're looking directly into your soul.

Not that Basil personally had anything to hide from her, of course. It was just hard to remember this fact when in her presence.

When he reached the library, Basil continued his quick pace through the atrium towards the main reading room on the ground floor. Moirne Koval was indeed sitting at the long table in the back of the room, various items spread around her. She was writing quickly in a small ledger, and as he approached, she glanced up at him and nodded curtly.

"Just a moment, Your Excellency."

Basil was not used to being kept waiting, but given the circumstances, chose not to be indignant. He strode to the ornate chair at the head of the table and sat down, taking in the scene before him. The room was well lit, and he could study the profile of the inquisitor with relative ease.

Moirne was a handsome woman, perhaps in her early thirties, with short jet-black hair and a strong jawline. She had wide shoulders, and while of slender build, he guessed she had a military background by the way she carried herself. It was not uncommon for inquisitors to rise from the ranks of one of the various armies in the region, being released from one service to that of a higher calling.

In Basil's experience, most inquisitors who came to the church in this manner were a bit on the brutish side. Of course, a zealous nature for upholding the Word of the Almighty One was an easy excuse for violence against the heretical.

Or those merely accused of heresy, if the rumors are to be believed.

Basil immediately admonished himself for thinking ill of Moirne's character. To date, any military upbringing she might have had only showed itself in her expectation that her orders would be followed.

The table they were now both seated at held a cornucopia of items. A book on anatomy, a map of the city, a sketch of the floorplan of a large building, and several bladed weapons of varying size were scattered about the inquisitor. There were also several clumps of herbs and flowers, as well as some carrots.

Basil could make very little sense of why the inquisitor had assembled all the various items, although the weapons did include the dagger that had been found embedded in the corpse. It had a very small blade, barely larger than a letter opener. He wasn't sure why the rest of the weaponry was there, noticing with some surprise that the inquisitor's own sword was part of the collection.

In the short time she had been at the abbey, he had never seen her without it strapped to her side.

Moirne continued writing for *much* longer than "just a moment" should imply, and Basil was getting annoyed by the time she finally finished and rose from her chair.

She faced him and formally bowed. "My apologies, Your Excellency. I was not expecting you, and you caught me mid-thought. I had to capture a certain point in my report before it escaped me."

Basil waved her apology away while cocking his head slightly to the side. "Your report? Does this mean you have reached a verdict?"

"I have, Your Excellency."

Thank the Almighty One!

It was all he could do to not smile widely in relief. "So, you will render a final judgment in the morning?"

"No, Your Excellency. I have already sent for my suspect, so that I may interview them immediately. However, I consider this a mere formality, as I plan to arrest them and charge them with the murder of Lady Toth's lady-in-waiting. Tonight."

Basil was confused. He blinked and shook his head. "Your suspect?"

But the accused was arrested almost a month ago; Brother Ezekyel sits in his cell even now. What is she going on about?

Moirne gave a small smile at his muted reaction. "I understand this may seem a tad confusing. I assure you, Your

Excellency, that my methods are sound, and my mind is certain. I will, of course, allow the suspect to plead their case. And if you had not sought me out tonight, I would have requested an audience first thing in the morning to provide you with a full briefing. As it is, you are most welcome to stay for the interview and draw your own conclusions."

Basil frowned. "Who, may I ask, is being brought in?"

"Lady Varissa Toth herself, Your—"

"*What?!*" Basil jumped to his feet, hands at his face. "By all that is holy, what have you done?"

"My job, Your Excellency." Her tone was even and her gaze firm.

She has gone too far by half. And it was me who brought her here. I will never hear the end of this at court!

The room and his world shrank inward as Basil fell back into his chair, too shocked to speak further. He sat motionless for several moments, his head bowed in thought. After a time, he stirred and looked at the contents of the table again, vainly searching for whatever links the items had formed in the chain of thoughts that had led the inquisitor to her conclusions.

Why in the Almighty's holy name would Lady Toth murder her own servant?

Finally, he looked at Moirne, more confused than angry. "I...I do not understand, Inquisitor."

She bowed to him again, a bit more gracefully this time. "I realize this may all seem rash, Your Excellency, but time was of the essence. I know the local populace grows weary of my presence. I also realize the forty days of sanctuary for Brother Ezekyel, as odd as that concept may be in this particular case, are close to expiring. But, most importantly, it became known to me that Lord and Lady Toth are departing for parts unknown in a day or two, meaning I have little time left to interrogate and incarcerate the baroness. Hence my late night and my rude use of your library."

She thinks I care about her use of the library! And yet, she hasn't said why she is accusing the baroness.

"We may grow weary of your investigation, Inquisitor, but that is only because the Almighty has already shown us who the murderer is! To my everlasting shame, Brother Ezekyel only awaits final judgment before being turned over to the city magistrate for the prescribed death by hanging for murderers. I only requested the inquisition's presence to show impartiality and to ensure the taint of the abyss does not extend to others within the confines of these walls."

"A praiseworthy move, Your Excellency, to be sure. Your courage and intuition to have the inquisition involved in this investigation will be duly noted in my report." If there was any sarcasm embedded within her statement, Moirne managed to remove any hint of it.

"My point being, Inquisitor, is that there is no one else to accuse! *Especially* Lady Toth!"

There was the sound of someone running down the hallway, and an instant later, a young acolyte entered the room. He had an excited look on his face, and he addressed Moirne directly.

"Inquisitor, your men are returning with— Oh, a thousand pardons, Your Excellency!" He noticed and then bowed deeply to Basil, who only stared at him in return.

Moirne glanced at Basil before addressing the young man directly. "Thank you, Petr. If you please, fetch some mulled wine and several cups for our guests. I am sure they will be somewhat chilled after their walk to the abbey."

"As you command, Inquisitor!" Petr bowed and raced out of the room as quickly as he had come.

Moirne cocked her head, listening intently, before addressing Basil. "Lady Toth and her escort are indeed almost here. I must beg Your Excellency to but observe and allow me to proceed as I see fit. I shall bear full responsibility for my actions, both to the doge of Myste and the Holy See."

Even as she was speaking, Basil could hear a commotion outside the room, as several voices were doing their best to talk over each other as they approached. He instantly recognized the deep bass of the baron, and he took the accompanying tenor to be the inquisitor's second-in-command. He did not hear the baroness but assumed she was with the two men. The argument seemed to be about the group's destination.

A mixture of soldiers appeared in the doorway, and it was unclear who was guarding whom. Basil was quick to note that, while the baron's men had numbers in their favor, the inquisitor's men looked more dangerous.

Each of the holy soldiers wore a small golden brooch above their heart, an encircled *crux decussata* that looked like a sideways "X" to the uninformed. The brooch and the hilts of their swords were the only visible colors on them, as they were swathed in the dull metal-grey armor and black uniforms of the inquisition from head to toe. They contrasted wildly with the House of Toth guard uniforms, a sky-blue coat of arms emblazoned upon a silver breastplate. The tension between the two groups was palpable as they entered the room.

Baron Angvar Toth and his wife, Varissa, walked in together, squarely in the middle of the turmoil created by the soldiers. He was of medium build with a full beard the color of brimstone, while her petite figure was almost overtaken by the long black braid that extended down her back. She was clearly his junior; Basil knew the age difference to be over twenty years. The baron was red-faced as he continued to harangue the tall, slender, dark-skinned man next to him.

"Damnit, man, you said we were going to see the archbishop! I ask you again, then why are we not going to the rectory? Why are we—" He broke off as he noticed who was in the room.

Without missing a beat, the man escorting the baron and his wife began to announce them. "Most Reverend Melnik, Inquisitor Koval, may I present to you the Right Honorable—"

"They bloody know who we are!" Angvar cut off the inquisitor's man with a wave of his hand. He then bowed deeply to

Basil, who had stood up when the large party entered the room. The baroness timed her curtsy perfectly to match her husband's movements as he continued speaking in a loud voice.

"Your Excellency! We came as soon as we heard you had called for us. No matter the hour, the Holy Church may rely on the House of Toth!" He pointedly ignored the inquisitor.

"But I…" Basil looked at the two courtiers in bewilderment. *What is he babbling about? I never sent for them!*

Moirne stepped forward, bowing her head quickly to the baron. "The Holy Church welcomes all true friends, my lord, and it is greatly appreciated that you came with such haste at this late hour. We have not been directly introduced. I am Inquisitor Moirne Koval, and I requested the presence of Lady Toth on behalf of the archbishop so that I might finalize my report on the death of her lady-in-waiting."

Basil frowned but decided to say nothing aloud.

What insolence! What would she say if I wasn't present? Very well, I will honor her request and let her proceed at her own pace, but she is, indeed, on her own now.

"You mean, her *murder*," the baroness said icily in response to the inquisitor's greeting. For as late as the hour was, her hair and dress were impeccable. However, she had dark circles under her eyes, as if she had not been sleeping well.

Moirne quickly bowed to her as well. "My sincere apologies, Lady Toth. Her *murder*. I have but a few details to confirm with you, and I had rather hoped a minor inconvenience tonight would be better than a major inconvenience tomorrow as you attempt to leave on holiday."

"Well, we're here now, so ask your questions and be done with it." The baron folded his arms across his chest. He, too, was finely dressed, almost as if he were ready for a hunt.

"Of course, my lord. Also, please know this most assuredly is not a formal inquiry. It is just that the weight of Lady Toth's words will do much to corroborate the statements of others."

The inquisitor half turned, and then with a pained expression, faced the baron again. "A thousand apologies, my lord, but the questions I must ask are somewhat private in nature. For discretion's sake, I will order my retinue to leave the room. Might I humbly request that you also dismiss your house guards?"

The baron looked at Basil, who smiled and nodded in favor of the inquisitor's request.

Yes, fewer ears now will mean fewer wagging tongues later.

Angvar frowned but glanced at his captain, jerking his head towards the door. "Don't go too far. This won't take long."

Both sets of soldiers started towards the door, the uneasy truce between them continuing to hold. As the tall, slender man also made to leave, Moirne called out first to him and then to the acolyte who had just returned with a tray of drinks.

"Uriel, fetch a chair for Lady Toth before you go. Petr, you have impeccable timing. Offer the lord and lady some wine to warm themselves while I retrieve my notes." Moirne then made herself busy at the table for several moments, altogether appearing as if she was ignoring the goings-on around her.

By the time the inquisitor stepped forward, journal in hand, the baroness had accepted a chair but not a drink. She sat with her hands folded in her lap, and the baron stood next to her with cup in hand. All the soldiers had cleared the room, and Uriel was just closing the door behind him as he left.

Seeing that everyone was settled in place, Basil sat back down in his chair, waving Petr away when offered a drink. The acolyte, clearly not knowing what to do, set his tray on the table and then slowly backed up towards the wall, as if trying to blend into the background.

Basil saw that the inquisitor's man had placed the chair Lady Toth was sitting in near the center of the room, away from the door and any other furniture. She would have been isolated from everyone else if her husband had not chosen to stand beside her.

Not a formal inquiry? Ha! He watched closely but quietly as Moirne took a few steps towards the couple and calmly addressed them both.

"My lord and my lady, I have taken great pains to not trouble you directly during my investigation, seeing as how the primary suspect is already in custody and my role is quite perfunctory in nature. I have completed my interviews, and I only wish to clear up some very minor details directly with you."

Lady Toth said nothing. Lord Toth muttered under his breath, "The *only* suspect is more like it," and made a *hurry it up* motion with his free hand.

Moirne smiled curtly and continued, looking at her journal. "So, to recount the basic facts of the case. Anna Molnar of Myste, lady-in-waiting to Baroness Varissa Toth, was found dead—*murdered*—approximately two hours after Compline on the 21st of Quintilis, some twenty-nine days ago. The body was found lying in the hallway that runs between the kitchen and servants' living quarters in the Toth family manor. Your summer quarters, I believe?"

She looked up briefly, receiving a small nod of confirmation from the baroness, before resuming her summary.

"None other than Baron Angvar Toth discovered the body, and the family's personal physician was immediately summoned to the scene. Cause of death was determined to be a single stab wound to the heart. The weapon was still embedded in the victim's body at the time of its discovery. This"—Moirne turned and briefly held aloft the dagger before returning it to the table—"is the identified murder weapon."

Lady Toth bowed her head, her fingers tightening slightly around each other. Lord Toth had finished his wine and was looking around for more. Before he could make any demands, Petr picked up the pitcher from the table and hurried over to refill his cup.

Seemingly unfazed by the minor disturbance, Moirne continued. "The physician also found a rosary clutched in the victim's right hand with an archaic *crux immissa* attached to it. The rosary, or rather, the crucifix, was traced to Brother Ezekyel Nagy of

Myste, who was immediately taken into custody, despite professing his innocence. All he would reveal upon initial questioning was that he was planning on leaving the monastic order, Anna had promised herself in marriage to him, and he had given the crucifix in question to her as a gift several years ago. He would *not* confess to the crime of murder."

Moirne paused briefly, as if she was reading a private note to herself, before turning the page in her journal and continuing her accounting of the facts.

"Brother Ezekyel claimed sanctuary upon his arrest, as was his right under church law. It was decreed by His Excellency, Archbishop Basil Melnik, that Brother Ezekyel would be confined to his monastic cell for forty days or until the inquisition could be summoned to pass final judgment, whichever occurred first. Anna was buried on the 25th of Quintilis, and without the ability to perform last rites for her soul, we offer prayer and supplication that her time in purgatory will be short."

Everyone crossed themselves, including the baron, as Moirne looked up from her notes.

"Those are the primary details of the case as they were provided to me upon my arrival a week ago. This information has since been corroborated by all that I have interviewed, with the sole holdout being that Brother Ezekyel has continued to maintain his innocence. Until this afternoon, that is."

Lady Toth looked up sharply, her shoulders shaking slightly. "What do you mean, Inquisitor?"

Moirne's voice was calm as she answered the baroness. "I mean that Brother Ezekyel has acknowledged the mortal sin he committed, and I have obtained a full confession from him."

The baron snorted. "Then I owe you an apology, Inquisitor! I couldn't understand why we didn't lynch the bastard the instant he was apprehended, especially when all the facts pointed to him being such a heinous monster. But now that you've beaten a full confession out of him, he is truly damned! That poor girl will surely enter heaven someday, but he will burn in the abyss for all eternity!"

"Yes, well..." Moirne cleared her throat. "If I may, there is still the small matter of a few questions that I have for Lady Toth about the case."

"Of course! By the Almighty, ask away!" Angvar's demeanor had become downright jovial upon hearing about the monk's confession, and he motioned to Petr to refill his cup once more.

Basil, on the other hand, wept internally at the baron's display and the admission of guilt by Brother Ezekyel.

One should not find joy in the damnation of others. We should all pray for Ezekyel's forgiveness and redemption surely as we pray for our own. We are all nothing but lost sheep crying out for the good shepherd.

Oh, my boy, my poor boy! I did not realize how lost you were. What drove you to such madness?

Moirne looked at the baroness. "My lady, did you know of Anna's marriage plans?"

Lady Toth shifted slightly in her seat. "Yes, she had confessed her feelings about...that boy...to me some time ago. They had grown up together and had been inseparable in their youth. He joined the church when she was promised to someone else, a wealthy merchant whose name escapes me. However, the merchant recently died while traveling in Oircadia. When...that boy...made it known that his feelings for Anna had not changed, she reciprocated in kind. As Anna's parents had passed away, she looked to me to bless the union."

"But you did not bless it?" Moirne prompted after a moment of silence.

The baroness frowned and shook her head. "I did not. I will admit that I selfishly did not want to lose her, as she was impeccable in her service to me. But I also did not trust...that boy...or his intentions. I cannot speak as to why, only that, unfortunately, my misgivings were borne out by events. In the end, I lost my dear Anna anyway."

"I am sorry to ask such a question, my lady, but I must establish motive. Was Anna going to tell the, uh, suspect of your decision the night of her murder?"

Lady Toth studied the ground in front of her for a time before replying softly, "I presume so. I knew they met on occasion, and I had ordered her to put an end to that as well." The baroness suddenly looked up at Basil. "I should have come to you, Your Excellency. But in my vanity, I thought I could handle such affairs directly. That...that *monster*...must have killed her out of spite when she told him that she would no longer see him."

Moirne was rapidly taking notes in her journal as the baroness spoke. When she was caught up, she turned towards the baron and bowed slightly. "My lord, I must confess that I was surprised to hear it was you who discovered the body, given the time of day and its location."

She had caught Angvar taking yet another drink, and it was a moment before he could respond. "Hmm? Oh, well, I always walk around the house before turning in. You know, uh, to check the locks. I only wish I had started my rounds earlier that night so I could have scared that little bastard off before he did anything."

"I see. And you take the same route every night?"

Angvar didn't seem to notice that the inquisitor's line of questioning had shifted to him. Instead, he merely looked puzzled. "Yes, I suppose I do," he replied after a short pause.

The inquisitor made another note, but she seemed confused about his response. "My lord, might I ask where you were coming from when you found the body?"

"Eh? What does that have to do with anything?"

"I am merely trying to create a full timeline of events. If you can tell me where you were coming from, or where you were headed, I may be able to determine when and how Ezekyel entered your house without being noticed."

"Oh. Well, I don't recall. All I remember is turning the corner and seeing the girl's body slumped against the wall. It was such a shock, and I stood there for a—"

"Which corner, my lord?"

"What?"

"Beg pardon, my lord, which corner did you turn? In which direction were you walking?"

All good cheer drained from Angvar's face. He was obviously not used to being interrupted, much less being asked such direct questions. "It matters not!" he snapped.

Moirne persisted, her tone becoming more strident. "I am afraid it does, my lord. You see, apparently the entire household knew of Ezekyel's visits to see Anna, but I have yet to find a witness who saw him at your manor on the evening of the murder. I need to ascertain his exact movements so I can determine who is lying and whether they are an accomplice in this crime of passion. I have the location of everyone else who is relevant to the case. I only need to know your path of travel. Can you not provide me with this simple information?"

"Do not use that tone with me, Inquisitor! You forget yourself!"

In a sudden tantrum, the baron threw his mug to the floor. Both his wife and Basil jumped at the sound, as the small vessel cracked upon the stones, leaving several large shards and a small pool of wine in its wake.

Moirne continued to look calmly at Angvar, as if sizing him up. He was breathing heavily now, staring wildly back at her.

"I tell you again, that it matters not! The *only* thing that matters is that the life of an innocent girl was taken! I found her grievously wounded, just moments after that sarding piece of shite had performed his foul deed! What more is there to know? *Nothing!* But here you stand, wasting our time and blathering on about nonsensical matters!"

The inquisitor had an amused look on her face, as if she had thought of a humorous rebuttal.

"How much liquid do you think was in that cup you just threw to the floor, my lord?"

Her question made absolutely no sense to Basil, and he did not appear to be alone in his confusion. Angvar's eyes bulged, and he spluttered rapidly, as if he could not comprehend the language that the inquisitor was using. "What?!"

"A gill? Half a pint? Let us be charitable to Petr's pouring and say half a pint. Now, how much blood would you wager is in a normal person's body?"

The baron balled his fists. "Why do you think I give a cobbler's damn about that, you insufferable cunt of a woman!"

Basil rose to protest the man's insulting language, but the inquisitor's voice firmly overrode whatever he was going to say.

"Would you believe, my lord, that an adult body can hold over a gallon of blood? Perhaps even half again?" She motioned to Petr as she spoke. "Sirrah, would you be so kind as to bring your tray of drinks over here?"

Petr, pale-faced, quickly crossed over to where Moirne was standing while she placed her journal on the table. She bowed slightly to him in gratitude then took one cup from the several on the tray. She motioned at the baron, as if toasting his health, and then slowly and inexplicably poured the contents of the cup onto the floor.

There was a shocked silence in the room except for the splashing of liquid. Small rivulets formed among the stones, and the wine slowly spread out from where the inquisitor was standing, creeping ever closer to where the baroness was sitting.

Basil had remained standing, completely perplexed at Moirne's actions. The baroness seemed to be frozen in time, wordlessly staring at the inquisitor. The baron looked to be apoplectic, and it took a moment for him to find his voice.

"Well, Inquisitor," Angvar finally sneered, "besides the wasting of yet more wine, what are you—" But he cut himself off with a curse as Moirne suddenly seized the pitcher from the tray and threw it to the ground.

The clay vessel shattered into a thousand pieces, its contents erupting out in every direction, splattering everyone.

"How dare you! How dare you attack us in such a manner!" the baron screeched. He immediately advanced towards Moirne, yelling at Basil. "Your Excellency, you will remove this unholy bitch from our presence *immediately*, or by the Almighty, I shall strike her down where she stands!"

He moved to grab the inquisitor, but before anyone else could react, Moirne shifted her stance with the precision of a boxer and cuffed him on the face so that he stumbled past her.

Roaring in anger and embarrassment, Angvar pivoted and

swung wildly at her. Grabbing his arm, Moirne used his own weight against him and easily threw him to the floor. He landed hard, his face making direct contact with the wet stones. He remained where he fell, stunned into submission.

Basil found himself rooted in place, not quite comprehending the events unfolding before him. There were sounds of commotion on the other side of the door, and he assumed the baron's guards had heard his cries and were attempting to come to his aid. However, no one entered the room.

Meanwhile, the inquisitor seemed to be ignoring everyone and everything except the baroness. "Where was the blood, my lady?" Moirne spoke in an even tone as she rolled her shoulders, as if the quick fight had been part of some exercise regimen. She gestured at the baron, who was motionless on the floor. "Lord Toth lies face down in roughly half a gallon of red wine. See how it spreads? See how it stains? If your lady-in-waiting was murdered where your husband says she was, where was the blood that must have been spilled from her body?"

Lady Toth's face twitched as she looked at her wine-spattered clothes, then her husband, and finally the inquisitor. She struggled to maintain her composure. "I...I assume it was cleaned up?"

"So thoroughly that no one in your household remembers seeing any blood upon the floor after the body was removed? Or even *before* it was removed, for that matter? Also, there is no stain left to be observed in the hallway. I have walked it myself to be sure."

The baroness blinked rapidly but appeared to be at a loss for words.

Basil, attempting to gain control of the situation, blurted out, "Come now, Inquisitor! As you have stated, the weapon was still embedded in Anna's body when it was found. Though deadly, it is quite small. Could it have acted like how a cork acts for a bottle of wine?"

He felt the weight of the inquisitor's grey eyes fall upon him and immediately wished he had kept his mouth shut as Moirne had requested.

He finished somewhat meekly, "I mean, perhaps the liquid was merely stoppered up within the vessel, so to speak."

The inquisitor answered him calmly enough. "Perhaps, Your Excellency. It is a fair point to make. Except that I believe the death blow was not as small as we were led to believe."

"What? How would you come to think that?"

"Because I examined the body myself, immediately after I had it exhumed."

"You *what*?" Basil was incredulous. "Of all the—"

Now the grey eyes flashed dangerously, and she cut him off with a look. "All holy rites were observed, Your Excellency. I am no ghoul. But you will be interested to know that the young lady's throat had been slit, almost from ear to ear. There would have been much blood spilled upon her death, methinks even more than what is presently represented here by the wine."

Basil stared at her, starting to understand what she was alleging but not able to bring himself to say it. Finally, almost in a whisper, he asked, "Meaning?"

"Meaning that I have come to the conclusion that Lord and Lady Toth have lied about both the manner and the location of the murder in question!"

***

Moirne watched as Basil fell back into his chair, his hands gripping the arms of it, as if to hold on to something tangible. Lady Toth was frozen in place, her face a mixture of anger and fear. Petr, still standing near the table and holding the tray of drinks, stared seemingly with pure awe at Moirne and her investigative prowess.

Ah, Dear Moirne...one part of your trap is sprung, but do not allow pride to blind you from the final truth.

Moirne walked over to where the baron lay on the floor, still motionless. Deftly, she drew his sword from its sheath. She could tell that it matched one of the weapons on the table, which she had obtained from one of his house guards during an earlier interrogation. However, if the baron's sword had been used in the murder, it had long since been cleaned and polished.

Lady Toth suddenly stirred, as if she had made up her mind about something. As Moirne turned to look at her, she cleared her throat and took out a handkerchief to daub her eyes. There was a forlorn, almost helpless look to her, as she addressed the archbishop.

"Your Excellency, I would confess my sins. I...I have been

complicit with many atrocities my husband has committed against the Almighty and Nature itself. I have shielded his behavior for many years, to the ruination of my name and now to the murder of my friend. I...I cannot go on living these lies."

Tears streamed down her face, and she made no attempt to brush them away.

Interesting...you would play this to the end. Well then, let us hear what you have to say before your husband regains consciousness.

Before Moirne could speak, the archbishop stirred in his seat. "Lady Toth, do you mean to say that it was *your husband* who murdered poor Anna?"

Lady Toth closed her eyes and slowly nodded an affirmative to Basil's question. The archbishop glanced over at Moirne with something of a confused look, and she attempted to be noncommittal in her reaction.

"Let us hear what Lady Toth has to say, Your Excellency."

I am very interested in what she has to say...

The baroness opened her eyes, focusing on the archbishop as she sat up straighter in her chair. She took a deep breath and then plunged forward, words spilling out of her.

"Your Excellency, the baron was having carnal relations with my Anna, for how long I do not know. She confessed this to me the day before she was murdered, and she swore to me that he was...that he was forcing himself upon her. Making her perform terrible acts. That he hurt her and warned her that he would kill her if she said anything to anyone. She implored me to believe that she had never willingly let him lie with her. And I did believe her."

She looked down at her husband, now trembling with rage as more tears formed in her eyes. "Sadly, I know intimately what this *beast* can do. If he had kept his cruel acts to our wedding bed, I would have borne it. But to do those things to another... No! I could not allow it!

"I told her we would face him together. He is a bully and a coward, and he could not stand against us. You see how quickly he falls against someone with strength of will! The pain and suffering would end, for both me and my Anna.

"I did not care where he went or what he did. He could join either a circus or a crusade, for all it mattered. He would leave, and his wealth would be ours as recompense. I would care for my Anna, and she would want for nothing. This was the fairy tale that I concocted for her."

Lady Toth paused to wipe the tears from her face with her handkerchief. "Anna was so brave to come to me. Because of me, my friend is dead! Because of me, my friend was *murdered*!"

The baroness spoke the last word with pure venom and then, gasping for air, bent over as she attempted to regain control of her emotions.

The room was silent as she composed herself. No noise came from the hallway, and even the fire in the hearth across the room had ceased its hissing and crackling.

When she continued, her voice was very small and barely

filled the vacuum. "He...he killed her in front of me. I...I must have blacked out, because the next thing I knew, he was standing over me, her blood dripping off his sword onto my face. I was so frightened. I *am* so frightened..."

Basil had been listening to her with lips drawn tight, his hands holding his rosary as he subconsciously fingered the prayer beads. Now he stood and slowly advanced across the room until he was even with the baroness. He then kneeled beside her and took her hand in his.

Even though she had asked him to remain apart from the interrogation, Moirne did not move to intercede. Instead, she bit her lip and remained silent as Basil spoke.

"Lady Toth, surely you know the church would have protected you if you had come to us. To me."

She shook her head slowly, lightly scoffing at his statement. "My word against his? I mean no offense, Your Excellency, but I find it highly unlikely you would have believed me. Regardless, he threatened the lives of our children if I said but one word to anyone. I could not risk losing them."

"I see. And the, uh, incident, it did not take place in the hallway as the inquisitor has concluded?"

"No, it did not. It happened in my dressing chamber. The blood stain that the inquisitor seeks is hidden under a new rug."

"And why would your husband pick Brother Ezekyel as his scapegoat?"

The baroness raised her shoulders in a helpless shrug.

"What I said about Ezekyel's relationship with Anna was true enough. They did grow up together, and he was heartbroken when she was promised to another. Recently, he had been coming around quite frequently. I suspect she confided in him, as well as me. Lord Toth probably did not want to take any chances that Ezekyel knew the truth and arranged that he be accused of the crime."

"And the rosary beads? Were they somehow planted on her body?"

"They were a family heirloom that Ezekyel gave Anna when he entered the monastery. She always had them with her. It would have been easy enough to put them in her hands if they were not already there."

"Thank you, my dear." Basil blessed her and then rose. He turned to Moirne, looking much older than just an hour before. "I am indeed grateful that you have discovered the truth, Inquisitor Koval. You have shown me much that I did not see."

Moirne bowed in appreciation, but not for the compliment the archbishop had given her.

I think he does your job better than you do, Dear Moirne. Perhaps he should become part of your retinue. But let us see if he asks the right question next.

She nonchalantly offered the baron's sword to Petr, who, after half a beat, took it and placed it gingerly on the table with the rest of the weapons.

The archbishop was walking back to his chair but stopped mid-stride. "But...But then I do not understand, Inquisitor, why

Brother Ezekyel would confess to this murder. Did he conspire with the baron?"

Moirne smiled at him, as he had indeed asked the right question. "I did not say he admitted to murdering the poor girl."

"But you said—"

Her smile vanished instantly. "I said that he confessed to a mortal sin. The mortal sin in question being adultery with Lady Varissa Toth."

The baron was starting to stir but remained on the floor, oblivious to the accusations made by and against his wife. The archbishop, stunned into silence once more, merely stared at Moirne. She ignored both men, shifting her gaze instead to Lady Toth. The baroness, ashen-faced, stared beyond Moirne, her focus somewhere far away.

Moirne took a few steps to stand directly in front of the seated woman before addressing her formally. "Lady Toth, do you confess to the sin of adultery?"

She stirred and looked up, defiance pulsing through her very being. "No! No, I shall not! It is the monk's word against mine!"

"I agree with you, my lady. Allow me then to read you some of his words."

Moirne went back to the table to retrieve her journal and thumbed through it briefly before arriving at the passage she was looking for. She turned to the archbishop, who still had a dazed look on his face.

"This is part of the confession I obtained from Brother

Ezekyel Nagy earlier today, in which he provided details of his carnal relationship with one Lady Varissa Toth."

Moirne glanced over at the baroness, ready to give her one last chance to maintain a modicum of modesty. Nothing but sullen silence was given in return. Shaking her head, Moirne began to read.

"The third occurrence took place on or about the 8th of Quintilis, late in the afternoon, but prior to Vespers. Lady Toth had sent for me using our prearranged signal, and I easily gained entry through the side door of the manor and up the back stairway to the lady's bedchambers. There, the baroness awaited me, naked except for a thin bed covering, and she had me fall upon her immediately, such was her lust."

The baroness bristled with anger. "Nothing but sordid, twisted lies! Those words are pure fantasy! There is no actual proof that monster has been with me!"

The archbishop had begun to shake, and Moirne looked up when she noticed his reaction. She knew from other discussions that he had never been good at handling the more depraved tendencies of his flock. She paused for a moment, then flipped a few pages ahead before continuing.

"On the contrary, my lady. Brother Ezekyel provided quite minute details of the encounter that can be physically confirmed if you insist upon the matter. Suffice it to say that he had ample opportunity to take note of several moles on your lower back, as well as an oddly shaped birthmark near your—"

"Enough! You understand nothing!" Lady Toth gripped her chair with both hands. Her face was filled with rage as she stared at Moirne.

Moirne had nothing but contempt for the baroness, and it showed in her voice. "What I understand is that you are a liar and an unreliable witness, who distorts the truth in their favor!"

"I am nothing of the—"

"*Silence*, deceiver!"

The command echoed around the room, and Lady Toth fell back in her chair as if she had been struck. All the fight went out of her immediately, and she said nothing else.

Moirne turned to address the archbishop. "As I told you earlier, Your Excellency, I have come to suspect that Lady Toth is the actual murderess, not her husband as she has just alleged. That will need to be adjudicated in a civil court. Nevertheless, there is sufficient evidence and testimony for me to unequivocally state that Brother Ezekyel Nagy is *not* the murderer of Anna Molnar. He is to be released from his cell immediately."

Basil looked like he was going to cry tears of joy, and he wordlessly looked to the heavens. Petr was staring unabashedly at her again, but Moirne's immediate attention was taken up by the baron, who had finally sat upright.

Angvar's nose was bleeding and obviously broken from the fall, and he winced as he touched it with his left hand. His pantaloons were soaked with wine, and the blood from his nose mingled with the red stain that had blossomed on his white tunic.

He looked altogether confused as to how he had wound up in his current state.

Before he could gather himself further, Moirne quickly stepped to the door of the library. Opening it, she found Uriel standing guard, sword in hand.

He looked over his shoulder at her, his long coal-black hair rippling with the movement. "My lady, is everything all right? I heard some fireworks."

"It is done, Uriel. Fetch your shackles; I require two sets."

"As you wish, my lady."

"Any troubles with Lord Toth's guards?" She looked up and down the hallway and saw nobody else.

He grinned. "Nothing we couldn't handle, my lady."

"Thank you, Uriel. Have the men detain them a bit longer. Quickly now on those shackles, as there may be some additional fireworks before our task is complete."

"Yes, my lady. I shall return at once!" The slender man loped down the corridor as Moirne turned away.

Lord Toth had managed to get himself into a kneeling position, and he glowered at her as she walked back towards him. "You spineless coward! What have you done to my wife?"

Spineless coward, indeed! It was all Moirne could do to keep from smirking. "Ah, Lord Toth. How good of you to rejoin us. You have been accused of murder. How do you plead?"

"What nonsense is this? What lunatic accuses me of such a thing?"

"Your wife, Lord Toth. Along with other inferred crimes, such as serial rape, marital rape, and adultery."

The baron opened and closed his mouth, but no sounds came from him as he stared at the motionless Lady Toth.

"I will personally add to your list of crimes to include attempted assault of a clergy person and deception. There are probably a few more I could list, but it matters little right now. I will be turning both you and your wife over to the city jailer in just a moment, as this case is no longer in the purview of the church."

As Moirne finished speaking, her second-in-command appeared in the doorway, and she glanced in his direction to confirm he had brought the shackles she had requested. She noted with satisfaction that, in addition to the shackles, Uriel had also brought rope, gags, and hoods.

"To the abyss with you, bitch!" the baron hissed, and he struggled to his feet. He had spied his sword on the table, next to the acolyte, and made for it. Petr stood frozen in fear, only to be shoved to the ground by the older man.

Lord Toth took up his weapon and whirled around to face Moirne. He waved the sword menacingly, coming dangerously close to striking the poor acolyte, who now lay prostrate on the ground in front of him.

"You won't have either of us! You'll hang for what you have done, I swear by the Almighty that—"

"*Enough!*" Moirne shouted at him. "The Almighty has already forsaken you!"

Suddenly there was a low hum in the room, and the fire sprang to life, fanning itself upwards and out from the hearth.

Angvar was rooted in place, seemingly out of fear. Moirne slowly advanced towards him, the air sparking around the periphery of her vision, the sounds of a tempest growing ever louder. She could feel holy power coursing through her body.

"You dare raise a weapon against me, *worm*? I should strike you down where you stand!"

She was close enough now that she could grab the baron by his tunic. He shrieked in terror as she did so, and she lifted him with ease off the floor so that his feet kicked helplessly in the air.

"See what awaits those who abandon the ways of the Almighty!" She allowed her grey eyes to go blank, showing the baron the nothingness of the ether. The man went limp in her arms as she levitated above the floor in the middle of the maelstrom.

The fire roared as if from the abyss itself, and there was a thunderclap that shook the room. The chair that Lady Toth was sitting on exploded, and she was thrown to the ground, unconscious.

Slowly, the noise and confusion abated. The fire burned low again.

Moirne stood in the middle of the room, the emptiness consuming her. She continued to hold the baron's motionless body for a brief moment before allowing it to slowly sink to the floor. His sword clattered harmlessly to the floor next to him.

I should have you strung up in the morning, but that is out of my hands now.

Uriel had remained standing at the door throughout the ordeal, and he had something of a look of satisfaction on his face as Moirne motioned him forward. Without speaking, he immediately went to work on binding the motionless lord and lady.

Only now did Moirne look at the other people in the room. Petr was whimpering softly, his eyes closed and on his knees in prayer. Meanwhile, the archbishop had slumped to the floor at the foot of his chair. He had seemingly been rendered unconscious by the tumult.

Moirne approached the acolyte and placed a gentle but firm hand on his shoulder. Slowly, he opened his eyes to look at her, and she smiled as a mother would to her frightened child. Petr looked around as if to make sure he was still among the living before giving her a weak smile in response.

Sensing the boy was both mentally and physically sound, Moirne grasped him by both shoulders and hauled him to his feet. "It seems you are none the worse for wear, Petr. Good lad! You are hardier than most, and I am glad you were here to bear witness to what was said and done."

"Most Reverend Mother, ask of me anything, and I shall do it! I would follow you until the end of my days!" He bowed over her hands, shaking in adulation.

Moirne swallowed hard at this but managed to maintain her outward good humor as her inner voice whispered at her. *He is indeed yours if you command him, Dear Moirne. But, no, let him be a child for a bit longer.*

"Anything, hmm? Well, Petr, you should be careful to whom you say that; you never know what they would have you do." She grasped his chin and slowly raised his head until she could look him in the eyes once more. "Be one with the Almighty and continue to serve the archbishop well. Pray thoughtfully and deeply about whether you wish to become an initiate. And be at peace. That is all I ask of you, Petr. For now, at least."

"As you wish, Most Reverend Mother." He trembled beneath her gaze.

She smiled at him again and winked. "Just Inquisitor, Petr. Just Inquisitor. Now, please, go see what you can do for His Excellency."

She could see that the archbishop had stirred and was now also knelt in prayer, feverishly working his rosary beads. Giving Petr a final pat on the shoulder, Moirne went to retrieve her journal from where it had been blown against the far wall. Once she had it, she went directly to sit at the table and began to write her notes of the proceedings.

When she looked up after a bit, Petr had gotten the archbishop back into his chair and was attempting to clean up some of the debris that the fire had shot into the room. The old man was looking at her, respect and awe that had not been there before showing in his demeanor. When she acknowledged him, he bowed his head in deference.

"If I may, Inquisitor Koval, I have a few questions."

Realizing the questions would be sensitive in nature, Moirne looked over at the acolyte. "Petr, leave that mess alone for now. If you could find where Lord Toth's guards are being held by my men and bring them a bit of sustenance. We should not treat them unkindly."

Clearly disappointed that he was being dismissed, Petr nonetheless bowed to both of his elders and left the room.

Moirne waited until the boy was gone before she answered the archbishop directly. "Please go ahead, Your Excellency."

Basil cleared his throat. "My first question is this: for the poor girl, Anna, why was such a grievous wound not discovered at the time of the murder?"

Moirne answered him with a question of her own. "Who actually saw the body before it was buried?"

"Well, Lord and Lady Toth, of course, and their personal physician. I, along with several of the local clergy, observed the girl when they prepared her for burial, and we—" His eyes widened with sudden clarity. "Ah, may the Almighty strike me down for my foolishness! I remember now, the body was shrouded and already in the casket when we arrived!"

Moirne nodded. "I thought as much. You are a good and decent man, Your Excellency, and the Toths knew you would have no reason to look under the shroud. As for the physician, when faced with a choice between his master's coin and his maker's damnation, he gave up the former to be spared the latter. I have a signed confession from him regarding the totality of the wounds inflicted upon Anna."

The archbishop motioned at the table. "I believe that I now understand the maps and diagrams and what you were looking for with them. Same with the weapons you have collected. But, out of curiosity, why is your sword on the table? Why were you unarmed for the encounter?"

Moirne allowed herself a sense of satisfaction. "My reasons were twofold, Your Excellency. One, to act as an assurance to any suspect that I meet with them openly and that they are not walking into an immediate fight. And two, to lull them into a false sense of security. As you saw, the baron was quite certain he could take me in a fight. He is not the first brute I have schooled, and I doubt he will be the last."

"I see. And the anatomy book, is that where you learned about the volume of blood inside a person?"

"Mmm, yes, Your Excellency."

"And the plants?" He looked at them more closely. "Good heavens, is that monkshood?"

Moirne nodded. "You know your species, Your Excellency. I picked that plant and the other specimens in the fields around the city. I must confess that, before I saw Anna's body, I was initially thinking the girl had been poisoned, with the knife wound applied later to act as cover. I was also worried that Brother Ezekyel might be poisoned before he could be properly interrogated. If that was planned, I am glad it was not successful."

"And the carrots?"

"My dinner," she deadpanned.

The archbishop stared at her for a moment and then chuckled. His shoulders relaxed slightly, and Moirne sensed that the stress he had been carrying was beginning to melt away.

Uriel had completed his task while they were talking, and he bowed to Moirne when she looked over at him. He had, perhaps out of some personal chivalric code, bound Lady Toth's hands loosely in front of her instead of behind like her husband's hands were bound. He had propped up both courtiers in a sitting position against the far wall, and there was slight movement from under both hoods. They were at least breathing, if not fully conscious.

Moirne was not concerned about either dying before their time. Uriel was an expert at keeping people alive until there was no longer a need to do so.

"Thank you, Uriel. Have Cedric and two others join you here and have the rest of the men release the baron's guards. They are to be told that their lord and lady remain here tonight as guests of the inquisition and that they are to return to their barracks and await instructions. Anyone who protests is more than welcome to stay as guests themselves. I will speak to their house steward in the morning."

Uriel bowed and silently left the room. Moirne noticed with some amusement that he took the baron's sword with him, as if it was a souvenir of the evening's events.

The archbishop had been listening intently, and now he looked at the two unconscious forms. "What is next for them?"

"They are no longer our concern, Your Excellency, at least from a criminal perspective. Since Brother Ezekyel has been cleared of any wrongdoing in the murder, that charge and everything else I have discovered can be given to the city magistrate to review and rule upon."

Basil looked somewhat concerned. "But, Inquisitor. The lord and lady both seem to be guilty of various mortal sins beyond the murder charge. Shouldn't the church maintain a presence in their overall judgment?"

"You and your office certainly may, Your Excellency, at your discretion. But my duty is done here. I will leave you a copy of all my notes, and you may use them as you see fit. It will not surprise me if you wish to excommunicate both of them. I will say this, however. I believe Lady Toth when she says her husband forced himself upon her lady-in-waiting. Based upon my examination of the deceased, there is no doubt that the poor girl was forced into multiple acts of cruel depravity."

Sadly, it would not surprise me if there were many other nameless victims of the baron over the years. But that cannot be proven, and I must resist insinuating more than I know.

Basil rapidly clasped and unclasped his hands but said nothing as Moirne continued.

"Because of this, Your Excellency, I truly believe Lord Toth is the greater evil of the two. An evil that preys on women."

The archbishop shifted slightly in his seat "Do you think him possessed? Should we not perform an exorcism?"

Moirne shook her head. "If only it were that simple, Your Excellency."

"You consider an exorcism simple?" Basil sounded incredulous.

"My apologies. An exorcism is certainly not simple to perform. I merely mean it would be a straightforward resolution to a straightforward problem. It would be easy to dismiss Lord Toth's behavior as merely being possessed by the Unholy One. No, he is just a man, with much to unpack as to why he acts as he does if we had the need or the desire to do so. Just a man, but an evil man beyond redemption."

The archbishop frowned at her last remark. "I do not believe anyone is truly beyond redemption, Inquisitor."

Moirne considered this briefly. "Then your flock is truly blessed, Your Excellency, as they have you to fight for their souls with full conviction. Lord Toth will pay for his crimes, but through your office, you can ensure he is given a chance to confess his many sins and seek forgiveness from the Almighty. The same with Lady Toth, as you deem necessary."

"Thank you, Inquisitor. My own soul will rest easier knowing this."

Uriel reentered the room, followed by three other soldiers. At Moirne's signal, they walked over to the two prisoners to take them away. Both were ragdolls in the soldiers' arms and had to be dragged out of the library.

Since the abbey did not have a prison, or even a basement,

they would be taken directly to the municipal prison. Moirne had made sure the city magistrate had known he would be receiving at least one prisoner tonight. She briefly pondered any local repercussions that might befall her or the church as the two courtiers disappeared from view.

With luck, their identification will remain a secret until the morning. An argument in favor of using the hoods, at least. If they are recognized by their clothing, so be it. Regardless, Basil should not fear any retribution from other courtiers for my presence or my ruling, given how minor the baron's role has been since falling out of the royal court's favor last year. If anyone cares he is in prison, it will be the debt collectors.

Basil had made no sign of leaving, and he stirred once more when he and Moirne were alone again. The fire was beginning to burn low, and the shadows crept in from the corners of the room as he spoke.

"One last subject this evening, Inquisitor Koval, if I may?"

"Yes, I imagine you wish to discuss the fate of Brother Ezekyel."

"It is as if you read my mind." The archbishop chuckled nervously.

"Your Excellency, he is technically guilty of single adultery and potentially sodomy. Unlike the Toths, we must look at his sins through the lens of the monastic vows he took. Chastity, poverty, obedience, and stability. I wager he has broken two, if not three, of these vows."

Basil sighed. "I know what you say is true, Inquisitor. He will be released from his cell, but he will be thrown out of the order as well."

Moirne studied the archbishop in the growing darkness. *You may be naïve, but you try to do what is right. Does that not count for anything?*

She paused a moment before sharing what she knew he had been hiding all along. "Your Excellency, I know that the boy is your kin through your sister."

His profile rocked slowly back and forth in the gloom. "That is a closely guarded secret, Inquisitor. I showed him no favoritism, but I know how it would look if our kinship became public knowledge. He was to be transferred in the spring, once his initiation period was over. But he is completely distraught over the death of the girl, and I do not know what to do with him. I dare not show him mercy if others would not receive the same in kind."

Moirne understood better than the archbishop knew. She had interviewed Ezekyel's mother and knew of the boy's suicidal thoughts.

There are already too many victims in this affair, Dear Moirne.

She knew what she had to do.

"Give him to me, Your Excellency. I will care for him."

"You...you would do that for him? For me?"

"I cannot promise a leisurely road; there will be hard and dangerous work, with little thanks from either me or those we toil for. Such is the life in my retinue. But he will be looked after and instructed in the ways of the church. And he will be far from here, where there are too many hard memories."

"But what of his mortal sin? His penance?"

Moirne smiled softly in the growing darkness. "We are all sinners of one sort or another, Your Excellency. But as you say, all deserve a chance at redemption. I will work to determine how his soul can be saved."

The old man reached out and took her hand in his. He squeezed it tightly and firmly. "Bless you, Inquisitor Koval. I will have him join you in the morning."

***

After the archbishop had taken his leave, Moirne sat in the darkness for some time. By now, the embers in the fireplace were dull points of light, but she made no effort to rekindle the blaze. She had enjoyed watching fires as a child, imagining the shooting sparks to be souls on their way to heaven.

What must I do to recapture that feeling? That faith of the innocent?

She sighed inwardly. Basil had obviously done the right thing in requesting outside assistance, especially given the original implication that one of the church's own was the guilty party. No doubt, the Toths had counted on the Holy See wanting to cover up things as quickly as possible and avoid asking too many questions. What bothered her was that the entire local clergy had been all too eager to accept that one of their own had done something as appalling as brutally murdering a young woman. None of them had thought of looking for another viable solution.

There should be more to any investigation than just praying for heavenly intercession!

There was a stirring to her left, and the faint smell of cinnamon told her that she was no longer alone.

"My goodness, my lady, what are you doing in here all alone in the dark? Ruminating on this evening's events, I suppose?"

"Leave me alone, Uriel."

"Ah, you know you cannot just wish me away, my lady. Besides, I wanted to congratulate you. I was listening in most of the time, and your handling of the situation tonight was masterful."

"Pfft! Situation indeed. A suspected love triangle that turned into a terrible abuse case! You could have warned me!"

"I know, I know, you hate surprises. But you know there are certain things I am not allowed to do. I did warn you about the impending departure of Lord and Lady Toth, didn't I? Although, I admit even I was surprised to see them dressed for travel tonight. They obviously had moved up their schedule yet again."

Moirne just sat in the dark and said nothing in return.

After a bit, Uriel coughed politely. "I see you have taken on a new project?"

"Yes, and you are hereby tasked to keep that boy alive until he realizes love is fleeting."

"Oh my, you really are in a sour mood. Nevertheless, I accept the challenge. To keep him alive, I mean. He will need to make up his own mind about love."

"Fine."

"Um...it is unfortunate about Anna, is it not?"

Moirne sighed. "Yes...most unfortunate."

"Do you think they really would have run off together and lived happily ever after? After all that had happened to them? After what they witnessed and what they endured?"

"What do you think? Or do you know?"

"No, I don't know, my lady. As I've told you before, all the results from any one choice are known before they occur, but once one door is opened, all the other doors leading from a decision are closed and forgotten. Less confusing that way. Also, I asked you first."

She stewed on the matter for some time before answering. "I would like to think they would have been happy together."

"I don't know that to be certain, but I will agree with you. Ah, you see? There is some hope left in you, after all!"

Moirne let loose with an exasperated curse. "God's nails, Uriel, why are you so vexatious?"

"Please don't say that. You know it hurts. I apologize for attempting to bring some good cheer to you."

"If you really want to bring me some good cheer, tell me I did right by Lady Toth!"

"Ah, Lady Toth. The true victim."

Moirne grimaced. "Indeed, the true victim. So much suffering at the hands of that monster of a husband. I wish I had seen it sooner than I did, and I did what I could for her. But there was only so much I could do, especially with the archbishop in the room."

"Mmm, yes. His decision to show up right before the interrogation was not supposed to happen. It was fortunate he was too embarrassed to push you on why Lady Toth and Ezekyel were having relations with each other."

"Yes, I know."

"And...you are at peace with her potentially being sentenced as a murderess?"

Moirne chewed her lip for a long moment and then sighed deeply. "I will ensure the city magistrate has my notes and recommendation. And regardless, she has many other crimes to answer for. But I truly believe she was not of sane mind when she killed Anna."

"But what would drive a human to do such a thing?"

Moirne sighed again. "Desperation? Misplaced passion, perhaps? She obviously knew of Ezekyel's meetings with Anna and had the chance to speak with him privately on numerous occasions. Perhaps he was merely kind to her, and she fell for him. Perhaps she was jealous of the true love she saw and acted out of spite."

"Perhaps the two women enjoyed his company together, and she did not want it to end?" Uriel's tone was lighthearted, and it felt wholly out of place to Moirne.

"You are too much by half! Do not place that image in my mind, and do not speak ill of the dead!"

"My apologies, my lady. I suppose we will never know the true reason."

"With time, Ezekyel may confess more fully to what has transpired over the past several months. Regardless, I believe Lady Toth could not bear the thought of Anna escaping from Lord Toth while she remained trapped. I suspect the baron may have thrown this very fact in her face, causing her to finally snap."

"Such a repulsive fellow. Still, the less our gentle archbishop knows about such things, the better."

"Very true. By the way," Moirne added, "thank you for not faltering in your role when you saw him with me."

"Yes, it was a wonderful performance all around, if I do say so myself. Although I am sorry for all the smoke and fire there at the end. I know you like to be dramatic, but I think it was slightly overdone this time."

"Overdone or not, I wish matters could have been resolved some other way. If only Lady Toth had told me the truth, the whole truth, from the start! Could she not see it was for her own good?" She pounded the table in frustration.

"Remember what she has gone through, my lady. She has no reason to trust anyone, especially some strange inquisitor who is here to send her to the abyss."

Moirne smiled slightly. "Touché."

Uriel waited a moment in the dark before changing the subject. "Besides, I believe our performance unwittingly picked up a new fanatic for you!"

"What? Oh, you mean the acolyte."

"Yes, our young Petr Venko. He would do anything for you, my lady. And I do mean, *anything*."

"That's disgusting, Uriel, and I could have you banished just for thinking it."

"I'm not entirely sure where your sordid mind just went. All I meant was that he would throw himself headfirst into the abyss if you asked him."

"We shall see. He needs a few more years of schooling, at minimum."

"Agreed. And you already have one new project. But I sense the fire in that one will burn brightly for quite some time. He will wait for you. Of that, I am confident."

"Let us hope so. I will need to replace you sooner or later."

"Come now, my lady, you know there is no replacing me. Not until we are at the end of our journey, anyway."

She knew he was right. "Have you at least made the arrangements for our departure tomorrow?"

"Yes, my lady. The shipmaster expects us before the afternoon tide, and I will have the men bring all our gear and supplies to the dock in the morning while you deal with the Toth steward."

"And where will you be?"

"I will be at your side, my lady. Perhaps to ensure you don't decide to visit the city gaol and take certain matters into your own hands."

She grimaced, as he had read her mind. “Touché, again. Angvar Toth cannot die soon enough for me.”

“And that is unsettling to me, my lady. I agree he is evil, but I also agree with the old man that even the basest of humans deserve a chance at redemption. There but for the grace of the Almighty go you all.”

“It is late, Uriel, and I do not want to argue this point with you. I am going to bed.”

“Yes, my lady. I will clean the library for you. You’re welcome. Don’t forget your journal and your sword. Oh, and your carrots.”

“Thank you, Uriel. For everything tonight.”

“I am yours to command, my lady. You know that.”

Moirne smiled. “I do. Good night.”

She collected her things before making her way out of the library and into the cold night.

CHAPTER ONE

Sail Her Down the River

It was thought that humans had been living where the city of Velych sat on the western bank of the Grumaius for well over a thousand years. No doubt trade was a major reason people had settled beside the great river and stayed there ever since. One had to look no further than the Kalchik family crest to understand the importance of the river to the city and the kingdom as a whole.

While most of the area's history had been lost to the ravages of time, it was known that being on the west bank had spared the initial human settlement many times over. First eldar raiders, and then orc nomads, had come down from or around the Riphean Mountains for time immemorial, but most had stayed on the eastern bank and had been content with laying waste to smaller hamlets and single homesteads. The river was wide and fast, especially during the wet months, and not conducive to crossing attempts in crudely made vessels. Even the pirates mentioned in old stories, who sailed up the river on larger, sturdier craft, seemed to have tired of adventure before coming so far north.

Velych itself had been founded over three hundred years ago. However, the city's fortunes, and those of the nascent Kingdom of Perizidon as a whole, had only begun to rise over the last century. Before this, the nadir had come when the Black Death stalked the land, and two-thirds of a mostly empty city burned to the ground in the Great Fire of 1348. Truly, the few survivors had said, the Almighty had cursed the land, and the End of Days was upon them. But subsequent bountiful harvests, timely alliances, and the decision to allow skilled tradesfolk to flourish within the realm had finally started a slow but sure recovery.

Once the kingdom's frontiers had finally been secured by Rurik the Peacemaker, his successor and Lianne's great-grandfather, Ansel II, had quickly turned his eye towards feats of engineering and architecture for his capital. At long last, the deep scars in the city landscape still left from the horrible fire were erased under the great king's guidance. A new main boulevard a full thirty paces wide was cut through the debris, with side streets wide enough for oxen carts to pass each other laid out at right angles to it. Stone construction replaced wood for all critical structures, including the massive city wall and the new gatehouses. The city docks were rebuilt and expanded, and artisans and clergy alike brought a new cathedral to life. Not even the short and tempestuous reign of Lianne's grandfather, Elric I, that followed could slow the wheels of progress. By the time Elric II had assumed the throne, Velych had grown in both size and stature, and all Perizidon flourished as a result.

It was time, the new king had decided, to attempt something truly monumental. For as long as the river was—many hundreds of leagues, in fact—not a single bridge spanned its waters. What better way to cement his legacy and prove that Perizidon was becoming much more than a small regional power than to conquer the mighty waters?

It was to be an enormous challenge, to be sure, as the river was nearly two versta in width as it wound its way past the city. Even if the small islands near the eastern shore were incorporated into the overall design, the main section of the bridge would need to be almost one versta in length all by itself. Then there was the rapid current during the spring thaw, the sporadic ice floes in the winter, and the massive amount of boat traffic on the river year-round to contend with. Lianne's father had merely tackled the impossible with the raw bravado of youthful ignorance.

Work on a bridge had begun in earnest in the second year of Elric's reign. His new bride, Leysa, had helped consecrate the location of the crossing with much fanfare. Money, time, and talent were all given in great quantities to the project. And yet, a decade later, there still had not been much to show for all the effort expended.

Huge abutments had been constructed on either shore of the river, but work on individual piers had gone extremely slowly. The proposed construction methodologies that two successive master builders proposed had done little to improve the overall situation. As wise as the king was proving to be in most matters, "Elric's Folly" was becoming a millstone around his neck as progress slowly ground to a halt.

Even worse, Elric's beloved Leysa had gone to her eternal rest the year before the tenth anniversary of the groundbreaking, leaving the king childless and devastated. Both the bridge project and the kingdom were left rudderless as Elric mourned. His council began to quietly reallocate the kingdom's resources to other needs, and it appeared that the project would be abandoned altogether. That was until Darnaya Kitko arrived in court.

She had come north, fresh from the *Politecnico di Myste*, with a letter of recommendation from the doge himself for an engineer's assistant position. It was later discovered that she was the second cousin of the doge's wife, but this small act of nepotism was ignored because it had already become clear that she could stand on her own technical merit. Not only had she immediately solved the problem of ice floes with the design of a new style of starkwater, but she had also made the critical recommendation to install a series of temporary berms in the river upstream of the city to help deflect debris around the bridge pier construction sites. Required repairs to the cofferdams had been reduced dramatically almost overnight, and the speed of pier construction accelerated to a previously inconceivable pace due to the additional labor and material that could be allocated. The project had been saved.

However, these technical advances did not come without upheaval within the king's council and in the royal court. Simply put, Darnaya was not just wise beyond her years; her veins were full of the piss and vinegar of a bad-tempered old man. The starkwater recommendation had been presented in a humiliating fashion, belittling the current master builder in front of the entire court. He had angrily called her out, only to see her idea bear fruit where all his had not. Resigning in disgrace, he had departed for parts unknown soon thereafter.

The fact that Darnaya was subsequently advanced over three more senior engineers to become the kingdom's first female master builder did nothing to temper her foul mood or sharp tongue. Unable and unwilling to play the political games of the royal court, she instead did her best to simply break the gameboard in two over her knee. New ideas were laid out in a manner that should be obvious to even the simplest lords and ladies-in-waiting, her mocking wit at the ready when it was obvious nobody knew what she was talking about. She would badger the master of arms on the maintenance of his siege weapons, and she would belittle the chancellor over the interest rates being charged by the money lenders. Brutally honest and sarcastic in nature, she suffered no fools and had neither respect nor time for anyone on the king's council except for the king himself.

While they hotly debated each other quite often on both technical and procedural matters, it was to Elric alone that Darnaya would defer, at least on occasion. She never spoke down to, or ill of, her sovereign. She would even curtsy to him when in court. It was perhaps the only bit of political nuance she ever cared to show.

With as many enemies as she created and maintained, there were plenty of courtesans spilling the wine as to why Elric did not dismiss her outright and rarely even chastised her rude behavior. It was clear that he had become fully reinvigorated with her appearance in court, shaking off his year-long melancholy after the death of his first wife and reasserting his rule.

Young and attractive with her long, strawberry-blond hair, ample chest, and wasp-like waist, it was the obvious conclusion that she was in his bed on a regular basis. Perhaps her sharp tongue had a soft side? Perhaps the king had just found a pleasurable way to shut her up? Or perhaps she rode him into submission, breaking him as easily as she broke court tradition and protocol?

Elric was indeed fascinated by Darnaya, although, if this manifested itself physically, he was always careful to maintain a shroud of mystery around their relationship. After all, he was married again, with his second wife Arina immediately bearing him an heir in Lianne. However, it was true that he greatly enjoyed Darnaya's company, even if their shouting matches in his private study could be heard well into the night. For what he had found in her, what they had found in each other, was something that both had been lacking—a worthy opponent in the arena of intelligence and wit.

This feeling of high-order equality was further bolstered when, over time, the real reason behind the doge's letter of recommendation was ascertained. Rather than behead Darnaya for gross insolence towards his person, the doge of Myste had acquiesced to his wife and had, instead, banished her to, in his mind, some backwater kingdom. Elric, therefore, knew that what drove her was not the need to be right, but rather the need to be respected. Thus, he gave her what she most truly wanted, and she returned it tenfold to him.

There could be no doubt that the results for his pet project were technically spectacular. Construction of the bridge continued to accelerate, and the design continued to be enhanced. Indeed, the structure fast became the pride of the kingdom, even before it was completed. Segmental arch spans and the use of *opus caementicium*, a building material thought lost to ancient Roma, had been employed to improve strength and sturdiness. Four magnificent spans, each thirty paces high and sixty paces wide, had been installed at even intervals along the main section, the bridge deck rising and falling gracefully on either side. Over double the size of what the original design had envisioned, these spans solved in an instant the issue of maintaining access to the upper river for larger vessels.

The realization of the bridge represented increased trade via both land and water routes, which also meant increased profits and tax revenue. Darnaya was feted by the merchant class, and the longshoremen raised their mugs in her honor. The fact that she publicly tweaked the noses of the royal court only made her even more popular with the masses. Master Gregor and Dragoman Chumak, annoyed as they were with Master Builder Kitko and her actions, were wise enough to know that the king had found the ideal person for the position. Calls for her removal among the courtesans were quietly muted, and the two of them merely ensured they had enough thick mead on hand for debriefing purposes after every council meeting.

The bridge opened with a joyous celebration shortly after Lianne's fifteenth birthday. She had ridden beside her parents in the royal carriage as the first people to officially cross the long expanse. As the white flagstone pavers stretched to the eastern horizon in front of her, her father had put his arm around her and hugged her close. "Gaze upon this wondrous structure," he had whispered in her ear, "but know that I would have you do such great deeds as to cast what I have done into shadow!"

The possibilities for her and the kingdom had seemed infinite.

***

Lianne gazed up at the bridge as the caravel she was on was unmoored from the city dock to start its trip south to Boloto, the capital of Astrikhon. From her vantage point, it gleamed brightly in the early morning sun, and she could see that it was already busy with traffic. Cart after cart moved methodically along the entire length of the main span. Though she was too far away to hear it, she knew there would be a cacophony even at this early hour.

The signal towers on either side of the river had just been doused, pointing to a prediction of clear weather for the day. A light breeze from the north was picked up by the two main sails of the vessel as they were unfurled, their triangular shapes filling quickly. The captain had told her it would be roughly three days to make the run to Boloto. It could be done in less than two if there was urgency, but this trip would be served better with a stately entrance as opposed to a rushed one.

Symon had departed two days before her to complete the necessary arrangements for local housing and transportation.

Everything should be ready in Boloto once Lianne's small party disembarked. All she was required to do for the next three days was to relax and be prepared for numerous meetings and ceremonies upon arrival. The captain's cabin had been given up to her for the short trip, and Melina had already made it ready for her use.

Of course, Lianne was going to do much more than just lounge on the side of the boat, watching the shoreline float by. One of Melina's overall duties when she came onboard was to assemble the various archival documents Lianne had brought with her on the long table in the cabin. She had been fully briefed by her father and Symon on the trade agreement that would be formally signed by Astrikhon during her visit, but she also wanted to brush up on the country's history and customs over the next few days.

Despite several nights of searching, she hadn't been able to discover much in the royal library about her kingdom's relationship with Astrikhon beyond some old treaties and maps. She had rounded up what she could in the way of interesting-looking documents she had not yet perused to bring along, with the grudging approval of Master Gregor. She felt she had enough with her to ward off boredom for at least half the trip down the river.

"'Scuse me, Yer 'ighness!" A burly sailor, with biceps the size of her thighs, barely waited for her to move before he shouldered past to secure a halyard. He smiled widely at her as he worked his knots, showing off several gaps in his teeth. His eyes were bloodshot from a night of carousing, and an odor that conveyed a mixture of ale and cow dung emanated from his person.

One of Lianne's guards had taken notice of the wholly impolite incursion into her personal space, but as he started to move towards the brute, she quietly waved him off.

"My apologies, Sailor! I am afraid I don't quite know where to stand."

"Na worries, Yer 'ighness, we'll letcha know if'n when you're in tha way!" He laughed heartily, but then he seemed to remember his place and gave her a quick salute and a nod. It was the epitome of respect, given the circumstances.

She smiled back at him, which made his somewhat toothless grin that much wider. "What is your name, Sailor?"

"Tymur, at yer service, Yer 'ighness! Ya need anythin' fer tha trip, I be yers ta command!"

Lianne couldn't place his dialect, and the accent was so thick she could barely acknowledge that he was speaking Common.

"Any o' these ruffians onboard 'ere give ya any lip, ya tell ol' Tymur, an' there won't be no problem fer long!" He drew his finger across his throat with one hand while patting an ugly looking knife at his side with the other.

Lianne had been around enough of the common soldiery to know how to respond. "Why, thank you, Tymur. But tell me, sirrah, what do I do if *you* are the one giving me lip?" She arched her eyebrow at him, hands on hips, as if she were a mother about to scold a petulant child.

"Then by tha Almighty, I'll slit me own throat, Yer 'ighness!" He bowed low, arms outstretched.

She laughed despite herself. "Let us hope it doesn't come to that, Tymur! But I will be watching you!"

"On me honor, Yer 'ighness!" He saluted again and then was off to finish securing the ship as it picked up speed on its way out of port.

A few of his compatriots had witnessed the scene, and out of the corner of her eye, Lianne could see them teasing him good-naturedly for his performance. She smiled to herself.

Better to show all of them that a royal can be a normal person as opposed to treating him like shite. Just remember what Father says: friendly but firm.

As she drifted back to her original spot on the railing, the commander of her personal retinue approached her.

The older woman stopped a few paces away and saluted before speaking in a low tone. "Your Highness, if I may. I would advise caution when speaking with the crew. They may not be lascars, but they are still an unruly lot and unpredictable."

"They cannot be any worse than your own troop, Major," Lianne retorted, a bit annoyed at what she thought was a condescending undertone to the warning.

"I agree, Your Highness, and that is why I advise caution." The soldier bowed, then retreated.

Lianne turned back towards the bridge so no one on deck could see her flushed face.

C'mon, Li, she's just doing her job. Marshal Gwyn probably told her to cut off the hands of anyone who dares touch you.

There were only twelve soldiers on board, essentially one for every sailor. The total number of her escort had been hotly debated in her father's council the week before she left. Not that anyone was worried about the crew members themselves. They were to be handpicked by the captain of the ship, who himself was a well-respected lower member of the court. Rather, Marshal Gwyn had been overly worried about pirates, and Dragoman Symon had been overly worried about not having enough soldiers to portray a military escort worthy of an heir apparent upon their arrival in Astrikhon.

Because of this, the former had insisted that a minimum of a dozen guards be with Lianne at all times during the trip, while the latter had insisted that a minimum of a full platoon should accompany her to Boloto. Other council members thought both numbers extremely high, with Darnaya sarcastically calculating how much an additional caravel could carry. "Perhaps we can stick another forty men in the hold, Symon. We can sling them in place like horses so they don't roll about too much!"

Elric had remained quiet throughout the argument until he was annoyed enough to jump in and end it. After confirming Symon would not back down from his position, the king had immediately ordered eighteen soldiers be crammed into every nook and cranny of the caravel that was taking the diplomat south. "If twelve more will be with Lianne, then there is the balance of your platoon, Symon. The matter is settled!"

Knowing that he had been outmaneuvered and that he

would be unable to travel in the luxury he was accustomed to, the dragoman had fumed in silence. Lianne had thought Darnaya was going to have a heart attack right there at the council table, as hard as she laughed. Even the chancellor had to hide a smirk; it wasn't every day that the proud dragoman was taken down a peg. When the marshal jokingly told Symon that he would make sure his men bathed before starting the journey, the portly man had stormed out of the chambers in a huff.

"Like a platoon will make any sort of meaningful military showing. Next thing you know, he would have demanded a full *brigade* accompany my daughter, and then we might as well invade the damn country!" Elric had muttered angrily to himself, but Lianne had heard the outburst just the same. Several others had heard it too, based upon the looks that were silently cast about the table.

At the time, she had tried her best to suppress her own smile. While Symon was certainly not her favorite of her father's advisors, he would be all she had at her side for the coming trip. She didn't want him to think she was part of some conspiracy to replace him, if such court intrigue existed in the minds of others.

After all that, her own caravel was still fairly snug. Including the guards, her overall traveling party more than doubled the normal contingent on board. It could have been an even tighter fit, but she had ignored her mother's protests and limited her immediate staff to just three servants, including Melina. She didn't mind traveling light, especially for what was supposed to be a short trip.

Of course, the definition of "traveling light" was relative to the person involved. Gowns, shoes, parasols, wraps, and all the various trappings required for the scheduled afternoon tea parties and evening balls had been loaded carefully into the holds of both ships until they barely had room left for the victuals needed for the short voyage. Various gifts and tokens had been loaded onto both caravels as well. One of Symon's last jobs upon arrival in Boloto was to confirm with his Astrikhon counterpart that the propriety of each item matched the prestige of the intended recipient.

Lianne's boat was in the main channel now, and the noises and smells of the city docks began to recede. As the vessel passed under the bridge, she looked upwards to stare at the underside of the arched span. At this close distance, she could see where the deck drains emptied, long blackish-brown stains showing on each pier where, every day, filth traveled down their entire length to the water's surface. Other than the stains, the underside of the bridge took on a greyish hue in the slight shadow, the large limestone blocks and mortar joints blending together to create a monolithic look.

Water lapped at the fenders as the caravel slipped past the mighty structure, the crew briefly stopping their work to openly mock a cog slowly heading upstream.

"Hey, lads, I left a big brown shite for ya floatin' at tha pier so yer tub don't feel lonely!"

"Don't take too long moorin' that piece o' flotsam. Ya only

got a full day o' light left!"

"Tell yer mum ta get that rash looked at 'fore I get back!"

"All right, all right, that's enough! Back ta work!" The first mate smacked a couple of the men in the head to make his point, and order was quickly restored.

For all their slovenly behavior, the crew worked quickly and efficiently, and it was evident that the captain and his first mate knew their business. The caravel quickly cleared the bridge and the immediate traffic surrounding it, and the coxswain pointed the vessel south along the western edge of the main channel.

Lianne allowed herself to view the landscape for a while, enjoying the wind in her hair and the sun on her back. It was extremely rare for her to be alone, as it were, with no immediate relations accompanying her. She knew next to nothing about her retinue's commander, other than she had saved Lianne's mother from a bear attack during a hunting trip over a decade ago. For that reason, she sensed the commander's presence had been something of an appeasement to her mother, knowing that she had been against Lianne traveling with such a small group.

Major Bannik had been cordial enough when she had been introduced to Lianne the previous evening, and there was obviously no concern about her loyalty to the crown. Grudgingly, Lianne resolved to listen to any words of advice or caution from the older woman a bit more graciously in the future.

Lianne reflected that she barely knew the soldiers, either, although this was to be expected given her station. Several had looked familiar from a distance, and she remembered most being posted within the castle recently. She had not taken the time to inspect them upon arriving at the dock this morning, but she resolved to do so before the day was out.

So much to remember! Perhaps Mother was right and I should have brought a full-time secretary with me.

Her three immediate companions, however, had been selected personally by her. Melina had been her maidservant for over two years now, having taken over from her older sister, and the two of them were as thick as thieves. Anichka, middle-aged but bright-eyed, was a seamstress without parallel and had saved many a gala for the Kalchik women with emergency repairs to any manner of vestments.

And finally, there was Olesea. Slightly older than Lianne and leaner in stature, she could have been mistaken as an older sister by a stranger. Lianne knew her to be sturdy, unwavering, and willing to take care of any task without complaint.

None of the three servants had traveled outside Perizidon before now, and all of them were excited about the prospects of seeing another capital city.

"M'lady?"

Lianne turned to find Olesea standing a few paces away, a head covering of sorts in her hand.

"M'lady, if you mean to stay on deck for a while, it would behoove you to wear a bonnet."

Lianne made a face. "Come now, Ole, do you really believe I

wish to look like an old maid with *that* on my head?"

Her servant smiled, fully embracing the familiar nickname. "Of course not, m'lady. It's just that it would not be proper to meet the king of Astrikhon with a bronzed face. I can look for a parasol for you instead."

Lianne knew she was right. "Very well, find one for me to use for the rest of the trip. But I should go inside now to do a bit of reading anyway."

"Yes, m'lady." Olesea bowed slightly. "Melina has finished unpacking your sundries and has laid out the table in the main cabin as you instructed."

"Ah, good. Thank you, Ole." Lianne looked at the hat in the servant's hands and shook her head. *So much to remember.*

She walked towards the back of the boat for the first time, Olesea in tow. The caravel was only forty arshin long and a third of that wide, so anywhere on board wasn't that far away. Two guards were posted at the door to her cabin, which took up roughly half of the space immediately under the quarterdeck.

Lianne smiled with recognition as she approached them. "Guard Oldenfeld!"

"Your Highness!" The young man practically shouted the honorific as he puffed out his chest, blushing furiously.

Olesea turned slightly, hand over mouth, and had a coughing fit.

Hopefully, your hide has recovered from whatever lashing your sergeant gave you, Lianne thought, recalling the details of her last encounter with the clumsy youth.

She looked at the other soldier, an older man with the start of a scar showing above his collar. His was another familiar face, and she also greeted him warmly.

"Ah, Guard Kushnir. It is good to see both of you again."

Ivan Kushnir responded immediately with the king's salute but didn't look at her. "At yer service, Yer Highness."

Remembering the heated council discussion about the number of soldiers that were to accompany her, Lianne was suddenly curious about how the specific guards had been selected for what she assumed was a coveted assignment. "If I may be so bold, Guard Kushnir, might I inquire as to how all the soldiers on board were selected?"

The soldier paused for a moment, and she couldn't tell if he was hesitating due to a lack of knowledge or an unwillingness to tell her the truth. He continued to look straight ahead when he finally answered.

"I'm sorry, Yer Highness, I don't rightly know. We was just given our orders directly by Cap'n Muromets. For tha mission, I mean. We wound up drawin' lots for which boat we got."

"Ah, I see." The answer was a bit deflating, but after a brief pause, she cleared her throat. "Well, at least I didn't get stuck with any loggerheads, did I?"

Ivan's face twitched as something of a smile tugged at his lips. "No, Yer Highness, I would say not."

I suppose if I really must know, I can ask Major Bannik about it. I assume she had final say on the list, even if the captain of the castle guard picked them all.

"Fair enough." She looked back and forth between the two guards and then nodded, as if accepting them in their roles. "If I am still in my quarters come None, knock loudly and alert me of the time."

They glanced at each other, and then Ivan responded. "Yes, Yer Highness. The guard will change at Sext, but we'll relay yer orders ta our replacements."

Lianne nodded and entered her cabin without saying another word. Olesea followed her into the cabin, closing the door behind her.

***

Dane Oldenfeld could hear the young women laughing through the wall of the cabin and then the murmur of voices. Suddenly, there was a loud shriek and yet more laughter. He couldn't help but wonder if the princess was talking about him, and he flushed deeply again. Thankfully, the slight shaking that coursed through his body was hidden by the movement of the boat as it slipped downstream.

"Pay 'em no mind, boy," Ivan said.

The older soldier continued to stare straight ahead, but Dane figured he was good at looking out of the corner of his eyes when he had to.

"It don't matter if they're talkin' 'bout you, or me, or tha man in tha moon. It's all tha same ta us on this side of tha door."

Dane cleared his throat. "Understood!"

Ivan was right to pay attention to their duty, and Dane should do his best to match the seasoned veteran. He knew he had been thrown a lifeline of sorts by being assigned to this royal escort mission in the first place, seeing how his spectacular failure in protocol in front of the princess had been just a few days ago. He attempted to stand fully at attention and stare straight ahead as his mind continued to race.

Just you wait and see, Ivan. I'll be the best soldier in the platoon, whether it be spit and polish looks, standing at attention, or marching in a straight line. But I know there's more to this assignment than just looking pretty. There's bladework to be done in Boloto, I'm sure of it. And I'll be there to protect our fair and fearless princess. You can all rely on me, Dane Oldenfeld, to save the day!

CHAPTER TWO

The Goat and the Dog

Sarl made his way down to the ground floor of the house, and he could hear the shapeshifter moving around in the relative darkness, along with the sounds of pieces of wood being tossed about. He assumed the *vovkulaka* was still gathering materials for a fire, and he laughed to himself at the thought of them getting splinters in their paws.

He went slowly, trying to clear his mind of at least some of the thoughts that were racing through it. His attempt to bed Katrya had just failed spectacularly, but it was apparently leading to a confrontation with the shapeshifter he had been chasing for some time now. How the beast was tied to Katrya's sister, Kira, wasn't completely clear to Sarl just yet, but he knew it had something to do with controlling the town of Stren.

That idiot sheriff, Yuri, is definitely up ta somthin' and it ain't just shaggin' his jailer, Kira. Seems like he wants more power than he's already got. But why would anyone else, let alone this shapeshifter, care 'bout this shitehole of a town in tha middle of nowhere? If I had ta guess, Kat an' her sister are fixin' ta leave this place, not take it over. An' that would ultimately put them at odds with ol' Yuri. But Kat dodged that question, didn't she. Least it don't seem like she's tied up with whatever's waitin' downstairs for me.

When Sarl sensed he had reached the bottom step of the

rudimentary staircase, he paused, waiting for his eyes to adjust to the low light and show him the layout of the large room he had only glimpsed for a moment when Katrya had led him into her sister's house. Sarl knew his profile was backlit by the moonlight streaming down from the upstairs sleeping area he had just left, making him an easy target, but he figured he was relatively safe for the time being.

'Cause if tha silly shite wanted me dead, I'd be dead already.

As he shifted somewhat impatiently in place, Sarl felt something soft next to his left foot. He assumed it was one of the garments he had hastily shed earlier in the throes of passion with Katrya. As he bent down to retrieve what turned out to be his undershirt, a flame flared to life in the hearth, and he instinctively stayed in a crouched position. His tunic was sure to be somewhere nearby, but he didn't bother to look for it. Instead, his gaze went to the other creature in the room as they became visible.

Even though they were standing next to the fireplace, it was still hard to make out any details other than the figure appeared to be a dark-skinned human. Sarl could see nothing that gave away the shapeshifter's other identity except for their eyes when they turned slightly to face him. The eyes shone red in the dark as they reflected the light of the flames coming from the growing fire. Sarl knew his own animalistic eyes would be shining pale green, and the two silently regarded each other from across the room for a long moment. It was the vovkulaka who finally broke the silence.

"Well met, Sarl Blackmoor of the Choros tribe," they

intoned, and they bowed at the waist. The red eyes stayed focused on Sarl, and there was no movement forward to greet him.

Sarl wasn't overly surprised to hear his name. If anything, this tidbit of knowledge confirmed in his mind that the creature was in league with Kira and Yuri.

But who's in charge of their little gang? Either way, be careful with this one!

He slowly stood back up, taking care not to make any sudden movements. "Whatever, *suka*. Ya got me here, so bully for ya. For what it's worth, ya seem pretty damn desperate ta talk with me instead of just killin' me."

The vovkulaka regarded him for a long moment, as if they were reconsidering whether killing him was indeed the better option. The level of light grew in the room in pace with the size of the fire, and now Sarl could make out a long, thin sheath strapped to either leg of the creature. The knives they held looked like more delicate versions of his own hunting knife, but he was confident they were every bit as lethal in the right hands.

Double-bladed is how you're runnin', eh? If tha blades are that thin, then they're made ta be handled fast, an' ya wanna be in an' out quick-like with yer strikes. So, what happens if someone actually grabs ya?

Sarl cursed his stupidity for being caught weaponless. He glanced over at the front door as a formality, expecting to see nothing. To his surprise, he saw that, while his satchel had obviously been moved and rummaged through, his weapons still lay on the ground where he had dropped them when he had picked Katrya up and carried her upstairs. His axe seemed to beckon at him invitingly from across the room to go and fetch it up, and he wondered just how quickly the shapeshifter could move.

"If you are wondering, I am very quick on my feet," the creature said with a bit of levity, obviously following Sarl's gaze. "But as you have inferred, my dear orc, I only wish to speak with you. There is no need to kill you. At least, not yet..."

Something of a snort passed Sarl's lips as he turned back and took a long, hard look at the shapeshifter in the brightening room. They were indeed dark-skinned with jet-black hair, and both the skin and hair seemed to bleed into their clothing. The effect was the creation of a shifting mass that made it hard to focus on anything except for the creature's eyes. The red color seemed to grow in intensity the longer he looked at them.

The vovkulaka continued. "Allow me to formally introduce myself. I am known as Kozel Golova, at least in these parts. I arranged to meet you here so that we might talk in relative peace and quiet. I much prefer this location as opposed to that filthy tavern you seem to adore, or some other public setting."

Sarl, still holding his shirt in one hand, took a few steps forward into the room. Only now did he return the other's greeting by performing a deep, mocking bow. "At yer service, Kozel Golova." He then crossed his arms and smirked. "Kozel, eh? What, tha Wild Boar ain't a good enough place for a 'goat' like yerself? Ya don't feel like mixin' with tha locals?"

Kozel smiled in response to the gibe about the literal meaning of their name and bobbed their head. "You are correct. This 'goat' is not going into that stinkhole unless absolutely necessary. The less I must mingle with the simpletons of Stren, the better. They bleat like sheep, and they all smell like that foul ale they guzzle with abandon."

Sarl chuckled and shrugged. "I agree tha ale ain't much more than piss, but yer missin' out some good goulash. Although, I'm pretty sure some of tha locals have had enough of me, so I may have ta stay outta there in tha future."

Kozel looked amused at this minor revelation. "A goat and a wolf hiding from the sheep? We indeed have the makings for being an odd couple."

"I'm just a dog, Koz. Ask anyone 'round here an' they'll tell ya that."

A slight frown crossed the shapeshifter's face, but it apparently wasn't because of the informal nickname Sarl had labeled them with. "Do not insult yourself, sir. There is nothing worse than false humility."

Sarl shrugged again. "Whatever." He looked around the room. "But, sure, we can talk here. I got some questions for ya, anyway."

"Of course you do," Kozel responded, the good-natured sound to their voice returning. "Just as I have some for you. We can take turns asking and answering each other. You do not know me, but I promise to be as open as I can afford to be and at least as truthful as you are."

That's an odd statement ta make.

"Whatever, Koz. I got nothin' ta hide."

"Oh, everyone has something to hide, Sarl. But whatever you are trying to hide, hopefully it is irrelevant to our conversation." Kozel glanced over at the staircase and then up at the ceiling. "But in the vein of secrecy, I would prefer that our discussion be completely private. I do not wish to tempt the lovely Katrya Toth into eavesdropping on what I have to say. Since I know for a fact that she understands very little of your beautiful eastern dialect, may we continue in that?"

Sarl had been hoping for this and was quick to agree. "I got no problem with that, Koz. Just watch how ya pronounce tha letter **и**." He paused briefly before continuing in his native tongue. "I mean, it's difficult ta say properly. At least for *humans*."

Kozel's eyes narrowed slightly but then nodded their head slowly. They turned briefly to tend to the fire, somehow accomplishing this while still paying attention to where Sarl was standing. After they had stoked the flames with a few more pieces of wood, they stepped back from the hearth, faced Sarl squarely, and responded in Orcish with barely any hint of an accent. "Very good, Sarl. Beyond that nose of yours, what gave me away?"

Sarl had already decided there was no harm in telling Kozel this part of what he had deduced. He began to slowly pace back and forth, still holding on to his shirt. "Several things, Koz. First, with tha amount of shapeshiftin' ya seem ta do, there should be bundles of clothes all over tha Wilds. Or maybe ya just like ta be naked when you're not a warg. But I've found nary a shirt nor pair of trousers out in tha woods, least not any that I think are yer style. An' ya don't seem ta want ta draw attention ta yerself, so walkin' 'round naked all tha time don't seem like somethin' you'd want ta do."

Kozel put their hand to their mouth as if to hide their expression but remained silent.

Sarl continued pacing and talking. "Second, with all tha hamlets an' towns you've visited over tha past few weeks, I seriously doubt ya got a safehouse like this one in every location. So, clothes or no clothes out in tha Wilds, I don't see ya havin' a chance ta change inta somethin' more respectable than yer skin in every place you've visited."

Sarl stopped pacing, having wound up several steps closer to the hearth. "An' finally, I don't believe tha wargs would abide yer presence very long if ya were human, naked or not." He shook his head slightly, as if he was disappointed in the shapeshifter, and put his hands on his hips. "If someone follows ya 'round long enough, Koz, there's only so much pretendin' ya can do without goin' ta much greater lengths ta cover yer trail, so ta speak."

Kozel had lowered their hand from their mouth and was now smiling openly, and not unkindly. "Well, that is all very observant of you, Sarl. I had not planned on someone following me around for any length of time, so shame on me for not being more careful. As far as the clothing goes, I appreciate that you believe I have a higher sense of fashion than most. But suppose you are correct with all your assumptions. What is your conclusion about me if you have decided I am not human?"

Sarl returned the smile, deciding not to show his teeth. "Well, if ya ain't a turned human, then you're either usin' old magic or you're an infernal. I ain't been around any wizards, human or otherwise, but I do know a bit 'bout old magic. Tha incantations take a long time, an' they make a person exhausted with constant use. Ya don't look that tired ta me, Koz, an' I gotta think ya don't got lots of time on yer hands every time ya wanna change shape. 'Sides, that metal smell of yers don't seem ta ever go away. So, my guess is that you're an infernal."

The vovkulaka's features continued to change their sharpness in the firelight, but the smile did not leave their face. "That is quite a reasonable conclusion to reach, given what you think you know. But certain items can be imbued with old magic, can they not? Perhaps I have some bauble about my person that allows me to shift my appearance at will. Surely, you must have thought of this possibility as well?"

Kozel stared at Sarl as they spoke with a seemingly knowing look on their face, but he couldn't be sure if they were making a veiled reference to his own pendant. He knew it was visible as it hung on its chain on his bare chest, and it seemed to get warmer as his thoughts focused upon it. It took a conscious effort on his part to not reach up and grasp the sending stone talisman as he thought of Elise, who had given it to him years ago as a sign of their devotion to each other. He stood as impassively as he could, and he lowered his arms to his sides.

"Eh, sure. Maybe ya got a special rock or somethin'. As a sign of trust then, show yer bauble ta me. Or tell me why ya smell, or how ya carry those knives when you're a warg. Better yet, explain why yer body is shiftin' 'round as much as it is, even when you're just standin' there."

Kozel's form immediately solidified, confirming in Sarl's mind that it was indeed a creature from the abyss. The rest of its chosen form revealed itself to be an average sized, almost featureless, human male. The shape was on the thin side, but not unnaturally so. The clothing it had selected was indeed of good material and cut. Whether the outfit was in fashion or not, Sarl didn't know and didn't care.

"Nice trick ya got there." Sarl took another step closer and leaned forward to inspect the new figure in front of him more closely. He squinted his eyes as he looked Kozel up and down.

The infernal didn't seem to mind the close inspection. It bowed slightly in response to the faint compliment, but it still didn't take its eyes off Sarl.

"Yes, well, it may not cause great physical exhaustion to maintain this form, but I cannot do it forever without some minor, uh, inconveniences, shall we say. Besides, I decided I owed you the courtesy of revealing a truer version of myself to you when we met."

Sarl leaned back up to his full height. "C'mon, Koz. We both know it was a test. Ya wanted ta see how much I knew about ya an' also whether I'd shite me trousers when meetin' somethin' from tha abyss."

Kozel's eyes widened slightly. "My dear Sarl! You really do hide some cunning behind that fabulous accent of yours, don't you?"

Sarl grinned widely, showing his teeth for the first time. "I ain't that cunnin', Koz. Just usin' me nose an' eyes is all. 'Sides, there's no reason ta shite my trousers, 'cause ya probably ain't gonna kill me now if ya didn't kill me earlier. But then, that begs a big question, Koz—why *didn't* ya kill me earlier when ya had the chance?"

"Hmm?" Kozel seemed to think for a moment. "Oh, during the warg attack on the priest. Father Malachi, I believe is his name? Yes, well, that was an unfortunate incident all around. If he dies, that only brings unnecessary complications to various plans, including mine. Although, there may still be complications even if he lives."

It muttered the last sentence, as if to itself. Sarl remained silent. He knew well enough that the creature was referring to an investigation by the church. There would certainly be an inquiry into the death of any clergyperson, even if the circumstances were not suspicious in nature. Just the attack alone would probably raise questions from a higher authority once it was reported.

But complications ta what, Koz? Why are ya throwin' yer lot in with Yuri, an' why do ya need him? It's gotta be more than control of tha docks or even tha rest of this sardin' town.

Kozel sighed deeply, putting its hands on its hips. "If I could order those damned wargs beyond the most basic of commands, I would have held them back from attacking the priest in the first place."

The infernal then pointedly cleared its throat before continuing. "But alas, *someone* drove them into a blood frenzy, and there was no stopping them from attacking anyone or anything that got in their way that afternoon."

There wasn't a hint of sympathy in Sarl's voice when he responded. "It's ain't that *someone's* problem that tha priest was in tha wrong place at tha wrong time, other than he sprung my trap too soon. I didn't even know he was there. But ya didn't answer my question."

Kozel furrowed its brow and seemed distracted for a beat. "About the knives? That just comes down to having a flexible harness that the sheathes can—"

"'Bout why I ain't dead yet, Koz."

The creature regarded him for a long moment before responding to the real question. "You are, of course, correct that I am not of this world. And if you know what I am, Sarl, then you should also know there are certain rules in place for my kind. No unsanctioned killings of the Almighty's true believers, lest they be turned into martyrs and made more powerful in their next life than they already are in this one. Under my current *modus operandi*, I will not act against that priest or anyone I believe to be his close compatriot, except in self-defense. This was especially true at the time of the, uh, incident we are discussing, because his holy blood had already been spilled by the time I arrived."

Inwardly, Sarl winced.

So, ya thought I was in league with tha priest. Which means I just shat tha pot by sayin' I didn't know he was there. Idiot! Always talkin' too much!

Outwardly, he scoffed. "That makes no sense, Koz. Yer wargs certainly didn't have a problem tearin' inta him! An' since when did anybody in tha abyss care 'bout keepin' tha laws of tha Almighty? Or did I miss somethin' 'cause I didn't get enough daily bible lessons growin' up?"

Kozel crossed its arms, and a deep scowl crossed its face for the first time. "The wargs are merely chaotic beasts and a means to an end! As I *just* said, I barely control them, and part of me is actually thankful that you have thinned their numbers. But, more importantly, who said anything about keeping the laws of the Almighty?!"

The infernal's eyes had turned dark brown when it had shifted into a full human form, but here they flashed momentarily red as it continued somewhat heatedly.

"I have no need for the church, nor do I believe the laws of the Almighty are universal. They hold no sway over me or those whom I serve. Those laws are merely a form of control over the masses, damning them to servitude in this life by promising freedom in the next. If only they knew. But that does not mean I believe in chaos. Far from it!"

Sarl let out a hearty guffaw at this. "Ah, c'mon! A little chaos never hurt no one. It's just what ya do with it once ya caused it!"

Kozel shook its head. "I should have known you would say something like that. Fine. Controlled chaos, if you accept the oxymoron, can be acceptable. Or rather, chaos that has a means to an end. But it is still not my preferred methodology."

Sarl looked askance at the infernal, and Kozel immediately picked up on his doubt. "I have no reason to lie to you, my good orc. Not all of my kind are chaotic in nature. I much prefer order and authority."

An' that probably makes ya more dangerous.

"Just so long as it's *yer* order an' *yer* authority. Eh, Koz?"

"Well, of course. How does that make me different from anyone else seeking power?"

Kozel had reverted to a calm composure, and the creature continued in what came out as a sanctimonious tone. "Besides, I do not despise *all* acolytes and servants of the church. Those that do not succumb to what they believe to be sinful? Or those that uphold their own traditions and sense of order? Those who are willing to die for what they believe? I respect them even as I seek to usurp them. I could certainly sense the untapped power that priest has within him; the power that comes from his faith. His unadulterated, true faith..." Kozel's voice trailed away as it seemed to reflect on its own words.

I think it actually admires tha priest!

Sarl remained silent as he tried to process everything that

was being said.

So, it really is power you're after. But an infernal still shouldn't care 'bout a shite village in the middle of nowhere. It's gotta be tha first step ta somethin' bigger... Wait, that's it!

The sheer number of villages that he had traveled around and through in the wake of Kozel and the wargs had suddenly hit Sarl like a thunderbolt. But just as he made this connection in his mind, the creature started speaking again, its tone sharper than before.

"In any event, back to my problem at hand. Namely, *you*."

Sarl couldn't tell where it had come from, but Kozel was suddenly holding a piece of paper in its hand. What he could tell was it was the church document he had received from Elise several months ago; the infernal had obviously rummaged through his belongings left on the floor and found it.

He did a particularly lousy job of feigning surprise as Kozel continued speaking.

"The timing of my arrival here tonight could have been better, as I did not have time to inspect that ridiculously large blade of yours. But the contents of your satchel were quite interesting. Specifically, this holy writ of yours."

Sarl's pendant seemed to grow heavier as he thought of the priestess again, and he fought to keep his emotions in check. "What, that old—"

"Do not feign ignorance with me!" Kozel raised its voice along with the document, cutting off any protest from Sarl. "This proclamation gives you full rein to pursue the wargs to the ends of the earth, or at least all over the Kingdom of Perizidon. It appears to tie you, albeit loosely, to the church. But I insist on knowing the details of your assignment."

Sarl knew he had to go on the offensive to maintain any semblance of control over the conversation. "Well, Koz, ya probably know tha church don't take kindly ta chaos either. But in particular, they don't like young women gettin' murdered or raped outta hand. An' there, they seem ta differ a bit in their approach from what you're doin'."

"Whatever are you talking—"

Sarl clenched his fists and took a step forward with a low growl. "Ya dumb goat, ya don't think I don't know what yer wargs have done outside Molotok an' elsewhere? What ya did yerself outside Myr?"

Kozel shifted slightly so that its weight was on its backfoot, as if anticipating a rush. "What *I* did? Outside of—" The infernal interrupted itself with a sound of annoyance. "Ah, yes. If anything, both you and the church should be pleased with the justice I dispensed to those thugs."

"I ain't talkin' 'bout tha thugs. Koz. I'm talkin' about that orc girl ya savaged!"

A look of confusion appeared on Kozel's face. "What? I never... Dovira? You're talking about Dovira!"

Now it was Sarl's turn to be taken aback. "Ya know her name?!"

"Of course, I know her... Ah, I see." Kozel raised its hands in the air and assumed a formal, almost apologetic, pose. "I think I know what you think you know. Please, Sarl, if you must assign blame for her unfortunate state, it must rest with her father."

"Her...her father is dead, ya shite! Same as the rest of her family!"

"They are all dead because of his actions. Will you allow me to explain?" The infernal slowly lowered its hands.

Mixed emotions raced through Sarl's mind. His partial bluff and his honest anger seemed to have diverted the conversation for the time being, but he didn't see why this should change his desire to tear apart the monster standing in front of him.

C'mon, meat, don't lose focus. Play for time...

"Time ta be as open as ya can afford to be, Koz?" He spit the infernal's own words back at it.

Kozel smiled and responded calmly. "There is little reason to hide this truth from you. Dovira's father and I had an understanding. I offered certain guarantees, and he gave something of value to me in return."

Sarl couldn't believe what he was hearing. "Are ya tryin' ta tell me that orc farmer actually made a deal with tha devil? What kinda dumb oaf do ya take me for, Koz?"

"I am sorry if a childhood bedtime tale of caution rings true, but even the worst tropes have a grounding in the truth. If you spoke to the locals at all when you investigated the scene of the massacre I left behind on that hilltop, you know that Dovira's family was relatively new to the area. But if you also used your eyes, you would have seen that their farmstead was already among the largest in the valley. I tell you, Hernac Mador was well on his way to providing security and stability for his family for years to come, just as he had hoped."

"Yeah? So, what happened?"

"Chaos happened...and a bit of hubris, to be honest. Those brigands randomly chose to rob his homestead out of all those available to them. And then they made their move when the entire family was there, instead of when they were out in the fields working. And finally, Hernac, he...well, let's just say he took my assurances of protection a bit too literally."

Sarl waved his free hand dismissively. "Right...so, ya cheated him just like those bedtime stories say yer kind always do?"

Kozel huffed at this. "I most certainly did not! Look, it is impossible to fully explain to a non-eternal such as yourself, but he called out to the wrong entity when he needed help. By the time I got his message, I arrived too late to assist him." The infernal shrugged but didn't seem overly apologetic. "You can go ahead and call it a technicality if you wish, but it is not my fault he chose not to follow contractual procedures."

It sounded like a pathetic technicality to Sarl. "Whatever, Koz. What did he give up to ya, only ta get shat on in tha end?"

"I just told you, what happened is not—"

"What did he give ya?!"

Kozel studied him for a moment, then replied simply, "His

firstborn."

"He *gave* you Dovira?!" Anger surged through Sarl again.

"She was promised to me when she came of age! Surely there are similar arrangements from where you hail."

"An infernal was gonna marry an orc girl? Really, Koz? Really?!"

Kozel grimaced and shook its fists at Sarl in apparent frustration. "Damnit, don't be so obtuse! Obviously, I wasn't going to marry her. But she was to be mine, body and soul, come her eighteenth birthday."

"Why?"

"That is none of your business."

"Okay, so what then? Ya just couldn't wait, so ya had her, *body and soul*, as soon as her old man was out of the way?"

The look of shock on Kozel's face was immediate. "What sort of animal do you take me for, sir?"

Sarl barked out a laugh and responded in a mocking tone. "Oh, I do *so* apologize that I accused an agent of tha abyss of doin' somethin' evil." He rolled his eyes and crossed himself.

Kozel's eyes blazed red in response. "I needed her pure and untouched, you idiot! She is useless to me now! I have done her a favor by addling her mind so she will never remember the ordeal!" It looked around the room, as if looking for something to strike. "She and her virginity were taken from me by those simpletons. Those *ingrates*! I would kill them all over again if I could! I will make sure they suffer in death until time itself dies, and that will still not be enough satisfaction!"

"Oh, stop yer yappin', Koz. You're just mad 'bout tha timin' of events, is all."

"What? How dare you—"

"Shut it, suka!"

Sarl shouted the infernal into silence, his hold on stability threatening to slip away despite his best efforts not to go into a rage. In that instant, he desperately wished that Elise was with him, and he called out to her in his mind. She understood his loss better than anyone else; after all, she had been there so many years ago. Just thinking of the priestess made Sarl's heart rate calm slightly.

C'mon, dog, focus! It's never been 'bout this Dovira, an' ya know it. It's just what she represents to ya. Or rather, who *she represents to ya. Ya can't trust this bastard, but that don't mean it ain't tellin' tha truth. So, do ya believe it or not?*

Kozel had been staring at him, with more of a quizzical look than anything else. Sarl decided in that instant that he didn't care what the infernal had done or not. Ultimately, it was just another impediment to what he needed to accomplish. He still wanted to help Katrya if he could, and he wasn't going to give any information away for free if he could help it.

Fine, call it out an' see what it does. If ya can't use tha shite ta help yerself or Kat, then just kill it like you've been plannin' ta do and get outta town.

"Sorry, Koz. Ya just remind me of someone worth killin', is all. I'm just tryin' ta figure out how one orc girl was gonna help ya take over tha whole kingdom."

The change of expression on Kozel's face was barely perceptible, but Sarl had seen enough eyes filled with hate to recognize that he had hit a nerve. Neither of them spoke, and Sarl assumed that the infernal was sizing him up again. They stood only a few paces apart now, but the momentary silence grew until it filled the room and threatened to spill into the cold night outside.

After a bit, Sarl sighed. "Fine. If ya ain't gonna talk, then I guess we're done."

He shook his head and stepped towards the front door. Kozel immediately moved to block his path, a hard look on its face. When it spoke, it was in a clipped tone that felt unnatural.

"Enough! I've already said that what I wanted that girl for was my business, and my business alone. I don't expect you to understand my machinations or end goal, and I certainly don't have the time or desire to explain them to you. But your attempts to distract me are at an end. You'll tell me what I want to know, and you'll tell me *now*."

"Yeah?" Sarl gave up trying to maneuver towards the door, appearing to stop mid-step. He kept his weight on his front leg.

"Yeah," Kozel retorted mockingly. "I need to know the *real* reason why you're here in the north." It waved Sarl's document in the air again. "Your loyalty to the orders you received from the church is commendable, even if misplaced. But I sense no great personal faith in you, at least none that I care about. There's certainly no martyrdom in your future. There's no heavenly reason why I should put up with your smug attitude if you're here just to kill a few wargs and seek misguided vengeance against me. So, why else are you here? The potential information you've got inside that head of yours is the only reason you're still alive right now."

Sarl consciously rubbed his head with his free hand. "So, not tha power of my faith, but tha power of knowledge in my grey skull? That's a tad scary ta think 'bout, Koz. An' you're not givin' me much of a reason ta share anythin' with ya, ta be honest."

"I will break you if I have to, Sarl. I don't think you would like that. This is your last chance."

The words were spoken calmly and quietly, as if discussing the weather, but Sarl could hear the dark malice behind them.

Sarl thought of the passe-dix games he had watched recently at the Wild Boar. It was time to gamble. "So ya can just kill me after I tell ya? Nah, I wanna deal 'fore I say somethin' worthwhile."

There was a short pause, and then a low chuckle came from the infernal. "Really, Sarl? How delightful. A trade involving the information in your head so that you can keep it attached to your shoulders, is that it? A pitiful exchange all around, but I might be amenable to it just the same."

It chuckled again, shaking its head in apparent disbelief. "The bedtimes stories haven't warned you off? Or do you think you can do better than Dovira's father in an exchange with me?"

Sarl shook his own head slightly. "I ain't lookin' for power or wealth. I just need ta know that Kat is safe from whatever ya got goin' on. Then we can talk 'bout what part of me may or may not get carved up."

There was another pause, and Kozel seemed to be staring at him even more intently than before. Finally, the infernal spoke in a dismissive tone.

"You do know that doxy has already done enough on her own to warrant a welcomed place in my master's eternal house, do you not? It matters not what I might allow to happen to her, or even what I think of her."

Sarl shrugged. "Us mortals are all lost causes at some point. Guess I want her ta have time ta find some grace an' not have ya take her away 'cause of some deal ya made with Yuri."

Kozel rolled his eyes. "That buffoon? I can honestly tell you that I have not dealt with him at all."

That's interestin'. Does that mean Yuri's tha one tied to tha whippin' post if somethin' goes wrong? But what are ya doin' that could go wrong in tha first place?

"Well, Kira then."

Kozel smiled, somewhat smugly. "Dear, dear Kira. More cunning than most and definitely worthy of a fate better than what awaits her here as second-in-command to that moronic sheriff. Her deal with me was born out of desperation, but it makes sense and is a reasonable gamble for her. I do like her, and I hope things work out for her. But then, what you will tell me plays into what she and I must do. Or not do, perhaps. That is the question."

"Is Kat tied to her sister's fate then?" Sarl pressed.

"Mmm, perhaps, but not because of anything I have done. Kira was quite insistent that I leave her sister alone, which I have done until now. But that, of course, is a blade that cuts both ways. If dear Katrya happens to be in the wrong place at the wrong time, well...I suppose the future can be a mystery even to me at times."

Sarl already had his answer and his proverbial money, but he rolled the dice one more time anyway. "So, ya won't let me deal for her?"

The infernal frowned. "Why do you care about her fate anyway?"

Sarl shrugged. "Seems like a nice girl, all things considered. She don't like Yuri, so that's a plus. An' she knows more of what's goin' on 'round here than most, so I might as well scratch her back a bit while she scratches mine."

That an' she reminds me of Elise, but I sure as shite ain't gonna tell ya that, suka.

Kozel looked at Sarl with a blank look in its eyes. "Whatever makes you sleep better at night, I suppose. But, no, I will not deal for that barmaid's pathetic soul. Katrya Toth's fate will not change based upon whatever you and I decide here. You should worry about your own skin instead of that trollop. Now, quickly, as the hour is late. What information will you trade for your life? For that is about all I am willing offer for what you may have to tell me."

So, Kat ain't part of the deal ya made with Kira, an' it don't sound like she's connected ta anythin' else ya want ta do here. That's good enough for me, an' that's probably good enough for her. Sarl smirked. "Ah, forget it, Koz. I'll tell ya what ya want ta know. It's not like I trust ya anyways."

"Then why did you just waste my—" The infernal's voice trailed off, and the look on its face became even more irritated. Sarl wondered if it had just realized it had told him too much about the two sisters, but it didn't matter either way.

"I'll tell ya tha truth, Koz, 'cause I don't care if ya know. Them wargs and tha order ta kill 'em are just a means ta an end. Tha church wanted them gone in a hurry, so they're usin' me as a hired merc. But I got other things ta do in tha kingdom, an' this gave me a way ta move cross country without bein' stopped all tha time or worryin' 'bout gettin' inta towns like this one. Followin' a shapeshifter all over tha countryside was good cover, too, if anyone ever asked 'bout ya. Which they haven't, by tha way."

Kozel still had a sour look on its face, but it seemed to be thinking. After a few moments, it crossed its arms. "'Other things'? What, pray tell, does that mean?"

"Ya think all I track are beasts for skins?" Sarl's grin grew larger, his teeth on full display, as he gestured over at his axe with the hand still holding his shirt. "That ain't no trapper's weapon, suka."

Kozel snorted. "What, you fancy yourself an assassin of some sort?"

"Merely a cutthroat, Koz. Although 'head loppa' might fit the actual deed a bit better."

"No official mandate to show me, Sir Head Lopper?" Kozel

sneered, becoming visibly angry.

"It's up here," Sarl replied, pointing at his head. "Ya said ya wanted what was in my grey skull, didn't ya?"

"Idiot! As inept as I find Yuri and his ilk to be, even they won't let you run around the countryside killing humans instead of wargs!"

"Who said I was tryin' ta kill humans, Koz?"

The infernal opened its mouth, then snapped it closed as the look on its face turned quizzical. After a long moment, it raised its eyebrows in realization.

"You're hunting your own kind?"

"Specific ones, yeah."

"But, why?"

"Tribal matters, Koz. I ain't gonna bore ya with tha details. Just know my orders were ta investigate tha Wilds 'round Stren and the mountain ta tha north, so I got lucky ya came back this way with those wargs of yers. That holy paper I picked up worked out better than I thought it would."

Kozel frowned. "I would like to believe you, but there are far too many open questions. Why did you come to the assistance of the priest, then?"

"'Cause he was good at killin' wargs, Koz. An' maybe if I could have talked with him, he'd know somethin' 'bout my real prey from all his travels."

"And why have you taken such a shine to Katrya?"

"I just told ya, 'cause she's tha kind of girl that knows

everythin' an' everyone in town. An' I'd rather talk ta her than that bitch of a sister she's got."

"And that sending stone around your neck, who are you in contact with and giving updates to about your escapades?"

"My...what?"

Shite, so it does know about it! Does that mean it knows about Elise too?

Sarl's skin started to tingle, and he imperceptibly tensed as the infernal shook its fist at him.

"*Damn* you and your fake innocence! That bloody pendant of yours oozes old magic. And if that wasn't annoying enough to my senses, it's been shining brightly for some time now! I can only assume that means you've been communicating with the person with the other stone. Who is it, orc? Who is your taskmaster?"

Sarl glanced down in surprise to see that the stone was glowing faintly, the bluish-green hue coming from it contrasting wildly with the reddish-orange light being cast around the room by the fire. He had never known it to shine like this, and he caught it up in his free hand for a moment to gaze at it.

Beware, Siryy Vovk, beware! You stand before pure evil, my love! Hold fast to what you know is true!

"What was that?!" Kozel demanded sharply. "A woman? What is she saying? I will not allow you to—"

Without warning, Sarl threw his shirt at the infernal's face and leapt forward with a scream.

CHAPTER THREE
Unmasked

Katrya Toth remained in bed for a few long moments after Sarl disappeared down the stairs into the darkness below, wondering who was waiting for him. For both of them, really. She didn't have much information on why the meeting was happening in the first place. Her older sister, Kira, had been fairly secretive about who wanted to meet with the orc, just that it had to be done quietly.

"See if ya can lure that oaf ta my place tonight. That'll be better than yer hovel or a room above tha tavern," she had told Katrya earlier in the day. "My, uh, friend, has a key ta tha back door and can let themselves in if they get there before ya do."

"If this meetin' is gonna be at yer place, then why can't ya just take tha orc there yerself?"

"There's been some sort of attack out in tha Wilds, an' Yuri's got me goin' out ta check on it. I gotta leave soon as we're done talkin'. And no, I can't ask Yuri or anyone else ta do this while I'm gone, Kat. Like I said, it's gotta be quiet like."

Kira had seemed distracted and a bit uneasy, and Katrya knew better than to press her sister with too many questions. Still, something seemed off to her about why Kira didn't want to involve the sheriff.

Ain't Yuri yer lover? Don't he know 'bout this friend of yers?

Katrya was still unconvinced about the whole situation. "But how do ya expect me ta lure that greyskin ta yer place? Other than tryin' ta gig me for local news, he seems more interested in goulash than girls, ta be honest."

Kira had looked at her sideways. "I *know* ya don't believe what ya just said. 'Sides, he's just another pig of a male who'll think with his tiny head when ya need him ta. Flash those pretty white teeth of yers, or maybe yer teets if ya have ta, an' he'll come runnin' like all tha rest. Same con we've always run."

Katrya had flushed hot with anger at the time, and she did so again now as she thought about her conversation with her sister. She couldn't admit to Kira that this con felt different than all the rest. It confused her, because using her Almighty-given assets to get what she wanted had never bothered her before. She could argue with herself that, in this instance, she didn't know what she was personally getting out of the exchange between the orc and Kira's friend. So, there was no way of knowing the benefits versus the risks of what she was being asked to do. She didn't even know the name of the person that Sarl was meeting.

A modicum of light made its way up to the sleeping area from downstairs, as apparently a fire had been lit in the hearth. Katrya leaned forward as bits and pieces of banter floated her way, and she was able to make out Kira's apparent "friend" introduce themselves as Kozel. She caught a few more words of the conversation before the two switched into Sarl's native tongue.

The Orcish language had always sounded harsh to her ears,

at least until an hour ago when Sarl had whispered some unknown phrase to her in their throes of passion. He had touched her *just so* when he had uttered the words, and she had melted. She flushed again, although not in anger this time, but at the memory of how ready she had been to receive him at that moment.

Shaking her head to clear it, Katrya quietly got out of bed and began to dress. She tried to think about her problem with Sarl in a more rational manner. What had he said right before he had gone downstairs, after he had guessed correctly about her and her sister trying to leave town? *Lemme see if I can figure out tha price of his ticket for ya.* Did he really give a damn about her and what she desperately wanted? Nobody had ever lifted a finger for her without expecting a kickback or a favor in return, except for Kira. Was this orc truly that selfless?

He can't be, ya ninny! But what kind of con is he runnin' then?

She hadn't seen the hook that he had obviously baited by agreeing to come along with her tonight, and that bothered her. She also couldn't tell if the bait was for her or for this Kozel person, and that *really* bothered her.

Beyond her own issues with him, what was Sarl doing in Stren anyway? Why was Kira so interested in him? And who was this mystery woman from his past that he was apparently still saving himself for? Loyalty to, or perhaps just thoughts of, an old lover had kept the orc from entering her, which just made her want to conquer him all the more.

Never mind this Kozel person downstairs; Sarl was the *real* stranger to Katrya.

She stared out the sleeping quarter's window at the moon and contemplated life's mysteries as the sounds of two people talking rose and fell beneath her.

Suddenly, there was a loud roar that had to have come from the orc, followed quickly by the sound of bodies colliding. Katrya had been around enough bar fights to instantly realize what was happening. She darted to the top of the stairs and proceeded halfway down to the ground floor before she could make out the unfolding scene.

Sarl was sitting on top of someone she assumed was Kozel, who looked to be a young man of slight build. The orc was still shirtless, and the light from the fire flickered across his menacing features. He leaned in towards Kozel and shouted something in Orcish that Katrya didn't understand.

"Potsiluy mene, persh nizh trakhnuty, suka!"

Sarl's sharp teeth snapped in cadence with his words, and he seemed ready to bite the young man's head off. Katrya was frozen in place at his ugly tone, sensing the anger rolling off the orc. Strangely, the pendant that he wore around his neck shone brightly as it hung on its chain between the two combatants. She had never seen anything like this before, and it was slightly mesmerizing. Both its bluish-green light and the muscles in Sarl's arms pulsed as he brought his face even closer to Kozel's.

Kozel's reaction to the orc was confusing to Katrya, to say

the least. He laughed. He laughed brightly, as if Sarl was the love of his life and had just said something ridiculously silly and sweet.

But then the young man looked right at *her*, and his eyes flashed red as a cruel-looking smile spread across his face. Katrya opened her mouth to scream, but no sound came out.

Sarl seemed to apply more of his body weight onto Kozel before he glanced in her direction as well. At that instant, Kozel appeared to sink slightly into the floor and slither out from under the orc. Now Katrya *did* let out a short shriek, not quite believing her eyes.

Sarl grunted and went to grab the young man again, but it was too late. Seemingly without effort, Kozel used his legs to kick the orc backwards, away from himself and the fireplace. He stood quickly and adjusted his shirt as the orc collected himself where he had landed, near the cooking area at the back of the room.

"Ah, Sarl. A predictable attack, to be sure, but I must say your quickness did surprise me. Too bad that it gained you nothing. I assume this means our conversation is at an end?"

Kozel had spoken in Common, apparently so that Katrya could understand him, and his eyes moved back and forth between her and the orc as he assessed the overall situation.

"Shut it, suka!" Sarl said grimly, and he spat on the floor for emphasis. "If ya didn't get what ya wanted from me, then maybe ya should just leave."

Kozel's laugh now came out as a sharp, short bark. "Hardly, good sir. If you won't tell me all that you know, then I must assume the worst."

A sleek, wicked-looking hunting knife appeared in each of his hands, seemingly out of thin air.

"And since you seem to have no true affiliation with the church, that only makes you one thing to me. *Expendable.*"

With lightning speed, Kozel leapt at Sarl, knives extended. The orc somehow dodged the initial lunge and then guessed correctly at which way Kozel would slash, rolling towards Katrya and the staircase as the blades cut harmlessly through the air. Sarl rose to a crouch as Kozel straightened, turned, and then matched the orc's pose from several paces away.

The orc glanced quickly over at Katrya and growled at her, "Get outta here, Kat. Either upstairs out tha window or out tha back. I don't think it'll kill ya 'cause of yer sister, but ya shouldn't take tha chance!"

"But who is he?" Kat hissed back at him. "And why is my sister mixed up with him?"

"Still not sure, but she better be good at playin' poker," came the reply. "An' like I said earlier, *it* ain't a '*he*,' Kat."

As Sarl finished speaking, he slowly circled away from her and towards the large table in the middle of the room.

"What?" Katrya was beyond confused now.

Kozel had obviously overhead them, and he spoke in a light tone as he mimicked the orc's movements. "Oh, my dear Katrya, your sister has left you rather in the dark, hasn't she? Do not fear, I will explain everything once I have dealt with the vermin infesting her house."

He rushed at Sarl again. The orc had already taken hold of one of the chairs by the table, and he slung it at Kozel in an attempt at deflecting the incoming attack. Kozel gracefully dodged the large projectile and continued forward all in a single motion, his right knife coming down in a large arc. The weapon caught the orc in his left bicep, but the following uppercut from its brethren slashed nothing but air as Sarl shifted out of the way. An angry red line formed on his upper arm, but he appeared none the worse for wear beyond that.

"Ah, first blood, quite literally, for me!" Kozel chortled. "Such *fun*, Sarl. Perhaps you'll make for a good sparring partner after all. It's been some time since I've had to administer a death by a thousand cuts."

"Whatever, suka," Sarl growled through clenched teeth. "If ya think ya can end it quick-like, then get it over with."

Why hasn't he gone for his axe? Can he not get to it? *Maybe...maybe* I *can get to it?*

Katrya had spied the orc's main weapon next to the front door, resting on the floor along with his satchel. She cautiously took another two steps down the staircase, but Kozel immediately looked in her direction and shook his head in almost an apologetic manner.

"My dear, I would beg that you do not interfere with the, ahem, ongoing discussion. Just wait and see if your current lover can somehow save you. I mean, he is quite correct that I don't want to kill you, but..." His eyes lingered on her for a moment, and then he shrugged and let the threat go unspoken.

Katrya felt her face harden. "I ain't no damsel in distress, *suka*!"

She spat out the insult she had heard Sarl use several times, and he chuckled from across the room as Kozel's eyes widened slightly. But if he had any concerns about Katrya understanding the recent conversation between him and the orc, they seemed to instantly fade. His arrogant nature recovered quickly enough.

"Yes, well, I suppose you'd have to be a damsel first, hmm?" Without waiting for her reply, he turned back towards his prey.

Instead of hurling another insult at Kozel's back, Katrya turned and ran back up the stairs, her feet pounding on the steps as she took them two at a time. Behind her, she could hear the young man speak loudly to Sarl, as if he knew she would be listening.

"Excellent! Now that the little minx is taking your advice and running away, let us end this dance without further interruption." The sound of something wooden being broken followed, along with several other indistinguishable noises.

Katrya went straight to the window and threw it open. It was still a cold night, but the wind had abated. She looked at the street below, the individual cobblestones indistinguishable from each other at this distance. The moonlight cast eerie shadows from nearby chimneys across her apparent path of escape along the rooftop, but the way forward was easy enough to see. She took a deep breath before proceeding.

"Thief! Thief!"

Her voice split the quiet night like a thunderclap. Immediately, from several streets over, there was a flash of light, and she knew that the night watch had heard her and had fully uncovered their lantern in order to respond to a call for help. She thanked the Almighty that they weren't too far away.

"Thief! *Thief!*" she called out again, a bit more stridently this time, and she directed her voice towards the light.

There was a moment's hesitation, as if the watchmen were finding their bearings, and then the light started moving towards her.

From down the street to her right, another light flickered on from a second-story window, and a dog started barking somewhere in the distance. Sensing she had done all she could to cause a public ruckus, Katrya turned away from the window to head back to the fighting.

Before she left the sleeping area, Katrya looked around quickly for anything that could be considered a weapon. She didn't know what she would do if she found something worthwhile to wield, but in any event, nothing useful stood out to her. She couldn't even recall there being any weapons stored in the back room on the ground floor. Kira always had her sword with her when she wasn't at home, and as far as Katrya knew, her sister kept any secondary weapons at the town hall.

As she was looking around, there were the sounds of another large collision and Kozel laughing merrily. Cursing under her breath in frustration at not being able to do more to defend herself, Katrya once again headed downstairs.

Now the scene that awaited her was much more chaotic in nature. All the chairs except one were now broken, bits and pieces of wood strewn about the large room. The table had been tipped over onto its side, and it blocked the entrance to the back room. Whether this was on purpose or by chance was hard to say.

The fire still burned brightly, but several logs had cascaded out of the hearth and lay smoldering on the floor. As far as Katrya could tell, the house was in no immediate danger of burning down, although there would be scorch marks left in the hardwood planking to commemorate the fight.

It appeared to Katrya as though Kozel had been pushed or thrown into the fire, and that was what had caused the issue with the logs. As he circled past the staircase, he shook himself and bits of ash and some dying embers fell off the back of his jacket. Oddly, the jacket itself did not appear to be singed anywhere.

She glanced over at Sarl and couldn't help but gasp. He clearly had been getting the worst of the fight, as at least half a dozen small cuts were now visible on his chest and arms. None seemed to be fatal, but blood was now smeared across his torso. There were potentially more cuts on his legs as well, given the tears in his pants that Katrya didn't recall seeing earlier.

Sarl still didn't have his axe, and the way he and Kozel were circling the room, it was obvious to Katrya that the young man was taking great pains to keep the orc away from the front door and his weapon. Instead, Sarl held a piece of firewood in one hand and the leg of a chair in the other as he seemingly looked for an opening to attack his opponent. His pendant shone more brightly now, casting a garish light across his features. He quickly glanced over at Katrya as she came to a halt at the bottom of the stairs and gave her a mixture of a grin and a grimace.

"Sorry this is takin' a bit, Kat. If ya ain't gonna leave, I'm open ta any suggestions ya might have."

"Oh my, you *must* be desperate if you're asking the lovely Katrya Toth for assistance!" Kozel laughed again, although this time there was a hint of malice in his overly cheerful demeanor. If he was surprised that she was still present, he certainly didn't show it. "Don't you know she's a lover, not a fighter? Every well-hung male in town knows that, don't they, *luv*?" He looked at her, mocking her informal term of endearment. "Probably some not-so-well-hung males, too, at least from the stories I've heard. You're obviously not that picky, are you, my dear?"

Katrya felt tears of anger forming, and she clenched her fists at her side. She had been called a whore—and much worse—over the years, but it didn't mean the insult simply rolled off her back. But instead of crying, she raised her chin slightly in defiance and took a step forward.

She spoke loudly while keeping her gaze fixed on Kozel. "Don't worry, *luv*. I called tha night watch, an' they'll be here shortly. Far as I know, ya ain't supposed ta be here, so I guess I just caught a thief tryin' ta rob my sister's house. An' since I musta slept with all tha guards, I reckon they'll believe me over any story of yers. Don't ya think so, *bitch*?"

Kozel looked at her as if for the first time, his eyes turning a dark red. "Clever girl…" was all he could manage. He cocked his head, as if listening for the sounds of someone approaching from outside, and his weapons lowered just a fraction.

"*Waaaaaaaaagh!*"

Katrya sensed rather than saw two shapes hurl through the air as Sarl slung his improvised weapons at Kozel and charged, yelling at the top of his lungs. The young man, apparently caught off guard for the second time by the speed of an attack, managed to deflect the pieces of wood but was barreled over as the orc crashed into him.

Kozel rolled deftly away to his left, but Sarl didn't pursue him. Instead, he rolled the other way, ending up next to the front door. Without turning around, he knocked the iron bar barricading the door up and out of its brackets with his left hand as he picked up his great axe with his right.

Sarl rolled his shoulders, seemingly growing in size as he gripped his axe with both hands. Katrya shuddered as the orc's countenance grew dark, flecks of saliva mixing with the blood on his chest as he bared his teeth at Kozel.

"Door's open, suka. But I think ya didn't run away in time."

"A berserker…fascinating…" she heard Kozel half-whisper in awe before Sarl charged again, impossibly fast and without warning.

The sound of weapons coming together rang out as Kozel barely parried Sarl's initial blow, but he was pushed back and was clearly now the one on the defensive. Sarl pressed his attack mercilessly, using his axe as a battering ram as he caught Kozel in the midsection. The massive hit doubled him over, and Sarl took advantage by kicking one of his legs out from under him.

Kozel expertly turned his fall into a roll, but the orc's weapon still caught him with a glancing blow across his back. The young man howled in pain but kept rolling, staying just ahead of several more slashing attacks. He wound up sprawled against the upset table and just managed to deflect the orc's last swing with both of his blades so that the axe embedded itself in the table a palm's width above his head.

Sarl roared and lashed out with another kick, and Kozel had no time to take advantage of the situation. Instead, he rolled away again, towards the fireplace, giving the orc time to dislodge his weapon. They faced each other, breathing heavily, the silence between them more forceful than any insult could have been.

Now there were the sounds from the street of footsteps running, and the front door burst open as Mykhailo, the night watch's leader, forced himself into the room. The rest of his squad followed him inside, suddenly making the large room somewhat cramped for space. All four soldiers had their weapons out and looked ready for a fight.

Mykhailo looked over at Katrya, glancing up and down, as if to see if she was injured, a concerned look on his face. "Ya hurt,

Kat?" he asked her, somewhat breathlessly.

"Nah, I ain't hurt. But ya need ta arrest that little *bitch* by tha fireplace. He ain't—"

Before she could finish, Sarl wordlessly charged Kozel again, his large weapon held to his side with both hands as if to engage in a sweeping attack. Kozel had something of a maniacal smile on his face, and he raised his weapons to meet the charge. But instead of sweeping his axe like a scythe through wheat, Sarl simply brought it in front of him and, ignoring Kozel's knives completely, pushed forward and brought the handle into full contact with the young man's face.

Kozel, stunned, stumbled backwards, dropping his knives in the process, and Sarl finished his charge by knocking him directly into the fire. Kozel didn't make a sound, and he appeared to be unconscious as his body landed limply in the middle of the fireplace.

Flames immediately licked hungrily at his flesh and clothing, and a mass of black smoke slowly started billowing out into the room.

Mykhailo had a stern look on his face and an exasperated tone in his voice as he swiveled towards Sarl, and he and the other guards readied their weapons. "Ho there, sirrah! That'll be enough outta ya, right now! You're gonna..."

His voice trailed away as the large orc turned his face towards the group of humans, a crazed look in his eyes.

"You're gonna..." The squad leader visibly swallowed after

starting to repeat himself, but he didn't lower his weapon. Instead, he went into a battle stance and signaled his men to fan out behind him.

"No!" Katrya cried out desperately. "He ain't tha problem! Sarl, luv, ya gotta—"

"It ain't over!" Sarl's voice came out strangled, as if it were an effort for him to form words.

Turning away from the guards, he took a step towards the fireplace, stepping on Kozel's knives that lay on the floor in front of the hearth. With a single motion, he grabbed both handles in his left hand and quickly wrenched them up while still standing on the weapons. The razor thin blades snapped in unison, and he threw the handles to the side before grasping his own weapon with both hands again. He faced the hearth in a crouch.

"It ain't over!" he said again in a low growl.

There was the sound of a familiar laugh from within the fireplace, and Katrya's blood ran cold.

"No, it is far from over, my friend." Kozel's voice was calm, and he stepped out of the smoke, seemingly unhurt. "It is only just getting interesting. But now that there are more witnesses, I must—"

He halted, having spied what was left of his weapons on the floor in front of him. A look of absolute grief played across his face. "My...my precious... What have you done?"

Sarl leered at him, teeth fully on display. "What's tha matter, Koz? Need some new toys, ya little *pizda*?"

"*What have you done?!*" the young man shrieked at the orc, holding his head in his hands and grasping his hair, as if he was about to pull it out in dismay.

Mykhailo took a step forward. "That's enough! You're both gonna stand down an' do exactly as I say. Orc, drop yer weapon or we'll make ya drop it. An' you, young sir, you're gonna—"

Katrya eyes were riveted on Kozel, as he paid no attention to the commands being given. For a moment, he seemed about to cry.

Suddenly, his eyes blazed red, and the rest of his face shifted out of focus. He pointed a finger at Sarl, and his flesh and clothing appeared to meld together into a black mass as his fingernails started to extend out to an absurd length.

Mykhailo's voice trailed away as the air seemed to filter out all other noise in the room as Kozel spoke in a guttural, dark tone.

"Ego dominus tuus sum et patieris!"

Katrya winced as the words wormed their way into her head. For a fleeting moment, it felt as though Kozel had forced his will upon her. Somehow the church's language felt perverted and twisted as he spoke, and her heart skipped a beat. The guards all staggered back a few paces as if they had been physically assaulted.

Sarl seemed to brace himself, and the grip on his weapon visibly tightened. He gave a short laugh and barked out in reply, "Drop tha costume, *suka khuylo*!"

Kozel raised his face towards the ceiling and howled. As he did so, his body grew in size so that it almost equaled the orc's mass, muscles bulging in his arms and legs.

Katrya could no longer describe the evolving creature in front of her as human, and now she understood why Sarl had referred to Kozel as *it* instead of *he*. As she looked on in horror, the head became misshapen as the nose and mouth turned into a snout full of long, pointed teeth. All manner of clothing was swallowed up into the black mass of thick fur that enveloped the beast's entire body.

She now realized that the stories about shapeshifters must be true, and yet this transformation seemed more horrible than any story she had heard. For while the monster standing in front of them had the appearance of a large, black wolf, there was a deeper sense of evil purpose about it. The only things that seemed to remain of the thin, young man who had been standing there only a few moments before were the creature's eyes, and they continued to blaze in a furious red as it surveyed the room.

The morphing had been so quick, so hideous, that none of the humans in the room had taken it upon themselves to react. They remained frozen in place, either from disbelief or from fear, as the abomination leered over them.

Sarl, though, who seemed to have known what was going to transpire, had taken a more defensive stance. The great axe's double-bladed head rotated slowly as he turned the weapon's handle over in his hands. In the bright light of the night watch's lantern, it seemed to Katrya that the cutting edges of the blades flashed silver as they turned.

There was no time to ponder what this meant, however, as Kozel seized the closest guard by the throat before anyone else could react. The poor fellow gave out a gurgle as he was raised into the air, his legs kicking ineffectually at the monster's side. As the other guards looked on in stupefied horror, the man dropped his sword as he beat helplessly at the large paw that held him.

"Veni, vidi, occidi!" Kozel croaked, and it looked straight at Mykhailo and the rest of the humans.

The man it was holding gave one last spasm before his head disappeared inside the maw of the beast. The other guards cried out in dismay as their brother-in-arms was brutally decapitated in front of them.

Katrya's own mouth opened and shut soundlessly, but before she could think to scream, she saw Sarl's shoulders tighten as he pivoted slightly and launched himself at Kozel.

Sarl came at the beast directly, his weapon above his head. Kozel quickly swung what remained of the guard's body into the path of attack, but the force of the orc's rush was such that he plowed through the grisly matter unimpeded. His axe flashed as it descended, and Kozel made an awful noise as contact was made with its extended arm.

The beast unceremoniously dropped the guard and lashed out at Sarl with one of its back legs. Sarl's frontal attack had left his own body unguarded, and he took the full brunt of the kick to his ribcage. He fell to the floor, winded, as the creature spun away, clutching its forearm. Dark blood, barely distinguishable from its black fur, now seeped from its limb and spattered onto the floor.

"Mori para, canis!"

The cruel words seemed to form in the air in front of Kozel's misshapen face, and it let go of its arm as it sprang on top of Sarl, claws extended and mouth open. The orc roared in anger and pain alike as the monster tore into him, and the two struggled on the floor in a tight embrace.

"Do something!" Katrya managed to cry out to the guards, who remained fixed in place, staring at the combatants as if not truly comprehending what they were seeing.

Seeing no reaction from them, she leapt forward and picked up the sword that had been dropped by their fallen comrade. Using all her strength, she attempted a sweeping blow across Kozel's back. It was as if the sword was trying to cut granite, and the blade merely skittered across the creature's hide.

Kozel laughed cruelly as it punched Sarl in the face, Katrya's feeble blow seemingly having no effect at all. As she raised her weapon to try again, it turned on her without warning and grabbed her arm that held the sword. She winced in pain as the monster squeezed tightly, and she dropped the weapon. All she could do was look into its blazing red eyes as its teeth hungrily approached her face.

The rest of reality fell away. Death had come for her, and she closed her eyes to receive its kiss.

"Idi na khuy, Koz!" From somewhere in the mists that surrounded her, Katrya heard Sarl cry out.

Kozel suddenly screamed and let go of her, and she stumbled backwards and fell to the floor. Dazed and confused, it took her a moment to understand what had happened. She had distracted the beast long enough for Sarl to make one final cut with his axe, and his strike had cut deep across Kozel's abdomen. It screamed again as it lurched backwards, grievously hurt and in obvious pain.

Someone was standing over her, looking down at her, and now they were advancing to where the orc lay on the ground. She vaguely recognized Mykhailo's profile as he reached down to grab Sarl with his free hand, struggling to drag him backwards towards the front door. The squad leader had recovered from his initial shock, and his sword was at the ready as he turned back towards the wounded monster.

Katrya got to her feet and staggered back towards the front door and the remaining humans. She glanced over at Kozel, who had made no move to attack Mykhailo when he had retrieved the fallen orc. In fact, the creature didn't seem to be paying attention to anything but the fire, and it stood with its back towards them. Dark liquid streamed from its midsection, and Katrya could see little puffs of smoke emanating from where it was striking the floor.

Before she could go to Sarl's side to check on him, a low, gruesome chuckle came from the beast. It raised its head once more to the ceiling as it laughed, but it broke off suddenly in a retching noise. Looking over its shoulder at the group huddled together, its eyes still burning, it spat blood on the floor and directly addressed the fallen orc.

"Ah, Sarl. My mistake...my hubris...for underestimating your cunning. If we both manage to recover...I look forward to a rematch." It spoke in Common, but with such a distorted accent it was difficult for Katrya to understand what it was saying. The monster's head seemed to bob in a modicum of respect towards the orc, before it turned fully to face her.

It regarded her coolly for a long moment, the silence stretching between them, as it held its arms tight around its gut wound. Mykhailo and one of the other guards moved close to her and took up defensive stances, but they seemed content with letting the creature make the first move.

Finally, it rolled its shoulders in a bit of a shrug. "Well met, Katrya Toth. We shall have words, anon. Oh yes...we shall have words."

Katrya hugged herself as she faced the monster, but before she could fashion any sort of response, Kozel made a feint towards the group. She and the two guards next to her took a quick step backwards, but instead of attacking, Kozel merely barked a short laugh, turned, and in one long stride was next to the overturned table. Shoving it aside with some effort, the creature disappeared into the back room without another word, a trail of blood marking its passage.

Mykhailo shook his head and crossed himself quickly, muttering what seemed to be a prayer under his breath. He again glanced over at Katrya to make sure she was okay before speaking to the guard to his immediate right. “Marko! Get ta tha town hall an’ sound tha alarm, *now*! We can’t have that monster loose inside tha walls! An’ find tha sheriff, we gotta tell him what’s happened.”

He then looked at the remaining guard, who was several paces away. “Felix, check tha back room an’ make sure that thing is really gone, then barricade tha back door an’ come back here.”

While Marko had already started to move towards the front door, Felix remained rooted in place, ashen-faced, shaking his head while looking at the remains of his slain compatriot. He whimpered softly, as if to himself, “I ain’t checkin’ nuthin’! We’re dead, we’re all dead...”

“We’re all dead if we don’t act. Get yourself together, man!” Mykhailo cursed and shook his head in frustration as Felix did not appear to even hear him. “Fine! I’ll check tha back room, just wait here.” He glanced down at his weapon and then again at Katrya. “Check on your friend, Kat. I wager we’ll need ta get him some help. Never seen anythin’ like that before. Yuri will want ta talk ta both of ya ’bout what happened ’fore we got here. ’Specially since that thing seemed ta know ya!”

Katrya nodded her head, to make sure Mykhailo knew she had heard him. He reached out and pressed her hand lightly, almost tenderly, before remembering himself. Releasing his grip, he moved towards the back room without another word.

Katrya found herself moving slowly towards Sarl as her surroundings fell away, out of focus. He had propped himself up on the wall by the front door, and she could tell that he was breathing heavily. As she drew closer, she could see the sweat covering his face. Blood oozed slowly out from his various wounds, and yellow pus was forming along the edges of where Kozel's nails and teeth had torn into him. The pendant around his neck looked cold and still, as if it had never been lit up like a beacon.

He looked up at her with obvious effort as she approached. "Guess Koz finally had enough, eh, Kat?" He tried to chuckle, but it quickly turned into a choking cough.

She knelt next to him, trying to assess the extent of his injuries but not knowing where to start. She gently squeezed his hand. "You was right, luv. It ain't a 'he' for sure."

"Yeah, but I wasn't sure 'til tonight that it was an infernal. If it was just a shapeshifter, things woulda gone a whole lot smoother. Hard way ta find out tha truth, huh?"

Katrya shivered and lowered her eyes. She had never been one to truly believe in heaven, or the abyss, or the existence of beings of true good and evil, but it was hard to discount what she had just witnessed.

Sarl weakly lifted his free hand and touched her face so that she looked up into his eyes. "Thanks, Kat, for what ya did. I owe ya one."

"Whaddya mean, luv?"

"I mean, if ya didn't call tha night watch, I...well, I'm not sure things woulda ended with me still breathin'. Thought I could take it, an' that sure didn't happen. Got lucky there at tha end with tha distractions ta hurt it bad enough ta make it run. But even now,

I don't think it'll be gone for long."

Her eyes widened. "Ya mean it'll come back? After that beatin' ya gave it?"

He gave her something of a sideways smirk. "I'm tha one layin' on tha floor, Kat. You an' yer guard friends bein' here were what made it wanna go lick its wounds. As disgustin' as that'll be..."

Katrya was surprised at this. She had thought he had given Kozel a death blow, despite the monster's bravado at the end.

Nobody recovers from a gut wound like that! Well, no human anyway...

"Then, how can ya stop it?"

Sarl sighed heavily and spoke with some effort. "I don't think I can, least not completely. Was able ta nick it hard, an' that'll take time ta recover from. But now I'm guessin' we need that priest of yers, or somebody else strong enough in their faith, ta banish tha thing back ta tha abyss ta really get rid of it." He sighed again and looked up at her. "An' yeah, I assume it'll be back ta finish whatever it's plottin' with yer sister."

Katrya swallowed hard. *Kira, what have ya done*?

She hoped that her sister had been duped by the monster into some sort of twisted deal that could be broken, but in her heart, she knew this was unlikely.

"You sure it's dealin' with my sister, an' not Yuri?" she asked, her misgiving showing itself in her voice.

"It said as much when we was talkin'. Guess it could be lyin', but it sure sounds like Yuri's tha patsy in their plan. Don't exactly know what tha plan is, though, our conversation ended up bein' a bit short." Sarl tried to chuckle again, but this time the resulting cough ended in him spitting blood. He looked visibly weaker than just a few moments ago.

Katrya looked around in growing desperation, the room coming back into focus. Felix hadn't moved and was still talking to himself, rocking back and forth. The other guard had left some time ago now, and the smoke had mostly cleared from the room to reveal the detritus of the battle.

Mykhailo came through the door from the back room, sheathing his sword and muttering to himself. Katrya called out to him, somewhat hysterically.

"Mykha! Please, he's hurt bad, an' I don't know what ta do!"

Ignoring Felix, Mykhailo came running over and knelt on the other side of the orc. He did a cursory examination and shook his head. "There's more here than just normal wounds, Kat. We got ta get him ta tha town hall or tha chapel, an' quick."

"Holy water…" the orc whispered weakly.

"What's that?" Mykhailo asked sharply, and both he and Katrya leaned in towards Sarl.

"Holy water on tha wounds…seen it work against warg attacks, might help me too…'less I ain't righteous enough." Sarl didn't try and chuckle this time, but a small smile still crept across his face as he closed his eyes.

Katrya let out a quiet sob, and Mykhailo glanced over at her before responding to the orc.

"Aye, holy water. Makes sense ta me. An' I don't know how righteous ya are, orc, but for what ya just did, ya got both my thanks an' my prayers." He shifted his gaze to Katrya and spoke to her quietly. "Kat, I got no one ta send if that bloody fool Felix can't get himself together. Not until reinforcements come, anyway, an' that may be a bit. Can ya make a run ta tha chapel?"

Katrya nodded quickly. The irony of her, of all people, running towards the church for help was not lost on her.

She quickly bent over and kissed Sarl on the forehead. "I'll be back 'fore ya know it, luv."

"No worries, Kat. I ain't goin' nowhere." He didn't open his eyes.

"Ya better not."

Katrya rose to her feet and dashed out the front door.

CHAPTER FOUR
Of Church and Children

The weather remained interminably damp as Grand Inquisitor Moirne Koval continued north from the watch house where she and her longtime friend Aerysiel had met the night before. The morning sun was weak and without warmth, and even its modicum of brightness was muted by the hour of Sext as rain and grey skies returned. Unlike the previous day, however, the precipitation was carried by a brisk, cold wind that buffeted against the inquisitor and her mare.

The tow path alongside the Grumaius River used by the donkey teams hauling barges upstream slowly became a muddy mess. After a while, the path was bad enough that, wherever there was a slight downslope, it threatened to slide anyone upon it into the river with little ceremony. In one location, Moirne had to dismount and lead her horse through the slippery muck for several hundred paces. It made for slow going, even for a well-seasoned traveler.

By early afternoon, everyone else on the path or the river appeared to have called it a day, as Moirne neither sensed nor saw any movement. The various donkey teams had had the sense to stop their plodding well before None, no matter how heavy the whip of their masters. The beasts looked miserable each time she passed a group huddled together by the crude tarp enclosures hastily erected by their human brethren. The various boat crews didn't even attempt to stop together in one place for safety, instead mooring wherever they could at short notice. On this day, the weather would be their protection against any bandits or wild creatures.

After several hours of trudging in the driving rain, Moirne knew she would have to stop well before Tuman. Even if she pushed through, she would reach town well after dusk and have to camp outside the city gates until the next morning. She could always force the issue with the town guard by using her rank within the church to enter at night, but that would mean revealing her true identity.

Besides, over the years, she had found that, in nonreligious situations at least, it was better to try and get her way without invoking the Almighty. Most common folk already feared or hated the inquisition, and she was careful to play upon these reactions only when truly needed. In any event, why impart bruised egos on some guards or endure a cold, damp night of camping when she had the watch houses at her disposal?

As before, the old watch houses built during the Time of Troubles and situated every few leagues along the road between Velych and Tuman were open to her due to her status within the church. Even if they had fallen out of use and soldiers of the realm had not been posted within them for quite some time, most were still in good repair. Moirne found herself eagerly looking for the next one to appear out of the gloom.

Unfortunately, the next watch house she encountered was one of the few along the road that had been damaged beyond use, as some long-forgotten fire had completely gutted it. The roof had collapsed, and there was no shelter to be had amongst the ruins. The forest had pulled back from the road and wasn't as thick overhead as it had been farther south, making any camping in the sodden underbrush around the ruins a dismal prospect. There was nothing to do except continue forward.

It was almost time for Vespers before Moirne made it to the following house, but this one at least was in good shape. Gaining entry, she unceremoniously led her horse directly inside to unsaddle it, and its mood brightened considerably once it realized it was out of the rain and cold. As with the previous structure she had stayed in, this one had an ample supply of old firewood. This time, however, she made use of it as soon as she located her flint and steel.

Braving the outdoors for a quick toilet and for drawing water from the river, Moirne was soon back inside for the evening. Her mare grazed for a short spell around the exterior but seemed more interested in staying dry than eating. It was soon back at the door, requesting entry, and Moirne didn't have the heart to keep the beast outside in the inclement weather.

The watch house soon took on the odors of a barn, what with the wet horsehair, leather accoutrements, and an ill-timed manure deposit. Moirne quickly mucked out the latter to set things right again. Overall, the smells did pull memories across the leagues and years from her time in another king's army, but no self-reflection accompanied them.

After quickly eating some hard tack and saying her evening prayers, Moirne stripped down to her undergarments and laid out all her wet belongings around the central fireplace. She then stoked the fire so that the house felt like a blast furnace. Her horse was used to flames and showed no concern regarding her actions, choosing to stand near the front door and nodding off soon after. Moirne positioned herself at the table, her bare feet stretched out towards the flames, and she attempted to find something of import in the case documents she had brought with her from Velych.

Moirne could occasionally hear the muffled sounds of ill-tempered weather from outside, but the house was still solid. There were no apparent chinks or holes in the outer walls to let any drafts inside. Surrounded by warmth, she was alone with her thoughts. Despite her best efforts to focus on her work, they soon turned towards her next stop along the way to Stren.

Moirne expected some sort of trouble was waiting for her in Tuman, even if she just meant to spend one night in town before continuing to push northward. She doubted any trouble would be tied to her ongoing investigation into shapeshifter sitings and warg attacks, but there would be trouble nonetheless. While Tuman was still regarded as just a garrison town, it was by far the largest and busiest of the six that encircled the capital city of Velych. This was due to its location at the confluence of the Gruminus and Grumaius Rivers. The docks in Tuman were almost as large as those at the capital to the south, and the crowds were rougher than those at the capital, given the proximity of the Wilds.

For those with criminal aspirations, it was easier to hide in Tuman as opposed to Stren or other, smaller villages to the north and west. At the height of her infamy during the Time of Troubles, the Bandit Lord of the Wilds hadn't even bothered to hide when she came to town. She had strutted about as if she owned the place, and with her control of the local trade routes, she essentially did. The River's Edge Tavern had served as her castle, and it was where she had held court for many a season.

Her gruesome death in front of the tavern, cut down by the king's men, had meant the end of her reign some ten years ago. Elric's flag now flew high over the town, the same as everywhere else in his kingdom, and the law of the land mostly held sway. It didn't mean, however, that all who lived under the king's flag cared for it or didn't wish for the return of the good old days. The local sheriff and his garrison kept most things under control, but due to safety concerns, Tuman was typically bypassed when the royal family made their annual voyages to Lake Sanguis farther upriver.

The application of local law and order wasn't helped by the small but steady influx of orcs who came to town from the east. They were more apt to stop in Tuman rather than Stina, given the higher prospects of finding either work or trade on the river. While most were well-meaning and hardworking, they were still loud and boisterous. They also loved their ale. There were very few nights that blood of some sort didn't flow in the streets, given the number of tavern fights and market disagreements that broke out.

All of this was, at best, of secondary concern to Moirne. Still, if she hadn't been traveling incognito, she would have felt compelled to stop in the garrison town long enough to check on the well-being of the local clergy. As it was, she would need to resign herself to making a few secondhand inquiries while passing through.

Tuman and the counties surrounding it had been deemed worthy of a bishophood approximately a decade ago, somewhat coincidentally with the end of the Time of Troubles. Moirne suspected the real reason behind assigning a bishop to Tuman was so that Archbishop Dorjan no longer had to make treks to the north, but that part of church administration normally did not fall under her purview.

In any event, the man selected for the position had proven to be forthright and hardworking. Bishop Nicholas had done much to calm local tensions since his arrival, at least from what Moirne understood. There hadn't been a reason to travel to Tuman for an investigation of the diocese since his arrival, which, in itself, showed well.

That meant, however, that Moirne hadn't seen the bishop in some years. She smiled at a distant memory of then *Father* Nicholas gently berating a young acolyte for accidentally scorching a tapestry with an ill-placed incense burner.

She briefly considered attempting to meet with him, like she had with Aerysiel the evening before, to see if he knew anything of the strange events being reported in the northern Wilds. But Aery hadn't mentioned anything of note happening in the forests near Tuman, and Moirne already had the church reports that the bishop would have seen as they made their way from the priest stationed in Stren south to the kingdom's capital. As much as she knew she would enjoy seeing the old man, even if he had nothing of substance to tell her, time already lost on the road north made her feel as though she needed to press forward as quickly as possible. Instead, Moirne resolved in her mind to pay her respects to him on her return trip back south once her current investigation was over.

Random thoughts about Tuman and the Wilds bounced around her head, and she found it impossible to concentrate on any sort of menial administrative work. After a time, she put her documents to the side and redressed herself in dry clothing. Letting the fire slowly die down, she sat in the growing darkness, idly smoking her pipe and focusing on nothing. Time slowly passed as she drowsed.

***

Moirne awoke with a start, as if someone had gently shaken her. The room was almost completely dark, the fire having been reduced to barely glowing embers. She found her horse standing next to her, it apparently having just nuzzled her to get her to let it outside to graze. Her pipe was still in her hand, and she grasped it firmly as she became fully aware of the real world and her dreams slipped away.

Upon opening the door to the outside, she found that the

rain had finally stopped. The night was cold enough that she could see her breath, and there were a few stars peeping out through the clouds above as they cleared. Letting the mare out, Moirne kept the door slightly propped open to let in some fresh air and went to tend to the fire.

She couldn't shake the feeling that someone or something—other than the horse—had caused her to wake. But she didn't have a lingering sense of foreboding, and nothing seemed amiss with her belongings or the house in general.

Chalking the experience up to whatever she had been dreaming about, Moirne waited until the horse was back inside before moving to one of the side rooms to sleep more fully. The rest of the night passed peacefully.

She was back on the road well before Prime. The day turned out to be clear and sunny, albeit still cold, with a brisk wind. Traffic along the road picked up in pace as she neared Tuman, and the southern gate was moderately crowded when she reached it shortly before Sext.

As her horse trotted up and reached the cobblestoned portion of the roadway just outside the gate, she could see that the guards were preparing for the midday shift change. The tables set up for cursory inspection of travel documents had any number of bedraggled peddlers and common folk milling around them, although the area around the portcullis was being kept clear. The large wooden gates situated on the interior side of the city walls stood wide open, as far as she could discern.

Being a garrison town, Tuman had the standard ditch that ran along the outside perimeter of the town wall. Being a river town, it had the added benefit of being able to flood the ditch to create an honest-to-goodness moat, but it did not appear this had been done recently. The ditch bottom was dry, although it was clear of debris and the side slopes looked to be in good condition.

Moirne noted that the drawbridge over the ditch no longer had any chains attached to it and was therefore fixed in a permanent "down" position. She assumed that the apparent loosening of security was due to the Time of Troubles gradually fading into the past.

Her horse's hooves clattered across the wooden planks of the bridge as she brought it to a slow walk and approached the gate. She stopped short of the gate but did not dismount, deciding that her appearance should warrant a modicum of personal attention from the guards.

Because of the imminent shift change, there were more soldiers present than usual, but it still took a long moment before any of them deigned to acknowledge the stranger sitting idly on her horse just outside the entrance. The road leading up to the entrance had been kept clear for at least half a league, so there was no chance that she hadn't been noticed approaching. Moirne smirked inwardly at the arrogance and illusion of control being displayed, but it didn't really bother her. If anything, it gave her more time to observe the general movements of the troops and note various defensive positions above and around the gate. There did not appear to be any archers in position.

She waited patiently for her turn to gain entry and, after a time, the officer of the watch approached her. He appeared to be slightly older than the rest of the guards present, but his beard was still full and had no grey visible in it from several paces away. His sword was strapped to his waist, but his head was bare. As he came up to her left side, two soldiers fell into position in front of her mare.

"Afternoon, m'lady." The officer spoke in a mild but firm tone. "We don't normally get single riders of the fairer sex this far north. Might I inquire as to your business in Tuman?"

Moirne bobbed her head in deference. He had guessed her sex despite her short hair and nondescript gear, and she silently gave him points for observation. "Merely passing through, good sir. I seek nothing more than a good meal and a dry bed, particularly after the last few nights."

"Just passing through to where, then?" The officer held out his hand, the unspoken command being for Moirne to present her travel documents. His voice and demeanor remained calm, and no feeling of heightened suspicion came from him or the other two guards. However, Moirne sensed that someone else was now watching her from afar.

"I aim for Stren," she replied simply as she produced a small document from a pocket sewn inside her cloak. Moirne turned slightly out of habit as she bent down and handed it to him before she remembered she wasn't wearing her crux decussata brooch on her tunic. It was, instead, hidden deep inside her saddle bags.

The officer accepted the paper from her without further comment and inspected it carefully. Moirne had memorized what the document said about her, and it was legitimate enough in that it had been prepared for her by the dragoman's office at King Elric's command. It merely stated she was in the employment of one of the courtiers in the royal court and was on an extended survey mission of their northern holdings. She had creased the paper several times over and had spilled some wine on it to make it look older than it really was.

"Tad late in the year to be conducting a survey this far north," the officer opined as he handed the document back to her.

She sighed heavily. "Yes, well, my lord only received reports of bad tidings up by Stren a few weeks ago. Seems to be some sort of disturbance in the Wilds that's keeping the trappers from their normal hunting grounds, and I get to go sort things out."

He pointedly looked at her sword and then gave her a wry smile. "I don't know about anything specific that might be going on, m'lady. But I suppose there's always something going on in the Wilds that can spook the trappers if they're behind on their pelt count."

While slightly disappointed that the officer wasn't in the mood to gossip, Moirne didn't let it show. She merely gave a short laugh in return as he turned and waved at the two soldiers in front of her to let her pass.

He looked back at her and gave her a short bow. "In any

event, you might think about taking a barge the rest of the way. The sheriff has never guaranteed the safety of the roads north of town, never mind what may or may not be going on in the rest of the Wilds. But worse than that, the tow path to Stren is in disrepair in several locations."

"Oh? What happened?"

He shrugged. "Landslide of some sort, perhaps due to the hard rains we had earlier this year. Like I said, you'd probably be better off on the water as opposed to beside it."

This was an unwelcome suggestion to Moirne, as she had no desire to step foot on any type of boat. Still, she had to play her part. "Isn't the ice bad this time of year?"

"Shouldn't get bad north of the confluence for at least several more weeks. The last big push to deliver supplies to Stren for the winter months has been going on over the past fortnight, but I reckon you'd still have your pick of vessels."

"I see." Moirne didn't bother asking who to see about passage on the river, since it would be obvious to any traveler that they would have to see the local dockmaster. "Well, something to think about. Thank you, good sir. Any suggestions on quarters for tonight?"

The commander thought for a quick moment, and he glanced again at her sword before answering. "If you're looking for a bit of peace and quiet along with that dry bed, I'd recommend staying by the western gate. Try the Red Squirrel, their sign will be easy to see. Your horse should be well cared for in their stables as well."

Moirne knew what he was really saying was to stay as far away from the docks as possible, and she doubted he gave everyone this advice. But he had probably surmised that a well-clothed traveler atop a groomed horse wouldn't be interested in causing the kind of trouble that would require the use of their weapon. Any trouble she might be here for would just give the sheriff a reason to extract a sizable fine out of her if she was caught.

She bowed, bending as deeply as she could at the waist without falling off her mount. She threw in a parting question to convey she had never been in town before, even if that wasn't truly the case. "Again, thank you, good sir. Pray tell me, is the church by the main square? I wish to give thanks for my safe passage thus far."

"Yes, m'lady, you won't miss it."

The street leading from the south gate to the main square was busy, but she was able to guide her steed through the crowd with relative ease. Most people gave her a wide berth, allowing her to casually look around, as if surveying the various storefronts and food stalls. Somebody was definitely following her now, but they were good enough at their task that they stayed out of her direct line of sight. She didn't waste time turning around and gawking.

It didn't take long to find her way to the large church that stood on the southern side of the town's main square. Before putting eyes on it, Moirne had remembered from a previous visit that it was of eastern orthodox construction.

Perhaps a tad archaic, but not out of place with where I am in the world.

Dismounting at its main entrance and tying up her horse, she looked up to study the structure. Not quite a cathedral, it was still of good size and constructed of well-cut stone. The central dome appeared to be four stories in height at its apex, and it was topped with an old crux immissa that spoke to the age of the structure.

The dome was surrounded by four small towers located at the major points of the compass. The whitewashed exterior shone brightly in the early afternoon sun, but the crowd milling around in the square seemingly ignored the beacon of the Almighty. There were earthly tasks to complete, and no doubt they felt their prayers could wait until the Sabbath.

Moirne, however, felt the urge to go inside. It would feel good to pray in a house of the Almighty, just as if she were any other weary traveler grateful for reaching a place of relative safety. She undid her sword and purposely lashed it to her saddle, and then she inspected the soles of her boots to ensure they did not have excess mud on them. With that done, she proceeded up a short set of steps and through a set of large wooden doors into the narthex.

Inside the church, it was quiet and unexpectedly devoid of any poor or downtrodden peasants asking for alms or simply seeking shelter from the weather. Moirne found this strange given the brisk conditions outside, but there was no one else present to inquire about any local customs. There was a chest fastened to the wall that she took to be the mite box. Fishing some coins out of a small pouch, she made a tithe offering before heading into the nave.

Sunlight streamed through large bay windows to illuminate the open space. No pews were present, although around a dozen wooden *stacidia* lined both side walls to provide seating for the elderly and disabled. The worship space was relatively simple, with no chandeliers hanging from the roof. In addition to the icon of the Son of the Almighty in the dome, a total of eight more were evenly spread about the space, with small candle boxes in front of each of them. One of them in particular caught Moirne's eye, and she stopped to take a closer look.

Saint Olga of Kyiv!

She crossed herself and reverently dropped to one knee in front of the large painting, her religious studies rushing to the forefront of her mind. Of all the saints she strove to emulate, Olga had always stood out as truly "equal to the apostles."

The first female ruler of the Kyivan Rus, her pilgrimage to Konstantine, her conversion to the Holy Church...but there's more to her story, isn't there?

If Moirne was honest with herself, it was the stories she had discovered on her own, outside those taught by the theological dons, that had made the strongest impact on her.

The avenger of her husband's murder, the cunning usurper of the Devlians, the patron saint of defiance and vengeance... Those are the chronicles that drove you to be a deadly instrument for the

Almighty. Do you still wish to fully emulate the mighty Saint Olga, Dear Moirne? Do you still want to be her second coming, to bring retribution to the unworthy?

Moirne swallowed hard, closed her eyes, and clasped her hands in front of her. She fought back the whispers of youthful arrogance with wisdom painfully gained with age.

Justice may not always be pretty, but remember that you do not have to always be its sword. Find your own peace. Find your own forgiveness.

Her prayer for intercession took some time.

***

When she was finally done praying to the Almighty, Moirne rose and adjusted her cloak as she turned to give the rest of the space a cursory look. At the front of the room stood two ornate candle stands, the only other objects of significance that she could see. They stood guard atop the single step that indicated the start of the *soleas* and the entryway into the sanctuary.

Moirne had no intention of entering the sanctuary proper, as there was no reason to inspect the altar table. While her office allowed her dispensation from various rules if the need arose, she also did not want to unnecessarily bring money or leather into the hallowed space.

The *iconostasis* that separated the sanctuary from the nave did not seem overly elaborate, and she did not feel a pull to inspect it more closely. As it was, she had already performed a longer prayer ritual than she had originally intended. As no priest or other religious person had appeared, she made her leave back the way she had come.

Outside, she found two children looking up at her mare, their backs to her and the church. Judging them by their roughly made but sturdy clothing, she figured they were the offspring of local traders or artisans as opposed to being either lower nobility or ragamuffins on their own in the street. Their heads were bare, the wind catching up their badly shorn hair and making it stand up on end, short as it was. Despite her own short hairstyle, she assumed they were boys.

They didn't seem to hear her approach, but she made sure her shadow fell across them so as to not completely surprise them. The one on the right reacted first, shrinking away from her and half-turning to look up at her with a scared look on his face. The one on the left turned more slowly to look fully at her, caution more than fear showing on his countenance. Both had to squint their eyes against the afternoon sun as they took her in.

"Greetings, young masters," Moirne said with a slight smile, and she inclined her head towards them. They were indeed both boys, and they looked similar enough to each other that they might be related.

The one on the left, who Moirne now deemed to be a few years older than his partner, gave her a short bow. "Ma'am," he said, and then he looked back over his shoulder at her mare. "That's a nice horse."

"Indeed, she is. Tahlia is her name."

"I like yer sword better." He motioned at the weapon strapped to the side of the saddle where she had left it.

"Mmm, yes. I find that most young men are drawn to it rather than my horse."

The younger child found his voice. "Does yer sword have a name like yer horse?"

Her smile widened a bit. "I am not a soldier, my child. I have no need to name my sword."

The older boy frowned at this. "But it looks like a soldier's sword. Do ya know how ta use it?"

"I do. It would be foolish to carry *any* tool without the knowledge of how to use it," Moirne said solemnly.

"Ya sound like our pa. Do ya know him?" the younger one asked.

Moirne bowed her head a bit more formally than the first time. "I do not believe so, but he seems like a wise and prudent man. What is his trade?"

"He builds boats!" the little boy said proudly.

"A shipwright, eh? A much-needed profession, and a good location for it, I wager."

"Do ya have a boat along with yer horse an' sword?" It was the older boy again, as if the now identified brothers were taking turns interrogating her.

"I do not. But perhaps I can hire the use of one from your father."

"Nah, he just makes 'em. You'd have ta talk ta tha

dockmaster if ya want ta use one."

"Yes, of course." While there were plenty of other people walking to and fro, Moirne caught a quick movement out of the corner of her eye as someone entered the shadows of an alleyway across from the church.

"Yer eyes look different. Are ya noble-born?" It was the younger boy's turn to ask a question.

Moirne chuckled and crouched down in front of the boys so that she was at their level. "I think my eyes are pretty, but they are not tied to my station in life. I am common-born, I reckon the same as you."

"Ya don't look common. Ya look like ya got money." The older boy seemed to be eyeing her cloak, which was in much better shape than his own garments.

"Years of hard work, lad." She instantly regretted this response, for it inferred the children's parents were layabouts. Fortunately, neither boy seemed to pick up on the unintended slight.

The older brother now seemed intent on taking over the conversation. "So, ya work with yer horse an' sword, then?"

She nodded. "Among other things, yes."

"Like what?"

"Like..." Moirne tried to think of something innocuous. "Like, my books." She reached inside her cloak and fished out her leatherbound journal. "For example, in this book, I write down information about the places I go and the people I meet. Names, dates, things like that."

"Why's that?"

"So that I can remember them. It is important to remember things in my line of work."

The older boy shifted slightly, as if eager to pounce, but he managed to keep the tone of his voice even-keeled. "What's yer—"

"Can ya write *my* name?" He was interrupted by his brother, who was looking at Moirne with wide eyes.

She smiled broadly and faced him. "If you'd like. What *is* your name, young master?"

The child drew himself up as much as he could, and he stood with his feet wide and his chest out. He proudly stated, "I am Vanko, son of Aleksandr!"

"Well met, Vanko." Moirne glanced over at his brother with a questioning look.

His face had darkened as he glared at the younger boy, and he shook his head and remained silent. She decided not to push him for his name, but she could now reason with good certainty that he, at least, was in league with whomever had picked her out at the gate.

Someone is in the mood to know my business. Not the guards, and not the church. So, how many gangs are on the docks these days, I wonder? At least they're not brazen enough to steal my horse or my sword in broad daylight. That and I'm being interrogated by children armed with cute smiles instead of thugs with ugly blades.

Opening her journal to the next available blank page,

Moirne dutifully wrote out "VANKO" in large block letters and then showed the results to both boys.

Vanko grinned from ear to ear. "That's me? I've never seen me name before!"

"That is indeed you." She quickly added "SON OF ALEKSANDR" behind what she had already written, taking a reasonable guess as to how to spell his father's name.

Upon seeing the results, Vanko clapped gleefully. "Now, write Anton's name, too! Ow!"

Vanko, in his excitement, had blurted out his brother's name and was immediately punched in the nose by the older boy. The young child immediately burst into tears and turned away in pain.

Moirne remained calm, but her eyes bore into Anton's red face. He was seething, his fists clenched, but he didn't raise them to strike his brother again.

She cleared her throat to get his attention and then spoke as a mother would to a petulant child. "Gently, Anton. I don't need to know your name to know what game you're playing at."

Anton folded his arms across his small chest and tried to bluff his way out. "I got no idea what—"

"*Enough!*" Moirne's sharp tone hit him harder than a slap to the face would have, and he visibly jumped. She regarded him for a moment before speaking in a much softer tone. "Where are you supposed to have me go?"

He blinked several times at this and looked directly at her, the look of fear in his eyes and the color draining away from his face. "How...how'd ya know?"

"I ain't no royal halfwit, boy. I used ta play tha same game when I was a young'un. Made proper coin from tha local toughs fer me effort, 'fore I got swept up inta tha army. Long time ago now, but ya never forget what ya learn on tha street."

It had been some time since Moirne had spoken in the dialect of her youth, but it rolled off her tongue as if she used it every day. The accent was southern, but the boy understood her well enough.

Anton stood a bit straighter. "We ain't street rats! We got a home!"

"Aye, ya do, lad, an' ya should be feelin' blessed fer it. Sounds like ya got a right proper pa, too, least good 'nough fer yer brother. But instead o' learnin' a trade or yer letters, you're out here runnin' jobs fer some small-time scoundrel. Fer what, a few copper coins at best? An' if lumps are comin', it's yer skin that takes 'em, eh?"

Anton looked down at his feet and didn't respond. Vanko was still whimpering, but the lack of attention to his plight had made him turn partly back towards Moirne to see what she was doing. Moirne wished she had some honeycomb or chamber spice candies to offer the boy and further break the will of his brother, but she had to work with what she had.

She kept her focus on the older boy and spoke to him again, reverting to her normal speech pattern. "Anton, look at me."

He did so, grudgingly.

"Anton, let me guess. You have several older brothers?"

He nodded. "Four of 'em."

"So, your father has more than enough apprentices down at the docks?"

He looked down at his feet again. "Yeah."

"And there's nothing else for you here? What trade have you been assigned instead?"

Anton's fists balled again, and he practically spit his next words out. "Pa wants me ta be a...a sardin' tailor!"

Moirne smiled gently. "No fame or fortune in being a tailor, eh?"

Anton shook his head furiously. She guessed his age to be no more than ten, but it was obvious his future was weighing heavily both on his mind and in his actions.

"I just thought..." He looked away in the direction of the docks, then up at the sky. When he finally looked back at her, his eyes were wet. "I just thought I'd be more than that. Tha Almighty didn't put me here on Terra ta sew dresses like a bloody seamstress!"

Moirne knew that Anton thinking above his given station in life might be deemed blasphemous by some in her position and outright dangerous by others. If everyone was allowed a chance to raise their status, how soon until the divine right of kings was challenged by the common mob?

But didn't you feel trapped when you were young, Dear

Moirne? And look at what heights you've pulled yourself up to, after such humble beginnings. You dare compare yourself to a saint, of all things!

She sighed to herself and attempted to focus on the young boy in front of her. "The Almighty works in mysterious ways, Anton. Did you know that a good tailor has probably saved my life?"

He wasn't expecting this sort of comment, and the look on his face was one of pure disbelief. "Faugh, 'nough o' that nonsense!"

Moirne placed her right hand over her heart. "I say the truth, sirrah. Do you see a lick of armor on me? No? Yet I tell you, there is plenty of protection within my clothing all the same."

"Whaddya mean?"

She tugged at her tunic, pulling it back slightly. "Fitted and padded linen undergarments, Anton, just as a knight might wear under their armor. Perhaps they won't fully protect me from the tip of a spear, but they will certainly assist against the blow of a cudgel or some other back-alley weapon that a brigand might wield."

"Yeah? So?"

"So, 'twas a linen armorer who made these up for me. Worth its weight in gold, as his creation has saved me from cracked ribs and a bruised ego at a minimum. It's kept me in several fights long enough to win them."

She was stretching the truth somewhat with her statement, as she had been wearing chainmail on top of the padding during the incidents being referenced. But the boy didn't need to know this. As it was, Anton's look of disbelief was slowly changing to one of introspection.

"So, you're sayin'..."

"I'm saying that there is the potential for fortune, at least, if you apply yourself to your trade. Even if that trade is tailoring. And fame may indeed follow, as well, if you are good enough to render service to a knight or a lord and word spreads of your work."

Anton gave a small smile at this but said nothing. Moirne hoped that she had at least given him something to think about and potentially get him off the streets. She lightly slapped her thighs and stood up to her full height, rolling her shoulders as she did so and looking around. Nobody was blatantly staring at them, and she couldn't see anyone in the alleyway.

Moirne glanced over at Vanko, who had stopped crying but was still furtively looking in her direction. She winked at him, and he quickly turned away. After a brief moment, he peeked back at her, a shy smile on his face. Now she really did wish she had some honeycomb for him.

Inspired by the thought, she took out her coin pouch and held it in the palm of her hand, in full view of the two boys and the rest of the street.

"Vanko, can you tell me if there's a place nearby that sells sweets?"

The little boy's eyes grew wide again, and he pointed vaguely to the north. "Oh, yes'm! There's a baker o'er there who makes tha best cryspels I ever had!"

She made a scene of rummaging around in her pouch before producing two copper denga. "Very good. Could you please get a few for yourself and your brother?"

"Yes'm!" The smile on Vanko's face threatened to spread past his ears. He accepted the coins with shaking hands and took off at a full run across the town square.

Moirne didn't bother to watch his progress and, instead, dropped back down into a crouch in front of Anton. He didn't seem to have paid much attention to her exchange with his brother, as he still had a faraway look on his face. However, when Moirne held a silver denga coin in front of him, his eyes quickly snapped to it.

"I want something more than sweets from you, Anton. I want information. But I am willing to compensate you for your time and trouble and to save your fingers from getting broken if you try and go for my purse."

She gave him a knowing look. The boy's face went red again, this time from embarrassment. He opened his mouth as if to protest but then quickly shut it and nodded his head.

"Good lad. Now, who runs the gang that put you onto me?"

He shuffled his feet a bit, but the coin held just a hand's width away from his face was too much temptation. "His name's Simeon, ma'am. He's got eyes at all tha gates, but 'specially tha south one. Anytime a stranger comes through an' looks like they got money, a runner goes out ta get a tail on 'em. We're just supposed ta find out what they're doin' here an' see if they need help findin' their way 'round town."

"Of course," Moirne said dryly. The delay at the gate made more sense to her now. Perhaps the guards weren't directly in on the take, but they obviously knew what was going on. It made this Simeon more than a small-time scoundrel, to be sure, if he could employ a whole rabble of youngsters, as well as intimidate or infiltrate the town guard.

"If I were to tell you that somebody is watching us from the alleyway behind you, could that be the runner who told you about me?"

To his credit, Anton didn't immediately turn around to look for someone. Instead, he scrunched his face up at the question. "Don't think so, ma'am. They're supposed ta go back ta their post at tha gate, in case somebody else comes through. Least that's what I do when it's my turn ta be a runner."

Moirne nodded and decided not to pursue the issue with Anton. "Never mind then, probably just a beggar. So, if you think me a good mark, where are you supposed to send me for trade or for lodging?"

He shrugged. "Small-time traders, they can go where they like an' be treated like anyone else. 'Less ya got precious stones or spices on ya, then we're supposed ta tell ya ta see Mikah 'stead o' Feodor 'cause Mikah got more pull 'round here."

Moirne kept the smirk off her face. She doubted that Anton knew anything about bribes, or weighted scales, or the countless ways you could make numbers work in your favor. All he would have been told was where to tell strangers to go.

"And how about food and lodging?"

"Tha River's Edge fer lodgin', ma'am. Best goulash in town, too, or so I hear. An' it's hist...historic an' all, is what they say."

Moirne couldn't help but let the smirk emerge now. She quickly huffed to try and disguise a bitter laugh. She obviously knew the historic implications of the tavern; after all, it was where her thoughts from last night had drifted. It didn't surprise her that it would be the headquarters of someone trying to conjure up ghosts of the past to help impress their followers.

"And what if I came to town by boat, Anton? Are there eyes on the dock as well?"

He shrugged again. "I ain't been allowed ta work tha docks, ma'am, so I don't know how they run. But I reckon that anybody comin' ta town that way has gotta see tha dockmaster."

Moirne nodded thoughtfully. She was willing to give Anton's father the benefit of the doubt and assume Aleksandr was an honest and hardworking man. No doubt it would be wise to keep a rebellious son of his off the docks so it would be harder to catch wind of what he was doing with his free time. Tuman wasn't a small village, by any means, but there would still be wagging tongues and sharp eyes about to render judgment on wayward children.

"What if I don't want to stay at the River's Edge, Anton? Will you get in trouble for not getting me to go there?"

He shifted his feet slightly but didn't look worried. "Nah, not really. Ya look too rich ta stay there anyway, 'less you're lookin' fer somethin' ta do."

"Oh? Like what?"

"Best goulash in town, ma'am, or so I'm told."

"Yes, you said that already. What else have you been told?"

"Well..." Anton looked around and then leaned in closer to her. His voice took on an excited tone, and he seemed to forget about the silver coin for a moment. "What I *know* is that Pa let me brother Beryan be put in tha stocks fer goin' there!"

"Really? Just for going there?"

"Well, not just fer goin' there, fer goin' there an' bein' drunk an' dis...dis..."

"Disorderly?" Moirne prompted, attempting not to chuckle.

"Yeah, that's it. Also, Pa was pretty sore that Beryan lost over a month's worth of wages at a dice game there. Yelled at 'im good, said if he ever went back, then he could spend 'is life loadin' ships instead o' buildin' them!"

Moirne smiled. It seemed as though she was right about Aleksandr's character. "I assume your brother hasn't been back since?"

The boy laughed. "No ma'am!"

A thought crossed Moirne's mind, and she decided to press Anton one more time. "So, if I want to risk my money in games of chance, that's something to do at the River's Edge. I will keep that in mind. But, Anton, do you happen to know if this Simeon fellow you work for runs the dice games there?"

"I dunno, ma'am. An' I don't really work fer 'im, least not

directly. Never met 'im, just seen 'im a couple times." His attention had gone back to the coin that Moirne was still holding in front of him, but he made no move to grab it from her.

She glanced over in the direction that Vanko had run off and didn't see him coming back yet. As she turned her focus back to Anton, she gently reached out and took his right hand in hers. Holding it in front of him at waist level, she placed the coin in the middle of his open palm but didn't let go.

"Now, Anton, most of what you told me is not worth an award, as you would have told me the information anyway in order to steer me where this fellow Simeon wants me to be. His name, I wager, is worth something, but not a full silver denga. So, I need something else from you to earn this coin from me."

A look of suspicion came over his face, and he didn't close his hand over the coin. "Oh yeah? What's that?"

There was a small commotion to the north, and they both looked over to see Vanko running straight back through crowd in the square towards them. In his hands were a couple of large pastries, and he had a very determined look on his face. There had never been a time in Moirne's life where she had actively wished to be a mother, but her heart went out to the young child all the same. She returned her focus to his older sibling.

"A promise to protect your brother."

"What?"

Moirne regarded Anton calmly as his eyes came back to her, along with a confused look that matched the tone of his voice.

Suddenly, she felt very tired, as if the weight of all her travels had decided to settle on her shoulders at that moment.

Still trying to save the innocent, Dear Moirne? I suppose it means you still have a shred of hope within you.

"Anton, listen to me. As you said yourself, you're no street rat. It shows, because you have much to learn in the ways of deceit and deception. I would rather you pick a more honorable apprenticeship, but that is your choice to make."

He swallowed hard at this, but before he could say anything, Moirne continued.

"Vanko is young and impressionable, Anton. I reckon he would follow you to the gates of the abyss if you led him there. You must promise me that, whatever you choose to do, you will protect your brother from harm. On the whole, he seems to me a bit tender for a life of crime." She closed Anton's hand over the coin and cupped it in both of hers. "Are you willing to make such a promise?"

Anton looked at her and nodded his head without hesitation. She nodded in return and released him as Vanko ran up to them, breathing hard.

"Anton, Anton! Here, take this, it's hot!" The young boy shoved a round piece of fried dough into his brother's free hand. Drizzled in honey, it was steaming in the cold air and appeared to be a sticky mess.

Anton accepted the pastry, and he wordlessly gazed at the contents in each of his hands.

"I got one fer ya, too!" Vanko announced proudly, and he

held up the other cryspel for Moirne to take.

She accepted it in good humor and made a point to take an exaggerated bite. It was delicious, and she sighed in appreciation.

"I told ya they was good!" The young boy was beaming.

Moirne had to swallow before responding. "You certainly did, Vanko, and they certainly are! But where is yours?"

His cheeks were already a rosy pink from the running, but perhaps they turned a bit redder. "I, uh, already ate it."

Moirne laughed heartily, loudly and long enough that several heads turned their way. Anton smiled at her display and, after a moment's hesitation, took a bite of his pastry. Moirne, having recovered, took another bite of hers. A warm, sticky silence enveloped them both as Vanko happily watched them eat.

CHAPTER FIVE

Up the River Without a Conscience

Umuk stared grumpily at the river flowing by his vantage point on the shore as he gnawed on some jerky. Other than stale bread, he, Uptar, and the rest of the crew of the *Vydatnyy* hadn't had anything else to eat for several days. The exact count was hard to remember, since everything they did onboard seemed to blend together.

Gotta be at least three stinkin' days. Least tha bread ain't maggoty.

He certainly wasn't the optimistic type, and not having to pick weevils out of his meal wasn't much of a silver lining for the situation he in which found himself. It certainly wasn't enough to change his opinion that the deal he and Uptar had been coerced into making several months ago was much worse than expected. As far as he was concerned, the dockmaster in Stren had reneged on most of what had been promised when they joined the ship's crew to get out of the sheriff's forced labor camp.

Figures, though. Never trust a human!

The *Vydatnyy* was, at its core, the main patrol vessel for the Kingdom of Perizidon along the upper stretches of the Gruminus and Grumaius Rivers. The ship's captain, a massive man by the name of Ruslan, was constantly reminding the crew that their duty was clear—trade must flow, no matter what. Any pirates on the water or bandits on the shore were to be dealt with quickly and with finality.

"What's that mean?" Umuk had asked the first time he had heard the captain's speech.

"Means we can gut 'em, take their stuff, an' nobody's gonna ask why we did it," came the response from one of the more seasoned crew members, accompanied by a shrug.

Umuk had laughed fiercely at this, not understanding the human's indifference. "Then what's stoppin' us? Killin' an' lootin' is what we all signed up fer, ain't it?"

As he knew now, quite a few things were stopping him from satisfying his bloodlust and greed.

First came the drills. He couldn't fathom why some idiots had to be taught how to row a boat, but every time a new crew member joined, it meant time spent with them learning the proper cadences. Working the rigging and other fiddly bits associated with sailing the boat, as opposed to rowing it...he understood these would probably take a lesson or two to get right. But these details had never been taught to him or anyone else not judged to be "able seamen" by the captain, whatever that meant. As it was, changing direction at speed, beaching and unbeaching the craft, and drilling for assaults that almost never happened had all been performed repetitively to the point of numbness.

Second came the housekeeping, or rather shipkeeping, chores. These tasks were handed out by Lev, the shifty-eyed first mate that Umuk couldn't stand. This was primarily because the rowers, or lob-cocks as Lev derisively called them, got stuck with all the shite jobs. Hauling supplies on board and keeping the boat clean were bad enough, but patrols on the river could last several weeks. That meant an inordinate amount of time was spent setting up camp every night somewhere along the shore, gathering firewood, digging latrine holes, standing guard, and then doing everything all over again somewhere else the next night.

At least onshore hunting parties were assembled at times, in order to obtain fresh meat, and Umuk had gotten to be halfway decent at spear fishing from the side of the ship. But with cold weather setting in, it had become harder to find any prey. Hence the hard jerky and stale bread on the tail end of their current patrol as they headed back north towards Stren.

Cleanin' an' sharpenin' weapons is a shite job, too, but it's usually got a purpose. But huntin' deer an' catfish ain't tha same as huntin' humans an' orcs. Deer don't scream so good, an' tha damn fish ain't got no loot ta take.

Giving up on the jerky as a bad prospect, he threw the rest of his ration into the water and sighed derisively. If the winter months weren't almost here, he would be seriously considering taking off into the Wilds on his own. Sure, it would put a bounty on his head, but he had already been in that situation before being captured during a tavern brawl in Stren. But breaking out now made no sense if he wanted a good chance of surviving; it was better to wait for the spring.

He glanced over at Uptar, who was napping a bit farther up

the shore, and he shook his head in disgust. The other orc had become very quiet over the months they had been on the river and had withdrawn from most of the crew. He would follow orders, but he rarely expended any additional effort or voluntarily did anything that benefited anyone but himself. Not that Umuk himself was a generous soul, but it irked him nonetheless.

That arse won't even talk ta me these days, an' after all I did for him while we was survivin' out in tha Wilds. He'd be dead if it weren't for me! Ungrateful bastard is what he is, that's for sure. Sard him, he's useless ta me 'cept for bein' a meat shield in a fight.

If Umuk hadn't been counting on the other orc for much help in the past, he certainly wouldn't be factored into any escape plans in the future. That was all Umuk could think about these days, yet another reason why he couldn't stand Uptar's lethargic behavior.

Seems like tha only escape that bloody idiot wants is ta escape inta his dreams. Shoulda just taken tha sheriff's rope 'stead o' this gig if all he's ever gonna do is sulk 'bout that dead bitch o' his. An' there ain't nobody else in tha crew worth their weight in shite, so I just need ta plan for myself. Just gotta hold out 'til spring, if I don't die o' boredom 'fore then!

Ultimately, Umuk's frustration was borne out of what he considered the worst part about working on the *Vydatnyy*. Because even when they did finally head out on the river for a patrol, barely anything ever happened! There had been nary a pirate ship to fight, and any bandits would just run away into the woods if they were discovered along the river.

Most o' them seem ta be worse off than we are anyways, tha damn grifters. Not like they'd get much from tha wretched flatboats we're guardin', even if they caught one. They all seem ta have shite for cargo, and nobody seems ta be smugglin' anythin' o' value. Sard this whole kingdom!

Umuk's disparaging opinion of barge captains and the apparent lack of contraband on their vessels was based upon what he had observed to date. For every ten boats the *Vydatnyy* stopped to inspect, perhaps one didn't have the proper documentation or was carrying something deemed not quite right. And as far as Umuk could tell, this just meant some coins were slipped to Ruslan and the other vessel continued on its way.

I know a bribe when I see one, an' that mangy cur o' a cap'n sure ain't sharin' whatever he's gettin' from his payoffs!

How plunder from captured pirate vessels or bandit camps was divided up had been loosely explained to him by one of the more senior crew members. But there were just too many quarter shares and eighth shares to think about for the mathematically challenged. All Umuk knew was that, to date, a quarter of almost nothing divided between all the rowers meant he had gotten two things—jack, and shite. And "late payment of administrative fees," or whatever fancy term the captain used for the bribes he was taking from the boats they stopped, didn't count as plunder.

Umuk also knew he wasn't the only one in the crew that felt as though they had been lied to when they signed on, or that the captain was holding out on the rest of them. Everyone was restless for a fight, except perhaps Uptar.

As long as we've been at this, we've barely seen a lick o' action. Only two barges properly boarded, an' even then tha cowards just gave up. Tha only fight that's been worth it this whole time is tha one night we laid over in Tuman, but even that was just a bar brawl. They wouldn't even let me kill that whoreson.

Umuk looked around at their current location, indistinguishable as it was from most places they stopped at. The ship was beached on the western shore of the river, as was typical, adjacent to the tow path that the barges used when moving upstream. Traffic was starting to get lighter as winter approached, but he had been told there was always somebody willing to risk a trip, no matter how bad the weather would get. It meant the patrols wouldn't stop even when the snow started.

He glanced over at the *Vydatnyy*, some twenty paces downstream from where he was sitting. The prospect of rowing through ice floes during a blizzard did not interest him in the least, even if Lev always boasted about how nimble the craft could be with the right crew.

This damn ship o' ours...he's always goin' on 'bout how fast it is, too. But if we're never gonna chase anyone, then who gives a shite? I'd rather have a bunch of mules drag us up the river 'stead o' havin' ta row all tha sardin' time.

If Umuk had known anything about ships, he would have known he was a crewmember on a rather impressive but ancient vessel. How old the *Vydatnyy* was, no one really knew. But she had been patrolling the kingdom's main waterways for far longer than any of her current crew had been alive, even longer than the dockmaster had paced the river's edge.

Legend had it that the venerable boat had once plied the dark, cold Suebic Sea far, far away to the west. How she had come to the backwater town of Stren, nobody could recall. Perhaps she had been carried in pieces, or rolled on greased logs, cross-country for leagues upon end between various rivers and streams. But, however or whenever she had come, she was like no other vessel in the kingdom.

The *Vydatnyy* had a sleek figure, several times longer than she was wide, and her oak-planked sides were still solid. Her keel was a continuous piece of solid wood, and it must have been a mighty tree, indeed, that had been felled to create her. A single mast made of pine rose amidships, supporting a massive sail. On the upper river, however, she mostly relied on her oars and the strength of her crew for movement.

The vessel could hold up to forty oars, twenty to a side, although she had been running shorthanded the entire time Umuk and Uptar had been on board. A few more crew members had been added since they'd joined, and the overall rowing complement was around thirty now. The first mate would still complain mightily about how much potential speed was being lost.

A wolf's head decorated the prow, rising up from the body of the ship on an elongated neck. It had been carved to depict a creature in motion, the tongue lolling out, the mouth open to reveal sharp teeth. The painted white teeth and red tongue stood out against the dark stain used on the rest of the ship, creating a fearsome visage. It meant that when the *Vydatnyy* was moving at speed, she truly looked to be on the hunt.

When the single large sail was deployed, its red and white colors stood out starkly against the background of the normal river setting, the diagonal lattice work of reinforcing ropes within the sail enhancing the colored diamond pattern. Nobody on the river could mistake the *Vydatnyy* for any other vessel, and many a barge captain would doff their cap as she cruised by. While she mainly stayed north of the confluence at Tuman, she was a well-known entity as far south as Kulak.

Harkening back to the dragon boats of legend, the *Vydatnyy* would have been outclassed in the open ocean or in ship-to-ship combat by more modern vessels. But she was more than adequate for overseeing the towed barges and smaller craft that plied the upper stretches of the primary river system in Perizidon. And with a knowledgeable steersman and able crew, she could still chase down any caravel that might happen to be on the water.

Umuk didn't know, or care to know, any of these details. But he sensed the boat's capabilities just by looking at it, channeling the innate ability of most orcs to pick out the fastest and toughest steeds in a wild herd. Maybe it was the blood that had seeped into the deck planking years ago calling out to him, but he knew the *Vydatnyy* had been built to pillage, not patrol.

The boat, in Umuk's opinion, was just like him. Neither was being shown proper respect or being given the chance to show off their true nature.

"Hey, Umuk! Give us a hand with tha anchor. We're 'bout ta set off!" Umuk looked up as one of the other rowers, a bald, scrawny human with a dirty beard, called out to him. He stood by the large iron boat anchor that had been wedged between two medium-sized boulders. There was a general stirring around them as everyone started to gather themselves to get back to work.

"Yeah, yeah..." Umuk grumbled. As he got to his feet, he glared at Uptar again, who looked like he was still sleeping.

That damn lazy shite always knows where ta go so he won't get picked ta do anythin'. An' it's not like we needed ta toss tha anchor overboard here anyways 'cause tha boat's wedged in firm enough ta shore without it. Sard me if that lubberwort first mate ain't just creatin' more work for everyone. 'Specially me.

Umuk's bad attitude didn't improve as the anchor was stowed, what supplies had been offloaded for the crew's midday break were put onboard again, and the boat was pushed back into the river. Because the barges needed to stay relatively close to the tow path, the river was kept dredged and free of debris along the western bank. This meant the water became too deep to stand in only a few paces offshore, and it made for wet business for the last crew members getting back into the *Vydatnyy*. Today this included Umuk, and it was yet one more reason to keep him in a sour mood.

The river was still quite wide in the section they were in,

perhaps a hard day's journey south of Stren. Still, the current was strong, and the wind was against them, so they had to pull at the oars with long, steady strokes to make any progress. Without any other boats in sight, they were able to maintain a steady pace in the middle of the channel for quite some time. The rowing motion was such that it dulled the mind with its repetitiveness, and Umuk lost track of time as he tried to recall better days.

Suddenly, he and the rest of the rowers were shaken from their repetitive stupor by a call from the lookout. Lev, who was standing amidships, instantly relayed the call back to the captain, who was standing by the steersman on the small quarterdeck at the rear of the ship.

"Barge ahead, sir! But she's on tha wrong shore! An' there's smoke!"

The *Vydatnyy* had entered a wide turn in the river, and looking to his right, Umuk could see that they were in one of the sections where the tow path had collapsed into the river several months earlier. Several barges had been put out of sorts in this location since then, as the donkey teams had to be brought on board while the barges were laboriously poled upstream for some distance. He didn't recall anyone ever drifting all the way over to the eastern shoreline, however.

Umuk glanced over his left shoulder to try and see what was going on ahead of them, but the lookout was in the way. At that moment, the man turned back towards the rear of the boat, making a rapid motion at the captain and the steersman. Immediately, the boat slew to the right side of the main channel, and as Umuk turned back, he saw the captain make a series of signals to the first mate. Lev, in turn, barked at the rowers immediately.

"Attention, lads! Prepare ta pull smartly now! Ready?"

"Ready!" came the call back from most of the crew.

Umuk just took a deep breath and set his feet as he finished his current stroke.

"*Pull!*"

The command sang out across the length of the vessel and the crew responded immediately. The longship heaved forward as it accelerated against the current, cutting a knife edge through the water.

The first mate cackled with glee. "Ya all wanted a fight, eh? Ya damn lob-cocks, you're gonna get one if ya get us ta shore in time! There be bandits ahead!"

Umuk's heart pounded in anticipation of some honest-to-goodness action. It was all he could do to not immediately get up and run to one of the weapons lockers, but he knew they had to get to shore first. He roared in frustration and pulled harder, forcing the rowers around him to match his pace through brute force.

Lev saw what he was doing and roared back in approval. "That's it, that's it! Get yer backs inta it like tha greyskin! He smells blood, that one. C'mon, ya shites! *Pull!*"

The longship was closing whatever remaining gap there was at astounding speed. Umuk was pulling harder than he ever had, and he had lost track of the cadence. A little voice inside him tried to tell him to conserve strength for the coming skirmish, but he paid it no mind. It was soon lost amongst the creaking of the oars, the shouting of the first mate, and the *whap-whap-whap* sounds of the ship cutting through small waves on the surface of the river.

"Starboard side, normal pressure! Larboard side, light pressure!"

The *Vydatnyy* heeled slightly to the left as Umuk and the other rowers on his side of the boat slowed their pull slightly. He figured they were close to shore now and Lev was trying to guide the boat in at an angle, as opposed to straight in, so they could go over the side all at once. He glanced over at where his axe was stowed near the mast and readied himself for glory.

There was a slight tremor as the longship cut through a small sand bank, and the first mate called out again.

"Starboard side, oars in, oars in! Larboard side, hold water, hold water!"

Umuk grunted as he held his oar blade vertically in the water, it and its brethren on the left side of the ship acting as a massive brake. They ground to a halt as they beached themselves, and Ruslan was over the side immediately.

Lev was already disembarking, as well, and he yelled at the rest of the crew as he went. "Drop oars, drop oars! Shore party, weapons out an' over tha side! Rally ta tha cap'n!"

Umuk, despite being on the far side of the boat from shore, was perhaps the second or third into the shallow water and then onto solid ground. The first mate had guided the longship right up against the shore, immediately upstream of a beached barge. The remnants of a large bonfire were still smoking heavily in a small clearing, perhaps twenty paces up from the water, and Umuk could see a number of humanoid shapes scattered about on the ground near the fire. From this distance, he couldn't tell if they were dead or just sleeping.

He took a quick look at the barge, which was also smoldering. It certainly was never going to leave shore again. There were several more humanoid shapes next to it, these obviously dead. A series of large casks from the barge's hold had been unloaded and were sitting on the shore. Umuk grinned as he looked at the casks.

Wine! Well, if they all ain't dead up by tha fire, then they're probably all too soused ta fight.

The captain motioned for silence as the rowers-turned-soldiers came ashore, and most complied after a few whoops and battle cries. He looked back at the lookout, who was still at the front of the ship, and they briefly flashed hand signals at each other.

Ruslan turned to address the shore party, some twenty strong. "Time to get to it! Brevine thinks at least six bandits lit out to the north when they saw us coming. If the barge captain's lockbox is anywhere, I'm sure it's with them!" He quickly pointed at Umuk and perhaps a half a dozen more crew members, including Uptar. "Get it back and there's a reward in it for all of us. Bring someone back alive, and there's a bonus for you lot."

Ruslan looked away and started to give orders to the others, but Umuk had already started running up the gentle slope of the bank towards the forest. As he ran past the bonfire, a few of the shapes on the ground started to stir. No doubt they were hungover, or even still drunk from a night of carousing with the barge's cargo, but they were someone else's problem as far as he was concerned.

The ground was fairly rocky at the tree line, and no boot prints were visible. However, Umuk could see a deer trail heading generally north from the bend in the river, and he assumed that's what they should follow. He paused and sniffed cautiously but didn't smell any humans nearby.

The others caught up to him, one of the humans already breathing hard. Everyone was armed with some sort of hand weapon except for Uptar, who had equipped himself with a longbow. Umuk didn't try and hide his look of contempt from the other orc, who just stared back at him with an unreadable look in his eyes.

Figures he'd take a coward's weapon when there's real game ta hunt.

Umuk was about to say something when one of the larger humans, a hulk named Stefan, motioned at him and then at the trees ahead of the group.

"Whatcha waitin' for? There an ambush or somethin'?"

Umuk smirked. "Not yet, meat."

"What then? Ya got a puddin' heart or somethin'? Let's go!" Stefan sneered and took off into the woods with a roar.

Two more of the group followed him instantly.

Umuk chuckled and then smiled at the remaining three humans in the party with his teeth showing. "Well, ya heard him. Try ta keep up!" He glanced over at Uptar but just shook his head in disgust and set out without another word, not really caring if any of the rest followed him.

The trail was barely wide enough for one person to fit through without breaking low-hanging tree limbs on either side, but the undergrowth had been beaten down enough that it was easy to find good footing. As Umuk made his way forward at a quick jog, both hands grasping his axe, he made sure to keep at least one of the humans in front of him in sight. As they snaked their way through the woods, no other pathways appeared, but he kept his eyes out for any signs of someone going off to the side.

After a while, the trail headed up a slight incline, and Umuk could see clear sky ahead of him. Increasing his stride, he loped to the top of the hill and soon came to the edge of a clearing. He was almost right on top of the three crew members who had been ahead of him, but he immediately stopped and stood to the side of the trail, trying to blend in with the trees. They kept moving forward, and he made no attempt to call them back.

He thought about stopping the two humans who had come up close behind him, but they blindly tore ahead into the clearing as well. Uptar, however, quietly stepped to the side opposite Umuk and nocked an arrow. Umuk looked back out at the clearing and sniffed the air warily.

Definitely humans over there, waitin' for us. An' some orcs, too?

A barrage of arrows erupted out of the woods on the other side of the clearing, immediately felling two of the humans in front and one of the trailers. Stefan, who was still standing, screamed in anger and burst forward with all the speed he could muster. He disappeared from view before another volley could be fired, while the human in back skidded to a stop and beat a hasty retreat to where Umuk and Uptar were hiding.

The clash of steel could be heard from across the clearing for several moments, along with several more screams. As the commotion continued, Uptar caught Umuk's eye and motioned that he was going to start circling to the right. Umuk didn't respond and merely watched the other orc carefully take a few steps back and then melt into the woods. Even without foliage on the trees, Uptar's skin color and the weak sun above made it incredibly difficult to see him after only a few paces.

"What...what should we do?" The human who had made it back from the clearing, the scrawny man with a dirty beard who had previously needed help with the ship's anchor, looked over at Umuk with fear in his eyes. The last human, who had been trailing far behind the rest of the group, had finally made it up the hill and stood next to them gasping for air, oblivious to the carnage that was in the clearing.

Umuk narrowed his eyes, trying to remember the names of the two men and failing. He gestured at the scrawny one. "Come with me, quiet like, 'round here ta tha left. As for ya," he said as he pointed at the latecomer, "stay here an' guard tha path back."

Both humans nodded silently. The noises from the other side of the clearing had now stopped. Since Stefan didn't come sauntering out, Umuk assumed he had come out of the exchange poorly. He quietly began circling to the left, staying in the trees and moving in the opposite direction from Uptar. He couldn't see the other orc now, but he figured the other greyskin wouldn't skive out on him.

Nah, not now. Maybe he just needs ta do some killin' ta put his mind right. But doin' some killin' here is gonna take a moment an' some thinkin'.

Umuk stopped moving after about ten paces, crouched down, and quickly counted the arrows that he could see.

One volley...looks like four hits, plus maybe a few that sailed wide. Gotta think there's at least six bowmen, maybe a few more, an' some others with melee weapons since ol' Stefan got met with steel soon as he went in over there. Assume tha big shite got one or two 'fore he dropped. So...ten left, maybe? Need ta split 'em up somehow. Are they gonna be stupid an' come out?

He turned to find the scrawny man crouched a pace or two behind him. Finally remembering his name, he motioned him forward and then cupped his hand to speak to him softly. "Goran, wait here. If ya see more than two of 'em come out ta look at tha bodies, make noise so they know you're here an' then run back ta tha trail. If it looks like they're followin' ya, run back towards tha boat yellin' for help."

Goran nodded. "How 'bout Branko? What should he do?"

"Who? Oh, Branko...like I care. If he's smart, he'll follow ya. But I think ya can outrun him if ya have ta." Umuk smiled darkly, and Goran nodded again.

Umuk slowly started moving left again, trying to catch sight of anyone on the far side of the clearing. A few moments later, there was some slight movement in the trees ahead of him, and he froze in place, his grip tightening slightly around the handle of his axe. He could hear the low murmur of several people arguing with each other, but it was still impossible to see how many bandits there were. The wind picked up slightly, and not in his favor.

There better not be any trackers in tha bunch.

Two bandits cautiously stepped into the clearing, an orc armed with a sword and a small, round shield and a human wielding a short bow with an arrow nocked. After looking around the perimeter of the clearing for a long moment, they slowly approached the two fallen crew members near the center of the space. While there hadn't been any movement from either man since they had fallen, Umuk nodded in grim appreciation as the swordsman put his blade through the neck of each one to make sure they were dead.

As the two bandits slowly approached the third crewmember who had been shot, Umuk could hear him belatedly call out for mercy. The swordsman looked briefly back at the far end of the clearing, as if looking for a sign. Whether he received one or not, Umuk couldn't tell from his vantage point. Nonetheless, he turned around and silently used his blade for a third time.

"See any more of 'em, Lana?" a baritone voice called out from the back of the clearing, and the archer shook her head in response. Neither she nor the swordsman relaxed their stances, however.

A tall, slender man, who Umuk assumed was the speaker, stepped out into the clearing. He was holding what looked to be Stefan's sword in his hands, and he was flanked by two more humans armed with short bows.

"Right, let's strip these three an'—"

The apparent bandit leader cut himself off as Goran took off at a run. Three arrows shot through the trees in his wake, but he kept going, and it didn't appear he'd been hit. Umuk sensed more movement to his right, and he assumed Branko had taken the hint to try and escape as well.

Lana and her swordsman compatriot sprang after the two men, and another two human bandits armed with axes broke cover and started sprinting after them as well. Their leader and his escort took a few steps forward, but they halted next to the first two bodies on the ground. Umuk knew if he was going to act, now was the time.

Trying to stay quiet, he took a few more steps to his left so that he was even to where the trio was now standing. He would have preferred to get behind them, but he figured there were at least two more bowmen he hadn't seen yet, and at this angle, they would have to shoot through their own people to get at him.

I hope that fool Uptar has tha right target picked out.

He sprinted out of cover, forgoing the traditional war cry of his ancestors to try and gain an extra half step of advantage. As the three bandits turned towards him in surprise, he heard the *thwock* of Uptar's first arrow impacting something solid. At the same instant the archer closest to him pitched forward, their head misshapen and bloody. The other archer made the fatal mistake of turning to see where the arrow had come from, only to be cut down with Uptar's second shot squarely in their chest.

The bandit leader feinted to his left, then jumped right before starting to run back towards the cover at the back of the clearing. Umuk tried to match his movements, shortening the distance between them as fast as he could, while still trying to block any potential shots at him from the woods. As he ran, the slender man put a hand to his lips and let out a sharp whistle.

Umuk made out two, perhaps three, arrows flying from where the bandits had staged their ambush. They were not aimed at him but rather towards the side of the clearing opposite him. He assumed the remaining bandit archers were trying to rattle Uptar and provide covering shots for their captain. No matter, so long they were kept busy.

An instant later, both Umuk and his quarry were at the tree line. The man turned to face him, but Umuk had noticed the archers who had stayed in the trees had lingered too long. He broke wide around the leader, surprising his foes, and managed to cut down one of the archers with a single stroke.

There was an outcry as the other two backed away hurriedly, trying to regain distance from Umuk. They had no shots now that he was among the trees, and they did not appear to have any melee weapons at hand. He noticed dispassionately that both remaining archers appeared to be female orcs.

Sensing he was not in immediate danger of getting shot in the back, Umuk turned back towards the leader. The man came slowly towards him, Stefan's old blade at the ready.

Umuk laughed, showing his teeth. "Ya ugly shite, ya know how long I've been waitin' for this?"

"Damn greyskin, I'll send ya back ta yer mother in pieces!"

There was a scream from the direction that the archers had fled, and Umuk immediately assumed Uptar was taking care of loose ends.

He leered at the man. "Yeah, sounds like a couple mothers ain't gonna be happy today." He charged, keeping his axe low.

The bandit braced himself and managed to block a sweeping attack, but Umuk's bulk was too much for him and he was knocked off his feet by the frontal assault. He rolled well, managing to put a tree between him and Umuk's next attack. There were a few more lunges and parries from both combatants, but neither could find advantage so long as the human was content with using trees for cover. The fight quickly devolved into a game of cat and mouse as the human evaded what attacks he could while slowly giving ground.

Umuk remained uncharacteristically patient. He knew he could easily take the man, but he played for position as they both waited for reinforcements to show up. He assumed Uptar had killed one archer and could take care of the other one, but he wondered how many of the bandits chasing Goran had turned back when they heard their leader's signal.

After a time, there was the sound of feet running and downed branches being broken, followed by the reappearance of the two bandit axemen. One of them had a bloody slash on his cheek, and both were out of breath.

The one with the cut face warily called out to Umuk's opponent from a short distance away. "Radenko, we gotta go. Tha whole shore party's comin' this way!"

"God's bones!" The leader swore. "Where's Lana an' Bojan?"

"They lit out already! Hurry up an' kill that grey shite, an' let's get outta here!"

Umuk sneered. "If it's that easy, then three on one should be child's play, suka! Come on, join tha dance!" He opened his stance slightly and beckoned at the two newcomers.

Radenko, sensing an opportunity, leapt forward to attack. "Now, lads! Rush 'im!"

As the human swung his blade, Umuk neatly parried the blow and sidestepped the rush, grabbing Radenko's sword hand as he passed. In the blink of an eye, Umuk ran the blade through the chest of one of the charging axemen, literally throwing Radenko on top of the already dead man with his follow-through. As he finished his pivot, Umuk brought his own axe up, catching the last man with a savage blow just beneath the chin. The man's body slumped on top of Radenko as his head bounced away into the underbrush.

Umuk breathed deeply. It felt good to be alive again.

He bent over and drew the sword out of the first axeman's body before kicking Radenko. "Get up, suka. Let's talk 'bout tha money chest I know ya got from tha barge."

The man struggled to get away from the bodies of his compatriots, his features and clothing the color of blood. He managed to crawl over to the base of a large birch tree and then turned over to sit upright against it, too stunned to speak. Umuk waited a moment before walking over, placing the tip of the sword in the middle of Radenko's ribcage.

"Tha chest for yer life. Think fast."

The bandit swallowed. "I'll tell ya whatever ya want, but not like this. You're just gonna kill me if I tell ya now."

Umuk chuckled. "Usually, yeah. But my cap'n wants someone alive, an' you're my last chance at givin' him what he wants." He leaned a bit on the sword, and Radenko groaned in pain. "But, ya see, I don't want ta share that money, so either ya tell me where it is 'fore anyone else shows up, or I'll forget what my cap'n wants."

"I already got tha chest," came a low, guttural voice that Umuk hadn't heard in a while.

He looked up to see Uptar standing about ten paces away, a young female orc in front of him. She was one of the archers that had run away earlier, and now her hands were crudely bound in front of her. Umuk could also see that Uptar had a small chest tucked under his left arm. His longbow was strapped across his back, and he held the woman's short bow in his right hand.

Umuk nodded at the chest. "That's tha money?"

Uptar nodded back at him. "Yeah."

"An' that's our live prisoner for tha cap'n?"

Uptar nodded again.

Umuk looked down at Radenko and shook his head. "Only need one. Sorry."

"No-no-n—"

Umuk put his full weight on the sword, and it easily slid through the man's chest. There were some gurgling noises as Radenko drew his last breath, but it was over quickly enough.

Uptar grunted, almost laughing. "Sorry, yeah!"

"Whatever, suka. Everyone else 'round here dead?" Umuk didn't clarify if he meant bandits or crewmates.

Uptar was equally ambiguous in his response. "Uh-huh. Quick now, we got somethin' ta do 'fore any others from tha boat get here."

Uptar pushed his captive forward, but she tripped on a tree root and fell to the ground. The orc ignored her as he tossed her shortbow to the side. He then walked towards Umuk, put down the chest, and then went over to what remained of Radenko.

"Whaddya doin'?" Umuk glowered at the other orc.

"She says he's got a key on him for tha chest."

Uptar quickly searched the dead man and found a string around his neck. Umuk could see that there was a small pouch and a long, skinny, push key tied to the string. Uptar broke the string and then took both items before tossing the key to Umuk.

Umuk glanced over at the female orc as he went to unlock the chest. She hadn't moved from where she had fallen and, in her frightened state, looked much younger than he had originally thought.

"If she told ya ta take tha wrong chest, then—"

"Then we deal with it," came the calm reply. "But I don't think we have ta worry 'bout that."

Uptar began to walk back towards his captive as Umuk turned to fiddle with the lock. There was a soft click, and he pushed the top of the chest back. Looking at the contents, Umuk could scarcely believe what he was looking at.

He turned the chest slightly so Uptar could see what was in it. "Sard me, mate, since when da barge cap'ns carry this much silver?"

Uptar chuckled. "That's just it. That ain't from just one barge."

"Whaddya mean?"

Uptar nodded at the female orc. "Milanka there tells me this group's been roamin' this side of tha river for a couple years now, hittin' homesteads an' small villages from time ta time. They've had time ta build up some resources an' money."

Umuk snorted, thinking of the trials and travails he and

Uptar had experienced on their flight from the east. “Hard ta believe that, given what we went through tryin’ ta do tha same sardin’ thing!”

The other orc shrugged. “They know tha countryside an’ tha humans in tha group can blend in with tha locals. Better than we could, ta be sure.”

“Pfah! Just pure luck! Or, that bitch is just lyin’ ta ya.”

“Like it matters. Anyways, she says they’ve been hidin’ close by for a while, ever since tha tow path went out. They’ve been able ta catch a couple barges that’ve come too close ta tha eastern shore. Usually, they just took their money an’ some food, then let ’em go.”

Umuk scoffed at this. “That’s bloody stupid! They were bound ta get caught sooner or later. Might as well take the cargo of tha first one they catch an’ run.”

Uptar shrugged again. “Everybody knows there’s bandits out here. So what if a couple barges get nicked? Folks will just say ol’ Ruslan ain’t doin’ his job. ’Sides, no one on tha docks is gonna care if a barge cap’n says he’s been robbed but his cargo is still all there.”

Umuk frowned. “Maybe, maybe not. Like I said, they’ve just been lucky!”

Uptar grinned, showing his teeth. “Sure, ’til now, anyways. Tha barge down there came aground late yesterday. The way Milanka tells it, once they saw what it was carryin’, most of their merry band couldn’t let all that wine go. Guess things got outta hand after that. Most everyone got soused, barge crew wound up dead. They was gonna burn everythin’ they couldn’t carry away today. But they took too long ta rouse, an' then we showed up ta ruin their fun."

Umuk grinned as well. *Maybe I actually do have some luck for once. But wait...*

He looked over at the female orc, then down at the chest, and then finally back at Uptar. "Ya know that I ain't sharin' tha loot with our bloody cap'n or tha soddin' crew, right? We gotta kill her an' hide this 'fore tha rest show up." *Then I only have ta worry 'bout yer sorry arse later, ya dumb shite...*

Uptar shook his head. "Nah, we don't. 'Cause I ain't told ya tha best part yet. Milanka said that bastard would also be carryin' this." He held up the small pouch that he had taken from Radenko.

Umuk watched as Uptar opened the pouch and shook the contents into his hand. He couldn't see what it was, but he could see that Uptar was practically beaming.

"More coins?" Umuk said hopefully.

"Ya could say that..." Uptar flipped something in the air towards Umuk, and he caught it with his right hand.

Opening it, he saw a small circle of stamped gold metal in the center of his palm.

A gold kopek!

Umuk was stunned into silence. The one little coin represented more wealth than he had ever had, practically more than he had ever conceived of. The fact that he was holding it in the middle of the Wilds next to a dead man seemed absolutely ludicrous to him.

Finally, he was able to form words. "How in tha abyss did this shite get one o' these?" He looked over at Radenko and then up at Uptar, still stupefied.

"Not one. Two."

Umuk laughed loudly. "Two? *Two?!*"

"Yup. I don't know how he got 'em, an' I don't care. Guess he was better at bein' a bandit then bein' a fighter. But these coins are our way out. One for each of us."

"No shite, mate! But that don't mean we shouldn't kill her and hide this!" Umuk gestured at Milanka and then the chest.

Uptar glowered. "Don't be an idiot! The cap'n will have us searched if we say we didn't find nothin'. Nah, now that we know tha chest got coins in it, we lock it up again an' throw tha key away. Then, we say we got tha chest but couldn't open it. The cap'n opens it with everyone watchin', an' then everyone gets paid. Meanwhile, we hide tha gold coins an' nobody's tha wiser."

Umuk stared at the chest, starting to fume. Perhaps it represented ill-gotten gains, but now that it was his, he wasn't going to give it up so easily.

Especially because some cowardly piece of shite says ta do it.

Umuk's mind was made up, and he shook his head furiously. "Nah, we hide it *all*. Tell that arse of a cap'n an' first mate either we couldn't find tha chest or tha remainin' bandits lit out with it. Why should we give all this up?"

"'Cause my way ain't gonna make everyone think we're lyin', ya dumb shite. 'Sides, ya—"

Umuk cut him off. "Ya think you're so smart, but you're really just muckin' everythin' up by not keepin' things simple." He pointed at Malinka again. "An' what, you're just gonna let her walk? Ya reach yer daily quota for killin' folks or somethin'? Or did she promise ta sard ya nice an' proper so you'll let her go?"

Uptar's body tensed briefly, but then he relaxed again and spoke in a strained but level tone. "Ain't nothin' like that. We made a deal, yeah, but it's her life for tha money. No way we woulda found that chest tha way they had it hidden."

As he spoke, he hauled the young female to her feet. As Umuk looked on, dumbfounded, Uptar took out a small paring knife and cut her hands free. She immediately backed away, rubbing her wrists, her eyes darting back and forth between the two of them.

Umuk took a hard look at Milanka and suddenly understood what was going on. "Nah-nah-nah, this ain't right. Too many loose ends with that skank runnin' 'round. Just 'cause she looks like tha other bitch that ya got killed in tha marsh don't mean that—"

"Shut it, Umuk! Ya don't know nothin'!"

"I know *everythin'*, ya dumb dog! Ya don't think I don't see what's goin' on inside that pointy head of yers? Ya think lettin' this one live is gonna bring tha other one back? Or stop yer dreams from makin' ya scream like some damn younglin' in tha night? *You're* tha idiot, Uptar, an' I'm 'bout done with dealing with idiots."

Uptar glanced back up the hill, and his voice almost had a

pleading tone to it. "Tha rest are almost here! Just trust me fer—"

"Nah, ya damn *pes*!" The words came out in a frenzy that only built as Umuk let his anger wash over him. It was obvious that Uptar had lost his mind, and Umuk was quite fine with clearing it for him permanently. "I ain't waited this long for a score just for ya ta give it away! This money's *mine*, ya hear? And that doxy cunt ain't walkin' outta here with nothin' but yer fat spindle in her mouth, 'cause I'm gonna lop it off an' feed it ta her! Ya sardin' shite, I'm gonna gut ya!"

Umuk leapt back to Radenko's body to retrieve his weapon, the gold coin and the money chest forgotten in the heat of the moment. He knew he could easily take Uptar in a fight, all he had to do was—

Thwock.

He staggered backwards, stunned into silence again, but this time because something powerfully sharp had penetrated his chest.

Thwock.

He looked down and saw two barbed shafts sticking out of him. Dropping the sword, he grasped at them feebly.

Thwock.

Umuk fell to his knees, the shock to his body too much to overcome. He felt so tired now, the pain already giving way to numbness. He tried to look up, but his vision was blurred, and he could only see dark shapes against a bright background. Someone was approaching him, someone familiar...

“Ya ugly shite, ya know how long I’ve been waitin’ ta do this?”

Thwock.

***

Uptar lowered his longbow as he walked up to Umuk. He studied the orc’s mangled body for a moment and then spit on it. “Good riddance, ya bastard.”

There was the sound of another bow string being drawn from behind him, and he smiled to himself. He spoke loudly without turning to face Malinka. “Ya already missed me twice, luv. Just go, ’fore tha rest of tha ship’s crew gets here. Or aim well this time, an’ kill me quick.” He couldn’t decide which option he personally preferred.

After a short pause that didn’t include an arrow entering his back, he slowly turned around. The younger orc had indeed nocked an arrow in her retrieved weapon, but she had only half drawn the bow and seemed to still be considering whether to shoot him or not. He didn’t know if she’d had an arrow hidden on her person the whole time or had just found one lying on the ground. Not that it mattered.

In the distance, there was the start of a murmur of people approaching from the river, and Uptar could make out calls for him and other members of the advance party. He assumed Goran and Branko were dead, meaning he was the only one still alive.

He gestured at Malinka, dismissing her. “Deal’s a deal. Yer freedom for tha money. Take tha deal an’ go.”

Malinka lowered her weapon, but she didn't make to leave. Uptar idly wondered where she and the other orcs who had been in the bandit party had come from. Perhaps they, too, were fugitives from an orc penal colony far to the east, just like the large group he and Umuk had escaped with some time ago.

An' now there's only me that's left from that group. Me an' my memories...

"Is it true? Ya had a mate that looked like me, an' that's why you're lettin' me go?" Milanka's voice was high pitched, and she was shaking slightly. Uptar realized she was probably much younger than he had originally thought.

Vesna...

"It don't matter. Just go."

"It *does* matter. Everyone back at tha other camp is gonna wonder how I got away when ya killed everyone else here."

Uptar sighed. "Pretty sure ya ain't the only one ta get away based on tha bodies I *don't* see lyin' 'round here. 'Sides, ya can just say ya ran an' hid from tha two of us while we looked for yer money box."

"The two of ya...it don't seem like ya shoulda been runnin' together, that's for sure."

"It's a long story, an' one I ain't gonna tell ya."

The murmurs from down the hill towards the river were growing louder, and Uptar shook his head in frustration.

"If you're gonna go, ya best go *now*. I can't vouch for how some of tha crew will treat ya if they find ya here."

A mix of emotions crossed Milanka's young face, as if she had many more questions for him. But whatever survival instincts she had finally started to kick in, and she turned to go.

Her chin raised a little as she risked a parting shot at him. "I'm warnin' ya now, I'll be workin' on me aim if ya try an' find me later ta shut me up."

"Then I'll make sure ta give ya a good five-year head start." Uptar smiled at her, but he didn't show his teeth.

She flushed a deep red and left without another word.

Uptar knew he didn't have much time before someone from the boat found him, and he sprang into action as soon as Milanka was gone. First, he retrieved the gold coin that Umuk had dropped and hid it in the front of his undergarments. Next, he went to the money chest, closing the lid and relocking it. When he was done, he took the key and threw it as far as he could into the forest. Hopefully, it would be lost in what little undergrowth there was, although he assumed no one would look for it in the first place.

Finally, he picked up the chest and tossed it on the ground next to Umuk. He looked down at the body of the other orc again, taking in his cruel-looking countenance. This time he didn't spit on it, and a feeling of almost pity wrapped itself around him instead of anger.

I knew ya wouldn't listen ta my plan, ya dumb brute, so I don't know why I gave ya a chance in tha first place. In our next lives, I'll just shoot ya straight away.

But ya could've been rich. Just take tha gold coin for yer silence, we give tha chest ta tha crew an' get our cut of that, too. I suppose I could've just killed Milanka an' left it 'tween us two ta sort out. But then we both know that would've just stuck a target on me back while ya figured out how ta kill me ta keep me quiet an' take my share. So, here we are.

It don't matter in tha end, 'cause everyone will believe me when I tell 'em that I caught ya tryin' ta run with tha chest. We all knew ya would run when given a chance, loot or no loot. Lev even took odds on how long it would take ya ta try.

Uptar looked back up the hill in the direction that Milanka had disappeared. He could have easily killed her when he had stumbled across her and the other archer beating a retreat from the fight. But it had been so obvious she had no idea what she was doing with the bow, and he couldn't bring himself to kill a defenseless young girl. Especially one that reminded him of Vesna.

He smiled ruefully at himself and fingered the talisman his dead lover had given him through his tunic as he looked back down at Umuk one last time.

Would I have let ya kill me for nothin'? 'Cause there was only one gold kopek in that pouch, ya dumb shite. It was yers for tha takin', an' now ya got nothin' but worms in yer future.

CHAPTER SIX

Holier and Humbler Than Thou

Kira Toth was beyond frustration, and she knew that her emotions were playing out fully on her face as she stalked across the muddy yard between the animal pen and the Shoikos homestead. None of her squad could see her presently, but she would welcome the opportunity to vent her wrath if one dared show their face. After all, collectively, they were the source of her anger. If only they weren't all half-wits, she might actually have time to conduct a proper investigation of what had happened to Father Malachi during the warg attack some two days prior.

"Damn *durni dity* is all they are," Kira muttered under her breath as she pounded the ground with each step. While she had always liked using Orcish insults to call out unsuspecting simpletons, she was starting to run out of terms to describe the incompetence of her troop. Other than Olena, they didn't seem to know which end of a sword to hold, let alone any basic foraging or camping skills.

Why gutter rats raised in the capital city thought they could come north and make their fortune in the Wilds was beyond her. Even just a few moments ago, she had been forced to stop Borys from ingesting blindweed berries because he thought "Them's pretty, so them's good ta eat, right?"

She sighed, knowing that it was her responsibility to train

the recruits as quickly as possible. If they survived, any lingering stupidity would be on her head for not knocking it out of theirs. Still, she wondered for the umpteenth time why she ever thought she could make them capable of anything more than the simple bashing of peasant skulls.

Not that it mattered to anyone but her, but Kira would argue that she had originally told Yuri she *thought* she could train any new members of the town garrison up to a respectable state of battle readiness *if* she was given enough time and resources. Of course, he didn't care to remember the *conditions* of her promise, and now it was too late to do anything about it.

She kicked an innocent stone out of her way and cursed again. She knew now that it would be hard enough to just control Stren with the force she and Yuri had mustered together, let alone attempt to sally out in force against a trained opponent. She hated to admit defeat, especially to the sheriff.

Still, Kozel had never thought the local garrison would have to do much of anything other than murder a few longshoremen and scare some peasants. He had even lectured her to stop wasting time on training "ruffians and scalawags" and instead focus on other tasks. Remembering this oddly made her feel a bit better in the moment, even if it meant admitting defeat to *both* Yuri and Kozel.

She sensed movement to her right, and she glanced up to see that Maryska Shoikos was also headed towards the house. Each of her hands held a good-sized wooden bucket by its handle, and it was obvious she was hauling water back from the well that stood some distance from any other structure. Seemingly practiced in this menial task, she walked briskly without any noticeable straining against the weight she was carrying, all the while taking care to not slosh any of the buckets' contents out onto the ground.

Kira shook her head in self-pity. She was sure that, if any of her newly minted soldiers were tasked with drawing water, at least two of them would fall down the well. Her mood soured again immediately.

She waited for the girl to reach the stoop of the homestead, holding the door open for her. Maryska smiled faintly and bobbed her head at Kira as she passed into the main room of the house. Kira followed her inside but was immediately conscious of the dirty condition of her boots. She decided to stand close to the door and not track mud all over the house, even if Maryska was making a bit of a mess of the wooden plank flooring with her own footwear.

Kira watched the farmer's eldest daughter as she headed to the cooking area and set half of her load down on the floor. The other bucketful of water was immediately poured into a large cauldron that was already sitting above a smoldering fire. Maryska ignored the second bucket for the time being and instead began to stoke the fire, taking medium-sized pieces of wood from a neatly piled stack next to the hearth.

She glanced over at Kira as she went about her business. "Don't worry about the floor, ma'am," Maryska said quietly, as if reading Kira's mind. "The boys make a shamble of the place all the time, and Mother will make one of them sweep it out this afternoon."

Kira nodded at this and wordlessly crossed over to the large table that was in the center of the room. Once there, she tore off a piece of bread from the large loaf that had been set out first thing that morning before sitting heavily in one of the wooden chairs that was by the table. In total, there were four chairs and two long benches spread about the room, as well as what appeared to be an old milking stool lurking in the far corner. All of the furniture, including the table, appeared to be well-constructed and sturdy.

As she smeared some honey on her bread, Kira idly wondered if woodworking was one of the many Shoikos family skills. If she didn't already know their history, both the floor and the furniture would have made her reason that she was sitting in the home of a fairly well-to-do and hardworking family. What wasn't evident from their earthly possessions, but was well-known all the same, was that Mykola and Hannah Shoikos were two of the most forthright and well-meaning people in the county.

In fact, they were *so* well-meaning that it was downright annoying to some, including Kira. They had been held up as paragons of virtue far too many times during Father Malachi's homilies for her taste. It was one of any number of excuses she could give as to why she had stopped going to mass some time ago.

Still, she had to admit that, if that damned orc was going to haul the injured priest to any farm in the county, perhaps even in the entire northern Wilds, he couldn't have picked a better location. Hannah was known to be an excellent apothecary, and her kind nature meant that she never turned away a patient in need.

A sudden thought occurred to Kira. Perhaps the priest took pains to mention the Shoikos family so much during mass as a way to keep anyone from spreading rumors about Hannah using old magic to conjure up her healing capabilities. It had been several years since anyone in Stren had been accused of witchcraft, but Kira knew far too well how superstitious the locals could be. Father Malachi, at least, was beyond reproach and was all the authority the inhabitants of Stren needed on what was good and evil in the world. If he vouched for someone, then that was usually the end of any discussion about their morality.

However, the fact that Father Malachi was beyond reproach and incorruptible was exactly what made him such a threat to what Yuri and Kozel were separately planning. It was also why Kira was at a crossroads in her own mind as to what to do about him and the current crisis the attack on him had created.

Personally, she liked the old man, despite his penchant for rambling sermons. Growing up destitute in Stren, she and Katrya had come to rely on the local chapel as a sanctuary for the poor because of him. Beyond that, he had saved them both from the gaol or worse when the old sheriff had caught them red-handed with stolen church property when they were barely teenagers. He hadn't even wanted a favor in return, a benevolent trait the sisters had learned over time was not held by many.

But still, in Kira's mind, Father Malachi had never confronted the root of corruption and unfairness of life in Stren.

While the church gave the downtrodden temporary respite, she didn't believe it did anything of long-term benefit. If anything, it kept the peasantry in their place by insisting their suffering in this life only meant their eternal life would be that much better.

As for the kingdom itself? As far as she could tell, it didn't matter at all to the common folk *who* was sitting on the throne. The Kalchik dynasty had certainly never done anything good for her or her family, if she could believe the drunken rants of her long-dead father. If someone else was sitting atop the heap, they would still just shite on the poor to keep their private hunting grounds and precious baubles. If the Rus wanted to invade Perizidon, so be it.

If I wanted ta believe my old man, us Toths had a coat of arms an' everythin' back in tha day in Myste, wherever in tha abyss that is. But somethin' went wrong and his parents fled north ta Velych, only ta be fleeced by the Kalchik king and marooned out here in tha Wilds. Who knows if what that tippled bastard said was even half true, but it don't surprise me that a king would take everythin' from someone for no good reason.

As far as Kira was concerned, it would be best if all the royals just met in the middle of some town square and beat each other to death with their crowns. None of them would ever lift a finger to help her better her own station. It was why she had turned to Kozel as the means for her to escape what life had intended her fate to be.

As she chewed her bread, she idly thought about the combined plots against Perizidon as she understood them from what Yuri and Kozel had separately told her. Both had indicated the Rus were intent on subjugating the entire kingdom under their rule, their attack on Stren being the start of an outright invasion. In the minds of the Rus, they were righting a wrong that occurred over two hundred years earlier when the territory that became Perizidon broke away from their empire.

Never mind tha fact that tha old empire had done nothin' ta protect tha locals from tha rampagin' orc tribes back then. Perizidon was just a piss poor fringe territory actin' as a buffer against tha Grey Horde. Now, I suppose, it's all about makin' Rusgorod great again.

Kira smirked to herself and took another bite of bread.

***

But why would the Rus target Stren, of all places? Kira had asked Yuri this question two summers ago, a short time after he confided in her about his treasonous plan against the ruler of Perizidon. Everyone knew that the town was in the middle of nowhere and far from any bordering realm.

Stren would see a smattering of orcs arrive from their tribal lands to the east, but a human coming to town from another kingdom was unheard of. Never mind that the Rus weren't exactly welcomed anywhere outside their own lands. How in the world was their army going to show up in Stren, let alone take it, without getting stuck at the border?

"They ain't gettin' stuck at tha border 'cause they're goin' 'round it," Yuri had drunkenly chortled.

"C'mon, Yuri! How can ya go 'round a border? That's what

closes up a country in tha first place!" Kira had been drunk herself, but not to the point of trusting Yuri's logic.

"Okay, okay, maybe they ain't goin' *'round.* But they're goin' *through* where nobody can see 'em." Yuri punctuated his remarks with a wild motion of his hand, sloshing wine out of his cup in the process.

If both of them hadn't already been naked and sticky from events earlier in the evening, Kira might have protested. Instead, she took a pull from the bottle they were currently sharing and pointed a finger at what she was fairly certain was his face.

"Fine, but where ya gonna go through, Yuri? Tha way I see it, we, yeah, *we*, tha Kingdom of Perizidon, *we* got forts on tha Rus frontier 'bout every couple leagues or so. They got tha same thing, least 'til ya get ta tha mountains. There's even a wall where tha main road is located, an' there's patrols as well."

Yuri belched and then nodded. "That's all true, luv, all true indeed."

"So where are they gonna go through without bein' seen, Yuri? What, tha Rus are jus' gonna sidle up ta some fort an' ask politely that everyone look right while they go left? That's plain stupid!" She stuck out her tongue at him and made a flatulent sound with her mouth to complete her argument before taking another drink from the bottle.

Yuri leaned away from her in mock outrage, but she knew it was really just to get a better view of her impressive breasts. She shook them at him, and he leered at her.

"Oh, Kira darlin', I'll show ya how ta go *through* somethin' all right." He made to reach down into her nether region, but she pushed his hand away.

"Not 'til ya admit you're full o' shite with this army business."

He made the same gesture and noise she had just moments earlier, but he relented from trying to grope her. "Fine, m'lady, I'll prove what I'm talkin' 'bout is true."

Mumbling to himself, Yuri attempted to get out of the bed they were sharing while holding his cup aloft, but this only compounded the amount of liquid trickling down and around his rotund figure. After a few moments of struggling, he let loose with a mild curse and drained the cup before tossing it on the ground. Kira giggled at him as he finally stood up, only to be shown his full backside while he made a rude gesture with his right hand.

"Careful, luv, I might have ta peg that nasty hole you're showin' me," she said, only to receive another rude gesture as he wandered out of the bedroom towards his study. Laughing, she called after him. "Ya know ya can't stop me, ya wandought! Ya only got one muscle in that entire bloated body o' yers!" Kira leaned back in bed, grinning wickedly, and set to finishing off the bottle she was holding. "You're just lucky tha Almighty put that muscle where it's useful..."

After a short time away, which included a series of noises that sounded like various objects being dropped onto the floor, Yuri stumbled back into the bedroom. He was holding a large piece of parchment in one hand and another bottle of wine in the other. He came to Kira's side of the bed and tossed the document on her midsection before starting to fiddle with the wax seal on the new bottle.

Kira took a moment to admire the view staring her in the face before looking down at the parchment. It was a map of the kingdom, and she picked it up to study it more closely. It showed her what she already knew, that Stren was leagues and leagues away from any passable route from Rusgorod.

She shook her head and started pointing out landmarks. "Yeah, okay, a map. So what, Yuri? Ya got tha Nebo Mountains here, an' they ain't gonna get an army through there. South of that, tha west route inta Perizidon is guarded by all them border forts I already mentioned. Even if they get through those, any Rus army would have ta go through Molotok, an' Myr, an' maybe even Tuman, 'fore gettin' here."

Yuri, having got the bottle open, took a long swig and belched again. "Look harder, luv. You're missin' somethin'."

Kira wrinkled her nose. "Phew, man, get thee ta tha bathhouse!"

Yuri giggled like a little boy and gestured at the map. "C'mon, Kira, tell me what ya see."

She gazed at the parchment for a few moments and then shook her head. "Ya got me, Yuri. Stren's not even tha right way ta go if tha Rus get past tha border, 'less you're tellin' me this shitehole is more important than Velych!"

"Forget Stren for a moment." Yuri pointed at the top of the map. "What's up here?"

She furrowed her brow. "There's nothin' up there. Just endless ice an' snow that's impassable. If ya believe tha stories of some lunatic orc trapper, there's a frozen sea if ya go far enough north."

Yuri chuckled. "Well, somebody over in Rusgorod *did* believe that lunatic orc trapper, or whatever version of tha story they got on their side of tha mountains. 'Cause that somebody followed tha Nebo range far enough north 'til it ran out, an' guess what they found?"

"Uh, ice an' snow, Yuri. I jus'—"

"They found a way back down here, Kira. On *our* side of tha range. Down ta Tha Mountain. Down ta *Stren*."

She looked at the map again. It showed Mount Iklo near the top, the Nebo Mountains to its west trailing off the edge of the parchment.

She took a deep breath and blew it out slowly. "But even if there's a trail, Yuri, how are they gonna march an army up there an' back? That's suicide!" She reached up and took the bottle from him to have a drink.

"That's tha beauty of it, Kira. They don't have ta!" Yuri grabbed at the map, ripping it in the process. Ignoring the damage, he grinned as he poked at Stren's location. "You're right, of course, tha Rus told me they can't send an army that way. Not even a couple hundred soldiers at a time. Too many supplies, too many pack animals, too slow. But then they thought, how 'bout just a handful of soldiers, ones 'specially trained for tha trip? It'd be easy enough ta sneak a small group through the northern wastelands where nobody is lookin'."

Kira started to scoff at the notion of a few soldiers invading an entire country, but then something sparked in her inebriated brain.

Having finished the bottle, she took the map back from him. "Did they already start this special trainin'?"

He nodded. "Last year."

"I assume they haven't started comin' over yet, if you're tellin' me tha truth 'bout this Rus contact of yers."

"Too late ta start lyin' ta ya now, Kira. Though I don't think you're gonna out me ta that bitch mayor of ours."

"Ha! That's fair." Their mutual hatred of the woman who had been assigned to oversee the town was the main reason they had started drinking together in the first place.

Yuri continued. "Like I told ya, I only started talkin' with tha Rus 'bout a month ago. But if they're tellin' me tha truth, they've been thinkin' 'bout this for several years. Now, they want ta start sendin' folks up, over, an' down ta Tha Mountain sometime next year. They'll do it slowly, slowly, only a couple at a time, so it'll take a while. But that'll give me...give *us*...time ta do our thing."

He had already told her that he wanted, even *needed*, her help, but Kira ignored the last part of his statement. Instead, she did some quick calculations in her head on the Rusgorod buildup.

"Okay, so assumin' they're only sendin' a small group every couple weeks or so, that's maybe fifty soldiers in a year. Give 'em a full hundred if ya wanna stretch it. They need a lot more than that ta win a war, an' that'll take years to build up. An' sooner or later someone's gonna see 'em, even if they're hidin' out in tha Wilds."

"They don't need a whole army ta take Stren! Not even a small one if we're already on tha inside! That's what I've been tryin' ta tell ya tha past few days!"

"Yeah, an' what *I've* been tryin' ta tell *ya* tha past few days is that *yer* numbers are all wrong! Even if ya bribe tha whole town garrison, there ain't enough heads ta smack tha rest of tha town inta submission."

Yuri groaned and looked up at the ceiling. "Then fix *our* numbers, Kira! That's what yer good at, fixin' me problems! Ya know I'll take care of ya in tha end."

Kira sighed. She already knew she was going to agree to help Yuri. After all, she and Kozel had already come to an arrangement, regardless of what Yuri wound up doing. The desired results of both of her so-called benefactors could work in tandem. She just wished Yuri had more of a plan than to rely on the Rus and her to take care of everything for him.

"Fine," she grumbled, "gimme a couple days ta think it out. I need ta think 'bout what ta do with tha mayor as well."

Yuri laughed. "That's what I like most 'bout ya, Kira, that big, beautiful brain of yers!"

She looked up at him with a bemused look on her face. "My

brain, huh?"

"Yeah! It does more work than...well...uh...oh my..."

Kira had tossed the map to the side and provocatively spread her bare legs. "Ya sure that's what ya like most 'bout me, darlin'? My brain? I think yer 'muscle' says otherwise."

Yuri put his hand on her shoulder. "Well, maybe I should say it completes ya."

***

Kozel had corroborated most of what Yuri had said. The Rus were indeed intending to have just a small shock force take Stren, but with inside assistance. The planned attack was now close at hand, and Kira's conversation with Yuri from the summer before last seemed like an eon ago.

Per the last message that the sheriff had shared with her, everything was scheduled for early Januarius, a bit after Epiphany was celebrated. While a winter attack by the Rus would be risky, it would slow any response from Tuman or the other garrison towns. But it was also why she felt so rushed in training her band of misfits.

Once Stren was taken, Yuri, she, and their rabble would be responsible for maintaining order within town. It didn't matter much how much "order" there was, so long as the Rus soldiery could move freely about the town and use the docks at their leisure. As far as either Yuri or Kozel knew, it was the intent of the Rus to continue to send small groups of soldiers "over the ice" to bolster the garrison at Stren. But per Yuri, it was to be a holding action, rather than a jumping off point for further attacks to the south. They were to deny the use of the town as a staging area for the Perizidon army and to deny the kingdom the flow of natural resources and material from the north.

The sheriff hadn't thought much farther than that. He simply knew that he would be able to dispose of the mayor, if she wasn't already dead, and rule his little fiefdom as he saw fit. How and when the Rus took over the rest of Perizidon was not his concern. But, once they did, Yuri had been promised a regional governorship position within their administrative strata. That sounded quite wonderful and was all he needed to know.

Kira had any number of concerns left unaddressed by this casual view of the future, but Kozel had managed to allay most of them. He wouldn't tell her how he knew, but he had it on good authority that a massive Rus army was poised to attack the western border of Perizidon in the spring. Once that happened, the holding force in Stren should be able to relax. Few, if any, soldiers would be spared by Perizidon to attempt to retake the town; they would have enough problems holding the line elsewhere.

In time, according to Kozel, the Rus holding Stren would be able to stage raids down the river and further disrupt trade. They would be the splinter in the hand of King Elric that couldn't be plucked until it was too late. At that point, Yuri could become regional governor, or something unfortunate could befall him. It mattered not to Kozel.

On that front, Kira knew she needed Kozel more than Yuri

to ultimately break free from Stren and the Wilds. Yuri would be unable or unwilling to give her what she wanted, and he would grow tired of her big, beautiful brain in time. And that was enough to seal his fate as far as she was concerned, big, beautiful spindle or not.

She was acutely aware that Kozel had several other schemes going on, what with his trips to the south and to The Mountain. But handling all the issues in and around Stren had kept her busy and not caring about what else he was doing. Despite not being able to train all the new recruits to a satisfactory level, she had still accomplished quite a bit over the past eighteen months.

She ticked a number of tasks off in her head, if only to make herself feel better. While it had taken longer than Yuri had liked, the amount of wine now being imbibed by the mayor was keeping her blind drunk and out of their way. The rumors of weird lights to the north of town and strange monsters wandering the Wilds that had kept people from nosing around The Mountain were still mostly working. The necessary stockpiles of weapons and supplies had been smuggled in via Tuman, and they could count on the majority of the Stren garrison to either rise against the crown or simply follow orders. The dockmaster wouldn't be a problem, so long as Yuri kept him paid off, and they had enough agents planted among the longshoremen that bottling up traffic on the river could start at any time.

Which brought her back to her problem with the priest.

She knew that Kozel was right in thinking that there would

be undue attention drawn to Stren if the priest died. It would mean an official investigation by the church, and an inquisitor would not be so easily dissuaded or corrupted as the mayor had been. Kira assumed Yuri wouldn't hold up well under interrogation, meaning the truth about what was being plotted would quickly be ferreted out. And once the inquisition knew what was happening, earthly justice would just as quickly be handed out against all traitors by the laws of the kingdom.

Kira also knew that such an investigation would take quite some time to initiate. Even if a report was sent to Velych today about the warg attack, it should take months for an official response. By then, it would be too late to matter in regard to their plans. Why care about an inquisitor showing up at the town gates if said gates were already barred?

Still, from a purely tactical position, she knew it would be best if the priest was taken off the board, whether it be by Yuri playing draughts or Kozel playing chess. No doubt Father Malachi had collected rumors and intelligence of what was going on in the Wilds, even if he hadn't properly connected all the pieces together. Whatever information he carried in his ledger could be withheld, and whatever information he carried in his head would be lost.

But Kira couldn't bring herself to be as ruthless as either Yuri or Kozel, at least when it came to Father Malachi. In her opinion, if he was merely incapacitated—as opposed to dead—then that would be good enough for the time being. And maybe, just maybe, *nothing* would have to be done with him. If she could just talk with him and figure out what had happened during the warg attack and what, if anything, he and the orc had discussed, that would go a long way towards deciding what her next steps would be.

An' if I can't talk ta Father Malachi, I at least need ta find that damn ledger!

Kira and her troop had arrived at the farm very late in the afternoon the day before. She had observed the still unconscious priest and heard a cursory report of the attack from Mykola Shoikos, but there had been little time to do much more than that last night. Soon after their arrival, Olena had caused a stir when she reported hearing wolf calls to the northeast. Kira hadn't heard anything herself, but she didn't want to take the chance of being caught unprepared if an attack came. As it was, setting up camp, the perimeter patrol, and the watch rotation had all taken much longer than she had anticipated.

Thankfully, there had been no warg sightings and the night had passed peacefully. Now, morning drills were over, and all the soldiers had been given their assignments for the balance of the day. Kira rather hoped she wouldn't have to deal with any of them again until well after Vespers. If given several hours, she felt she could properly interview both Shoikos adults and visit the site of the attack. If she was truly fortunate, the priest might recover enough to regain consciousness.

But since he was knocked unconscious durin' tha fight, I doubt ol' Malachi can shed much light on that damned orc's story.

That grey shite, I know he's up ta somethin' an' I can't put my finger on it.

As Kira mulled all these things over in her mind, Maryska finished fussing with the fire. She turned her attention to the second bucket she had carried from the well and began to ladle clean water into various vessels. One of the first vessels was an earthen jug of good size, and this she brought over to the table to replace an identical container that seemed to be empty.

She motioned at several drinking mugs that also stood empty on the table. "Would you like some water, ma'am?"

Kira grimaced slightly. "Don't suppose ya got some mead instead? Can't really trust water 'cause ya never know what's in it."

"That may be true in town, ma'am, but our well is pure, and its bounty has never caused disease. Father Malachi blesses it on a regular basis."

"Well, he blesses tha wells in town, too, an' it don't seem ta matter."

Maryska regarded her quietly for a moment. Kira wondered if the girl would retort that, in addition to their well, her family's souls were also pure, or at least purer than most of the town folk.

Surely that's tha reason tha Almighty has blessed ya with drinkable water, along with all tha other blessings ya got, Kira mockingly thought.

But Maryska was either too humble or too polite for such arrogance. She simply turned and went back to the counter by the hearth, returning to the table with yet another jug. She poured a full mug of mead and offered it to Kira.

It tasted like sweet heaven to Kira, and she quickly downed her entire portion. "Thank ya kindly, Mary. Uh, just leave that here." She reached out to take the jug of mead from Maryska, who had turned to go back to the cooking area. She poured herself another mugful but slowly sipped at this one. As she did, she watched the girl begin to add various herbs to some of the other vessels she had ladled water into a few moments ago. "Ya makin' more medicine for tha priest?"

"Yes, ma'am. The holy water you brought with you was most appreciated and helped immensely last night, but we have already used it all up. We still need to clean Father Malachi's wounds several times over, and Mother wants to place another poultice on his leg. There are also two potions that she wants him to sip from as he is able."

Kira glanced in the direction of the side room where she knew the priest was being tended to by Hannah Shoikos. "Seems a bit strange ta make tha potions now if he can't drink 'em for who knows how long."

Maryska looked over her shoulder at Kira, a quizzical look on her face. "But, ma'am, he'll take them with his breakfast."

Kira choked on her mead and barely managed to not spray it out across the table. "What?! He's awake?"

"Yes, ma'am. His fever broke very early this morning, and Mother—"

"God's nails, girl!" Kira had already scrambled to her feet, and it took all of her self-control to not walk over and choke the now petrified teenager. Instead, she turned and stalked towards the bedroom she knew the priest was in, silently fuming.

Why in tha abyss did no one tell me he's conscious? He's tha sardin' reason I'm here in tha first place!

She reached the door to the side room and barged through it without ceremony.

CHAPTER SEVEN

Diplomatic Games

Dragoman Symon Chumak of Perizidon was annoyed, and he didn't care if his Astrikhon counterpart knew it. In fact, he rather hoped his mood would spur the fawning sycophant into action. Still, he silently counted to three before speaking in a slow, level voice.

"As I have already said, Dragoman Balakiv, I do not have the list. I gave it to your associate this morning."

Mikhal Balakiv wrung his hands in apparent distress, and his eyes darted about the room as if looking for someone to blame. "But, my dear Symon, she has told me that she never received it and—"

"Then she is wrong!" Symon barked, now beyond irritated that Mikhal had either not noticed his honorific was being used in cold courtesy or, worse yet, didn't believe the situation warranted it.

That and he obviously believes that dumb wench of his instead of me.

The other man looked down at the table they were both seated at for a long moment, with his fingers pressed together before him, almost as if in prayer. When he spoke, it was seemingly with all the earnestness he could muster. "I *will* make it right in the end, Symon, I *promise* you. But we simply must have a list to match your wonderful gifts with the intended recipients in His Majesty's court."

It was all Symon could do to not pull out the ceremonial dagger he was wearing and stab the other man repeatedly. Of all the things that were incomplete or improperly done for Princess Lianne's visit, his counterpart remained fixated on the trivial.

Like I bloody care which cheap trinkets go to each of your insufferable courtiers.

Instead of reaching for his dagger, he drummed the fingers of his right hand on the table. "Oh, I agree, Dragoman Balakiv, we must have a list. But surely you do not believe it is my responsibility, or yours, to recreate the initial accounting?"

"Of course not, Dragoman Chumak," the other man responded immediately, finally using Symon's honorific and looking at him directly.

"*Fine.*" Symon managed to keep most of the growl out of his voice, but he couldn't help but take a verbal stab at least. "Does your associate still have the use of her eyes since last I saw her?"

Mikhal laughed nervously. "Of course she does, my dear fellow."

"And I assume she can read and write?" It was all Symon could do to not sneer.

"Of course, Dragoman, of course!"

"Then, since she has obviously misplaced the original list, she can recreate it. Have her take an inventory of the gifts."

"But—"

Symon cut the other man off. "*Then*, after that, have her list the names of the courtiers in your king's court on the same piece of parchment. I assume she is politically nuanced enough to know who should be put at the top of the list of names and who should be at the bottom?"

"Well, yes, but—"

"Then just match up gifts to people. Have her draw lines between the two columns if she must." Symon shrugged nonchalantly to convey how easy he believed the task to be.

Mikhal seemed about to faint. "My lord! Something this delicate must have more input than a lowly scribe's!"

Symon rose to his feet. He was done being diplomatic for the day, and the verbal thrusts came quickly now. "Then give me the list when it is completed, my lord, and I will present it to your king and ask his opinion on the matter. That is, if he is not too busy deciding which villa my future queen will use during her stay, or where the foodstuffs are for her guards, or *which bloody pier her vessel can moor at tomorrow*!"

Mikhal had also stood, a shocked look on his face. His eyes wide, he backed several steps away from the table, again wringing his hands. "I will see what I can do, Dragoman," he muttered as he continued to back up, out of the room.

There were some muted commands from the corridor, and then Symon could hear the pounding of feet.

The Astrikhon diplomat stuck his head back through the door frame. "Ah, good sir, I have sent an attendant to relay your wishes to my assistant immediately. I will personally check on the other matters of concern as well. Please, avail yourself of any of the drinks or sweets that have been provided while I am gone. I shall return presently."

Mikhal's head disappeared, and there were the sounds of more footsteps heading off down the corridor at a rapid pace.

Symon sighed and leaned on the table with both hands. He was either getting too old for these types of shenanigans or had simply spent too much time dealing with the same fools. While it had felt satisfying to vent his anger on the other man, he knew that little good would come of his outburst long term. His reputation as the "Prick from Perizidon" would, no doubt, be fully cemented in place now.

He also knew that Mikhal's position was completely hamstrung by his master. Even now, he couldn't help but feel a tad bit sorry for his pathetic counterpart.

Although, really, it's his own damn fault he's in such an idiotic situation. If Elric was as dictatorial and overbearing as Haldir is, king or not, I would have killed either him or myself long ago.

As far as Symon could tell, Mikhal was actually a very smart man. He was quite accomplished in the ways of diplomacy, so long as discussions were limited to hunting, music, jousting, or any other subject where an administrative decision wasn't required. Symon supposed one of the reasons why Dragoman Balakiv kept his position was directly related to his ability to make everyone happy while promising everything and nothing at the same time.

That and the fact he apparently doesn't mind the king holding his spindle hostage and being told when he can sard his own wife with it.

It was well known throughout the capital of Astrikhon, even to foreign dignitaries such as Symon, that Haldir would routinely summon Mikhal to his private study at any time of the day or night. Then, for the next several hours, the king would render decisions on any outstanding diplomatic issues, all the while haranguing his dragoman about his personal shortcomings. Once he had received his instructions and verbal lashing, Mikhal would then scuttle away and set about making sure his master's wishes were carried out to the letter.

Symon recalled what his personal docket on Mikhal said about the history of the man. An orphan, he had been taken in by the church early in life to keep him alive and off the streets. Mikhal had blossomed academically, if not theologically, so much so that the archbishop himself had paid for the lad's entrance to university. Since graduating with honors, he had worked tirelessly up the ranks of the kingdom's administration to his current position. He had certainly earned his position through talent and achievement, but Symon suspected he maintained his position through his ability to be spineless.

It was rumored that, despite the constant abuse, the king had made Mikhal fabulously rich, far beyond anything he could have imagined as a boy. Symon smirked to himself. Blind loyalty, at least, was apparently rewarded quite well in Astrikhon.

Mikhal probably knows that the Almighty has already showered him with enough favors for a lifetime, so he can afford to have his manhood taken away. Besides, there is nowhere else for him to go now, is there? He has been bought and paid for, so he remains at the side of an insufferable bastard.

Despite the modicum of pity that Symon felt for Mikhal, he was both out of patience and had his own mistress to serve. It was unclear to him why the other dragoman had clearly been given orders to worry about anything and everything else going on in Astrikhon except for Lianne's visit. To not even know where she and her entourage would sleep was not just impolite, it was downright insulting and dangerous.

But, obviously, he already knows where the princess will be staying. Or at least his king already knows. It's all about control in Haldir's eyes, which is why he hasn't felt the need to inform me of anything. If he thinks me a prick, then stop giving me reasons to behave like one!

Symon adjusted his robe and motioned to one of the manservants who had been standing unobtrusively by the library's main door the whole time. "You, there. When your dragoman returns, tell him that I have gone for a walk to clear my mind. If he wishes to find me, I suppose that I will wander by the docks at some point."

The young man, who had stepped forward when called, bowed stiffly and returned to his post. Symon glided past him and into the deserted hallway, but not before selecting a rather large pastry from the side table.

It is time to be less than diplomatic with everyone else in this blasted city. I'll sort things out myself, no matter whose toes get trampled upon in the process.

***

The sun shown down on Symon the next morning as he paced slowly back and forth in an isolated part of Boloto's harbor. The Astrikhon capital was a good-sized trading city, the first major stop for northbound merchants who had navigated their way from the Karadeniz Sea through the vast delta of the Grumaius River. Even now, with the onset of the winter months, Symon could see the pennants of several dozen fiefdoms, free cities, and kingdoms flapping in the cold wind atop the masts of their respective vessels.

Of course, it was his own kingdom's pennant that he was currently concerned about. Word had been relayed from the border scouts overnight that Lianne's caravel had crossed into Astrikhon territory the afternoon prior. Symon had known that the ship's captain would follow the prearranged order to hove to for the night, anchoring just an hour or so north of Boloto. This would allow a stately entrance to be made the next day, with as little or as much fanfare as was desired by the locals.

Yesterday, Symon had seen to it personally that Lianne would have a safe and quiet berth to disembark at. The dockmaster had proven to be a respectable and competent matron who had solved the issue of where the Perizidon vessel could moor and take on stores within mere moments of his request. She had even set up a harbor pilot to be on notice as soon as Lianne's captain signaled his approach to guide them in as quickly as possible.

Symon was still distressed over the apparent lack of celebration that had been prepared for the princess by the Sokolov royal family. It was true that this was to be an informal visit, but Lianne was still royalty. Not only that, but she was royalty bringing with their person a much sought-after treaty.

At least she'll have a roof over her head tonight, instead of being given over to some dingy manger. That may have been good enough for Iesu, but he only had swaddling clothes to contend with, not taffeta silk dresses!

What amount of personal begging or bribing Mikhal had performed since he had left Symon's presence yesterday, Symon didn't know or care. All that mattered was that he had messaged Symon last night that everything was finally settled regarding the basic needs of the princess and her entourage for the duration of her stay. This morning, Mikhal's assistant had even sullenly provided a complete list of gift recipients for Symon's review.

The other dragoman had begged off meeting the princess at dockside due to some unknown diplomatic emergency, but Symon hadn't pressed him on whether the emergency was real or imagined. He preferred meeting Lianne without other dignitaries hovering about, as it would give him time to give her updated information on who she was meeting and when.

Symon looked up as the sergeant in charge of his retinue of soldiers approached him and bowed.

"My lord, I believe I see our ship entering the main channel!"

"Eh? Where?" Symon looked up and squinted out in the general direction of the harbor entrance.

"There, my lord. A bit to your left." The soldier pointed, allowing Symon to sight down his arm.

"Ah, yes, I see it now. Good eyes, sergeant, good eyes indeed!"

The sergeant dipped his head at the compliment and stepped back to where he had been standing with the rest of the escort. It would still be a bit of time before the vessel made its way to where they were, and Symon made use of it by conducting a cursory inspection of the men's uniforms and his own robes.

The caravel made its entrance gracefully, the harbor pilot easing the boat up to the dockside. When the boat was just a few hands away from the pier, the local handlers the pilot had brought with him onboard jumped off and began working the mooring lines fore and aft. They were soon joined by several of the crew, and there was the normal hustle and bustle of making things secure.

After a few more moments, the commander of Lianne's guards and overall military leader for the mission was the first person down the gangplank.

After briefly taking in her surroundings, the woman strode over to Symon and bowed formally. "Dragoman Chumak! It is good to see you, my lord."

He returned her bow, although not quite as deeply.

"Likewise, Major Bannik. I assume no issues with security on the trip downriver?"

"No, my lord. No issues on the river or with the border crossing."

"Excellent. I am pleased to report that Sergeant Vokun and his men have served me admirably over the few days we have been here. All should be ready for you and the rest of the platoon."

She nodded and gave him a curt smile, one without humor. "I am glad they did their duty, my lord."

The sergeant had approached while they were speaking, and he crisply saluted his superior. "Good to see you, ma'am. The men are ready for your inspection."

Major Bannik returned the salute, bowed again to Symon, and went to look over the other men. They hailed her loudly as she approached, as if happy to be under direct military command once more.

Symon suppressed a smile at the guards' formalities, but he knew he had his own show to perform now.

All the world's a stage after all.

Lianne soon made her appearance with two of her ladies-in-waiting, disembarking smoothly and making directly for Symon.

He bowed deeply as she approached. "Your Highness! I trust all is well?"

She gave a short but proper curtsy in return. "Dragoman Chumak. Yes, all is well, except for a short bout of sickness on the way south."

"Sickness, Your Highness? I am sorry to hear that. You, at least, appear to have recovered from your ailment?"

The princess cast a quick glance at one of the young women who was escorting her, and Symon detected a mischievous look dart between them.

"I was not personally taken ill. Rather, it was Anichka, my third companion, who was sick for a time yesterday. But she is recovering nicely and will be along shortly with the first of the baggage."

Symon, of course, knew the seamstress, but he hadn't known her to be prone to what he assumed had been motion sickness. Nevertheless, he nodded. "Ah, I see. There has been a brisk wind the past two days, so I assume there was a bit of chop on the wider parts of the river."

The young woman whose name Symon recalled was Olesea snorted derisively, and then she immediately turned red and bowed. "Beg pardon, my lady."

Lianne frowned at her lady-in-waiting, but after a moment, grudgingly responded to Symon. "Well, I believe her sickness came from my insistence that she try her luck at Karnöffel."

Now he understood, and Symon did his best not to smile too widely. "Hmm, yes. I seem to recall that Madam Anichka is an absolute wonder with her needle, but not so much with her abilities at playing cards."

"Ain't that tha truth," muttered Lianne's other companion, who Symon knew to be her maidservant.

"Melina!" The princess turned to the other young woman with a shocked look on her face. She had clearly noticed Symon's arched eyebrow at the servant's impertinence.

"Well, m'lady, next time we play she can be yer partner!" Melina blurted out. She immediately remembered where she was, turned redder in the face than Olesea had, and curtsied low to both the princess and Symon.

"Beggin' yer pardon, m'lady! An' yers, m'lord."

Symon frowned and stared in turn at both Olesea and Melina. Neither of them would look him in the eye, and it was obvious to him that the princess was absolutely mortified at their performance. Reading the room, as it were, he decided he should attempt to smooth things over rather than cause even more of a public scene.

"That will do, ladies. A bit of mirth, or perhaps some kvetching, at the end of a voyage is all well and good. But I must remind you that we are all ambassadors of our king now, and we must present a good and common front to the people of Astrikhon. Let us leave any public displays of uncouth behavior here at the docks with the sailors."

Hopefully Her Highness will do her duty in private and at least threaten the lashing you both deserve.

It was Lianne's turn to turn a slight shade of pink, but Symon couldn't tell if she was embarrassed for them or angry at him. Nevertheless, she remembered her upbringing.

"You are, of course, correct, my lord. Please forgive their

impetuous nature."

With the princess, he was more charitable. "Please, Your Highness. I may remind them of their duty, but I remind myself at the same time. There is nothing to forgive that I have not done myself on occasion. Your father, as well. When there is time, and we are alone, I will tell you about his escapades during his first voyage abroad to Myste. Utterly shocking and reprehensible, and yet the world still stands."

Symon raised his hands and shook them tremulously at the three women, but he attempted to give them a broad, friendly smile, as well, to show them his last sentence was to be taken as jest.

Lianne seemed somewhat taken aback, but after a moment she laughed. "Thank you, Dragoman Chumak, I most certainly will remind you to tell me that story."

The two other women mumbled their apologies and looked appropriately chastised.

The princess looked around, much in the same way as the major had done a few moments before. Symon waited patiently for her to change the subject, which she did shortly.

"I must say, it is good to both have solid ground under our feet and to see a familiar face in a strange land."

Symon bowed again. "It is good that you are here, Your Highness. Your introduction to the House of Sokolov and the formal signing of the treaty between our two kingdoms will do much to secure peace along our southern border for the foreseeable future."

Lianne motioned to Olesea, who immediately stepped up and handed her an envelope. "Speaking of important documents..."

She looked back at the other two young women, and they suddenly discovered they had something important to discuss a few steps away, while looking out over the water. Now with a modicum of privacy, she turned back to Symon and presented him with the envelope. He looked at the front and could see his name written in a flourishing script.

Jarek!

"Your Highness?" He looked at her, curiosity in his voice.

She smiled at him, and he could feel the warmth behind the expression. "Your husband worries about you so much, my lord. He came to me in confidence and begged that I send you a message from him. I thought it would be better if he wrote the words himself and sealed them away for your eyes only."

Symon could feel his face growing hot, and for once, he struggled to keep the proper amount of decorum. He bowed deeply, holding it for a long moment in an attempt to clear his eyes. When he stood up straight, he had mostly managed to compose himself.

"I thank you, Your Highness, for your thoughtfulness. I shall enjoy reading his note later tonight."

"Very good." She glanced back at the other women, who were still engaged in their own conversation, before addressing him directly. "Dragoman Chumak, know that I am relying on your very capable hands to guide me through the next several days. But also know I do not wish to dally here any longer than is necessary. We shall both do our duty, and then we will be home before the holidays to be with our loved ones."

He could have hugged her. "Yes, Your Highness. Thank you, Your Highness."

Instead of embracing Lianne, Symon offered her his arm, which she took. The other women fell in behind them as he started to walk at a stately pace towards the end of the pier. As they passed the soldiers, who were now standing at attention, their commander fell in at the side of Lianne, perhaps half a pace behind her.

Symon assumed half of the soldiers would fall in at the back of the small procession, with the rest staying behind to guard the boat as it was unloaded. He also had no doubt that the ship's captain would see to the baggage and pay off the harbor pilot. Ahead of them, several horse-drawn carriages that Symon had arranged awaited, ready to whisk them to the mansion that was to be a home away from home for the princess during her stay.

Symon smiled warmly at nobody in particular. It felt good to be orchestrating a well-oiled machine after the past few days of chaos.

He turned slightly towards the princess and began to speak in a low tone. "Now, Your Highness, please allow me to brief you on today's events..."

They were almost to the carriages when the clatter of approaching horses was heard. Whoever was approaching was coming at a full gallop. Major Bannik immediately stepped in front of the princess, her right hand on the hilt of her sword as she gestured with her left. Soldiers fanned out on either side of Symon and the women. They, too, had their hands on their hilts, but they were well disciplined and waited for the command to draw their weapons.

Three horsemen appeared at the front of the line of carriages, all dressed in full regalia denoting the Kingdom of Astrikhon. Two of them were ensconced in armor and held spears in their off hands, but the one in the lead was dressed more finely and did not appear to have a weapon. The three brought their steeds to a halt some ten paces away from the party, the leader dismounting quickly and gracefully. As he faced the princess, he smiled and bowed low to the ground.

Symon could scarcely believe his eyes, but he quickly turned to face Lianne as well.

"Your Royal Highness! Might I have the honor of introducing His Royal Highness, Prince Hadeon Sokolov of Astrikhon!"

CHAPTER EIGHT

Peas in a Pod

In what seemed like no time at all, Lianne found herself sitting in one of the carriages with the prince of Astrikhon as they pulled away from the docks. Hadeon's two mounted soldiers were alongside them as they began to move at a moderate pace into the city. The rest of her party were either still being put in the other carriages or would have to wait for additional transportation to arrive. She hadn't noticed what had happened with the prince's horse.

At least Major Bannik didn't draw her sword and put it to his neck when he dismounted! He is either insanely brash, or naïve, or both!

After the prince had made his surprising entrance, introductions had been short and to the point. Hadeon had acted very familiar with everyone, even going so far as to personally greet her ladies-in-waiting. However, if Symon had been irritated by the various breaches in etiquette the prince had displayed, he had kept his anger to himself.

I think the prince won Olesea over instantly, at least. Knowing her, she's vexed that she's not here with me. Or rather, him!

Lianne looked down to hide her smirk. Hadeon had insisted that she ride with him into the city, which she had accepted after only a slight hesitation. He had even opened the door to the first carriage in line for her, somehow moving faster than the footmen who had been waiting alongside it. He had then immediately jumped in behind her, although he had taken care to sit opposite her instead of next to her.

The carriages themselves were quite ornate, as they each had a solid wooden roof and extensive carvings on all their sides. While the interiors were still exposed to the elements via open windows that the occupants could peer out of, Lianne's, at least, had heavy curtains that could be pulled across the openings for privacy. The seats were cushioned and very comfortable, and blankets had been provided if she found the brisk air too cold for her liking.

Out of the corner of her eye, Lianne had seen Major Bannik approach her carriage and assume one of the footman positions on the runner adjacent to the door she and the prince had just used. She had glanced in at Lianne but said nothing as the carriage started to roll away under the power of four matched horses. If the displaced footman had protested, he had been ignored. While Lianne didn't believe Hadeon to be a deranged lunatic, she was still glad for the presence of the major and for her quick thinking.

What would Mother think of this? I'm practically unescorted in here! Symon must be beside himself. At least the prince has not attempted to draw the coverings over the windows.

After several moments of silence, the prince coughed lightly into his left hand, and Lianne looked over at him.

He had a rueful look on his face, but it quickly dissolved

into a jovial grin as he spoke. "I do apologize, Your Highness, for being so brash as to come to the docks unannounced and to greet you so informally. Both my dragoman and my mother warn me quite often about rushing into situations such as this. But I just could not wait until later today to meet my counterpart to the north!"

The interior of the carriage was sheltered enough from the wind that she was able to respond to him in a conversational tone. "It is quite all right, Your Highness. I have been looking forward to this trip and building the relationship between our kingdoms."

She knew it was a bit of a stilted statement as soon as she spoke, and some of the prince's enthusiasm left his face.

All the same, he continued to smile. "Excellent. Well, there is a formal audience with my parents this afternoon, and I assume you would like some time to rest from your journey. This carriage and the others are headed directly to your temporary residence, and your baggage train will arrive immediately after you and your escort. You will then have several hours on your own to recuperate. But in the meantime, Your Highness, is there any way in which I can assist you?"

Lianne swallowed and glanced out the window, trying to think of something to say. The cobblestones rattled away underneath the wheels of the carriage at a constant rhythm, as if marking the moments that began to stretch between them.

Come on, Li! It's not like you don't have a thousand questions to which he might have the answers. No sense in losing a potential ally due to rigid formalities you don't particularly care for anyway.

A sudden thought came to Lianne as she glanced back at Hadeon. She knew the prince to be a year or two older than her seventeen years, but he was exhibiting the same exuberance and innocence of youth that her younger brother Lucas did. The thought surprised her, but in a good way.

Finally, she cleared her throat and responded to his question. "I must confess, Your Highness, that I had hoped to learn more about your country before I arrived. Perhaps you can enlighten me a bit before I meet the king and queen."

"I see. Well, if you wish, Your Highness, you can certainly test me on how well I have listened to my civic lessons over the years." Hadeon then leaned forward and spoke in a conspiratorial way. "Only, please do not tell my don if I falter. I rather dislike getting my knuckles rapped."

Lianne laughed at this, immediately putting her hand in front of her mouth so as to not completely break etiquette.

The prince leaned back, perhaps with a bit of relief playing across his face at her reaction, and he continued in an off-hand manner. "I can certainly quote any number of statistics for you. The size of our army, our largest export, the number of acolytes we provided to the church last year...all the minutia you could ever care to know."

Lianne clasped her hands in her lap and smiled. "Oh, I assure you, my don has drilled the very same numbers into my head about my own kingdom. And perhaps my knuckles were rapped along the way as well."

Hadeon laughed loudly at this. He did not cover his mouth, but he did turn away slightly so as to not show Lianne his tonsils. "It is good to know that princes and princesses are treated equally before the universal throne of education!"

Lianne felt herself warming to him, sensing he was a kindred spirit. She decided to risk a slightly teasing tone. "So, Your Highness. If I asked you the size of your army, would you actually tell me?"

He squinted his eyes at her and put his hand to his face, slowly stroking his short goatee. "Well, my lady, are you a spy for your king, or are you merely curious?"

Lianne immediately noticed the slight change in how he addressed her and matched him in turn. "Neither, good sir! I am a rogue agent for the infamous League of Bandits!"

She raised her chin and attempted to look haughtily down her nose at him, which garnered another laugh.

"Oh dear, yet another enemy of the kingdom, and one that I was unaware of. Hopefully, I make it out of this carriage alive!" Hadeon rattled the side of their enclosure for effect.

Immediately, the footman standing on the runner outside the door opposite Lianne peered inside through one of the openings. "Yes, Your Highness?"

"What? Oh, er, how long until we arrive at the princess's residence?"

"Very shortly, Your Highness. Just three more turns, I

believe."

"Ah! Very good." Hadeon vaguely waved, and the footman looked away. The prince looked back at Lianne, somewhat sheepishly. "My apologies, my lady. Where were we?"

The princess hesitated, then said, "Please, sir, call me Lianne."

He smiled widely at her and didn't appear flustered at the breach in protocol created by someone other than himself. "Very well. Lianne, it is. But only if you will call me Hadeon."

"Of course. Hadeon, it is."

He looked away again, and another moment of silence encapsulated them both within their individual thoughts.

Rather than let this one drag out, Lianne coughed lightly to get the prince's attention, mimicking his own previous action. "So, Hadeon. I believe you were about to confess some military secrets to a bandit queen."

"Ah, yes!" He thought for a moment longer before answering. "Well, Lianne, if I knew you to be a bandit, and a notorious one at that, I would tell you we have a 25,000-person standing army, with another 25,000 that can be called up within a moment's notice, and the resources to hire some 10,000 mercenaries on top of that. And that, of course, does not count all the common folk who will form lynch mobs and hunt you down on their own for stealing their grain and cattle."

"Of course," Lianne said a bit dryly. She wondered if he was being sarcastic about the lynch mobs but let him continue.

"Now, if you were a spy, you would immediately halve all of the figures I just stated to come up with more reasonable values, seeing as you would probably already know quite a lot about our administrative functions and where taxes are spent." He leaned forward again in his seat, but this time without a smile. "However, if you were a potential ally and friend, I would cast caution to the wind and be forthright with you. While we are not officially at war with the orc tribes, much capital and many personnel are spent holding their raids at bay. We have perhaps three thousand soldiers constantly patrolling our northern border, and they are a major drain on our resources.

"Our navy patrols the southern reach of the Grumaius, and it also ventures out into the Karadeniz Sea to keep the worst of the pirates and smugglers out of the river delta. That consumes perhaps a thousand sailors and marines, as a number of the outer islands are garrisoned. Add another thousand more soldiers or so to patrol Boloto and other towns, man our other frontiers, and provide a small reserve, and that is what we must make do with."

"So, divide your initial number for your army not by half but by five or so?" Lianne asked after quickly adding up his real values in her head.

That number is quite close to what Father says we can afford to put in the field during peaceful times.

Hadeon nodded emphatically. "Yes, that is indeed the case. We do have peasant levies that can be called up in an emergency, assuming it is not the harvest season. And there is money in the treasury to hire a sizable force of mercenaries for a short spell. But as I assume you know, it all comes down to budgets, budgets, budgets."

Lianne nodded. "True enough. I do not envy my chancellor's job, but I also do not look forward to being ruled by them with every decision that must be made."

"Exactly! Raise taxes and the artisans will revolt! Place tariffs on imports and the doge of Myste will merely direct his merchant ships elsewhere! Reduce the standing army and get invaded by orcs! There are some days that I wish I had an older sibling."

The princess chuckled. "Heavy will be the crown upon your head. On mine as well."

"Yes! And that is what I hope you and I can discuss at some length. Or rather, how we can lighten each other's crowns."

"Oh?" Lianne frowned slightly. "The treaty that I bring with me...surely that brings a modicum of relief to both of our fathers and thus to our future selves as well. Is there a reason why you wish to discuss policy without our dragomen or other advisors present?"

"Not policy, per se, it's just..." Hadeon seemed to be searching for a better way to speak his mind, but then just threw his hands up in front of him. "Bah! I am making a mess of this introduction."

The carriage was slowing as he spoke, and Lianne could see that they were pulling up to a large mansion. It was set back from the street, with a sizable garden area in front of it. There didn't appear to be a fence surrounding the perimeter of the property, although a short hedgerow prevented passersby from wandering in wherever they pleased. A half dozen soldiers were waiting for the carriage, and they snapped to attention as it stopped.

The footman who had previously stuck his head inside now opened the door on the far side from Lianne, and she descended from the carriage gracefully, while protecting her modesty. Major Bannik had already come around from the street side, having dismounted from her runner as soon as they had stopped. Lianne nodded to her, thankful for her presence among the small host of strangers.

Lianne turned around as the prince hopped down from the carriage.

"Li—" he started to call out before catching himself. He coughed and then gestured at what Lianne thought to be the leader of the soldiers who had been waiting for them. "Sergeant Chernov, *leave* four men here to assist with the other carriages and have the rest join whoever is standing watch at the back entrance of the house."

The sergeant barely blinked as he briskly saluted. "Yes, Your Highness."

Hadeon then turned and motioned at the major. "Sergeant, this is Major Bannik. She leads the security escort for Her Royal Highness, Princess Lianne Kalchik of Perizidon. I need you to brief the major regarding the security measures that have been put in place around this residence. Bring me any requested changes or concerns she might have."

“It shall be done, Your Highness.”

“Excellent.” Hadeon looked at Lianne and made a short bow before addressing her formally. “Your Highness, might I trouble you for one moment longer?”

“But of course.”

They smiled at each other, and he extended his arm. Lianne glanced over at the major, who merely nodded back at her. The rest of the carriages had not appeared yet, but the princess assumed they weren’t too far away. Whatever Hadeon wanted to tell her in confidence would have to be done relatively quickly.

Lianne took the proffered arm, and the prince slowly steered her into the property. However, he then turned right into the garden rather than walking towards the house, and he waved at the grounds with his free hand.

“This used to be the residence of my grandmother, the queen mother. She spent as much time as possible in her flower gardens in her old age, and anyone was more than welcome to join her so long as they helped her with the weeding.”

“Do you really mean *anyone*?” Lianne was shocked. Even though she believed her family to be fairly well liked within their kingdom, there wasn’t a chance in the abyss that they would let a random stranger enter the grounds of their private residence.

“Oh, yes. She was truly loved by everyone in the city, if not the kingdom. As I am sure your major has noticed with dismay, my grandmother insisted on having the perimeter fence around her residence torn down. When my father protested, she told him that good weeders were hard to find, so why make it hard for them to come help her? I think she only later agreed to the shrubbery along most of the perimeter because too many people were stepping on her mallows."

Lianne looked around as he led her to a small patio with a gazebo. Even with the coming winter, they were far enough south from Perizidon that there was still quite a bit of greenery surrounding them. "This space must be absolutely stunning in the springtime."

Hadeon sighed. "It is at that."

Lianne sensed there was a personal connection to the grounds for the prince, something that brought him comfort. "Would you often help your grandmother with her gardening?"

"Yes, whenever I could get away from my books and my escort. I loved playing in the dirt as a child, and I loved being with her. No one would dare say anything to my grandmother directly, but sneaking in here to be with her is the main reason why my knuckles are so scarred now."

Lianne chuckled at this confession as Hadeon released her arm so she could sit down in the gazebo. He remained standing at its entrance, a few paces away from her, looking past her towards the street.

After a moment, the faraway look on his face passed, and he focused back onto her and the present. "Lianne, my grandmother was a wonderful person, and many people besides just me have fond memories of her and her gardens. But the reason she lived in this house for so long was that her husband died quite young, making my father king when he was yet in his teens."

Lianne wracked her brain to remember what Master Gregor had lectured about the history of Astrikhon, plus what little else she had found on her own. "Your grandfather...King Horik IV, yes?"

He nodded somberly. "Yes, that is correct."

"He died in battle against the orcs, did he not?"

"That is the story that history has been told to remember, yes. It is well known that he was killed by the orcs the last time we attempted to invade their homeland. It is not well known that he was killed after being captured in battle and that the army only recovered his head."

Lianne swallowed. "Oh...I am sorry to hear that."

"Yes, well, it is ancient history to you and me, something that happened long before either of us were born. But it is not ancient history for many in the royal court here. Memories and grudges run deep here, I am afraid." He looked at her oddly, as if gauging how she would react to his pronouncement.

"It is exactly that type of insight that I wish I had more of, Hadeon. As I said on the ride over, I had hoped to learn more about your country before I arrived. To better understand your customs and your history, I mean. Not just how many acolytes you provided last year."

Hadeon smiled. "Thirty-three. Just over our quota."

She smiled back at him. "Twenty-nine. We met ours, but only just."

He left the doorway and took a seat on the bench next to her. "Yes, well, I must admit that I had the same desire about learning more about Perizidon before your visit. Beyond mere facts and figures, as you say. It's just..." He furrowed his brow.

"Yes?" Lianne's skin was suddenly tingling, and she leaned in towards him.

"It's just that...well, to be blunt about it, my courtesans, and even my don, seem to thrive more on rumor than fact when it comes to long-held beliefs associated with your kingdom. To make matters worse, certain items seem to be missing from our archives. I am told the documents I seek are there, but I cannot find them. They pertain to a very important time in our combined history, and I wanted to—"

Lianne reached out impulsively and grabbed his arm. A slight jolt ran through the prince's body, and he stopped talking immediately but did not pull away. "Hadeon! Tell me, exactly what time period are you speaking of?"

"The Time of Betrayal, when—" He coughed, cutting *himself* off this time. He looked at her and started again. "My apologies. What I meant to say was, the time period centered around Perizidon making peace with the orcs."

"And the assassination of our king?"

"Uh, yes, your King Rurik. That as well." He looked down at his arm that she was still clutching and then back up at her. "What am I missing?"

"Exactly the same thing I am missing!"

He looked at her with a confused look on his face. "Beg pardon?"

Lianne shook her head quickly, as if to clear it. "History, Hadeon! We are both missing the same pieces of history!"

She released his arm and stood up. Such was her energy that she immediately began to pace quickly around the small gazebo.

"My apologies, let me explain. Like you, I visited our archives before my trip south, to try and find information on the relationship between Perizidon and Astrikhon from roughly a century ago. I daresay for the same reasons that you were looking, even if from a different perspective."

He nodded and crossed his arms. "Broken alliances and dead kings do have a way of stirring things up."

"Yes, indeed. And events such as that are usually written about at length, if not when they happen, then certainly some time afterwards when the truth comes out."

Hadeon smiled, somewhat ruefully. "Even more so when multiple versions of the truth are most likely present." Suddenly, he sat straight up on his bench. "Wait a moment! Are you telling me that you also found nothing in your archives?"

Lianne stopped pacing. "*Exactly*. Nothing of importance, anyway. Just, oh, I don't know, some minor border treaties and what-not."

"That is extremely interesting..." Leaning forward, Hadeon folded his hands together under his chin.

"I cannot even locate—" Lianne started to speak, but the

prince held up a hand to silence her, not unlike what her father did when he was thinking. It vexed her somewhat, but she allowed him a moment with his thoughts.

He soon spoke again, but as if she wasn't even there. "But who would prosper at the suppression of this information? Surely not our fathers, or our father's fathers. Why would they both conceal the same thing, or rather everything? Could our dons possibly collude with each other in striking our collective archives? But what would they, or anyone else in our royal courts, for that matter, gain by doing this? Unless..." He looked up at her. "My apologies, Lianne, I am babbling to myself. What were you going to say?"

She gave him a quick smile to let him know she bore him no lasting ill will. "Nothing. Or rather, nothing more than the same thoughts you are having. Who would benefit from hiding the truth from everyone?"

Lianne was actually grateful that he had cut her off, as she had been about to say that she couldn't even find a copy of the treaty between Perizidon and the orc tribes.

That's obviously what he meant by the Time of Betrayal. Memories and grudges run deep here, indeed. He was trying to warn me about his father and the court here! Telling him that the physical document at the heart of his country's ill will towards mine is either missing or doesn't exist is probably not something to share just yet. His heart seems to be in the right place, but who knows what he would do with that knowledge. Careful, Li!

There was the sound of multiple horses approaching, and they both looked over at the street to see the rest of the carriages drawing near. Three were approaching leisurely from the dock, but there was another one approaching from the other direction at breakneck speed.

Hadeon swore to himself and stood up. "Lianne, I am found out. That carriage coming from the castle is the personal vehicle of my father's dragoman, Mikhal. No doubt someone has told him about my brash behavior, and he is sweeping in as quickly as possible to mend whatever diplomatic fences I have torn asunder. I am afraid we will need to pause our private conversation for the time being."

It was all Lianne could do to not swear as well. Just like what had happened with her conversation from about a week ago with the inquisitor when Moirne wouldn't elaborate on the complicated history of Lianne's lineage, she hated loose ends and stories that were not concluded properly.

The inquisitor... God's bones, I almost forgot about her mission for me with the archbishop here! Perhaps the church knows something about this missing piece of history. They must have their own archives, obviously. If not in our respective capital cities, then in the holy city of Konstantine.

I must figure out a way to broach the issue when I have my audience with the archbishop. Ugh, but how am I to get word to him in the first place that I must see him? Hopefully he will be at court later today.

While these thoughts flashed through her head, Hadeon had crossed over to her and had extended his arm again.

"If it is acceptable to you, *Your Highness*, I would prefer that we only mention our joint admiration for the queen mother's gardens to our collective escorts."

Lianne wholeheartedly agreed with him. She decided against giving him a conspiratorial wink but accepted his arm. "Of course, *Your Highness*. That is quite easy to say, as it is the truth."

"Excellent!" He smiled briefly, but then he brought his head close to hers as if he was worried someone was hiding in the hedge. He spoke in a low voice. "But, as to our apparent joint discovery, the immediate thought that I have is that some third party is at cross purposes with both of our kingdoms! Why else would someone allow these old wounds to fester except to maintain a divide between us? To keep us from building strength through unity like the old fable? Easier to break each twig by itself than the whole bundle, eh?"

"God's nails!" Lianne could not keep herself from swearing aloud this time as the thought sank in, and she immediately blushed.

Hadeon continued as if he hadn't noticed or didn't care about her blasphemy. "Exactly! Something is amiss, Lianne, and has been for some time. I must think about how to approach this discovery with my father, or anyone else for that matter. I am just glad that a first step towards better relations between our kingdoms is already occurring with your visit, with or without some grand conspiracy running amok behind the scenes." He reached over with his free hand and squeezed her arm good-naturedly.

Then, winking, he immediately swept the same hand across the horizon and began to talk in a loud voice. "Ah, Your Highness! You honor the memory of my grandmother with your sage comments on fertilizer! Now, if there is time, let me show you where she used to plant her most beloved annuals..."

Lianne could see that a thin man had leapt from the carriage that had arrived from the direction of the castle, and he was already hurrying towards them as quickly as protocol allowed. Further discussion on important issues would indeed have to wait.

CHAPTER NINE

Let's Make a Deal

The early evening hour of the same day Moirne had entered Tuman found her sitting in the River's Edge Tavern, sipping a mug of spiced wine and appreciating its warmth. The day had turned even colder after her encounter with the boys outside the church, and she was very glad not to be camping out in the Wilds. The wind that was rattling the windows of the tavern did its best to drive this point home as she subtly looked around the room at the other tavern patrons.

She had taken the gate commander's advice and had secured accommodation at the Red Squirrel on the western edge of town. Her mare was tucked away in a nearby stable for the night, no doubt also glad to be out of the weather. By all rights, she should be warming herself in her rented room, looking through mundane administrative documents. And yet...

And yet you're here instead, Dear Moirne. Or is it to be Saint Olga tonight?

Moirne sighed and took another sip from her mug, this one a bit longer than the last. Neither the wine nor her thoughts were doing much to ease the sour feeling in her gut that had grown ever since she had entered town.

Maybe I should have just had another pastry with the children and then stayed in my room.

Whatever trouble she had expected to find in Tuman, the apparent rise of a new local gang fit perfectly into her thinking. It clearly wasn't her responsibility to interfere in the secular machinations of the kingdom. If she did anything, she should merely identify herself to the sheriff, report her findings, and be off to Stren in the morning. But how often in her investigations had religious and secular concerns merged into one overall pattern of transgression?

Far too often. But, no, you need to focus on the bigger picture. And that's why you're here tonight.

A conversation with the Red Squirrel owner had confirmed what the gate commander had said about the road north of Stren. It would be rough going for any traveler on foot, starting some five leagues north of town. The riverbank had recently collapsed in two locations, making the barge tow path unusable for quite some distance. Donkey teams heading north had to be brought on board their barges, and then the barges had to be poled through this long stretch of the river. It had led to much consternation amongst the barge crews, but it was too late in the season to send a repair party out to set things right.

There were other roads leading north that she could take, but they wandered farther to the west than she liked. Using any of them would delay her arrival in Stren by several days, if not longer, depending upon the weather. Her horse wouldn't mind being pushed if it came to it, but it was not an ideal option.

Of course, along with the other land routes were the normal

rumors of outlaws in the Wilds, but nothing of substance as far as Moirne could ascertain. Confronting the odd ruffian did not concern her in the least, as there was no doubt in her mind she would overcome them. But dealing with them would likely mean having to reveal her true identity, as well as bringing any survivors back to town for dispensation of civic and church justice. And the restless feeling in her gut continued to tell her that personal discretion was the best way forward.

It would be different if there were any reports of wargs in the area that needed to be investigated, but they and the malevolence they breed seem to have stayed to the west and north of here. Perhaps Aerysiel and her treants still hold some sway, at least more than she thinks. Or perhaps just more than what she's willing to let on to an old friend. In any event, I must press for Stren before easy access shuts down for the winter.

Moirne never liked traveling by boat, given her long-held phobia of murky water and what may be hiding within it. Even long bridges had been known to give her pause in the past. But given the circumstances, after her inquiries at the Red Squirrel, she had reluctantly decided to at least investigate the option of taking a flatboat north from Tuman to Stren.

Even with the inclement weather, the docks would be open late into the evening with the last bustle of harvest season traffic. However, she had been told at the Red Squirrel that the dockmaster and his scribes would not see any strangers or conduct new business until the current frenzy of work was over. Her best bet for securing passage north as soon as possible would be to come to an agreement with a captain directly and then let them deal with the bureaucratic process. And any captains not at the docks driving their crews to load faster would be spending the evening at the River's Edge drinking and, most likely, gambling away donkeys and priority berthing rights. Her evening plans were therefore set.

Moirne had changed out of her travel clothes, not only so she could get them cleaned, but also to blend in a bit better with the local crowd. She still wore a nicely made tunic, but her riding pants had given way to a long skirt. It made her look a bit more feminine, and it also hid her boots. She had muddied them up on the walk over from the western gate to the docks, but they would still be seen as a mark of prosperity if anyone took a close enough look.

She had wisely kept her cloak for the short walk across town to protect against the worsening weather. The bitter wind also meant that even the locals were wearing several layers of clothing, making it easier to hide the padded undergarments she had told Anton about.

Better safe than sorry. You never know when a brawl might break out.

However, she had left her sword safely secured in the weapons locker at the Red Squirrel. It would do her little good in the close quarters of a bar if she found herself in a fight as opposed to a brawl, and there was no sense in showing it off to any locals who hadn't seen her about town earlier. She was far from being unarmed, of course, what with a dagger strapped unobtrusively to her waist and the free use of her limbs.

In the end, her voluntarily decision to leave her sword behind mattered little. When she had arrived at the River's Edge, she had been mildly surprised that the patrons were observing the use of the tavern's weapons locker for their long blades. The two brutes stationed near the main entrance also seemed to be taking their job seriously.

Still, the fact that they have two brutes here means they expect a rough and rowdy crowd tonight. And it's not even market day.

Moirne had taken her meal at the bar, discovering that Anton had been right in his assessment of the tavern's goulash. She had polished two bowls off with gusto, making small talk with the young bartender while making sure he noticed her coin purse. The crowd was still light due to the early hour, so she had the balance of his attention.

He had the markings of a half-breed, being bald and having mottled skin, but he showed no other signs of mental or physical ailments received at birth. After she had ordered the second round of goulash, he had finally gotten over the fact that she wasn't a local and had warmed appreciably to her. With her second mug of mulled wine, he had given her both his name and, upon being asked, some advice on which captains she should approach.

"I'm tellin' ya, miss, ya want one o' tha older cap'ns," Barinov said as he slowly wiped the counter with a dirty rag.

Moirne noticed he did this continuously if not busy serving patrons, as if the motion was compulsory.

Now, as he continued to speak, he leaned in closely as if they were co-conspirators in some mysterious plot. "Them young'uns be too impatient, too eager ta get ta where they need ta be. They ain't seen enough winters yet ta judge tha ice floes when tha weather turns bad. 'Sure,' they think, 'my barge is up close ta shore, I ain't gonna get sunk by some berg.' True, I says in return, but what if some big chunk o' ice angles in an' cuts yer haul line?" He made a gesture with his free hand as if waving goodbye while pursing his lips together. "Pshht! Off ya go, mate, outta control! An' if tha confluence don't swamp ya, maybe that sardin' bridge they built downriver will finally stop ya!"

Moirne didn't think getting a tow line cut happened that often, at least by river ice, but she looked appropriately horrified. "Come now, sir! Surely any captain in their right mind would have more than one rope handy? Or at least a grappling anchor at the ready?"

Barinov winked at her and gave her a toothy grin, showing off part of his Orcish heritage. "Ah, miss, ya got yer wits about ya! Jus' means ya got more in that pretty head o' yers than tha average jobbernowl that's haulin' freight up tha river! I think maybe one o' them youngsters should be payin' ya ta travel with 'em 'stead o' tha other way round."

They both laughed at this. Moirne allowed a bit of color to enter her cheeks, and she appeared to wobble a bit in her chair at the compliment. "You flatter me, kind sir. Please, just let me know when the right captain comes in, young or old, and hopefully, I can conduct some business with them."

She quietly slipped a silver denga across the counter as she made her request. The bartender's rag never stopped its wide, circular motion, and a brief moment later, the coin had disappeared within it.

"Thank ya, kindly, miss. I'll be sure ta point out some good'uns fer ya when I see 'em. Till then, yer wine's on tha house." Barinov inclined his head slightly to her, then continued. "Is there anythin' else I might interest ya in? Entertainment o' some sort? A game o' chance, perhaps?"

Moirne smiled. "I heard there might be some games of chance played nearby."

"Oh, *quite* nearby, miss. If ya fancy rollin' tha bones a bit, I'm sure tha good folks 'round here won't mind." He suddenly frowned. "But, just so ya know, tha bishop don't take kindly ta passe-dix fer some reason. So don't let no local heathen trick ya inta playin' it."

"Oh? Why's that?" Moirne knew what the bishop did, that playing passe-dix was seen by some in the church as akin to casting lots for Iesu's clothing under the cross. But she didn't want to let on that she was too knowledgeable of the holy doctrine.

"Well, if ya lose, eh, ya lose." The bartender shrugged off what seemed like the inevitable result for someone like her.

"And if I win?"

"If ya win, ya might have a sore loser on yer hands. Then, all a sudden, ya might find yerself gettin' hauled in front o' tha inquisition fer playin' tha soddin' game in tha first place! Best stick ta hazard, miss, unless yer willin' ta gamble with yer soul." Barinov crossed himself and looked upwards.

Moirne hid the grin that threatened to form on her face, both at the thought of investigating herself on behalf of the church and the fact that a game of passe-dix was already ongoing at the large table in the far corner.

"I understand, sir. Still, I'm not willing to wager my earthly possessions against weighted dice, no matter the game."

The bartender placed his free hand over his heart. "I hear ya there, miss! But don't ya worry, tha dice here be legal if Simeon's got anythin' ta say 'bout it."

"Simeon? Who's that, the owner of this establishment?"

"Aye, miss, tha owner."

Moirne nonchalantly tossed back the remains of her mug and placed it on the bar for a refill. She wasn't sure if the bartender had made an intentional slip or not when mentioning the name of the leader of the new local gang. Still, he had confirmed what Anton could not earlier, that Simeon was overseeing operations at the tavern. She decided not to push Barinov on the issue and, instead, waited for him to refill her drink before asking a different question.

"Well, what else might there be to do with my time while I wait for my ship to come in?"

The bartender must have thought there was something suggestive in her tone, as he glanced at her sideways. “Beggin’ yer pardon, miss, are ya askin’ what I think you’re askin’? I mean…”

Now Moirne did grin. “Ha! I assume if the good bishop frowns on games of chance, then whoremongering is right out.”

Barinov actually blushed. “Er, yes miss! O’ course, miss! I mean, I would never, uh, think that—”

She waved him off. “I know you meant no insult. I merely wanted to know if there were any feats of strength or games of skill that one could partake in or wager on. Or is that sort of thing reserved for market day or festivals?”

“Uh…” It took a brief moment, but the bartender collected himself. “Nothin’ formal most nights, miss. But, sorta related ta that, ya never know when a brawl might break out.” He jerked a thumb over at the front door where the two brutes were in the middle of collecting yet more weaponry. “Mandiv an’ Boyko usually keep things civil-like here in tha bar. But if a couple o’ rascals can’t let things go, they can always go settle their differences out back in tha Square. Makes fer good entertainment fer everyone else, an’ there’s usually money changin’ hands on who’s gonna win.”

Moirne raised her eyebrows. “Sanctioned fighting? Like the Roma gladiators of old?”

“Nah, they ain’t allowed ta use weapons, miss. Just their bare ’ands.”

“Ah, so boxing!”

Barinov smiled broadly, showing his teeth again. “Ya got it, miss! If ya never seen a *bonum pugilem*, then ya don't know what you're missin'!"

Moirne had indeed seen quite a few good fighters throughout the years, and she personally knew the difference between a boxing match and a tavern brawl. Memories of one match, in particular, that had left her with a broken nose but her opponent unconscious raced to the front of her mind, distracting her from wondering how much Latin the bartender knew.

She shook her head to clear it and came back to the present. Raising her full mug, she tipped her head at Barinov. "Well, I've seen plenty of fights. As exciting as they can sometimes be, let us hope the evening doesn't turn violent."

He laughed, although not as kindly as before. "Miss, it always turns violent here, one way or another. If ya like yer boxin' or yer bettin', just wait a bit." He bowed and then left her to wait on a couple who had sat down at the bar a few seats away.

***

A younger version of Moirne, perhaps the version from her army days, would have been found blacked-out in a nearby gutter the next morning with the proposition of free drinks for the evening placed in front of her. But an hour later found her slowly sipping the same drink that Barinov had left her with. She would have watered it down if she trusted the local water supply, but the risk of intoxication was far better than the risk of catching the blue death.

Over the intervening hour, the tavern had slowly filled, although it was still only at half capacity. It was still possible to catch most of the conversations around her without too much struggle. Barinov had covertly pointed out a few captains to her as they had come in, but she had not approached any as of yet. She was biding her time to let them fill their bellies and hopefully calm any temper they were still holding onto after a long day on the docks.

The locals were mostly debating how soon the first snows would come to the area. The last large shipment of the year of materials and supplies had started to head upriver to Stren over the past week, and those still waiting to leave were getting worried they had waited too long. Once the weather turned, it was anybody's guess how quickly the tow path would get buried under several feet of snow and ice would start to appear on the upper stretches of the Gruminus.

Moirne didn't want to look too interested in one particular conversation, but it was hard to ignore the loud voices of some men to her left. There were three of them seated around a small table near the bar, and Barinov had mentioned briefly to her that all three were captains worth talking with later in the evening. She could tell the youngest-looking one was extremely agitated, and the ale in his mug sloshed onto the floor around him as he gestured to and fro to emphasize his words.

"I'm tellin' ya, those clodpoles up on tha docks in Stren better not be slowing me down on tha turnaround! Ain't no way I want ta get stuck up there an' have ta force me way down through tha floes."

One of the older men he was speaking with grunted and shook his head before taking his pipe out of his mouth. "I'm tellin' ya, Olek, then ya best get movin' north 'fore tha Sabbath. I'll wager it'll take least a day ta unload ya an' over twice as long ta make ya square for tha trip back."

"Over two days ta load up a few beaver pelts an' quarry rocks?!" Olek finished his current drink in one large gulp and then banged his mug on the table. He threw his arms up in disgust and looked up at the rafters. "Where's tha justice in that? I suppose tha longshoremen think they can just charge what they like an' do what they like, eh? Can't we go talk ta our dockmaster 'bout this?"

The other older man at the table, this one with a shock of white hair and, curiously enough, spectacles, spoke up. "C'mon now, ya know tha problem ain't with our lads. They'll load an' unload any boat quick as lightnin'. But Stren's always had their own men move tha loads back an' forth tween dockside an' storehouse. That's how their dockmaster Bartosh has done things since he took over. Worked just fine 'til recently."

Barinov had already come around the bar to replace Olek's drink, and the young man quickly took a healthy swig before sighing heavily. "I know, I know. But each time I goes ta Stren, there be more an' more men standin' 'round tha docks up there, an' less an' less seem ta know their arse from a hole in tha ground. It's like they're addin' people for no reason."

The first old man with the pipe grunted again. "Least yer getting' there. Heard tell there be pirates back on tha 'Minus again!"

"Sard that, Yakev! Ain't no pirates, mate." A fourth man, sitting alone at a table on the far side of the group from Moirne spoke up.

Yakev wheeled in his chair to stare down the interloper to the conversation. "Oh, really? Then how do ya explain what happened ta Marcus an' his boys, eh? That barge o' his just catch fire on its own? There was nothin' left but a hulk burnt down ta tha waterline. We couldn't even do a proper salvage on it!"

"That ain't—"

"An' him an' all tha crew laid out on tha shore with their throats slit, how 'bout that, eh? Maybe some damn eldar came back an' got tha trees ta do that?" Yakev shook his pipe at the man, obviously annoyed that his word wasn't being taken as gospel.

The man smiled with a bemused look on his face. It appeared that he had suffered the wrath of Yakev in the past and didn't think much of the bluster. "That ain't pirates, that's just bandits. Them bodies was found on Dead Man's Bend, an' *everyone* knows that ya don't stop on tha far side of tha river."

There was a murmur of assent, and even Yakev grumbled something under his breath that seemed to agree with the statement. He stuck his pipe back in his mouth as the other man continued.

"Don't know why that doddypoll Marcus stopped there for tha night, 'specially goin' upstream. If anythin' is gonna draw in random scum from tha Wilds this time o' year, it's gonna be tha foodstuffs an' wine he was carryin'. They ain't dumb, they know what we're all haulin' north."

"I think Vasily's got ya there, old man," the bespectacled man said as he gently poked Yakev in the shoulder.

"Shut it, Pavlo! We're *always* haulin' wine north these days, everybody knows that," Yakev growled in a meek retort.

Vasily's smile grew slightly. "I grant ya that, Yakev. But I think tha stories of old would tell ya them eldar treants would rip people apart, not slit their throats."

"Damn sheriff needs ta do somethin' 'bout it," grumbled Olek into his mug, but this statement drew immediate hoots of derision from the older men at his table.

"Ho now, talkin' 'bout doddypolls, ya *have* met our esteemed sheriff, right? Can't take a piss without askin' tha bishop ta bless tha waters comin' outta his spindle!" Pavlo spit on the floor for emphasis as the others thumped their mugs on their respective tables in agreement.

"Or Simeon tellin' him which side o' tha pier ta use!" Yakev added with sudden bitterness in his voice.

Moirne sensed a sudden chill cross over the other men.

While none of the other patrons scattered around the room seemed to notice what had been said, Olek choked on his drink and immediately put a hand on the old man's forearm. "Quiet, Pa! We ain't alone."

Moirne felt Olek's gaze briefly settle on her and then move on to the bartender. Barinov was busy serving drinks to the table playing passe-dix and obviously hadn't heard the old man's comment.

Yakev scoffed. “I ain’t scared o’ that little hoodlum. Just ’cause he’s beddin’ down with tha dockmaster’s daughter, he thinks he can run tha town. That’ll change soon as she gets bored with him. ’Sides, ain’t nobody listenin’ ta us ’cept that noble-born at tha bar.”

Moirne winced internally. Apparently, she had been more obvious with her eavesdropping than she intended.

Might as well own it. They’ll only get more belligerent if you feign ignorance after being called out.

She turned to fully face the foursome. Yakev greeted her with a knowing look and a mocking smile, while the others had varying degrees of scowls on their faces.

She smiled back with what she hoped was a slightly guilty look. “You caught me, good sir. I must admit, I am quite interested in the stories you’re telling about the trials and travails facing you as you travel north.”

“Yeah? An’ why’s that?” Olek asked, his scowl darkening slightly.

She glanced over at Barinov, who was making his way back to the bar. “The kind bartender told me that I might inquire about passage to Stren from you gentlemen.”

Pavlo guffawed at this, but Yakev drew himself up a bit straighter in his chair.

“Gentlemen, eh? I dunno ’bout all that, m’lady, but what’s a noble-born want with Stren at this time o’ tha year?”

"At *any* time," Vasily said quietly as he looked her up and down.

Moirne rose from her chair at the bar, motioning slightly at Barinov as she did so. He nodded and immediately began filling a quartet of mugs.

She turned back to the men and did a slight curtsy, smoothing out her skirt as she did so. "Derya Asken at your service, good sirs, and I am far from being noble-born. I am merely doing the bidding of my master back in Velych and am striving to reach Stren as quickly as possible."

***

It took several rounds of ale and some major embellishment on Moirne's part about the reason for her being in the north, but most of the men gradually warmed to her. It helped immensely when she pulled out her own pipe and offered Yakev some of her southern blend of tobacco. However, when it came to haggling over a ride to Stren, her options halved immediately.

It turned out that Pavlo and Yakev were both mostly retired, each having spent the better part of three decades on the water. They only took loads south from Tuman these days, that leg of the river being easier to navigate. While they were polite about it, it was obvious that no amount of silver would make them amenable to going to Stren on the brink of winter.

Olek had sailed with his father since he could walk, and despite Barinov's earlier warning about younger captains, seemed to be the most cautious of the bunch. Taciturn and tightlipped at first, he eventually seemed to decide that she was more than a wayward pretty face. He had his own pipe but for the time being stuck to his self-admitted main vice of ale.

Vasily appeared to be between the other three in terms of age, and he remained mostly withdrawn throughout the general conversation. He stayed seated at his own table, only interjecting with pointed questions from time to time. It was clear to Moirne that some part of her story wasn't sitting well with him, but he wasn't ready to publicly accuse her of anything for the time being.

Barinov had told her earlier that Vasily was the best riverman out of the four, but even after over fifteen years of hard work he was still considered an outsider by some since he hadn't grown up in town. "I hear he came from tha capital when he was a teen, an' he ain't never told his story ta no one. But he claims ta know tha whole river all tha way from Stren down ta tha Karadeniz Sea, an' ain't nobody in a position ta call him a liar."

Sooner or later someone from down south will recognize you from the past because of your haircut or your eyes, Dear Moirne. But if he keeps quiet, there's no reason to change your story now.

Moirne carefully sipped from her mug, having switched from mulled wine to ale at the insistence of Yakev. She was approaching her tolerance level, even with two bowls of goulash in her belly, and she had the vaguest start to a headache. She needed to close a deal, and fast.

"Well, good sirs, I am sorry that I must press you for an answer. I need to be on my way in the morn, be it by road or by river. I will gladly pay my way on one of your ships if—"

Olek held up a hand, interrupting her. "Barges, miss. They're just barges. Don't make us out ta be more than what we are."

"What you *are* is the best option open to me. Now come, you have me at a disadvantage, so name your price and be done with it."

Olek smiled at her, and not unkindly. "Easy, Derya. We won't leave ya at tha dock in Stren with nothin' but yer shift on, now. Although Vasily may want ta take a peek at yer ankles as part of any deal!" He laughed heartily while Vasily shook his head with only a hint of a smile.

However, Yakev immediately reached over and smacked him hard on the shoulder. "Manners maketh tha man, son! Apologize ta tha young lady!"

Olek blushed, although whether out of anger or embarrassment Moirne couldn't tell.

She leaned forward and put her hands on the table. "Please, sir, I take no offense. But if it will be me and my mare on the road north on the morrow, I ask that you tell me now so that I may rest and prepare for the ride."

Pavlo had been quiet for a time, as if in thought, but now he spoke up. "Olek, you're tryin' to make it out on tha river tomorrow 'fore tha longshoremen change shifts at Terce, right?"

"Yeah, if they can load those bloody oxen in time," the young man replied.

"An' Vasily, you're stuck here one more day anyways, on tha account of that wine shipment bein' late from Velych. Right?"

"It's always tha bloody wine," Yakev muttered, but Vasily merely nodded.

Pavlo spread his hands wide. "Well, yer barge still has room in its stable for one, maybe two oxen, right?"

Vasily sighed. "I see what you're doin', Pavlo, but I ain't takin' those damn oxen off Olek's hands for nothin'. He already tried ta unload them on me this afternoon."

"Ya ain't takin' them for nothin', 'cause you'll get tha full haulin' fee once they're delivered!" Olek retorted. He turned to his father. "I'm tellin' ya, I don't like how tha wind's blowin'! If I can't leave early on tha morrow, then ya best get Putinski ta go north 'stead o' me."

Yakev grew red in the face himself and poked his pipe at Olek. "I'll do nothin' o' tha sort! That man's a crooked-nosed knave with shite for brains. I already saw him off last week while ya was comin' north from Velych, an' he ain't ever workin' on tha river again if I can help it!"

"What's the hauling fee for oxen to Stren?" Moirne asked quietly, almost as if to herself.

"Eh? What's that, miss? Speak up!" Pavlo motioned for the other men to stop their quarreling.

"Six silver each," Vasily answered, a bit too quickly. Olek stirred, but before he could say anything Vasily pressed on. "But, my dear lady, you don't understand. There'll be transfer fees ta pay out, an'—"

"Which are, no doubt, absorbed in the hauling fee you'll collect," Moirne stated flatly.

"An' tha berthin' fee that—"

"That you're paying already."

"But what about tha extra delay if I take on—"

"You've already indicated you're leaving a day later, so any further delay for taking on oxen will either be the fault of the longshoremen or your own."

Vasily frowned. "Well, it's bad luck ta have a woman onboard a ship, so I don't see why—"

"Well, I don't see why that's a problem if I am not on your *barge* to begin with." Moirne turned to address Olek directly. "Sir, I am willing to pay you four silver each for passage to Stren for myself and my steed. That will compensate you fully for leaving two fully grown oxen at the dock here, based upon the kingdom's standard rate of *three* silver each for this section of the river. Since I assume you won't slaughter the poor animals where they stand but will arrange passage north for them at a later time, you and your father should come out quite well on the overall transaction."

Pavlo and Yakev glanced at each other and then pretended to be busy with their mugs as she continued.

"Furthermore, if you allow me to take my mare off the barge to graze at night, you can save some of your fodder for the next trip. And I am willing to stand guard and do my share of manual labor along the way, meaning you can run a man short if you so choose."

She smiled as demurely as she could. "And I would hope that my mare, at least, will smell better and have better manners than the oxen."

Olek looked over at Vasily and then back at Moirne, grinning. "Well, now. Looks like someone knows their business. How soon can tha two of ya be ready ta leave?"

"We can be at the dock at Prime, sir, ready to embark."

He extended his hand. "Deal. 'Cept I ain't gonna run a man short, so I leave it up to ya on what ya want ta do while on board. Also, if ya call me 'sir' one more time, I'll throw ya off me barge inta tha river."

Moirne chuckled. "Very well, Olek. Thank you."

They shook hands, and Olek immediately turned to look over at Vasily. "So, ya want them oxen or not?"

Vasily was staring at Moirne, but if he was angry over the proceedings, he wasn't letting it show. "Nah, they can rot here in Tuman for all I care."

CHAPTER TEN

Trouble in Tuman

Moirne made her way to the bar to seal the deal with another round of ale, and she noted that the tavern had continued to fill with people. As she waited for Barinov to serve her, suddenly there was a minor ruckus at the front door. Several orc trappers had entered and immediately began to argue with the brutes about having to leave their bows and large hunting knives in the locker. Moirne assumed that, if the weather was better, they wouldn't have come into town in the first place, let alone stay after being told to disarm themselves.

Heads began to turn, and the undertone of crowd noise quieted slightly. But after several tense moments, the orcs relented, albeit with some loud cursing in their native tongue. Without a brawl to watch, most patrons went back to what they had been doing.

The trappers immediately commandeered a table near the middle of the room. They called out their order to Barinov in broken Common as he came over to serve Moirne, rapping the tabletop loudly with their coins in hand. They didn't seem to mind he was a half-breed, or at least they didn't appear to treat him more rudely that anyone else. Still, he shook his head and looked annoyed as he quickly completed Moirne's order.

"Friends of yours?" she asked him with a wry smile on her

face as he pushed five mugs towards her.

"Pfah! Damn trappers. Always smellin' like a tannery an' always lookin' fer trouble. Least this lot seems ta have copper on 'em." He leaned in so she could hear him over the rising din. "If ya wanna conduct any more business, miss, I'd suggest ya do it now. It's only gonna get louder in 'ere, an' pretty soon tha singin' is gonna start."

"Singing?" Moirne didn't see a stage, and the tavern didn't look like the type of place that would hire a minstrel.

"Yes, miss. You'll know it when ya hear it."

Another patron called out for a refill, and Barinov was gone before providing a satisfactory answer to her question.

Vasily had already left by the time Moirne got back with the round of drinks, and after quickly downing his mug, Olek made to leave as well. "I need ta make sure yer bunk's ready an' get tha paperwork ready ta go. Nothin' like throwin' somethin' new at the scribes first thing in tha mornin'!"

Moirne nodded. "Thank you, Olek. I shall see you first thing on the morrow."

Olek pointed at her as he stood up. "I'll see you at Prime, Derya, and not a moment later!" He quickly bowed low over her hand, although he did not brush it with his lips. Looking up at her, he winked. "I best tell tha wife that I'll have a proper woman onboard for tha trip north. Don't need her ta hear that from tha crew after I get back!"

He laughed, then gave his father a playful punch on the

shoulder and tipped his cap to Pavlo. With that, he headed towards the door, quickly melting into the growing crowd.

Pavlo reached across the table to take what would have been Vasily's mug. "I'm glad that all turned well for ya, miss. Are ya headed ta bed yerself, or are ya stayin' for tha boxin'?"

Moirne held her own full mug in her hands, but she had yet to take a drink from it. "I really should head back to my room. Besides, I thought matches only happened by chance."

Pavlo chortled as he took a drink. "Tha only thing left ta chance 'bout tha matches is who's gonna be in tha next one! It's a rare night when at least a couple don't happen, 'specially this time o' year when there's nothin' better ta do."

On a whim, Moirne asked, "I don't suppose that Simeon fellow will be there to watch?"

Yakev looked at her sideways. "An' why in tha blazes do ya wanna see that little shite?"

She shrugged. "Heard a lot about him. It's always good to know something about those in charge."

"All ya need ta know 'bout him is that he's no good," Yakev grumbled.

Pavlo made something of a grimace. "I tend ta side with my brother in that tha less ya interact with that man, tha better. But if ya want ta catch a look at him, no doubt he'll be watchin' at least some o' tha fights since he owns tha place."

There was a commotion to the right of them as the dice game broke up unceremoniously. One of the gamblers appeared to be extremely angry about the outcome of a roll, and he stood up with his fists balled. However, he was immediately showered with ale by everyone else at the table and verbally insulted until he turned and scurried away, alone and defeated.

"They let any mangy dog in here," growled Yakev to no one in particular.

"Well, ya almost got tha first match of tha night, miss, right on cue," Pavlo chuckled. He took a quick look around the tavern before addressing Moirne again. "But I bet I know tha main event that's comin'. Ya got a guess?"

It was getting harder to carry a conversation in the rising din of the crowd, and Moirne had to lean in to hear the old man. "Well, the obvious choice is those trackers who just got here."

"Aye, very obvious. But fightin' with each other or with someone else?"

"Hmm..." Moirne looked around the room, finally stopping on a table in the far corner of the tavern. She could see a number of large men deep in conversation, obviously keeping to themselves. They were all wearing longshoremen vests, and some of them were wearing hooks on their waist belts.

She gestured discreetly at the table she was looking at. "I'd say, if the trappers are looking for a fight, they'll want a good one. And those gentlemen over there look like they'd give them what they want."

Pavlo slapped the table in good humor. "Yes, indeed! I'd say you're spot on with yer guess, though I think yer idea of a 'gentleman' is a bit different than mine. But longshoremen an' trappers don't mix well no matter where they are. Hardest part will be gettin' them in tha Square 'stead o' them just brawlin' in here."

Yakev had gone quiet and appeared to be watching the front door. Suddenly, he tugged at the sleeve of Pavlo's tunic. "Hey now, I think we're gettin' tha first match o' tha night after all!"

Moirne turned in time to see the losing gambler from the passe-dix table pushing his way back through the crowd, holding a short sword of some sort. He had obviously grabbed it from the weapons locker at an inopportune time for the brutes, one of whom was now giving chase.

The man was loudly cursing as he advanced, weaving back and forth in a drunken rage. "Ya scavy harlot! I'll teach ya ta try an' use rigged dice 'gainst me!"

Instinctively wishing to stop a fight before it started, Moirne reached out with a foot as the man passed her at a half run, and he went sprawling. People jumped out of his way as he fell so that he landed hard, face-first on the cobblestone floor. The sword clattered away from him in the direction of the table he had been making for.

The pursuing brute was on him in an instant, seizing his neck with a meaty paw and hauling him to his feet. The man, nose bloody from the fall, gasped for air as he tried to kick himself free.

Someone in the crowd started yelling, "Choke 'im out! Choke 'im out!" and the chant was quickly picked up by the whole bar.

The brute turned slowly, obviously enjoying the notoriety, grinning while dangling the man like a puppet in front of him.

"Hey, Boyko! Why don't ya leave that piece o' shite ta me?"

A scrawny looking woman, with hair as black as Moirne's, stepped forward from the table the drunk had been running towards. She had obviously been drinking, too, and she had to steady herself on several onlookers. Her eyes rolled back and forth inside their sockets, but she managed to shake a fist in the direction of the brute as she addressed the man he was holding.

"You're a shite, Putinski! Tryin' ta...tryin' ta shank me, are ya? Tryin' ta kill me, after tryin' ta steal me money?! Ya spindle eatin', beef-witted, dirty little churl! I oughta—" She paused to spit and then doubled over, heaving.

Having been denied a proper throttling, the crowd now cheered the woman's effort and egged her on to do more.

"Ya tell 'im, Ganna!"

"Give'm what's for, ya crazy bitch!"

"Take up 'is sword an' stick 'im! Stick 'im good!"

"Take 'im ta tha Square an' beat tha piss outta 'im!"

"Throw that drunkard outta here. He ain't worth tha air he's breathin'!"

Moirne turned with an arched eyebrow to look at Yakev as his voice joined the general chaos. Given the rather unique name, she had already assumed the drunk gambler was the same person that he had fired a couple weeks ago. Pavlo just laughed and took another drink.

At least Yakev just wants Putinski gone, not dead. This is a lynch mob if I ever saw one. Where's the bloody sheriff in all this?

A shrill whistle came out from the back of the crowd, and the laughing and jeering died away. Moirne could tell that someone was coming through the packed onlookers as they parted to create a pathway to the brute. It could have been Moses himself, except without the pillar of cloud leading him on.

A very short man, perhaps even a dwarf, stepped out into the circle that had been roughly formed around Boyko and Putinski. Ganna was still on the edge of the crowd to one side, having recovered somewhat from her bout of sickness. But all eyes were on the new man as he quietly surveyed the scene, hands on his hips.

Boyko started to speak. "Sorry, boss, I shoulda—"

The brute was waved off before he could finish his apology. The man looked around the crowd, his eyes seeming to stop ever so briefly on Moirne. It was for but an instant, but it was as if he recognized her from a description he had received earlier in the day from her interaction with the children.

So, you're Simeon...

Slowly, he walked over to Putinski's sword and picked it up from the floor. It looked like a veritable long sword in his small hands as he held it closely, inspecting its blade.

"Well, now," Simeon finally said in a low baritone voice that Moirne had not expected, "raising a blade in anger in any tavern in Tuman is punishable by six months hard labor on the docks. Even if you are quite tippled." He looked at Putinski. "Anything to say in your defense?"

Putinski continued to struggle in the grasp of the brute, who loosened his fingers around the throat of the man enough so he could speak.

"That little harpy tried ta rob me blind, Simeon! I mean, usin' bad dice in here, that's worse than usin' a sword, you've said so yerself! I want justice 'gainst that hedge-born bitch! I want her bleedin' heart in me hands!"

Simeon had held out one hand as soon as the word "dice" was mentioned. Even before Putinski had finished speaking, one of the men standing next to the passe-dix table had picked the dice up and brought them over to the gang leader.

He inspected them carefully for a moment before speaking. "These are house dice, Putinski. *My* dice. So, are you accusing *me* of cheating?"

Putinski went pale and stopped struggling. "Nah, 'course not, Simeon! She musta changed 'em somehow, an'..."

Simeon shook his head slowly as he pocketed the dice, and Putinski's voice trailed off. The short man raised his voice slightly so the entire crowd could hear him. "I saw no markings or signs of malfeasance on the dice. But let us hear what Ganna has to say for herself."

Simeon walked over to the woman, still holding the sword, and gently took her left hand up in his. Moirne noted that he stood to the side of Ganna, in case she decided to purge more of her stomach onto the ground.

Her head rolled back and forth slightly as she looked down at him. "Hey-hey, yer grace!"

"Hey-hey, indeed, my dear. How are you tonight?"

She belched, and Simeon moved a pace further to the side, but nothing else followed.

"I ain't doin' so well, Simeon. Ya know that little *bitch*, Poo...Putinski?"

Simeon grinned widely but managed not to chuckle along with some of the crowd. "Yes, I do indeed."

"I think...I think that shite tried ta poison me! Made me drink all that dark ale with 'im. Ya know tha stuff, it just hurts me gut after tha fourth or fifth one. An' then..." Ganna raised her head, trying to get her bearings. It was then she remembered Putinski was only a few paces away. She spit in his general direction, and her face went dark with rage. "An' then, ya puke-eatin' poltroon, ya try an' cheat at dice, an' everyone here knows it, but ya got tha balls ta say *I'm* tha cheater. I should gut ya where ya stand!" She made a feeble attempt at the sword Simeon was holding, but he merely moved it out of her reach.

"Ya *are* a cheater, ya doxy cunt!" Putinski raged.

"Doxy cunt?! I'll give ya a doxy cunt!"

Ganna let go of Simeon's hand and grabbed her skirt. She managed to hike it high enough to reveal her hairy nether region before she fell backwards into several waiting arms. The crowd whooped in delight.

Simeon let them have a moment before raising a hand for silence. Once he more or less had everyone's attention again, he turned from Ganna and addressed the room. "Well, we seem to be at an impasse. If justice is to be meted out, as apparently demanded by both parties, we must request the presence of the sheriff to help us settle this matter!"

There was some hissing from the assembly at this, but he continued.

"Unfortunately, I happen to know that our hardworking sheriff is, well, *indisposed* at the moment in one of the upstairs bedrooms. And I, for one, do not wish to disturb him while he is exerting himself!"

Simeon made a shoving motion with his fist, and everyone jeered.

"So, if we all want justice...*real* justice...then let us take this argument to the Square!"

Moirne looked askance at the small man as the crowd went wild. Most of the crowd had obviously known how the matter was going to be resolved. The doors to the back room had already been flung open, and there was a general surge in that direction. Boyko proceeded to frog march Putinski towards the room, while several of the gamblers started guiding Ganna in the same direction. Neither seemed to protest what was about to happen, although Moirne guessed at least one wasn't sober enough to process the turn of events.

Yakev shook his head as the clamor of the crowd moved

away from where he and the others were sitting. "Nothin' but mob rules. Damn sheriff needs ta do more than get his whorin' for free."

Pavlo finished his drink. "I dunno. May still be better than sendin' tha two ta tha cells. They'd just rot in there, or somethin' worse."

Moirne looked at him. "Whatever do you mean, something worse?"

He shook his head. "Take that punishment o' six months hard labor for wieldin' a sword in here. Tha longshoremen ain't ever gonna allow a scab ta do work for free on tha docks, so tha sheriff would just ship ol' Putinski north ta Stren ta serve his time. Got some deal goin' with tha mayor up there."

Moirne furrowed her brow. "Somewhat inconvenient, but I suppose it matters not where the time is served."

Yakev snorted. "Yeah, 'cept barely anyone ever comes back. Some end up dead, others just disappear. An' most..." He shook his head, looking slightly confused. "Most just stay."

Pavlo nodded. "An' I hear tha real reason why Vasily don't want them oxen is 'cause he's already made a deal for haulin' a batch of prisoners up ta Stren this trip. Pays well, 'specially if ya want ta crowd a few more bodies in than ya should. Just gotta make the paperwork look right and slip some copper ta tha right clerk."

Moirne's gut growled at her even louder, and it wasn't because of all the ale she had consumed. Something definitely seemed off with the whole arrangement, something more than just a semi-legal transfer of prisoners.

Are they all actual criminals, or is this how Simeon takes care of potential usurpers to his little throne? And if no one comes back, are they just being press ganged into some sort of service up in Stren? Or is this outright slavery?

As she pondered this, there was a loud cheer from the back room and some indistinct announcements. Moirne assumed either betting or fighter introductions were ongoing. But what she heard next made her sit up straight in amazement.

The crowd had started to sing!

The singing started somewhat softly and offkey but gained in volume quickly. It sounded like a sea shanty of sorts, although once Moirne could make out the words, she realized they had nothing to do with working on the docks.

Ya got trouble, my friend, trouble in Tuman!
You're in it now, 'cause there's a fight that's brewin'
Better take a deep breath, an' set yer feet
Put up yer fists now, lad, an' give us a treat!

Moirne looked over at the two men with an arched eyebrow.

Pavlo grinned. "Tradition, miss! Just go with it."

Yakev also grinned at her while shrugging. "It's a song only a drunken sot could love, which means everyone in there loves it. On good nights, they'll make up a new verse on tha spot."

Moirne's curiosity got the better of her, and she rose to her feet to check out the match. The men stood as well, but it was clear they were not headed in the same direction.

"Pleasure makin' yer acquaintance, Derya, but we're off. Gonna be a long day tomorrow, as we'll be loadin' boats goin' both ways on tha river. Now, don't you make my son wait!" Yakev made as if to poke her with his pipe, but then he gave her a fatherly smile and offered his hand.

Moirne gave a short curtsy and then shook hands with both of them.

Pavlo leaned in with a last word of advice. "Do yerself a favor, miss, an' don't stay for tha main event." He nodded at the table of trappers, who were well on their way to being completely soused. "It'll get ugly once they decide ta stop drinkin' an' start bashin' skulls."

Ya got trouble, my friend, trouble in Tuman!
It don't matter ta me, if you're orc or human
If ya get hurt tonight, well don't get pissed
Shoulda thought o' that 'fore ya raised yer fist!

The crowd continued to sing as she made her way towards the back room. The Square turned out to be a large room with a wooden plank floor, and Moirne was eventually able to squeeze her way to the front of the onlookers. There, she came up against what looked like a choir rail that encompassed an area roughly ten paces on all four sides. Inside the railing, Putinski and Ganna were bathed in sweat, struggling to hit each other.

A round column was housed in each corner of the railed-off space, and these extended up to support the ceiling. While there were no gaps in the railing, it was easy enough for combatants to clamber over or get hauled out under it. The space outside the railing was big enough to house a crowd of five to six people deep all around, and one side even had a slightly raised platform for better viewing.

Moirne noted there was a copious amount of sawdust on the floor inside the railing, no doubt to help soak up whatever blood and other liquids were spilled during a contest. Two wrought iron chandeliers hung from the ceiling provided more than enough light for fighters and spectators alike.

What Moirne could easily see in the bright glow coming from overhead was that the two combatants were far too drunk to fight well. They stumbled about the confined space like newborn calves as the crowd hurled insults—and occasionally ale mugs—at them. Every now and again Putinski or Ganna would land a lucky hit, but even then, it was usually just a glancing blow. Both of them had blood on their bare knuckles and were breathing heavily.

Moirne shook her head at the mockery of a boxing match. “Some justice...” she muttered to no one in particular.

Ya got trouble, my friend, trouble in Tuman!
Hurry up now, lad, ’cause there’s more fights queuin’
We’re bettin’ you’ll win, or mebbe we’re not
Jus’ look out now, ’ere comes tha next shot!

Almost in time with the word "shot," Putinksi finally landed a hard blow to Ganna's gut, and she immediately doubled over, retching. A large groan went up, as she was apparently the sentimental, if not betting, favorite.

Bending over so quickly appeared to save Ganna, as Putinski swung wildly above her head, and she stumbled towards one of the corners. Several calls of encouragement went up, but Moirne could see that money was already exchanging hands throughout the crowd, as if the bout was over.

"C'mon, lass! Don't give up!"

"C'mon, Ganna! Don't let tha shite win!"

"Ya got 'im right where ya want 'im!"

Something in the way the last outburst was called out made Moirne looked sharply at Ganna. She was still bent over, seemingly listless against one of the support columns. But her eyes had lost their glassy look, and she tensed as Putinski staggered closer to finish her.

God's nails, it's fixed!

All of a sudden, several voices throughout the crowd broke out in an apparent new verse to the shanty.

Ya got trouble, my friend, trouble in Tuman!
You're just a silly ponce, an' yer lass came callin'
She's so sick of ya, tryin' ta milk her teets
An' now she's here, ta knock ya off yer feet!

Ganna practically launched herself at Putinski, who had no idea what hit him. She caught him square in the jaw, and he stumbled backwards, arms flailing as he tried to catch himself. Her attack was relentless, and she pummeled him a half dozen more times before he fell to the floor unconscious. Sawdust flew into the air at his impact, creating a halo effect around the triumphant Ganna as she stood above him, posing for the cheering crowd.

While some had surely lost money on the result, nobody seemed to care in the heat of the moment. Simeon appeared from somewhere on the other side of the room, ducking under the railing and advancing to the middle of the space. He pointed towards the ceiling with his right hand and then at the assembly. Moirne could barely hear him above the din.

"And the winner, in front of the Almighty themself and all you esteemed layabouts, is our own little lady, Ganna!"

The crowd cheered again and immediately started pelting Putinski with whatever was at hand as he was dragged off by Boyko. Bits of food, crockery, and other detritus bounced off his listless body as everyone started in on one final stanza. This verse was obviously a crowd favorite and probably sung at the end of every match.

Ya had trouble, my friend, trouble in Tuman!
You're all bloody now, an' yer shirt is ruined!
We could tell ya, lad, that ya fought with class
But really, me boy, you're just a horse's ass!

A boisterous cheer went up as the patrons started to make their way back to the main room. Moirne let the noise wash over her as she tried to stay in character. Rigged fights, a corrupt or inept sheriff, and a potential slavery ring were all mixing together to bring her to the breaking point. Technically, they were all still kingdom-related issues, although if the slavery charge held true, then she could intercede for the church on moral reasons.

A chilling thought suddenly hit her.

What if the bishop is in on all of this? Surely, he isn't. Did I perhaps misplace a report about him?

She thought back furiously to her interview with Archbishop Dorjan not even a week ago back in Velych. No, he hadn't mentioned anything unsavory going on in Tuman. But then she had been pressing him about reports tied to unholy works of the abyss, not anything tied to more earthly vices. She ground her teeth in frustration.

Saint Olga indeed. You can't even sniff out a simple fixed fight until it smacks you in the nose.

She briefly thought about finding Bishop Nicholas right this instant and getting the truth out of him, but she had zero proof that he was one of the guilty parties. That wouldn't stop some of her fellow inquisitors, to be sure, but she personally needed something tangible to confront him with. Besides, from what she knew of the man, it seemed completely out of character for him to be caught up in something so morally corrupt.

Don't go chasing ghosts or guesses, Dear Moirne...

Moirne quickly resolved in her mind that the potential slavery ring was the key to any potential intervention here in Tuman. Proving it existed would start many wheels to turn and potentially many heads to roll. But rather than tarry here, it was yet one more reason to get to Stren, to see what was happening to the prisoners who were sent there.

As the crowd started to disperse and head back to the main room of the tavern, she had the sensation that someone was studying her from across the Square. Glancing about, she saw that Simeon was busy helping Ganna out of the ring, the two of them sharing a muted laugh. Barinov was, no doubt, serving drinks up front, Boyko had already carried Putinksi off somewhere, and none of the captains she had been speaking with earlier were still around.

So who...?

She perhaps caught a glimpse of someone tall to her left, but they were gone when she turned.

Or they were never there to begin with. Ghosts indeed... Get a grip on yourself, Moirne!

It was a cold walk back to the Red Squirrel, but she slept soundly once she made it to her rented room.

CHAPTER ELEVEN
Stranger in a Hostile Land

It was several hours after Lianne's encounter with Prince Hadeon in his grandmother's former garden, and the time since then had been fully taken up with settling into her temporary residence. Now, she busied herself with the final preparations for her formal introduction to the Astrikhon royal court. She found herself more nervous about it than she had anticipated.

Truth be told, Lianne was starting to feel the weight of the importance of the first impression she would make and how it would play into all subsequent dealings. She knew the treaty she had with her was a good start to finding common ground for the future. However, she also was sure there was still plenty of room for misgivings between the two kingdoms.

Her father had hinted at this point with her in a roundabout way when they spoke privately the evening before she set sail to Astrikhon. It was the first time since Lianne's interview with Grand Inquisitor Moirne that she had been able to talk with her father alone, and she had hoped he could shed some light on what the inquisitor told her.

"Yes, the inquisitor has been raising her personal concerns about the Rus to me for some time now," had been his response to hearing that Moirne had told Lianne about the possibility of an invasion from the west.

"Her *personal* concerns, Father? But not the concerns of the church?"

He had nodded at her with a grave look in his eyes. "Quite right, my dear. The inquisitor has always been very clear with me about what information she provides in her official capacity and what she does not."

"And you obviously trust her?"

"I do, Lianne. But as you are doing with all of my close advisors, you must make up your own mind about what advice to follow and who to trust when you cannot directly corroborate what they say."

Lianne felt herself flush slightly as she wondered if some of her opinions about her father's council members had reached his ears, but she nodded all the same. "I merely wish to trust but verify, Father, as you are wont to say."

"That works quite well in most cases, yes. But there arise some occasions when you must decide what to believe based purely on faith."

"Yes, Father."

He had smiled at the uncertain tone in her response. "Come, let me assuage your doubts about the inquisitor. I will give you some assurance that, at least in this instance, my belief in her and the truth of the world measure up well together."

He had stood up from the desk in his study and had gone to a large bureau on the side wall. From the top drawer he pulled a map of the entire continent of Evros and the seas surrounding it, bringing it back to the desk. Lianne rose from her seat to join her father to look at the geography from the same perspective, and it gave her pause to see the true size of the Rusgorod empire in comparison to her own kingdom. She again wondered why their king, her own blood through her mother, seemed so bent on the destruction of her father and Perizidon.

"I believed the inquisitor's misgivings about the Rus when she first brought them to me several years ago, not only because of our friendship, but because of past actions of your great-grandfather. But at the time, our spies had not uncovered any plans of King Ioseb against us other than his normal machinations. So, what was I to do with this bit of intuition? I asked a few of my council to put their minds to work on how to crack this nut."

Her father gestured around the map. "Bribes to certain officials in Malorossiya. A secret delegation sent almost all the way around the known world to Polotsk, far to the west of even the Rus. Weapons and raw material trading manifests obtained from Myste at great cost. And finally, infiltrating an agent or two through the Nebo Mountains to perform some old-fashioned lurking about within Gavan and the surrounding countryside. All of this has helped paint a fuller picture of what the inquisitor insinuated."

Her father paused as Lianne first looked around the map and then back at him.

"And, Father?"

"And," he said with a deep sigh, "after comparing our latest information with what the inquisitor told me right before she left,

Marshal Gwyn and I believe we truly are on the downward path to war. Our estimate is we have perhaps two summers at the most before the Rus invade."

Lianne had been completely dumbfounded. "What?! How can this be?"

"I will show you the various reports upon your return from Astrikhon, if you like."

She had brushed this aside. His word, at least, she would always take on faith. "But, Father, just a few nights ago you were going on about how the Rus have no legitimate reason to think of us as their primary adversary!"

"And that is still true. But we can still prepare for strife behind a peaceful front."

Lianne was frustrated. Even if she believed her father, it didn't mean she didn't also feel somewhat misled by his calming words the last time they spoke. "We were just talking about inviting the *damn Rus* to my investiture this coming spring!"

"We did. And we still are."

"But, Father..."

Despite the grave situation being discussed, he still smiled and winked at her. "What better way to confirm what they are doing behind their wall than to send a messenger through it on an official diplomatic mission? You can *distrust* but verify, as well, my dear daughter. Something to remember when you meet with King Haldir and his council."

Her father had not been quite as forthcoming with his

opinion on whether or not a greater evil was stalking the northern wilds of his kingdom, only saying that he typically left ethereal matters to the church. He knew the inquisitor was headed north to investigate the issue, and he also obviously knew of Moirne's request that Lianne deliver reports for her to the archbishop in Astrikhon. But, just like Lianne, he did not know the contents of the reports, and he was not going to press the issue.

Lianne had pushed her own questions on that matter to the side for the time being, as well, and now she tried to focus on the instructions and information that Symon had given her earlier in the day.

The dragoman had given her cues on the formal introductions that would be used and the standard protocols that should be in place. However, he also warned her that the king was somewhat tempestuous and was known to ask direct questions to throw other diplomats off-kilter.

"One would hope that he is not overly abrasive on his first meeting with you. But if something, uh, impolite occurs, Your Highness, please know that it is not personal."

Lianne grimaced at herself in the looking glass she was using to adjust her dress.

So, he's an arse to everyone. That will make the encounter interesting, to say the least.

She attempted to remain neutral in thought before she met the man, and it helped somewhat that she took Symon's opinions of other people with several large grains of salt. She rather hoped she was not as pretentious as her father's dragoman could be and that this would help her cause.

To this end, she had gone against the diplomat's advice on what to wear for the occasion. Instead of the voluminous rose-colored gown he had suggested, she selected a simple emerald-colored dress that she thought complemented her hair nicely. It was embroidered along the hem and the sleeves in gold leaf, and she wore a short cape to match it, along with very little jewelry. Her regalia consisted merely of her tiara, but she knew most eyes would be drawn to it, even if she had been completely ensconced in royal trappings.

Loaned to her by her mother, and hers by birthright when she formally ascended the throne as queen, the tiara was, indeed, a symbol of the grace and beauty of past consorts to the throne of Perizidon. Designed in the garland style as a heart flanked by continuous running scrolls, interspersed with star and cornet-shaped flowers, what set the golden family heirloom apart were the various precious stones set throughout in a circular fashion. It would dazzle in the sunlight or in bright firelight, creating an angelic halo around the head of whomever wore it.

Lianne knew the tiara to be somewhat simple compared to other royal headwear, but she liked the fact that it wasn't overly ostentatious. The lightness of it was also a great blessing when it came to suffering through long banquets. It was Melina's favorite, as well, and the sparkle from the headpiece that reflected in her eyes the few times Lianne had worn it in the past made for long-lasting memories. A feeling of stately calm seemed to emanate from it now as Lianne put on her white gloves and Melina made some final touches to her hair.

"Ah, m'lady, ya look regal for sure!" Melina stepped back to look at Lianne, pride and excitement showing in both her voice and her body language. "I wish I could see tha looks on tha faces of all tha lords and ladies who'll see ya for tha first time!"

Lianne smiled broadly at the compliment. "Thank you, Mel. But just you wait, we'll *both* look glamorous tonight at the banquet in front of the Astrikhon nobility. I'll have to assign you a personal guard just to keep the suitors away!"

"An' why would ya go an' do that, m'lady? Don't ya like me anymore?!" The two young women laughed.

There was a light knock at the door, and Lianne's maidservant went to answer it. Symon was standing outside in the hallway, with his hands behind his back and a stern look on his face. He did not enter the room but, instead, waited wordlessly for Lianne to exit. He nodded curtly at her as she came into his view, appraising her appearance in a single glance. She either passed muster or there simply wasn't enough time to force her to change out a piece of her ensemble.

The royal castle was a very short ride from the mansion Lianne was staying in, being only a couple hundred paces down the main avenue that ran through the middle of the city. The horses were kept at a walk so that the Perizidon security escort, led by Major Bannik, could march on either side of the carriage as it slowly rolled along the cobblestone pavers. Astrikhon guards from the castle formed a cordon of sorts for the procession to go through. There were a number of gawkers that watched her pass, but no one called out or waved.

Symon, who alone was riding with Lianne, leaned over and spoke in a low voice. He seemed to want to reassure her over the relatively small size of the crowd watching them pass. "Since this is an unofficial visit, Your Highness, there have not been any public proclamations made regarding your presence. No doubt most people here just see you as a common noblewoman visiting the court."

Lianne smiled at the irony of being called a common noblewoman, but she nodded her head at her dragoman. "That is quite all right. I am more concerned about the reception *inside* the walls as opposed to outside them."

He bowed his head slightly. "I trust all will go well enough, Your Highness. Despite my opinion of his base nature, King Sokolov should not want to create a diplomatic scene with you. Not when he is this close to securing a border and increasing trade all in one breath."

Their carriage was already turning into the castle's main courtyard when a disturbance caught Lianne's attention. She couldn't quite tell what was happening, but one of her guards had apparently seen something or someone in the crowd that they didn't care for and had veered off the cleared path to investigate. At least one Astrikhon soldier was running towards the disturbance as well, but it was behind where the carriage was now. Lianne knew it wouldn't be proper to stick her head out of a window and gawk. She glanced quickly at Major Bannik, who appeared unconcerned about the situation, so she instead diverted her attention to taking in the surroundings.

The castle was impressive enough, the battlements rising into the late afternoon sky with the royal pennant of Astrikhon flapping lightly in the wind. As they slowed to a stop, she could see that Symon's counterpart was waiting for them with a small security detail. Whatever commotion had occurred outside the castle walls was apparently not large enough to raise an alarm inside them, so she put the matter out of her head.

Unlike the Astrikhon prince, Lianne hadn't been able to make up her mind on how she felt about Dragoman Mikhal Balakiv after one brief meeting. He certainly had been polite, practically bowing all the way to the ground when he met her earlier in the day. Unlike Hadeon, he had followed all normal protocols of royal society, but he had maintained a smile on his face and seemed genuinely happy that she had made the trip.

For an older man, he was quite handsome, as well, maintaining a full head of light-brown hair with the trace of youth's curly locks. He had a very short beard, which made his Roma nose even more prominent, but he had a wide mouth and sparkling blue eyes that Lianne felt most people focused on instead. She thought him to be perhaps twenty years her elder, with just the start of crow's feet showing at the corners of his eyes.

And yet, there had been something standoffish about him. Not disquieting, and certainly not rude, but a certain sense of there being a mask in place that Lianne sensed very few people were allowed to see beneath. Upon reflection, she decided it wasn't all that surprising, given his position. Perhaps it was just the stark contrast he presented after the completely open, almost puppylike greeting she had received from the prince.

With age comes wisdom, or perhaps just stodginess. Maybe that's why Symon is such a stick-in-the-mud. What will I be like when I'm old, I wonder?

Trying not to focus on philosophical questions, Lianne dismounted gracefully from the carriage to be received by the Astrikhon dragoman.

He smiled, took her hand in his, and bowed gracefully over it. "Your Highness! So good to see you again and to formally welcome you to the royal residence of the Sokolov dynasty."

Lianne curtsied in return as Major Bannik and Symon came around the carriage to stand slightly behind her. Both had formal attire on, the soldier's breastplate broadly bearing the Kalchik heraldry upon it. Mikhal released Lianne's hand, took a step back, and bowed formally to Symon and then to the major but did not greet them personally. Lianne sensed a slight movement to her right and assumed Symon had acknowledged his counterpart in some small manner, but the major appeared to remain motionless.

Mikhal offered Lianne his arm, which she took, and, turning in unison, they marched in a stately manner into the castle proper.

They entered a wide corridor that went straight into the heart of the structure, with various hallways and doors on either side. The center of the corridor had been covered with a series of dark-red carpets with gold fringe that muffled the footsteps of their small party as it advanced.

Since it was supposed to be a smaller, more intimate reception, and not an introduction to the full court, Symon had decided that none of Lianne's ladies-in-waiting would accompany her. Lianne had thought about insisting that Olesea, at least, be brought along, but it wasn't worth upsetting her dragoman over the issue. Major Bannik, on the other hand, had simply joined them without any discussion on the matter.

Strength before beauty, or perhaps just security before elegance.

Mikhal whispered something to Lianne about a tapestry they were passing on her left, and she nodded absentmindedly without really paying attention. She could see a young man dressed in fine livery at the end of the corridor, standing in front of a set of large, closed doors. Two Astrikhon guards flanked him. No doubt the throne room was on the other side of the doors. Lianne took a deep breath to steady herself, resisting the urge to glance back at Symon.

He may be a stick-in-the-mud, but he certainly knows the steps to this particular dance we are about to join. Remember what he said about their king.

As they neared the end of the corridor, the two guards

simultaneously turned, and each opened a door. While the corridor wasn't overly dark, it seemed downright dingy compared to the amount of sunlight that streamed in from the throne room. Mikhal paused their progress forward so she could be properly announced, and Lianne was glad for the moment to allow her eyes to adjust. As it was, she could only make out several dozen blurred figures waiting in the brightness ahead of her.

The young man who had been waiting with the guards turned out to be the herald. He bowed low to Lianne, and then he wheeled and advanced into the throne room several paces. Lianne idly wondered if he had to call out his declaration with his eyes shut or if resistance to sudden changes in light levels was part of his qualifications.

"Your Royal Majesties and esteemed lords and ladies of the court, may I present to you a royal guest from our neighbors to the northwest! May her visit lead to increased understanding and everlasting peace between our two peoples! Bid welcome to Her Royal Highness, Princess Lianne Kalchik, daughter of King Elric II, and heir to the throne of Perizidon!"

The herald bowed and then stepped aside, his duty done. Mikhal waited half a beat before stepping forward, and Lianne followed his lead. The carpet reversed colors as they stepped over the threshold and became a solid gold with a dark-red fringe, and now it was also continuous all the way to the dais, which had a large throne centered upon it.

As was the protocol that Lianne had been told, Mikhal

bowed to his king and then released her, stepping to the side opposite the herald. She knew that Symon and the major would proceed only a few steps into the throne room and then wait to be called forward only if deemed necessary. She would be entirely alone, and already she could feel the eyes of the crowd boring into her.

Nothing to it, Li. It's only what you've been trained to do your whole life.

The room was eerily quiet as Lianne advanced through it, although the courtiers did not appear to be outright hostile. There were only about four dozen people, evenly spread on either side of the carpet. The room itself was spacious and probably could have housed a crowd four or five times the current size. The afternoon sun shining through large bay windows was the reason for brightness in the room, and the space was quite warm, even without many bodies to heat it.

As she walked, Lianne could see patterns of light playing across the faces of the crowd as her tiara caught the sun, including the faces of the three members of the royal family that stood waiting for her on the dais. She fought to keep a neutral look on her face as she glanced at Hadeon, though it was almost impossible not to match the wide smile on his face as reflected sunlight danced in his eyes.

At least there is one friendly person in the room. Hopefully his mood has rubbed off on his father.

Lianne quickly glanced at the king, and all thoughts of

smiling left her mind immediately. Haldir stood in the middle of the dais, in front of his throne, arms crossed and with an extremely dour look on his face. If she didn't know any better, she would have thought he had been awakened from a nap mere moments before she appeared.

God's nails, it looks like he doesn't want either of us to be here. Careful, Li...

A tall, slender woman stood on the other side of the king, and Lianne assumed she was the queen consort. Symon hadn't said much about her, only stating that she had never been a direct part of the treaty negotiations. She was wearing a close-fitting dress made of a silvery material that shimmered in the reflected light from Lianne's tiara. A slight smile played across her lips as if she was enjoying the added attention the light was providing her.

She's beautiful, I'll give her that. But that waist is impossibly thin. She has to be wearing stays of some sort under her dress. Looks bloody uncomfortable!

Lianne stopped the prescribed distance away from the dais and performed a deep curtsy. She then folded her hands in front of her and looked steadily up at the king. As she did so, reflected light from her tiara played across his face, as she was standing in the middle of a patch of sunlight. He scowled and looked as if he wanted to bat the light away like a pesky insect.

Sighing heavily, Haldir stepped off the dais so that the light was no longer in his eyes. He came forward so that they were only a couple paces apart, performed a perfunctory bow, and then looked her in the eye.

"It is too bad that your father cannot be here."

He spoke in a conversational tone, but it was still loud enough for practically everyone to hear in the quiet space that surrounded them. It was an impertinent start to any conversation, let alone their first, but Lianne was ready for it.

"Yes, Your Majesty. He knows your time is precious, and his presence would require all the trappings of an official state visit. You and I, on the other hand, may dispense with the business at hand in an expedited manner, if that is what is required."

He smirked at this. "Hmm, yes, the business at hand, as you say. I assume your dragoman back there has the final treaty document at the ready?"

"He does indeed, Your Majesty. We can present it to you now, or we can perform the signing more privately with your council, as you see fit."

Haldir waved his hand dismissively. "Yes, yes, we can attend to that later. I am sure that, between Symon and Mikhal, they can start the signing ceremony without us and rustle up enough platitudes and arse-kissing to keep things moving until we arrive."

"Symon can indeed be long-winded if he wants to be, Your Majesty. However, my father has not commented on his kissing ability."

This caused a slight coughing fit from the king, and he seemed to relax slightly. "Well, Princess, I am sure Mikhal can do enough for both of them if the need arises."

"If you say so, Your Majesty."

"I do say so." Haldir glanced back at the dais. "I believe you have already met my son?"

Lianne bowed her head at Hadeon, and now she smiled slightly. "Yes, Your Majesty. He welcomed me in your name at the docks and did me the honor of escorting me to my temporary residence."

Haldir stared past her at the back of the room with a dark look on his face, and she assumed he was silently castigating his dragoman. Whether it was because Mikhal hadn't stopped Hadeon in time from meeting Lianne or should have done what the prince had in his stead was unclear. The awkward moment was brief, and the king returned his gaze to her.

At least he looks at me in the eye and not at my bodice.

"It is good to hear that Hadeon cares about honor in times such as this. Come then, let me introduce you to my wife, Corinna."

He extended his arm to her, which she took loosely, and then walked her the few steps to the dais where the other two royal family members had remained standing. The queen consort was even more striking close-up, with large hazel eyes that matched her long hair and silky skin that matched her dress. She wore a simple tiara, similar to Lianne's, but with a matching brooch and earrings.

They curtsied to each other and appraised each other briefly. Lianne was struck by how young Corinna looked.

More like an older sister to Hadeon than a mother would have been my guess. Perhaps she's his stepmother?

"It is a pleasure to meet you, my dear." Corinna's speech was heavily accented, almost as if Common wasn't her native tongue.

"The pleasure is mine, Your Majesty."

"So, you are Arina's daughter?"

She's asking about my mother. How strange...

"Yes, Your Majesty. Do you know her?"

The queen consort smiled, showing perfectly straight, white teeth. "We met once, a very long time ago, when we were but children. I, of course, know her story and how she escaped the clutches of that *dupek* who still sits on the throne of Rusgorod. It is good to meet her daughter. I hope you have half the backbone of your mother."

Lianne curtsied again. "I do, as well, Your Majesty. I will be sure to pass along any message of greeting you may have for her."

"Very good, my dear." The teeth flashed again, contrasting against Corinna's thick, red lips.

Lianne found it hard to look into her eyes and not be mesmerized.

There is no way you are the same age as my mother!

Haldir motioned to his son, who came forward immediately.

Hadeon had managed to subdue the grin on his face to something a bit more in line with protocol, and he bowed deeply to Lianne. "It is good to see you again, Your Highness," he said to her, with perhaps just the slightest emphasis on her title.

It was all Lianne could do to not laugh and respond using his given name, and she tried to look demure as she curtsied back at him. "I share your sentiment, Your Highness."

The king appeared not to have noticed anything out of the ordinary pass between them, and he addressed Hadeon in a somewhat subdued tone. "Good sir, since you are already acquainted with our royal guest, I would ask that you introduce her to the lords and ladies gathered herein. Do not dawdle like some might, as I want you to come to the council room as soon as possible."

Lianne was shocked at what the king was inferring.

He's already done with me and these proceedings? What in the abyss is going on? Symon said to expect impertinence, but this is beyond the pale!

If Hadeon was surprised by his father's request, he did not show it. "Certainly, Your Majesty. Would you prefer if Dragoman Mikhal handled—"

"I would not," Haldir snapped, interrupting him. He glanced at Lianne and then leaned in towards his son and whispered something she couldn't catch, emphasizing whatever was said with a strong poke of his forefinger into Hadeon's chest.

When his father had finished speaking to him, Hadeon smiled meekly and nodded. "Yes, Your Majesty."

Haldir turned back to Lianne. "It is good that you are here, Princess, and I echo the sentiments of my herald in that I hope we continue to have peace between our two nations. That, of course, depends upon you continuing in your father's footsteps and making amends for the egregious sins your kingdom has committed against mine in the past."

Lianne felt the blood drain away from her face, but before she could fully absorb the boorish statement, the Astrikhon king continued.

"And speaking of your father, he must be prescient. For my time is indeed precious, especially today. I hope to see you at the banquet tonight, where we may follow the lead of our dragomen and talk about nonsensical matters. But, for now, I must leave you in the capable hands of my son and attend to an urgent matter with my council. Until this evening, Your Highness."

He bowed low to her and then turned and walked quickly towards a side door without waiting for her return valediction. The room remained quiet behind Lianne, as if all of the courtiers were used to their monarch storming off without notice, and she neither heard nor sensed anyone else making to leave.

Hadeon cleared his throat and stepped forward. "Please forgive my father's behavior," he said quietly to Lianne, who was doing everything in her power to not clench her fists and hurl insults at the back of the king. The prince watched his father disappear from view before speaking again. "There are unfortunate events unfolding in the north that we have only learned about in the past few hours, and his mind is elsewhere."

Lianne glanced up at him with a withering gaze before hissing through clenched teeth, "Tell me, *Your Highness*, do you think that condones his boorish conduct?"

Hadeon took her hand up in his and bowed over it. He came

up with a rueful smile. "No, it does not. But, please, let us talk about such things when we are in a more private setting. For now, I would do his bidding and introduce you to those that would help you find your way within our society."

Lianne was still facing the front of the throne room, and she assumed that only Hadeon and his mother had seen whatever anger had played across her face at Haldir's rude exit. She glanced up at the queen consort, to gauge her reaction to the proceedings. The slight smile from before was back on her face, and she seemed to give a small shrug of her shoulders. It was as if she was telling Lianne that what had just transpired was normal and to be expected.

Perhaps to be expected, but to be accepted *is another matter altogether...*

Lianne made a motion with her hands as if smoothing the front of her dress. She took a moment to mimic the serene look of Corinna on her own face, then turned to fully face Hadeon.

"I would be honored if you would introduce me to the court of your father, Your Highness."

The next hour or so was spent in a reception line of sorts, as Hadeon presented Lianne to each individual in attendance. There were dukes and duchesses, counts and countesses, and a few more minor nobles to be met. But that was not all. Artists who were held in high esteem of the court, merchantmen and women who had bought their way into favor, and even several heroes of the kingdom who had made their mark fighting orcs on the frontier were paraded in front of Lianne. She had to admit it was an interesting and eclectic collection of people, although about halfway through, it dawned on her that a major subsection of higher society seemed to be missing.

Where are the clergy?

She put the thought to the side for the time being, smiling and curtsying at a handsome-looking duke and his wife.

Corinna had quickly joined her son in helping with the introductions, especially with some of the more elderly nobility. Lianne didn't know where the two dragomen had made off to, or if they were even together, but there was no time to inquire about them. However, she could feel the presence of Major Bannik behind her, a silent bodyguard who, no doubt, was keeping a close eye on the proceedings. The few soldiers in the receiving line looked at her in apparent respect, bowing to her in addition to Lianne as they passed.

When the pleasantries were over, the sun was low in the sky and the light in the hall was starting to falter. The herald made an announcement that the welcoming banquet would start shortly after the hour of Vespers, giving the crowd a bit of time to prepare themselves. Most of those who were still in the throne room slowly dispersed, with only three young women standing together in one of the corners talking quietly amongst themselves. The queen consort took her leave, and Lianne found herself somewhat alone with the prince.

He looked at her with relief and good humor playing across

his face. “Well, Your Highness. That wasn’t too bad, I hope?”

She managed a smile, although it felt artificial and merely painted on her face after all the pantomiming she had performed over the past hour or so. “I must admit that I am glad this was an informal introduction to your court as opposed to a full-scale production.”

Hadeon chuckled. “Well, if the entire royal court had been assembled, there would have been perhaps only two or three dozen more nobility who would have warranted a personal introduction. And another merchant or two, and a few more generals. Oh, and the entire royal council, of course. But the rest would have had to make do with gazing at you from afar.”

Lianne glanced around to make sure no one was within earshot. She was glad to see that even the major was giving the two of them space to talk discreetly with each other. “What about the church, Hadeon? Is it normal for their leaders to be absent at these events?”

He seemed to light up when he heard her use his name but then frowned all the same. “Yes, indeed, the church. The archbishop is very elderly and does not necessarily care to attend such mundane events such as this. Uh, his words, not mine.”

Hadeon cast an anxious look at her, and she motioned slightly with her hands to show that no harm had been done to her ego.

He continued in a sober tone. “As to other senior members of the clergy, they typically do not attend these events out of deference to my mother."

Lianne was surprised by this. "Your mother?"

He coughed slightly into his hand. "Yes, well, let us just say she did not have an agreeable childhood and blames the church for various...misunderstandings and mishaps." He looked away, and Lianne knew not to press further on matters dealing with religion.

She could not, however, resist the temptation to ask about his mother's age. "The queen consort...she said that she met my mother when they were both young. I must admit that seems, well, strange."

Hadeon looked back at her. "Oh?"

"Well, given that your mother is so young. She hardly seems old enough to be your biological mother, to be frank."

"Ah, that. Yes, I suppose with you being new to our kingdom and royal court, her appearance would be somewhat surprising. But, please believe me, she is indeed my mother and bore me into this world. As to what manner of witchcraft she uses to maintain her beauty, it is beyond my comprehension."

Lianne was stunned at this statement.

Witchcraft! Is he being serious? No wonder she doesn't want clergy around. But what about the inquisition?

Hadeon had continued talking, not noticing how his statement had taken her aback. "It has been some time since I have been inside her private rooms, but even as a young child, I was amazed at the number of vials and pots she had surrounding her looking glass. The only time she has been truly angry with me is when I took it upon myself to paint my face with some of her makeup."

Lianne snorted, losing most of her royal dignity in the process. "What did you say?!"

The prince looked at her sheepishly. "I was perhaps ten at the time, and I was thinking the many colors she had would make for a wonderful war mask. I was only trying to look fearsome for my fencing lesson later that day."

Lianne, shaking with quiet laughter, pictured in her mind a younger version of the prince with a garish face getting berated by his mother. At the same time, she realized that his use of the word "witchcraft" had only meant to signify his cluelessness to what most women did to become, or remain, beautiful.

"Well, I will say that your mother seems to have much better results with her mixing and matching than you did. She is extremely youthful in appearance."

"Yes, her daily results please both her and my father. To me, it seems like a waste of time to struggle so mightily against the wages of time." He shook his head, but whether at himself or his mother, Lianne could only guess.

She looked around the room as she composed herself, noticing that the trio of young women were still talking with each other in the corner of the throne room. She vaguely remembered them all being daughters of various nobility and that they had been among the coldest of people in their reception of her. Her suspicions as to why were confirmed by the way they were now glaring at her and Hadeon.

"Well, Hadeon, be it through cosmetics or stylish dress, there are many women who feel their looks are the best ways to capture a man's heart."

He made a huffing noise but then followed her gaze towards the corner. Once he saw who she was looking at, he smiled at the young ladies and bowed to them, which they returned with their own smiles and curtsies.

The prince then looked back at Lianne, moving slightly as he did to block her view of her apparent rivals for his attention. "Yes, I realize that. To your point, the young lady in the middle of the trio over there is quite lovely indeed. Without any needed assistance from potions or petticoats, I might add. She would use her good looks to woo me, to be sure. But she is much more than a pretty face, which is why I am actually attracted to her. There are many within the court who believe we will be a good match, when the time is right."

Then I am obviously a rival to her, and a dangerous one at that.

"I see. Do *you* believe the two of you will be a good match?"

The prince attempted to be casual in his response, but Lianne could tell there was mutual attraction between the two. "Hmm? Oh, I suppose. She is smarter than I am, is a good rider, and comes from a family that has long been loyal to the crown. We have known each other our whole lives, so we are already very comfortable around each other. Truth be told, however, I don't believe either of us are quite ready for a betrothal, let alone marriage."

You could have fooled me, the way she seems to want to plunge a dagger in my chest.

"And the other two? Friends of hers?"

He rolled his eyes. "Hmm, yes. 'Friends,' indeed. Let us just say that I will not speak ill of them and, therefore, have nothing further to say on the matter."

Lianne grinned. "Navigating court politics is always so much fun."

Hadeon sighed. "Yes, quite. But, speaking of court politics, I am afraid that I must take my leave of you and go attend to my father. He was quite adamant that I join him as soon as possible, and no doubt he will berate me for not running to his side as soon as we were done here."

Lianne did her best not to frown and fall into a bad mood again. "He does seem to have an interesting grip on his court."

"That is one way of putting it, yes."

"Might I ask what has occurred that has him in such a bother? Or does he always behave...oddly?" Lianne was going say "like a churlish peasant," but decided to remain as diplomatic as possible.

"Orcs," Hadeon responded simply. "An incursion of orcs has occurred."

Lianne caught her breath, her opinion of the situation and the king's behavior changing instantly. "Hadeon! Is it bad?"

"I do not believe so, but I will know more in an hour or so. Please, now, do not be alarmed. Unfortunately, this is not an uncommon occurrence for us. Hence the large garrison to the north that I mentioned to a certain bandit queen earlier today."

They smiled at each other, and he bowed. "I will see you shortly at the banquet, Lianne. If you need anything in the interim, have a lady-in-waiting speak with my manservant, Aleksei. And thank you for your patience and understanding this afternoon."

She curtsied in return. "But of course, Hadeon. We shall speak again soon."

Lianne noticed that the prince went to speak briefly to the young women in the corner before making his exit out the side door that his father had previously used, but she was too wrapped up in her own thoughts to think much of it. Symon had reappeared in the main entryway to the throne room and had been waiting for her to finish her conversation with the prince. She walked towards him, with Major Bannik coming up behind her.

Symon made a short bow as she approached and then spoke in a hushed but stern tone. "Your Highness, I must apologize for the king living down to my opinion of him. I have already informed my counterpart that we do not look kindly upon being treated so rudely. He has, no doubt, scuttled away to tell his master some watered-down variant of my message."

"It is not your fault, Dragoman Chumak. You did warn me that His Royal Majesty might act like an ill-bred swine herder."

He didn't smile at her rough choice of words. "Yes, Your

Highness. Still, from what I could tell, you handled the situation as well as could be hoped. Both your mother and father will be pleased."

Lianne bowed her head slightly at his compliment, rare as they were.

Symon glanced over at the major but then continued his conversation directly with Lianne. "You appeared to be in good hands and in good spirits with the young prince, so I took the opportunity to steal away and make some preparations for tonight and the rest of your stay."

That and you probably didn't want to make small talk with Astrikhon nobility for any longer than you had to. Especially if you had just told off Mikhal in front of some of them.

"Thank you. Speaking of which, there is a bit of time before the banquet, and I rather need to refresh myself."

"I suspected as much, Your Highness. I have obtained the use of a sitting room off the library for your use. It is only a few paces away, and your female companions are waiting there for you."

"Excellent! That will do perfectly. Now, if you would walk with me for a moment."

Lianne led the others into the main hallway outside of the throne room, turning into a smaller corridor when Symon indicated the way to go towards the room he had secured.

Once they were away from any Astrikhon guards, Lianne turned towards her dragoman and spoke in a low voice. "The prince has just informed me that the king and his council are dealing with a serious situation on their northern border. That was the reason given for his inauspicious departure."

Symon nodded his head, again looking over at the major. "Yes, Your Highness. I was made aware of what is going on at the border less than an hour ago by a reliable source. It is still not a viable reason for the king's behavior towards you, in my opinion."

Lianne knew better than to ask who the reliable source might be, and she didn't bother agreeing with him again about Haldir's behavior. Instead, she looked around to make doubly sure the three of them were alone. "How bad is it, Symon? Hadeon says such things happen on a routine basis, but I am not so sure."

The dragoman furrowed his brow. "I tend to agree with you, Your Highness. From the very little that I know, this incursion of orcs seems to be larger than most, at least based upon recent history."

Major Bannik stepped forward, breaking into the conversation. "Dragoman Chumak, are you saying an *invasion* has started?"

Symon turned to her, a look of appeasement on his face. "Now, now, we cannot be too hasty, Major. I would not call it an invasion just yet."

The soldier made a strange noise in the back of her throat, and her hand unconsciously drifted towards the hilt of her sword as the statesman continued.

"Reports are still coming in, and our hosts have not gone on full alert security-wise. Whomever, or whatever, has broken through the border is still some fifty leagues from here."

The major was obviously unappeased by his statement. "Nevertheless, we must assume the worst, Dragoman. We should prepare to leave here immediately, perhaps as early as tonight!"

Lianne took a deep breath. She hadn't even thought of the need to break off her visit.

Surely King Haldir and his council aren't that concerned, are they? The major must be overreacting for the sake of my mother.

Symon seemed to be thinking along the same lines. "Major, while I applaud your caution and for putting Her Royal Highness's safety before all else, I do not see the need for such a drastic measure. The Astrikhon army is well-equipped for dealing with this issue. No warnings have been issued to the local population. Even if this becomes a true emergency, we have plenty of time to consult with our hosts and react accordingly. Remember that, officially, we are not even supposed to know what is happening."

The major seemed to want to say something more, but she merely pressed her lips together and took a step back.

"I share your opinion, Dragoman," Lianne said. "We should not show ourselves to be people who panic at the mere hint of trouble. Let us see how things play out tonight and on the morrow. However, I would think that the ship's crew should be kept somewhat close at hand to the docks tonight. Just in case, of course."

Major Bannik dipped her head. "A prudent decision, Your Highness. I will have their liberty canceled and ensure your captain has supplies taken in for our return trip no later than tomorrow afternoon." She looked at Symon. "My lord, with your permission, I will have the same discussions with the captain of your ship."

He nodded his head. "Thank you, Major. I agree, it is a prudent decision. The crews will not like it, but that is a small price to pay for a bit of vigilance."

The major gave Lianne the king's salute and immediately strode back down the corridor towards the castle entrance.

Lianne watched her go until she was out of earshot before turning back to Symon. "I must know, Dragoman. How tight of a rein was she told to keep on me?"

"Very tight," was his quick response. "Your mother is quite worried about you, Your Highness. In the major's defense, this news about the orcs is, indeed, unsettling. If nothing else, it makes for very bad timing. We should look to finalize the treaty tomorrow morning before the king and his council become completely absorbed by other events."

Lianne thought quickly. "If it is, indeed, an invasion, or even just a serious attack, I would think that the king and his generals will want to shift as many soldiers off our border to their north as quickly as possible. It should make the signing of the treaty with us a high priority."

"That is quite true, Your Highness. However, it will still be good to put ink to paper and leave nothing to chance for either side. With that accomplished, we can decide how long to tarry here in Boloto from purely a perspective of courtesy."

Lianne suddenly remembered her other task for the inquisitor.

Shite, I must talk to Olesea at once about getting an audience with the archbishop. It sounds like it should happen as soon as possible.

"Very well, Dragoman. I am sure you need to prepare for the banquet, as well, so I will take your leave for the moment."

"Indeed, Your Highness. I will come for you a bit before Vespers." Symon bowed to her and marched off down the corridor in the opposite direction of the throne room.

"I hope you are on your way to find a stiff drink, and that you have one for me," Lianne muttered. She sighed and went to look for Olesea and her other ladies-in-waiting.

***

"God's teeth, Oldenfeld! What in the abyss were you thinking?!" Sergeant Vokun paced back and forth in front of Dane, his clenched fists shaking. "But that's always the problem with you, isn't it? You *don't* think!"

Dane stood silently at attention, what few wits he had about him knowing that anything he said, anything at all, would make the situation worse than it already was.

But it wasn't my fault! Not this time, because I saw someone with a knife in the crowd! I was just trying to protect the princess from unknown assailants and assassins. How was I supposed to know it was just a dim-witted butcher who had wandered over from his stall to watch a parade go by?

His sergeant continued to rage at him. "How many times do we have to go over this? When you are on escort duty, you march, you observe, and you follow orders! Did anyone give you an order to break formation and go into the crowd?"

Dane remained silent, which apparently was *also* the wrong thing to do, because the sergeant was immediately less than a hand's width away from him, spitting words in his face.

"*Answer me, soldier!* Did *anyone* give you an order to break formation?"

"No, sir!"

"Did *anyone* tell you to apprehend cleavers, tongs, and other tools of trade from the crowd?"

"No, sir!"

"And did *anyone* tell you to embarrass Her Royal Highness in front of the Almighty, the kingdom of Astrikhon, and, worst of all, *the major*?"

"No, sir!" Dane winced internally. He had hoped beyond hope that Major Bannik hadn't seen or heard about the disturbance he had created. But, of course, she had. She was the ultimate professional soldier, after all.

That and she has eyes in the back of her damn head.

Sergeant Vokun rocked back and forth on his feet, seemingly deciding between striking Dane across the face or punching him in gut. Ultimately, his own professionalism won out, and he did neither. Instead, he took a step back, did a crisp about-face, and marched the few steps to the door of the temporary barracks room that had been created in the bowels of the princess's residence. However, his apparent contempt for Dane was such that he didn't bother to turn around to issue him orders.

"You're confined to quarters until the major decides what to do with you. But whatever she decides, the first thing you'll do for *me* when you get out of here is clean every single chamber pot in this damn mansion. Maybe, just maybe, by looking at shite all day, you'll figure out how much shite you would have put our entire delegation in if you had hurt an innocent peasant. *Bloody idiot!*"

Dane waited a short moment after the door was closed before slumping onto the nearest bunk. Despite his best efforts to do his duty, he had failed again. He had gotten in trouble before the trip, back at the Kalchik castle, for not reacting to a potential troublemaker that turned out to be just the princess's brother. And now he had just gotten in trouble for doing the exact opposite thing in overreacting to what he thought was a potential troublemaker! He just didn't understand why he kept screwing things up when he knew, he just *knew*, he had a date with destiny.

He sighed heavily, then chuckled at himself. The way his luck was going, there would be an assassin hiding in the privy hole he'd be dumping all the chamber pots into, but he'd drown the poor fellow in piss before either one of them could do something heroic.

Well, I'm still here in Boloto, no matter the punishment. I can still do right by the princess if the major will let me, somehow. I just have to figure out how to save myself before I can save the day...

CHAPTER TWELVE

Conversation with a Devil

Kozel was in agony. He couldn't remember when he had ever been in so much pain. Of course, eternity stretched to either side of this specific moment, so obviously something on the universal timeline was worse than this. But, at this instant, it was impossible for him to focus on much more than his insides trying to work their way out of his current form.

He paused to get his bearings, to try and sort things out in a semi-rational manner. He was somewhere to the west of Stren, out in the Wilds and away from all the putrescent stink of the town and the humans that inhabited it. If he could, at this moment, he would burn it all to the ground.

First things first, be a realist. How did you get here?

He focused on the physical, rather than philosophical, response to his internal question. He had walked here, obviously, wherever "here" was. Or rather, he had stumbled and dragged himself here. Not that there was anything wrong with his legs. It was just hard to walk when you had to hold your intestines in to keep them from spilling onto the ground.

I would laugh at your pathetic condition, but it hurts too much to do so. So, where is here?

He tried to think. How far had he traveled? How had he gotten out of town? When and why had he transformed out of his dangerous and menacing vovkulaka form into this pathetic and soft human form? Details, details...details that he couldn't quite remember.

But you can remember who did this to you, right?

Oh, he could definitely remember how he received his injuries. Yes, *that* he would remember that until the End of Days. That cursed orc, who had cut him to the quick, who had broken his playthings, who had dared to mock him. That monster with his secrets, who had humiliated him more than any mortal being ever had before or ever would again.

Yes, whatever will we do with that perversion of nature? That mangy cur?

He would see the dog defanged and damned. He would fashion a necklace out of the greyskin's teeth and wear them as a trophy. He would tear the orc asunder and drag the corpse into the abyss himself. He would do all that and more.

Don't stop there. What other wretched things will you do to him? Tell me!

Kozel winced and tried to stop the inner dialogue. He needed to get a grip on himself, on this version of reality. He knew he couldn't actually die on this plane of existence, but the pain made him almost wish he could. The pain... He needed to focus on something else.

Hatred and loathing. Focus on your hatred for that damnable orc and use it as a poultice. Pack your injuries with it, wrap it to you tightly, and let it succor and sustain you. Just let it marinate for a moment, or a millennia...

"Kozel? Kozel darling, you need to wake up!" A familiar voice, and not his own, called to him from somewhere nearby, and he awoke with a start. He found himself sitting on the ground, resting against a large tree. He paused to get his bearings, to try and sort things out in a semi-rational manner. He was somewhere to the west of Stren, out in the Wilds and away from all the—

"Kozel, stop it! You're spiraling. You need to focus, my dear, or you will never get anywhere. We need to talk. Come to me, *now*!"

The last word vibrated in his mind. He had to obey. Struggling to stand up, he found that he had let his hands slip from his abdomen while he had been resting by the tree. Most of his insides had indeed worked their way out of him, and it took some time to remedy the situation. But he had all the time in the world, didn't he? At least the voice didn't seem to mind waiting, so long as he was showing some sort of progress in following its order.

Finally, he was standing, perhaps not as a whole person, but as an unholy one. The play on words amused him, more than it should have. He tried to laugh and think of another joke.

A priest, a succubus, and an eldar walk into a—

"Kozel!"

"Yes, yes, I'm coming," he responded, although not tersely. It was best not to make anyone madder at him than they were already. He looked around for the way to go.

There was a door where a door shouldn't be, seemingly stuck on the side of a large boulder. As Kozel approached it, it seemed to shimmer briefly, as if it had been waiting until he acknowledged its existence to fully enter the physical plane. As he staggered up to stand in front of it, it acknowledged him in kind and slid noiselessly to the side. He passed inside the boulder, and some hidden mechanism closed the door behind him.

Dim, artificial lighting cast from above showed him an interminably long corridor that went straight on ahead of him, the end lost somewhere in the gloom. The corridor appeared to curve slightly upwards, and he couldn't see any doors or intersections. The smooth, blanks walls were made of a consistent, grey stone that had no cracks or aberrations showing in it. The floor was made of the same material and looked easy enough to walk on, even in his current condition.

"You could have added a handrail or a moving walkway," Kozel groused, but the voice didn't respond. He sighed and started slowly on his way, holding his midsection together with both hands. He thought about marking one of the walls periodically as he went to ensure that he didn't become disoriented and start walking in the wrong direction, but he ultimately decided against it. The voice did want to speak with him sooner rather than later, after all. He would find his way when it was time to do so.

Sometime later, Kozel looked up and saw a door on the right in the distance. As slowly as he was walking, it still took some time to reach it, but at least it didn't relocate itself or flicker out of existence. As he approached, he saw that the door was windowless and appeared to be made of some sort of metal. It was tightly fit with both the floor and the wall, as if constructed so that no sound would filter through it from either side.

INTERROGATIONS – ROOM 9 was neatly printed on a small sign that was attached to the wall next to the door. At one point, there had been an array of dots under the words, but someone had taken the trouble to shave them down. Kozel ran his fingertips over where they used to be, but he couldn't feel anything but some rough edges. All he did was leave a streak of blood that smeared the sign for the visually unimpaired.

The door opened easily enough, swinging silently outwards into the hallway. It revealed a small, nondescript room that was lit somewhat better than the hallway but in the same artificial manner. A table and three chairs located in the middle of the room were the only pieces of furniture, and the walls were bare.

One of the chairs was by itself on the far side of the table, and he assumed that was where he was supposed to sit. There was a large eye bolt attached to the table in front of it, and as he walked around the table, he noted that the isolated chair was the only one anchored in place to the floor. He smirked to himself.

An interrogation, or an inquisition? One and the same, I suppose. Well, if they want to manacle me to the table, they'll just have to deal with my blood and guts spilling out onto the floor. Both will probably end up there anyway.

Sighing, he worked his way to the isolated chair and sat down. It was made of cold, hard metal, and it forced his body to conform to its shape. The other two chairs didn't look any more comfortable, and he didn't feel like changing locations anyway now that he was seated.

Holding his stomach, he tried to compose himself for what he assumed would be a long wait. The room smelled and felt stale, as if forgotten by time itself.

***

"Hello, my dear."

Kozel had been contemplating the blank surface of the table in front of him, and he had no idea how long the other person had been standing in the doorway. He would have stood up, but he wasn't sure how much of a mess that would make. Instead, he tried to sit up straight and gave them his best smile.

"Mistress Lilia. A pleasant surprise, indeed."

She regarded him cooly for a moment before responding. "It has been far too long, darling. How wonderful to see you."

Kozel could feel the irony dripping off her words, matching his own. She was alone for the moment, although he knew how dangerous she could be even without any muscle to back her up. As Lilia entered the room, the door closed behind her with an audible *click*.

Her long, golden hair was pulled back in a single braid, and for some reason she was wearing dark rimmed spectacles. Her clothing, while masculine in cut, was still able to fully emphasize the human female shape she had assumed, and her high-heeled shoes sounded menacing on the smooth floor as she walked to the table. Her makeup was immaculate, and her overall appearance made Kozel feel disheveled and dirty.

Lilia placed a full folder on the table in front of her as she sat down directly opposite him. She folded hands that ended in razor sharp nails neatly over the folder, obscuring what was written on the outside of it. She looked calm, but her bright-blue eyes flashed red for just a moment as she smiled back at him.

She allowed him to take one of her hands in his, dirty and bloodstained as it was, and he bowed low over it and brushed his lips against her skin. The sickening sweet smell of vanilla rose up to meet him, and he gently released her and sat back.

Animalistic features played across her visage for the merest of moments before she spoke again. "Ah, my sweet, delectable Kozel. A gentleman to the end, no less. It is one of your qualities that has endeared you to me over the years."

Kozel bowed his head slightly but didn't verbally respond. He had managed to catch the title written on the folder when he kissed Lilia's hand, confirming it was his case file. It had gotten considerably thicker since the last time he had seen it.

Lilia continued. "I will cut to the chase, my dear. As you know, the central office constantly monitors all field operatives to ensure appropriate performance metrics are being maintained. There has been rising concern among all involved that certain goals within your sphere of influence may not be reached in a timely manner. Do you disagree with this concern?"

Kozel coughed slightly. "On the contrary, Mistress, I am painfully aware of certain recent shortcomings."

Her nostrils flared slightly at his choice of words, but that was the only noticeable reaction he could elicit. "I am glad that you concur with this assessment. It has been quite some time since you have filed a formal progress report, so both your progress and your mindset have become increasingly unclear."

"I would like to think that my progress, while somewhat slowed recently by a series of unfortunate events, is still within acceptable parameters. As to my state of mind, it has never been clearer. But, uh, I understand why there may be concern and am quite happy to provide you with a full and proper update." Kozel hurriedly added the last line, as Lilia's eyes had narrowed and her hands had clenched ever so slightly over his docket as he had spoken.

"I see. Well, we shall discuss these 'unfortunate events,' as you call them, shortly. But first, you need to show me the damage dealt to you."

He had not been expecting this type of demand, and he stared at her blankly. "The what?"

She huffed with exasperation. "I can see your broken forearm quite clearly, but you keep hiding your midsection. Stand up, *now*!"

Kozel found himself complying as quickly as he could. *Might as well give her the whole show.*

It certainly was a disgusting show, and enough time had passed so that at least part of him was starting to rot. The smell of death wafted out from him as his body disgorged itself onto the floor.

Lilia was still seated, but she crossed her arms across her chest and looked up at him over the top of her glasses. “So be it, your wounds are grievous in nature. But why are you being so dramatic about this? It’s not the first time you’ve been beaten in a fight, and nobody here cares if you want to carry on playing the martyr. Just transform already and be done with this nonsense!”

He regarded her with some irritation, trying hard not to rise to the bait. “I…can’t.”

“What do you mean, you can’t? It’s more like you *won’t*!”

Kozel slammed both fists on the table. “Do you honestly believe I want to remain in this condition? Are you bindworthy, woman?!”

She was at his side in an instant, her true nature revealing itself. Without saying a word, she was holding his spiritual essence in her hands, inspecting him, showing him how insignificant his role was in the machinations of the Unholy One. He had wasted what few gifts he had been granted, and now there was nothing but eternal pain awaiting him as she slowly consumed him over a thousand eons.

***

He awoke to find himself sitting in the chair, physically whole again. His arm was back in one piece, and his insides were back where they were supposed to be, although he could feel thick scar tissue from the recent wounds under his clothing. There was also a faint throbbing at the back of his mind, as if some memory was trying to work its way out to his consciousness.

Looking across the table, he saw Lilia writing notes in his file. Her hair had been taken out of its braid and dropped loosely around her, hiding her face. Her clothes had changed, as well, into something much more casual than before.

He must have shifted slightly in her peripheral vision, as she spoke to him without looking up.

"If you are truly back, darling, I will be with you momentarily. I need to complete my report on your debriefing."

Kozel was slightly perplexed at first about her statement before realizing she now probably knew more about him than he did. He refrained from responding and, instead, looked around the room. It appeared to be the same room, although there were a few noticeable changes to it since he had last been conscious. He wondered how much time had passed, even here.

The ceiling's pattern had changed in a way he couldn't put his finger on, although it was still difficult to tell where the artificial lighting was coming from. A small black box with a flashing red light now occupied one of the corners of the room, high enough to be out of reach. A large mirror had been installed on one of the side walls, and he stared at himself for quite some time while waiting for Lilia to finish writing.

"That orc really took it to you, didn't he?" She was still looking down at her notes, and the tone of the question was neutral enough that Kozel couldn't tell if she was mocking him or not.

He sighed, rubbing his scarred midsection. "Yes, he did. I

underestimated the brute."

"Hmm," was the only reply, but now she did look up at him. Her face was as neutral as her voice, and she wasn't wearing spectacles any longer. After a moment, she prompted him to continue. "In what way?"

"Well, for one thing, the fellow is quite cunning for his type. You might even say intelligent, at least in a worldly sense. After all, he was able to deduce what I was."

"That's not *too* surprising, given his race's olfactory senses."

"True, but he backed that up with some surprising logic. That, and it certainly helped that he knows his way around old magic, so he could eliminate some options."

"Yes, that talisman of his. We had no record of it on file. There always seems to be another item to add to the registry. Did he actually understand how to use it?"

Kozel thought about this for a moment. "That is an excellent question, Mistress. He was obviously communicating with someone, but it was more like having an open wavelength that transmitted basic thoughts and feelings as opposed to a concise conversation. But that someone on the other end..."

"Yes?"

He nodded to himself, thinking of the last message he had overheard. "A woman. She definitely knew how to use her stone."

Lilia continued to stare at him and to speak in a neutral tone. "So, you knowingly let your adversary communicate with some unknown purveyor of old magic while he was figuring out who you were and what you had been doing in Perizidon?"

Kozel opened his mouth, then closed it. The silence between them stretched as he tried to think of something witty to say in the moment. He realized that he could not. "Yes, Mistress."

She made a quick note in his file. "Please, my dear, continue. In what other ways did you underestimate this orc?"

Kozel ground his teeth. He wasn't used to being talked down to like an ignorant apprentice, but there was very little he could do about it now. "I am quite confident he is a berserker. Whether or not that is an innate talent or tied to some other form of old magic he had about his person, I do not know. Perhaps it was a spell tied to his weapon."

"Ah, yes. His weapon. Describe it to me, please."

"It was a large, double-headed axe. Certainly not a trapper's first weapon of choice. It was meant more for a battlefield than for hunting beaver or deer."

"How is it at hunting wargs?" There still wasn't a hint of mockery in her tone, but the question cut deeply all the same.

"More than adequate," he managed to get out without growling.

"Mmm, yes. We appear to have lost almost two dozen of the beasts in your sector over the past few months. They don't spawn on trees, you know."

"I didn't ask for them in the first place, and they are uncontrollable!" Kozel snapped defensively. "They can all die and come back to rot here in the abyss for all I care."

Lilia smiled, showing sharp, canine-like teeth. "Ah, so your backbone is still in there after all! Excellent, my dear. Well, I could certainly arrange to redirect any future reinforcements elsewhere if you prefer."

Kozel raised his chin slightly. "As you wish, Mistress. They are obviously useless to me."

"Obviously," she repeated dryly. "But back to this axe. Did you happen to see any runes or markings on it?"

He thought briefly. "Nothing that I can recall."

"Nothing to suggest why it cut you so deeply? So easily?"

"I just told you he was a berserker, the strength behind—" Kozel stopped short, an impossible notion forming in his head.

Did I truly miss some incantation written on the weapon? On the handle perhaps? What is wrong with me?

"Sard me..." he muttered.

"Not today, my pet. You don't deserve it."

Lilia wrote another note in his file before continuing. "We will come back to the orc's weapon. For now, anything else that you can recall from your ignoble defeat? Did the fact that the orc had reinforcements and you did not perhaps come into play? Perhaps those wargs would have been helpful if they had been with you?"

"Forget the damn wargs!" Kozel said heatedly. "They would have never gotten into town without attempting to maul the guard and raising the alarm! The meeting would have never occurred with them carrying on like they always do."

"Then adjust the location of the meeting, darling. And you

will mind your tone with me," she said coldly.

The throbbing in the back of Kozel's mind spiked for an instant, making him wince. "Yes...Mistress." He collected himself. "His reinforcements, such that they were, I would have defeated easily in turn. Nothing but weak-hearted humans."

"From what I can tell from your memories, the leader of the soldiers had a bit of initiative. And that harlot the orc was bedding showed enormous pluck, given the circumstances."

"What do you want from me, Mistress?" Kozel asked in as toneless a voice as he could manage. "To completely debase myself? Yes, I underestimated that little bitch as well. I had assumed she would just run away, but she apparently has feelings for that accursed greyskin."

"Something her sister, your beloved Kira, failed to mention to you, hmm?"

"Kira is *not* my beloved. If you have searched my memories, then you know that I have never seriously thought about violating her."

She batted her eyelashes at him. "Oh, Kozel darling, you are such an infernal being of virtue. Are you saving all of your essence for me? Because you know I will take it regardless. I can get to be so *ravenous* at times."

There was a sudden urging in his nether region, and Kozel groaned audibly. He grasped the edge of the table, forcing himself to remain in control. "Of course...Mistress..."

She released him as quickly and as forcefully as she had

taken charge. "You may not have taken that sow of a human to bed, my dearest, but you certainly favor her above all the other swine. I would think she would at least offer up all her thoughts to you, if not her wretched flesh."

Kozel dared to think for the briefest of moments that Lilia was actually jealous of Kira, but he stored the thought away instantly for fear of what would happen if he voiced it. "She may not have known herself. About her sister's feelings towards the orc, I mean."

"Hmph. Perhaps. In any event, Katrya Toth's actions were to call out for reinforcements and to stand and fight with *her* beloved. That, at a minimum, provided more distractions than you had accounted for, yes?"

He sighed again. "Yes, Mistress."

"Very well." She made a final note in his file, then closed the folder. Standing, she walked over to the mirror and made some adjustments to her appearance. She looked back at him as she tousled her hair. "This entire episode with the orc, I assume you see it as one of your so-called recent series of unfortunate events?"

"Yes, Mistress."

She turned to face him, leaning back against the wall next to the mirror. "The other significant ones being?"

He listed them quickly. "The unexpected strength of faith in our enemies to the south, the unwanted chaos introduced by those damnable wargs, and the senseless death of Dovira Mador. Also, because of these events and more, there is the cumulative effect of not having time to travel to Gavan to press the Rus to strengthen their force in the north."

She sauntered back to the table and sat on its edge, looking down at him.

"First, my dear, the southern resistance to our message was a known risk from the start. Pushing hard to usurp either the church or crown in that region was foolish and a waste of time, and you know it. Second, you have already stated your annoyance with the wargs, and it has already been noted." Her voice softened ever so slightly as she continued. "As to the death of that virgin orc, I do agree with you that it was both tragic and untimely. In fact, the central office commends you on resolving the issue before our more chaotic brethren could take advantage of the situation."

Kozel grimaced. "You are sure they were involved?"

Her chuckle was low and chilling. "Oh, Kozel, those wonderful mortal souls you dispatched to us confessed to everything. They all sang quite nicely, even before they were done being processed. Sadly, they had been taken in by a local hag, who had a personal grudge against that farmer."

"I knew it! I knew I smelled the taint of chaos on that savaged girl! But why is some hideous miscreant allowed to interfere with our operations to begin with?"

Lilia shook her head in apparent commiseration. "I wish I knew. The chaotic types always proclaim to be working for the ruinous downfall of all creation, the same as we are. The enemy of my enemy is my friend, I suppose."

It was all Kozel could do to not sneer. "Like we would have anything to do with what they would put in the place of the enemy. Pure anarchy befits no one!"

"Well, the hag has been dealt with, my dear. And you at least stopped their chaos with a bit of your own." She smiled at him, somewhat mischievously this time. "I suppose those wargs did come in handy after all, eh?"

He huffed ungraciously. "You know the saying that even a broken clockpiece is correct twice a day? I am still waiting for the second instance of them being useful."

She laughed and cupped his head in her hands. "Touché, darling!"

It felt like her fingers left burn marks on his cheeks as she released him and went back to her seat across the table. She seemed to be in a better mood than before, which bothered him as to what was coming next.

"Regarding your lack of time for travel to see King Ioseb, that was always considered an optional and nonessential task. It is hereby taken off your mission board."

"But, Mistress!" he protested. "There is important news to relay to the king regarding ore deposits in The Mountain."

She looked at him, shaking her head. "Can you hear yourself, my dear Kozel? Ore deposits? *The* Mountain? Stop thinking like a human and stop sounding like another simpleton from Stren."

Kozel was across the table and at her throat in an instant,

even though he knew it was only because she allowed it. He cared not what she did to him, but he could not, *would* not, let the last slight go without a response.

"Do not ever say I am from that fetid town! Do not *ever* say that!"

There was the briefest instance of unimaginable pleasure as she bound him to her, her hair tearing into him as it wrapped around his throat. They would be one, and they would create worlds together.

And then there was only emptiness, her maniacal laughter fading into the background as he found himself back in his chair, the desperate craving for her unsatiated.

"Oh, *darling*!" she purred, as she adjusted her top. "I told you not today, perhaps not ever, but you can make such a case for yourself when you want to. Just save your arguments and your strength for more important matters than this."

Lilia settled back in her own chair as Kozel struggled with his composure.

"Remember, my dear, that ultimately, we do not care who wins this little war. Rusgorod is well on their way to being the despotic empire we all know they can be, but whether they control the little shite territory of Perizidon matters not for our end goal. So long as the Kalchik line falls, whether from without or within, our current mission will be fulfilled. *This* time, we will not fail."

Before Kozel could comment on Lilia's last statement, she leaned forward and pointed a finger at him as if it was a dagger.

"That means your stupid ore mine, that town of Stren, the whole of the Wilds for that matter, are only places on a map to be taken by one side or the other. Even that saddle-goose of a king, Ioseb Geladze of Rusgorod, is but a clueless pawn in our little game. Stop worrying about the pawns!"

She sat back again, inspecting her nails. "As it is, we believe there are already enough Rus soldiers camped on Mount Iklo to take that rump of a town. With or without the support of the thugs that idiotic sheriff and your beloved are assembling, I would imagine."

Kozel was breathing normally again. "To take it, yes. But to hold it?"

Lilia waved her hand dismissively. "Who cares? If the Rus cannot hold it, they will burn it to the ground as they retreat. That serves our purpose well enough."

"But why allow chaos to win such a cheap and easy battle? The rule of law, the power of order, should—"

She put her hand up, interrupting him. "It should, and will, take its rightful place, my dear. Rest assured that our lord and unholy master will rule over all dominions with total authority and with every single detail accounted for. Do not concern yourself with the path as much as the final result. 'Chaos with a means to an end' is how you put it to the orc, was it not? One of your more thoughtful statements in that whole exchange."

Kozel was about to say something rash but then reconsidered. "Well, who am I to not trust the will of the Unholy?"

Lilia's eyes flashed red as she smiled at him. "Exactly, Kozel darling. Exactly."

He sat up straight, his hands folded neatly in his lap. "So then, Mistress. What would you have me do instead of travel to Gavan?"

"Well, let us speak of knights and bishops still on the board instead of pawns, my dear. Let us return to this loathsome orc of yours. Or do you consider *him* merely a pawn?"

Knowing the question was a trap, Kozel did his best to spring it slowly. "He is a formidable opponent, Mistress. But I left him on the floor, badly injured, and it will take some time for him to recover. Even if I, or someone in my stead if I am to be replaced, am not allowed to finish the job quickly, he should still be in Stren when it is taken. The Rus, or perhaps even that sheriff, can dispatch him easily enough in his current state. I am sure Kira can pin some sort of crime on him if need be."

She nodded. "That sounds reasonable enough. Just let him bide his time, then?"

Kozel could feel the jaws of her trap closing, but there was nothing he could do. "What concerns you, Mistress?"

Lilia perched her chin on her hands, presenting almost a coquettish look. "While we have been having this lovely chat, my dear, have you given any more thought as to why you suffered such horrible wounds at the hands of a mortal? Even a brute of a mortal?"

"The orc's weapon, Mistress. It must be that, not the orc

himself. But I had no time to inspect it, so I can only—"

She reached across the table and slapped him hard across his face. "You mean you didn't *bother* to inspect it, you arrogant fool! Instead, you invited the orc to a gentlemanly discussion, and you built him a fire! You might as well have bought him dinner and let him suckle at your breast while you were at it!"

Kozel reeled from the blow, more mentally than physically. Doubt clouded his mind like never before.

Have I become that numb to the potential dangers of the physical plane? Was I really outplayed and outmaneuvered that much by a greyskin and a backwater whore?

Lilia waited until his eyes focused back on hers before continuing. "We were able to study your wounds while you were...indisposed...and discovered a few interesting details about this weapon. First, there were very faint traces of holy water in your system. We assume that imbecile stopped by the local chapel in Stren and dunked his blades in the baptismal font. That seems like an appropriate thing to do for the uninitiated. But, more importantly, we were able to identify some rather unique burn marks around your wounds. We believe they point to why the cuts made by the axe wouldn't close and why you eventually lost your ability to transform."

Kozel knew better than to suggest the burns came from the fireplace he had been pushed into and merely nodded, waiting for her to continue.

Lilia looked at him squarely in the face. "Do you know the

full story behind this *euncheol* you so desperately seek? How and why it came into existence?"

Kozel gasped, his gut feeling like it had been split open once again. "How...?" He shook his head. "The metal...it exists? It *actually* exists? That...that cannot be..."

"Cannot be possible? Oh, my dear, darling, Kozel, it can be and *is* very possible. If only you knew."

The orc's weapon...is made from that?! *After all this time, after all my searching,* this *is how I discover that silver iron exists?* Kozel stared silently into space, attempting to comprehend what Lilia had just told him.

"Tell me what you *think* you know about your precious metal," she prodded him after several moments.

He looked at her, anger, frustration, and disbelief coursing through his veins. It was all he could do to not scream. "All the human legends say that the eldar discovered the metal deep in the ground, and they secretly hoarded it as they built their empire. Nobody knows where their mines were located, or how the material could be forged. Nobody even truly knows if this 'silver iron' even exists! All the so-called examples of this metal that I have found stored away in crypts and treasure troves have been nothing but well-crafted forgeries and lies."

Surely, this is a lie as well. She must be wrong, or she must be tormenting me for some purpose...

Something barely short of desperation tore at him now as Lilia looked at him with eyes that seemed to mock his very essence.

"*Please* tell me you taunt me with this fantasy, Mistress! I have searched for this metal for so long, and you want me to believe that this, this mangy *dog*, wields a weapon of legendary proportions? It simply cannot be!"

She sighed deeply. "You really have spent too much time among the humans, Kozel. You have taken on their petty desires and have forgotten that we are above such things as earthly possessions. But, perhaps in this one instance, I can be somewhat charitable in tolerating your overly dramatic behavior."

"Whatever do you mean by that?" he muttered, hating her all the more.

"That your beloved *euncheol* is not borne of Terra."

"What?!"

Her face grew grim, and her next words resonated with longing hatred. "When the war in the cosmos happened at the beginning of time, and our master was cheated of victory, we were cast out from the place that shall one day be ours again. But the archenemy, in their arrogance, believed that they had won the war for all of eternity. Thus, their soldiers threw down their weapons and their armor, and they pledged fealty and peace amongst themselves.

"Such was the archenemy's haste and foolishness in ridding themselves of their tools of war, they were simply cast aside without a thought. Falling like rocks from the sky, these items were torn asunder or burned apart as they plummeted down across all creation. What remained of this celestial material struck the ground with such force as to be buried far beneath the surface of Terra. There, the scattered pieces waited to be found, reforged, and used once again.

"The eldar, being the first race, *did* find this metal, as your human fables state. Without true faith, they could forge the metal into items of great beauty and great terror, but they could only master its physical properties. It helped them hold sway over many lands for over a millennia, but it was not enough to stop their inevitable decline. Since then, we have done our best to hide the results of their craftsmanship and erase the memory of even the existence of such a metal as best we can."

Kozel stared at Lilia, a chill running down his spine. If her story was true, then he instantly understood why the metal had been hidden away from humanity.

If the eldar had no souls, no wonder they could not fully appreciate or gain control over the metal. But humans...

He shivered at the possibilities. "What such weapons could do in the hands of those who fully believe in our accursed enemy!"

Lilia nodded soberly. "Yes, my dearest. So, while I do not approve of the manner you went about discovering the properties of the orc's weapon, it is well and good that you did, so that the issue can be properly investigated."

He bowed his head slightly, succeeding in swallowing his sarcastic retort to her backhanded compliment.

She carried on as if not noticing the scowl on his face. "So, now we have an unknown orc, in possession of both a holy writ and a weapon of untapped holy power, somehow showing up exactly where he shouldn't be. Not only that, but he appears to be in regular communication with someone with intrinsic knowledge of old magic. And finally, he just happens to stumble into the most devout priest this side of Konstantine in the middle of the Wilds while fighting off your wargs."

She looked at him with a concerned look on her face. "As you can imagine, the central office has already passed this information on to the high lords. For they believe as I do, that we have a dangerous rogue element on hand that has not been accounted for in our planning."

Kozel looked at her closely, sensing a slight change in her demeanor.

By all that is unholy, that's not concern in her eyes—that's fear! Perhaps there is a way out of this mess where I can regain trust after all. But I must have that weapon!

He cleared his throat and spoke carefully. "Mistress, is there any...unease...on the part of, uh, *others*, that the archenemy has staged all of this? To actively draw us out?"

She was silent for a long moment before responding. "*Others* have indeed raised that issue, my dear. But I have argued that your preliminary assessment in the field was the correct one: the orc has appeared coincidentally for unrelated reasons, as unfortunate as that may be. For him to be installed by our adversaries to directly foil our plans would speak to a level of duplicity and cunning they are not known for. We must remember to think like they do in cases such as this.

"The orc told you himself that he was not in Stren to meet with the priest. You have already sent that wench of yours to confirm this directly with the priest, which was a prudent step. If there has been any damage to the overall mission, it has been field triaged to the best of our abilities, and we have been given time to react."

For the first time, a look of smug satisfaction appeared on her face. "Because of this, I have successfully argued that you should remain in your current position. You will continue with your overall assignment, and you will continue to report to me so long as I deem your, uh, results, to be satisfactory. So, despite your recent shortcomings, you will not be detained for rehabilitation."

Well, some good news at last. Time to lick the boot that kicks you.

Kozel bowed so low that his forehead almost touched the table. "Your unworthy servant thanks you, Mistress. As always, I serve at your pleasure."

"Mmm, darling, I just knew you would say that. But my pleasure must wait, as much as it pains me to say it. For you have a new field order that must be carried out immediately. The priest, Malachi Ghent, must die."

Kozel did a double take. "The priest, and *not* the orc?"

"The orc is a stranger who would find it hard to make allies if he even wanted to, and he seems to know nothing of the power he carries. The priest is revered by the local population and has been a known threat for quite some time. Even now, the prayers coming from Stren for his healing are as incessant as the mewling of hungry children! This Malachi is the real danger to us and the mission, *not* the orc.

"The fact that getting rid of him would have spawned more inquisitorial interest than could be reasonably tolerated has long kept him alive and unsullied. But now, the next phase of our plan is so close to kicking off that nothing can be left to chance. That includes the chance, be it ever so low, that this priest could come into possession of a mighty holy weapon. No, the odds have decisively swung against him, and he must be taken off the board. Immediately."

Now Kozel smiled, scarcely believing what he had just heard. "So, I am to be unleashed? The gloves are coming finally off?"

"Not completely off, my dear, as there must be some tact involved in how this is accomplished. We do not need to barge into the sanctuary of the enemy, as it were, and announce our intent. That and you are still in a weakened state, and I would just hate for that priest to take a piece of you away from me."

He briefly reconsidered, and his smile broadened. "There is already a solution close at hand, Mistress. One that does not directly involve me."

She thought for a moment. "Kira? That lowborn human would fulfill this task for you?" Before he could respond, she added in a surprised tone, "You would have your beloved do this for you?"

"She must do as I command, Mistress. And I offer her services to you as a gift of fealty."

"What do you mean that she must...?" Lilia's eyes opened wide. "Your deal with her! Oh, my darling and cunning Kozel! You magnificent beast, what must that seed-eating harlot do for you?"

You really are jealous of her, aren't you, my dear Lilia? Vanity truly is your weakness.

"She must deliver to me the results of three mortal sins of my choosing, no matter the cost to her personally. Murdering the priest in cold blood will count as her first task being fulfilled."

Lilia's enthusiasm seemed to wane slightly. "Mmm, that sounds quite delicious, my dear, but that doesn't seem like much in the grand scheme of things. How many mortal sins has she already committed in her short lifetime?"

"Oh countless, if you go by the letter of the law. Which those in power will, even if she personally will not see it that way. But the requirement of our deal is that my demands are mortal sins she *knows* to be wrong from the outset, ones that she would not do otherwise without my bidding. Committing them will shatter her personal code of ethics and I daresay will break her spirit. She will be left adrift and alone."

Lilia licked her lips, and her nipples became visible through the thin gown she was wearing as they hardened with her arousal. "Oh, Kozel! I had no idea you were such a scoundrel! I can almost taste her already."

She rose gracefully and started to walk around the table

towards him, her form slowly shedding clothing as she came closer. Her long hair slowly twisted about her so that he could only see a hint of her most delectable parts, teasing him as the strands swayed back and forth.

"But, darling, how do you know she won't escape your grasp in the end? All this effort wasted if she calls out for forgiveness, even with her last breath. And after you've tempted me with such a delicious treat." She straddled him, moaning as she did so, as if begging him to impale her on the table. As he reached up to lightly touch her sides, she played with his hair and looked at him with smoldering eyes. "My dearest poppet. How can you be so sure you won't disappoint me in the end? How do you know this Kira Toth will be mine to devour?"

Kozel knew full well that Lilia had no real concept of true grace, just like he did not. The fact that the accursed enemy seemingly offered full repentance to any human who truly asked for it was an inconceivable idea, if not an utterly ridiculous one. But to outright mention the enemy's true love for humanity could be deemed treasonous, and someone was always listening. He glanced at the mirror, assuming that someone was watching them from the other side. Even now, Lilia was skirting close the edge of ruination for both of them.

He attempted to answer her carefully, even as she distracted him with her simpering. "If I can break Kira's spirit and make her believe that salvation is impossible, then she will do our job for us. For how can she be freed from sin if she never asks to be freed?

How can she ask for something she cannot even comprehend? She will slip quietly into the abyss, an unredeemable soul, and then she will be yours."

Lilia placed her hand on his chest, his shirt burning away at her touch. "You would do this for me, my dearest? My *love*?"

He felt his final inhibitions stripped away, and he could resist her no longer. "I...I would do anything for you, Mistress..."

"*Anything?*" she repeated impishly. "Would you do *this* for me?"

Her form transformed before Kozel's eyes, and now Kira was sitting naked atop him. She pressed close to him, tearing at his flesh.

Her lips brushed his ear as she desperately whispered to him in a familiar, husky voice. "Ya sure ya don't want this form instead, luv? Ya think ya can handle me?"

He could smell honey on her breath, and the rapid switch from Abyssal to Common threw him for just an instant. He grasped Kira's sides firmly to center himself, holding her close.

Lilia immediately pulled back, frowning at the apparent intimate action. "So, it's like that, dearest?"

"No! Mistress, I—"

She disappeared from view, and Kozel's chair was yanked away by some unseen entity behind him, leaving him flailing. Rough hands grabbed him and threw him face down on the table, and there was the low rumble of harsh laughter.

A familiar voice tore into Kozel, speaking in the Orcish

language that he loathed. "I'll do tha handlin' in here, *suka*! Come find me when tha priest is dead, an' maybe I'll have another go at ya! Go, *now*!"

There was a flash of light, and Kozel was cast out into nothingness.

CHAPTER THIRTEEN

One Night of Solace

Sarl drifted in and out of consciousness for what seemed like an eternity. He couldn't remember where he was or why. There had been a fight of some sort, and he had...lost?

That's bloody unlikely! Tha last time I lost a fight was...

He struggled to remember anything beyond the here and now.

Well, sard me sideways. Maybe it was a draw?

He came to his senses enough to realize he was lying on a cot somewhere that smelled faintly like shite, bile, and blood all rolled together. He couldn't tell which of the three odors were emanating from him. His vision remained hazy, but he could tell at least two humans were standing over him.

"Tie him down before...the holy water...his wounds..."

Their words were spoken too quickly and quietly for him to understand what they were saying, but then it felt like someone was securing his arms and legs to the bed. He wanted to swat them away, but his hands were heavy. His head lolled to one side, and he had to concentrate on his breathing. It seemed to be getting darker.

There was a flare of light to his left, and a face appeared above his. It looked so familiar, but he couldn't remember any names beyond his own. What felt like a few drops of rain landed on his cheek, and he wondered why he was lying outside and if it was about to storm.

"Sarl, luv..." The face disappeared from view, and he passed into unsettled dreams.

***

Yuri looked down at the injured and unconscious orc, hands on his hips, annoyed and perplexed.

It was two mornings after the apparent ghoul attack in Stren, and everyone in town was still in an uproar. Mykhailo had been smart enough to send a guard to rouse him immediately after the attack, but that was about all that had gone right for Yuri in the aftermath of the incident. Even the bloody mayor had heard some version of what had happened and was asking questions that couldn't be answered.

An' damn it all, it's tha one time I need Kira tha most an' she's off dealin' with another mystery out in tha Wilds!

He had at least, in his mind, the sense to keep the damn orc in Kira's house where the attack had taken place. Not that it ultimately helped keep news of what happened out of the taverns, but it had given him and the town guard a few hours to work with that first night before everyone fell into hysterics.

Yuri had no idea why that little harlot Katrya had decided to bed the damn orc in her sister's dwelling, but he was going to stay out of any ongoing family squabble and just let the two sisters argue. He actually found it amusing on a perverse level that the younger Toth might be marking out new conquered territory at the expense of Kira.

Maybe I need ta start callin' her Cat instead of Kat, hee-hee-hee...

Also unexplained, and much more vexing, was why the supposed monster had come knocking at Kira's door. Was it just lurking about town for some reason and had chosen a house at random? Was it looking for Kira? Or her sister? Or the damn orc?

It was probably lookin' for tha greyskin, since that's who it brawled with. Maybe those wargs tha orc's been huntin' are its pets? By tha Almighty, suddenly all my problems are due ta cats an' dogs!

Mykhailo wasn't in his pocket, but Yuri knew him to be honest, hardworking, and accountable. Because of that, he had read the squad leader's report several times over, trying to puzzle through everything that had occurred during the fight. A sullen Katrya had corroborated most of what Mykhailo had written, although that didn't mean much to Yuri, since he knew the two had a heated and passionate history from a few years back. It wouldn't surprise him if they were covering for each other about something, but then he couldn't figure out what that might be.

Dammit, Kira! For once, I really need yer big brain an' not yer big breasts. Although I wouldn't mind seein' all of ya right now... Mmm, yeah, I mean... Aargh, focus Yuri, ol' boy, focus! Ya got troubles all over, with a capital T.

It was hard to admit, but the troubles around town came from the only big misstep he knew *he* had made. When he had arrived at the scene of carnage and seen the decapitated body of Taras on the floor, never mind the badly injured orc, he hadn't thought of confining the other guards who had been with Mykhailo to their quarters. That way he could have figured out a story that could be spun for the general population.

But that pathetic coward Marko an' his ramblings messed everything up. I should just string him up for dereliction of duty...

The traumatized guard who had witnessed the attack had shown up at the Oar House as soon as he was off duty that next morning, banging on the door until someone let him in. Marko was raging drunk before Sext, and by midafternoon, the whole dockside was in an uproar over his story of what had happened. Everyone knew that a vile monster had appeared from the abyss the previous night and had slaughtered the first of many victims.

What made things even worse was that Kira hadn't come back yet from the Wilds with a report on Father Malachi. The current rumor circulating the market was that the priest had been mortally wounded in a surprise attack by the Unholy One itself and that Kira and her patrol had been slaughtered as well. There was nothing standing between the town and the minions of the dark lord coming to wreak havoc on all of Stren.

Yuri had set a stricter curfew than usual, but in any event, nobody had been out that next night. The taverns had closed early due to a lack of patrons, there had been a run on prayer candles from the chapel, and threshold charms had sprung up on almost every household. It had been almost impossible to get anyone to man the gates, and absolutely no one had been willing to patrol the streets. He himself had spent a nervous night at the town hall, the large central fire blazing and all the light fixtures lit.

Thankfully, a hole leading straight to the abyss hadn't opened up in the main square and swallowed the town, so frayed nerves had mended somewhat yesterday. But in order to really set things right, he still needed more answers than he currently had.

Before everything had gone to shite on the first day, daylight had led to the discovery of a trail of blood that had started at the back of Kira's house and had gone over the wall behind a nearby stable. Yuri had sent a patrol around the exterior of the town perimeter, and they had easily found the trail again. It led generally westward from town but had disappeared into the forest instead of following any known path. Curiously, the amount of blood left behind was enough that it seemed to have been made by several large beasts. It was certainly more than what could be generated by a single humanoid.

An' now, of course, nobody wants ta follow tha trail out into tha Wilds. How am I supposed ta warn Kira that somethin' may be comin' her way?

It surprised him to find himself legitimately worried about her well-being.

Guess it shows how much I really need her here now. But really, tha last thing I need is for this news ta reach tha Rus an' they start thinkin' I can't handle a small bit of civil unrest.

The front door to Kira's dwelling opened, and Yuri looked up to see Katrya come in from a cold, grey morning. She was laden down with several satchels and bags, and she passed him without a word and began unloading them onto the table near the middle of the large room.

He glanced back at the orc, who remained silent and motionless except for a barely perceptible rising and falling of his bandaged chest. Katrya, no doubt with help from Mykhailo and some others, had moved Kira's bed from upstairs and placed it under the stairwell, and that was where the greyskin had been ever since a few hours after the attack. Yuri noticed, with a bit of annoyance, that Sarl's limbs were no longer bound to the bed frame. He knew it had been done originally to keep the orc from moving too much while he was being treated, but it would have been nice to keep the ropes in place for any initial interrogation as well. Yuri was hopeful the orc would recover at least enough to be conscious so he could get the greyskin's version of what had happened.

"No change yet, huh?" he asked Katrya, more for a conversation starter than anything else.

She muttered something under her breath that he couldn't catch and continued to unload her bags. Yuri could see several large earthen pots with covers that had been strapped in place, and he assumed she had visited the chapel for more holy water and had gotten stew from somewhere.

He walked over to where she was working. "I need ta know when that greyskin wakes up, ya hear?"

She glanced up at him, disdain evident in her eyes. Judging by the circles under them, and her overall haggard appearance, she hadn't slept much the past two nights.

"Yeah, I hear ya, Yuri. Ya only tell me tha same thing every damn time you're in here."

"Well, it's important. I really need ta know that he wasn't meetin' that...that thing for some foul reason."

"God's nails, Yuri! I already told ya, I brought him here ta turn a trick, an' that thing broke inta my sister's house while we was here! Ya gonna ask Kira why a monster wanted ta loot her house when she gets back? Huh?!"

Yuri took a step back. "Easy, Cat, easy..." He doubted he could make a convincing "C" sound instead of a "K" and decided that the joke wasn't worth it. "Ya know I gotta do my job."

"Yer job..." She shook her head. "Then maybe do *yer job* and post a guard at tha chapel. Somebody's been takin' holy water out of tha font. There's barely any left."

"Ya mean, somebody besides yerself?" Yuri patted one of the large vessels on the table.

"'Course that's what I mean. Nobody else in town has been wounded by an infernal, have they? Or are ya not doin' *yer job* of guardin' tha gates ta keep it from comin' back?"

It was all Yuri could do to not slap the rude little bitch. Instead, he leaned in close to her and spoke softly. "Carry on all ya want, Kat. Just know, when yer sister comes back an' that orc wakes up, there are gonna be a lot more questions asked an' a lot more things goin' on 'round here. Maybe yer old friend Mykhailo will have ta do some trackin' for me out in tha Wilds ta see where that monster went. Maybe this orc will need ta spend some time at tha jail gettin' his memory straight. An' maybe, just maybe, Kira will agree with me that stickin' yer arse in a cell next ta tha orc for assaultin' poor Bohdana is tha right thing ta do ta maintain a little law an' order in this town. Eh? What do ya think 'bout all that?"

Katrya looked like she was going to haul back and slug him, and he wished with all his heart that she would. But instead, she looked down and away and said nothing.

"Oh, what's tha matter now? Cat got yer tongue?" Yuri couldn't help himself and laughed. "Just make sure ta find me tha instant this here lover of yers wakes up. Now if you'll excuse me, Mayor Freya is actually awake this mornin' an' needs attendin' to."

He took one last look at the orc before shaking his head and walking out into the street. The sky fit his mood, dark and looking like a bad storm was on the horizon.

Maybe that damn monster from tha abyss will freeze in tha snow that's comin' an' save me some trouble. Dammit, Kira, ya need ta get that cute arse of yers back here on tha double!

Yuri grinned at his ever-present rhyming mastery and stomped off to tend to the mayor.

***

Drifting back into consciousness, Sarl sensed there was someone in bed next to him, and they had cold feet. Keeping his eyes closed, he attempted to assess his personal physical condition before anything else.

It hurt to breathe too deeply, and he could tell that his chest and upper arms were heavily bandaged. His head felt like someone had just finished smacking him around with a hammer, and he was incredibly thirsty. However, by shifting slightly, he could tell that he still had all his limbs and that none of them were restrained.

Well, I've awoken ta worse things, I suppose.

He didn't sense any bright lights through his closed eyelids, so he assumed it was nighttime. Which night it was, he had no idea. It certainly wasn't the same night as the fight, but how many had passed since then?

The figure next to him stirred, as if sensing he was awake, and he could feel their body turn. They must have been studying his face, as a hand lightly touched his brow, as if measuring his temperature. Fingers moved through his hair, and lips pressed lightly against his cheek. He could smell lavender and smiled.

"Sarl? Ya there?"

He opened his eyes to a dimly lit room. He could just make out Katrya's face hovering above his, her worried look giving way to one of relief.

"Hey, Kat..."

Before he could get any more words out, she leaned down and kissed him firmly on the lips. Her hands pressed against his shoulders as she kissed him, as if to pin him in place so he couldn't escape. Despite his bandages, he was able to bring his arms up in something of an embrace, but he quickly discovered that holding her too closely was too painful for the wounds on his chest.

As if sensing his discomfort, Katrya pulled back to look him in the eyes. She smiled and, giving his shoulders a squeeze, left the bed. She was soon back with a mug, and at her beckoning and with her assistance, Sarl proceeded to take sips from it. It was a bitter-tasting liquid, but such was his thirst that he drank it without complaint.

"How long I been out?" he asked when the mug was empty.

"It's tha third night since tha fight," she responded. "Things were touch an' go for 'bout tha first two days, but you've been sleepin' peaceful-like since this mornin'."

"Where am I?"

She snorted. "Still in tha same room, luv."

This surprised him. "Yer sister's place?"

She nodded in response. Sarl did his best to look around, and it appeared he was lying in a bed that had been placed on the ground floor of Kira's house. He was under the staircase, off to the side of the large main room. He couldn't tell how much of the mess from the fight with Kozel had been cleaned up, but it wasn't a big enough issue for him to be concerned about.

He looked back at Katrya. "An' how does Kira feel 'bout me bein' here?"

Katrya put the empty mug on the floor and held his hand. "She's still out in tha Wilds, so she don't know. It didn't seem right ta move ya in yer condition, an' there really ain't nowhere else ta take ya anyways. Nowhere that ain't a shitehole, at least."

"So not yer place, huh?" He winked at her, and she huffed in mock irritation as she grinned.

"You really are an arse, ya know that, right?"

"Always, Kat. Always. But, seriously, why not take me back ta tha Wild Boar? Yer boss, ol' Bainor, he don't want me lyin' 'round in one of his rooms above tha tavern, gettin' rent money for doin' nothin'?"

She looked away. After a moment, she muttered, "Bainor an' me ain't talkin' right now."

"Oh? How's come?"

"Well, I went in ta see him tha mornin' after tha attack ta get yer stuff that ya left with him. Yer sweet 'Dana' was there, an' I guess she was still sore at me from tha night before. We sorta had words 'bout some things."

Sarl doubted that Bohdana, one of the other tavern barmaids who had flirted with him earlier, was *that* angry about him going off with Katrya instead of her. He assumed there was a long-standing feud between the two women. "So, uh, why does Bainor care that tha two of ya—"

Katrya made a short raspberry sound with her lips and looked back at him with an exasperated expression that immediately shifted into something more like chagrin. "Sorry, luv, I keep forgettin' that you're new 'round here. He's her uncle."

Sarl, opened his mouth to say another arsehole-worthy comment, then thought better of it. "Ah, I see. So, he picked a side in tha argument?"

"Yeah...I mighta helped him pick a side when I laid her out with a good left."

Sarl started to laugh, but it was hard to catch his breath, and he wound up in a coughing fit instead. Katrya looked away again, her hands fidgeting in her lap, as she waited for him to recover.

"Remind me not ta make ya too mad at me, Kat."

"She's had it comin' for a while. Anyways, I best not show my face in there for a bit. Bainor will get over it, or my sister will make him get over it once she's back."

Yeah, yer sister...

Sarl hadn't had too much time to think about the jailer being Katrya's sister, other than her apparent connections to both Yuri and Kozel. But the mention of her sparked several thoughts now.

"So, Kira's still out talkin' with tha priest an' that farmer?"

Katrya shrugged. "Far as I know. She said it might be a few days."

Sarl didn't know who in Stren, if anyone, would know of the severity of the priest's wounds beyond what he had reported. But it was easily understandable to him why Kira might be having a bit of trouble talking with Malachi.

"An' what 'bout Yuri? I assume he's poked his nose in here. He can't be too happy I'm messin' up his love nest."

"Oh yeah, he's been here. The night watch told him 'bout tha attack, an' he came here straight away. It was actually him that said ta keep ya here. Pretty sure that's 'cause he didn't want nobody seein' ya and even more stories gettin' out 'bout what happened."

Sarl smirked. “More stories?”

“Yeah, there’s plenty already all ’round town as it is. Ya can’t hide somebody dyin’ in a place like this, especially when they die ’cause their head got taken off by some monster. From what I know, Mykhailo tried ta downplay what happened in his report, but one of tha other guards went on a drinkin’ binge an’ told everyone at tha Oar House what he’d seen. Whole town is in an uproar now.”

“I bet,” Sarl mused.

Hopefully, that means it’ll be harder for Koz ta sneak in an’ either cause more trouble or try an’ finish me off. But it may not have ta come back if it can get Kira ta do its dirty work now, right? ’Cept I don’t think that bastard would let anyone gut me without at least bein’ there ta see it. I may be safe for a bit, but I better not push things by stayin’ here.

He attempted to sit up, and immediately the hammering sensation in his head returned. He winced and fell back against his pillow.

Katrya bent down beside the bed and came back up with a good-sized bowl that had a wet towel in it. She picked the towel up and squeezed excess liquid out of it before applying it to Sarl’s forehead. His pain immediately eased considerably, and he smiled weakly at her.

“Thanks, Kat.”

She gestured at the bowl. “Ya sure were right ’bout that holy water, luv. It cleaned up yer cuts straight away, and it seems ta help with everythin’ else, too.”

"Huh...just think what it's doin' for that priest of yers, then. He's definitely more worthy of attention from yer Almighty then I'll ever be."

Katrya frowned. "How's he gonna get holy water out in tha Wilds?"

"I went ta tha chapel an' got some for yer sister 'fore she left."

Katrya nodded her head. Sarl wondered if she was going to ask if he was the one who had broken the lock on the cover of the chapel's font, but her mind was apparently elsewhere.

"I'm worried 'bout Father Malachi an' my sister. I mean, with that thing out in tha Wilds. Mykhailo told me that they found a trail of blood headin' west, but there ain't nobody here that wants ta follow it."

For once, Sarl thought for a moment before speaking. "Well, I don't think that ugly shite will want ta meet up with yer priest anytime soon, given his condition. As for yer sister...well, unless she's crossed it somehow, I don't think it'll touch her either, Kat. 'Cause of...well, ya know."

She sighed and slowly shook her head. "I just can't believe she'd deal with that...that thing."

"Desperate people take desperate measures, Kat. Look at what you're doin' with me."

He meant it as a joke, but instead of laughing, she bit her lip and went to smooth the towel on his forehead.

"Don't go thinkin' too highly of yerself, luv. Yuri really

wants ta talk ta ya, so he figured somebody had ta try an' nurse ya back ta health. He ain't too happy with me stayin' here ta do it, but nobody else wanted tha job."

Sarl looked closely at her face as she leaned in close to him. There was determination in her looks, but he could sense the underlying desperation in her as well. Her eyes seemed to flit back and forth, the look of a cornered animal never leaving for long.

Still searchin' for tha best way outta here, Kat? But are ya really gonna ditch everyone else in this shite town an' tie yerself ta me? Are ya really gonna ditch yer sister?

"Ya ain't barely left my side, have ya, Kat? Is that why Bainor's sore at ya, that ya ain't showin' up for work?"

"Shush, now," was all she said in return, although her face grew red. She fussed with the towel for a bit longer before he gently grabbed her wrist. Whether her support and care were born out of pure selfishness or not, he knew he'd be in much worse shape—or even dead—without her.

"Kat, I won't leave ya here ta rot. I owe ya that much."

Her eyes went wet, but she remained silent as she disentangled her wrist from his grasp and took the towel back.

He studied her for a long moment before saying something he knew she didn't want to hear. "But I think you're gonna have to choose me or yer sister."

Katrya let out a shaky breath, and the tears left her eyes and slowly rolled down her face. She nodded, almost absent mindedly. "Is that what that thing told ya?"

"Sorta, yeah. It said that yer sister warned it off hurtin' ya, but it sure ain't gonna go outta its way ta help ya neither. Even if ya wanted that kind of help."

"How's it helpin' Kira?"

"It didn't say outright, but from what it did say, I'm thinkin' she wants it ta help her get outta here. Or at least be in charge here."

Katrya scoffed at his last sentence. "Nah, no way does she want ta be in charge of this shitehole. Unless that's tha only way to get out, like ya said. I just..." She sighed again. "I just really can't believe she'd deal with that thing."

Sarl didn't know what to say in reply, so he wisely kept his mouth shut and dropped the topic.

The two of them chatted about unimportant things for a time, and Sarl was able to eat. He was ravenous and was delighted to find that Katrya had secured some of the Wild Boar's excellent goulash, her feud with Bainor and Bohdana notwithstanding. He ate his fill and then some. He didn't want to admit it, but it tasted even better without the tavern's awful ale around to wash it down.

Katrya changed his bandages, and they were both surprised at how well the wounds were healing. He would definitely have some new scars, but that didn't bother him in the least. She grew quiet as she smeared a poultice across his chest and reapplied the wrappings, and Sarl decided not to tease her about it as she worked.

It was late into the night by the time Sarl attempted to sleep again. He felt stronger than even a couple hours ago, but he also sensed he'd be on the mend for a bit longer. Katrya simply kissed him on the forehead and settled in next to him on the bed, to which he had no complaints.

Eventually, she turned and carefully put her head just below his, her cheek against his chest, as if she was listening to his heartbeat. He held her loosely, his hands interlocked around her back. Whenever she stirred, her hair tickled his nose, threatening to make him sneeze. He hardly minded, as it felt natural to hold her in this position, and he would inhale deeply every time her movement woke him up. There was the hint of lavender in her hair that always seemed to accompany her, but something about her closeness made her scent more exotic than usual.

His mind raced, and it was impossible for him to sleep. The next time she shifted, he gently kissed the top of her head, and in return, she squeezed his left side ever so slightly. It was as if each of them was drifting out of their own dream worlds, not quite believing the other was there and needing the physical reminders as an anchor to reality.

Sarl broke his loose grip around her, and his left hand drifted down to the side of her torso, lightly stroking her skin.

She shuddered and pulled away slightly at this, but she didn't seem overly upset. "Stop it, luv. That tickles..." she murmured, nuzzling him at the same time.

Sarl shifted slightly so that they were lying more beside each other on the bed, and he did as she requested, placing his hand on her hip. "Weak spot, huh?" he whispered back, chuckling.

She huffed at him, lightly. “Mmm, maybe...”

Now, she shifted, and her movement lightly brushed his hand out of the way as she slipped hers around him instead. Their bodies were still close together, side by side. A warm feeling in Sarl’s gut began to grow as she began to stroke the back of his leg, and his mouth went dry.

“I think ya found *my* weak spot,” he whispered.

Her response was to grip his buttocks and squeeze gently. In return, he squeezed her whole body closely and desperately wished for the moment to never end. Whatever pain he still had in his chest and arms was being completely ignored by both of them now.

Katrya released her grip but kept her hand on his body, sliding it slowly up and forwards. She paused briefly when she reached his upper thigh, and the scent coming from her hair seemed to intensify. Sarl slowly swung his hip open, indicating his need and desire for her. She continued forward, slipping inside his trousers, her light stroke setting him ablaze.

Her hair shifted away from his nose as she slid down his body, and he released her midsection with his right hand to grip the bed frame instead. He lay back in a supine position, and her continued movements compelled him to widen his legs. Katrya seemed to sense that she was in control, and she pressed her advantage. It was all Sarl could do to keep breathing, and his chest heaved in rhythm with her actions.

As she worked, she stripped him of both clothing and any

lingering sense of impropriety until he lay bare before her. He moved to invert her above him, but she wriggled away and calmly placed the palm of her left hand on his stomach, anchoring him in place with her cool touch. His vision blurred, and he gave up doing anything but enjoying her presence and the path she was taking him down.

Eventually, Katrya's form appeared above him, and she kissed him forcefully on the mouth as she mounted him. A slight grunt escaped her lips as they joined, but otherwise, she was silent as she began to sway. He gripped her hips and sought to keep her close, wanting to give her as much of himself as he possibly could, but she obviously had other ideas.

Arching her back and slowly increasing the speed and ferocity of her thrusts, her hair fell back behind her as she looked up at the ceiling.

The dim light of dawn coming through the dirty windows in the front of the room was still enough to paint her body in a dazzling white, almost blinding Sarl. There was nothing for him to do except to follow where she led. He moaned her name as her essence consumed him, and all sense of time slipped away. Soon enough, though, she extracted every drop of being that he had.

When Sarl could finally focus again, he found Katrya gazing down at him, something of a wry smile on her face. His hands were still on her hips, but his grip had gone slack and there seemed to be little strength in any part of him now. It was all he could do to smile faintly back at her.

Katrya leaned down and kissed him again squarely on the mouth. “Good mornin’, luv,” she whispered before dismounting and moving back to her original position next to him.

The last thing Sarl remembered before exhaustion took him was her head on his chest and her hair tickling his nose.

CHAPTER FOURTEEN

Bad Intentions

Hannah was already looking up at the doorway when Kira burst through it, a contorted look of anger on her face. She had obviously heard the commotion from the other room. Now, even as Kira slowed to take in the scene before her, Hannah's knuckles visibly whitened as she clenched the bandage wrap she held in both hands.

"No, no, *no*!" she hissed. "Not now! Father Malachi needs his rest and is in no position to be interrogated by the likes of *you*!"

"Tha likes of *me*? That ain't very mannerly of ya ta say!" Kira frowned as she pointed an accusing finger at the other woman. "Maybe ya shoulda told me he was awake an' let *me* decide when he can talk!"

For an instant, Hannah looked like she was going to curse, but instead she closed her eyes and muttered something under her breath. While she calmed herself, Kira walked over to the foot of the bed to get a better look at the patient. He was not a sight for the faint of heart, and the blood-soaked mattress bore witness to what he had gone through. Kira knew in an instant that Hannah must have been pushed to the utmost limits of her not-insignificant healing capabilities to keep the priest alive even for this long.

He was breathing evenly, at least, and most of the blood on the mattress or wrappings didn't appear to be fresh. As Kira observed him, his eyes fluttered open as he seemed to sense somebody new in the room. He didn't attempt to focus on her face but rather turned his head slightly from side to side.

"Who's...who's there?" he whispered faintly.

"It's Kira Toth, Father," Kira responded calmly. She could tell that he recognized her voice immediately.

"Ah...Kira...you came all this way...just to see me?"

The old man smiled and attempted to raise his hand in greeting. Hannah looked quickly back and forth between the two in surprise, but she remained silent as Kira went to kneel at the bedside by the priest's head. She took the offered hand up in hers, holding it gently.

He closed his eyes again and spoke in a halting, but clear voice. "I suppose...you came to hear my confession, eh? The tables turned, for once? I must warn you...there may be others better equipped than you...to give last rites..."

Kira couldn't help but smile at this gibe.

Damnit, old man! Ya always know what ta say ta me!

"Ya know me, Father, I gotta get yer story 'bout tha wargs if you're up ta tellin' it. I can wait a bit for ya ta get yer bearings if ya need tha time. But as for last rites, we both know you're gonna outlive me, so I expect ta receive 'em from ya, not give 'em ta ya."

Hannah muttered something else under her breath that Kira chose not to hear.

The priest squeezed her hand, more firmly than she would have expected. "Just a simple prayer then, dear Kira."

She looked evenly over at the other woman as she answered him. "Well, if I'm gonna pray for anyone, it'll be for ya, Father."

The priest opened his eyes and looked up at her. "Any prayer…said in earnest…is gladly accepted." He glanced over at Hannah. "But for now, I would ask…that you join me in a prayer…of gratitude. For the Shoikos family. I would not be here to be…interrogated…by anyone if not for them."

Kira swallowed and Hannah looked away and down, both of them embarrassed by what the priest had said.

Before Kira could say anything else or pull away, Malachi closed his eyes and began to whisper in Latin. "Oh, give thanks unto the Almighty, for they are good; for their mercy endureth forever. Oh, give thanks unto the God of gods; for their mercy endureth forever…"

Kira bowed her head slightly, but she maintained her gaze on the priest. His face and body had been cleaned and his wounds expertly dressed, and yet from the mere sight of him, she knew he was lucky to be alive. Experience told her that far fewer wounds had killed many a man. Her mind raced with questions as she listened to Hannah quietly recite the psalm in unison with Malachi.

As the prayer ended, there was a sound at the door, and both women looked up to see Maryska standing in the doorway. She was holding a platter of sorts with several mugs and bowls on it, and she pointedly addressed Hannah.

"Mother, it's time for Father Malachi's medicines."

"Thank you, my dear." Hannah stood up, took the tray from

her daughter, and then placed it on a small table that stood on her side of the bed.

As Kira followed her actions, she noticed the table had an open shelf near the floor, probably normally used to store shoes or miscellaneous objects. What she saw there was of much greater interest to her than shoes.

Tha priest's ledger! That's gotta be it!

Hannah began to work with the various medicines at the table, and Maryska entered the room to gather up the accumulated soiled rags and bandages from around the bed. Neither looked at Kira as she quietly schemed about getting the book, but after a long moment of silence, Hannah addressed her curtly.

"Medicine, now. Questions, later."

Kira's face hardened, but before she could form a retort, she felt pressure on her hand again. She looked down at the priest, and he smiled weakly at her again.

"I'll make sure...they don't poison me..." He nodded faintly in the direction of the door. "Please, my child..."

His simple request moved her more than Hannah's demand. Kira nodded in return and slowly disentangled herself from him.

"I'll be back in a while, Father. Don't ya worry 'bout that." She bowed to him and went to make her way out of the room.

As she reached the doorway, Hannah coughed sharply and caught her up in a steely gaze. "If you must return, at least go and wash your hands and face first! And leave those boots of yours in the other room! I will not have any more filth in here than can be helped."

Kira raised her eyebrows at the venom in Hannah's voice, but she nodded silently and left the bedroom. Maryska followed her out but continued outside with her collection of bloodied waste. Kira was left alone with her thoughts in the large common space of the homestead.

Crossing over to the table, she helped herself to another mug of mead and drank it hastily. She wanted to curse at the top of her lungs but didn't want to give Hannah the satisfaction of knowing she had gotten under her skin.

I got yer filth right here, ya unsufferable holy cunt!

Tossing her mug back on the table, Kira made for the front door. She almost ran into Maryska on the way out, startling the girl as they crossed paths on the stoop.

"Tell that...tell yer ma that I'm goin' ta inspect tha site of tha attack on Father Malachi. An' I'll make sure ta clean up 'fore she has ta acknowledge me presence again!"

Kira strode off, deciding not to care what Maryska or any of the other Shoikos family members might think of her. Without any hesitation, she struck out towards her goal on her own. There was plenty of daylight left, it not even being Sext yet, by her reckoning, and she wasn't overly concerned about visiting the attack scene all by herself.

A couple wolves ain't no concern if they're still out there, no matter how big they are. 'Sides, if I took any of tha troop with me, I'd probably end up stranglin' them.

Kira's path took her almost directly west from the farm, following what amounted to a worn horse trail through the thinned-out woods. Based upon what both the orc and Mykola had told her, she didn't have far to go, perhaps a bit more than half a league. The day's weather was brisk but dry, and the fresh air helped clear her head as she walked.

The site was easy enough to find, with the wagon still laying on its side and its contents scattered about. It hadn't rained since the day of the attack, and she was able to easily make out the tracks of various wargs and two humanoids around the wagon. The bodies of three wargs lay close to it, all with various visible wounds. It appeared that a large object had been dragged away to the north, and Kira assumed it was the remains of the priest's horse.

Walking only a few paces past the wagon, she quickly discovered four more warg bodies. They were strewn about a large oak tree, and she surmised this was where the priest and orc had made their stand together. Even from a distance, she could see the stab wounds and large slash marks on the wargs that paid tribute to the weapons that had been used in their slaughter.

All of the corpses reeked horribly, as if they were far more decomposed than they should have been after just a few days. The fly situation was terrible, especially for this late in the year, and they seemed compelled to attack Kira as she stepped in to take a closer look at one of the bodies. She could only make a hasty inspection of it before being forced back. The main thing she could ascertain was that, aside from the one head the orc had taken as a prize, the corpses did not appear to have been disturbed by anything or anyone other than the flies.

It was easy to find the remains of the priest's horse, which had been dragged about fifty paces away to a small clearing. Unlike the wargs, the poor nag's body had been almost completely consumed. Kira found it odd that absolutely nothing was left of its inner organs. Even the intestines appeared to have been eaten, or at least removed.

A quick reconnoiter of the surrounding woods did not turn up any more warg bodies, although it appeared there had been at least several more in the general vicinity due to the amount of broken underbrush. She did find the remains of a buck farther to the west, its condition being similar to the priest's nag. It was a recent kill, and she supposed it was just another victim of the ravenous beasts.

Overall, the evidence confirmed in Kira's mind that a warg attack of some sort had actually happened. She grudgingly decided that the basic framework of the orc's story made sense, but she still had many questions. She knelt at the back of the wagon to look at the ground more closely.

I still can't tell why tha wargs attacked tha priest in tha first place. Is it just a case of bein' in tha wrong place at tha wrong time? Seems too much of a coincidence. By tha wheel an' hoof marks, he was movin' when they jumped him. One went for him, tha other two went for tha nag.

Ol' Malachi must have got tha one in tha throat an' was

thrown clear, an' then...I guess tha orc took out tha other two? But where did he come from? Was he already here, just waitin' ta meet Malachi?

She glanced back at the oak tree, trying to recreate the rest of the fight in her mind.

Then, four more beasts came in ta press tha attack, an' almost immediately after tha first three. There wasn't time ta make a defensive position, at least. Assumin' they all attacked at once, it's pure luck only one got through. Luck, or maybe providence...although real providence would've had that damn orc take a bite ta tha leg 'stead of Malachi!

She spit on the ground in disgust.

Just too many coincidences...

Trying to make more sense of things, she went about inspecting the wagon and what remained of its contents. Father Malachi's wardrobe, meager as it was, lay immediately next to the wagon. Inside the wagon, she found some rudimentary cooking utensils and a small axe, presumably for making kindling. Having the priest's strange dagger already in her possession back in Stren, she wasn't surprised at the lack of additional weaponry.

After all, he ain't tha kind ta carry an extra mace 'round with him.

A small chest lay nearby, along with an assortment of quills and ink pots. The priest didn't appear to have a personal journal, and Kira already knew where his official ledger was, so she paid little attention to the writing paraphernalia. A larger, unopened chest proved to contain the symbols of the Eucharist, along with a simple serving tray and goblet made of silver.

After inspecting the items closely, Kira bound the chest up again. She then paused to take another look around the general area of the wagon, noting the rest of the items she could see spread about.

A bible, a simple cross, some rosary beads...some crusts of bread an' a water flask...candles...all tha earthly items you'd expect a priest ta have. So, what could be missin'?

She suddenly laughed aloud at herself.

That sardin' orc! He took tha priest's lockbox!

Just to make sure she wasn't missing anything else important, Kira started to slowly walk in an ever-widening circle around the point of attack. As she checked the ground for any additional clues or objects that shouldn't be there, her mind raced, attempting to poke holes in her theory that the orc had stolen tax and tithe money alike.

She supposed that Sarl could have just salvaged the lockbox from the attack site and given it to the farmer to hold, just like he had the ledger. But the orc hadn't mentioned the lockbox at all to her, and he would have known its importance. The family hadn't mentioned it to her either, but surely they would have if they had known about it.

But they didn't tell ya 'bout the priest wakin' up, now did they? Or tha ledger for that matter.

Kira dug through a pile of leaves with her sword, uncovering only some rotting branches, as she continued to think. As much as she disliked Hannah and her ilk, she couldn't pin the absence of the lockbox on them. Withholding information about the ledger, or merely forgetting to tell her about the priest, seemed altogether different than not telling her about some missing money.

Holdin' out 'bout that lockbox would be akin ta stealing from both tha church an' tha king ta them. There ain't no way they'd do that. An' there ain't no other tracks of someone comin' through here after tha attack, someone who coulda seen tha lockbox an' took it. It's gotta be that bastard greyskin who took it. So, what'd he do with it?

She stopped walking in circles and looked up at the sky through the bare branches of the trees surrounding her. It was still light, but she should probably get back to the farm soon. If nothing else, she would need time to inspect whatever traps and warning bells her soldiers had managed to fashion. And now she had even more reason to talk to the priest as soon as possible.

She sighed, sheathed her sword, and put her hands on her hips.

Ain't no way Sarl brought tha lockbox ta town. Too risky ta be seen with it, plus he was carryin' that warg head already. So, it's out here, somewhere. Tha big shite probably buried it nearby, an' he figures he can just wait for a spell an' then come get it with nobody tha wiser.

Yeah, we'll see 'bout that once ol' Yuri knows we got a reason ta make yer life unpleasant, ya bitch. Suka, my arse! I like where this is goin'.

Kira was almost certain the orc wasn't a simple bandit who had staked the road out to rob the priest. If that was true, there would have been no reason for him to then save Malachi from certain death. But it still meant she had something to accuse him of to get him to cooperate. It also meant Yuri had a reason to string him up if he didn't cooperate.

She smiled at this. She and Kozel would get answers to their questions one way or another.

Having decided she had seen everything there was to see, Kira headed back to the wagon to pick up the chest of religious items. While it would be a bulky load to carry, the chest didn't weigh much, and she was intent on taking it back to the farmstead. Even to a nonreligious person such as herself, it felt wrong to just allow it to remain in forest, unprotected as it were.

Almost as an afterthought, she took a moment to stuff the priest's cross into her belt and wrapped his rosary beads around her wrist. She doubted that Hannah would think much about her "despoiling" Father Malachi's personal religious effects, but she knew he would appreciate having them back.

Without a backpack or satchel, the priest's massive bible would be too much to take back on this trip. As Kira went to put it back in the wagon to protect it from the elements, she suddenly caught movement out of the corner of her eye.

Pretending to have not seen anything, she quickly dumped the bible in the back of the wagon and then put the chest back on the ground. Crouching down to fiddle with the straps that bound it closed, she casually glanced around.

What few birds and squirrels were about had stopped their chattering. Kira couldn't see any more movement, but she sensed something in the bushes to her left, perhaps twenty paces away. She carefully sniffed the air, but the wind was working against her.

That damn orc? A warg? It's just one beast, but whatever it is, it's big...

"Well?! Be ya man or beast, quit yer skulkin' an' face me, ya shite!"

Kira stood up as she challenged the unknown assailant, drawing her sword and bringing its tip up. She balanced herself on her toes, leaning slightly forward, ready for anything.

But what rose up to meet her from the bushes just *ten* paces away was nothing she had expected.

A loathsome creature indeed, it looked like a large, black wolf standing on its hind legs. A darkness seemed to shade it from the sun, as if a cloud had just descended above it, and its red eyes glared at Kira. It slowly took a step forward, pointing at her with a talon-tipped finger.

Kira steadied herself against the wagon, unwilling to give ground. She could see the monster had been injured in the past in several places. The raised arm had an odd angle to it in the forearm, as if it had been broken and then reset incorrectly. There was also an ugly scar across its belly that looked like it was just starting to heal. She guessed whatever fight had caused the wound had happened recently due to the dark, encrusted blood that still clung to the beast's fur.

"So, ya bleed, eh? Guess I'll just have ta finish someone else's job!"

In an instant, it was upon her, grabbing her sword arm at the wrist and squeezing hard. She grunted, resisting the force meant to make her drop the weapon. Using the wagon to brace herself, she lashed out with a well-placed boot to the creature's midsection, catching it with a full blow.

A mixture of a howl of anger and a scream of pain came from its snout, the fetid breath causing her eyes to tear.

She couldn't stop it from ripping the sword out of her hand, and it threw it away as it took a couple steps back. As she readied herself for it to pounce a second time, it howled again, but instead of advancing it merely looked skyward.

The large shape seemed to collapse in upon itself, and it was hard to tell what was transpiring right before her. Now the creature actually looked humanoid in shape, like a thin man. It looked like...

"God's nails, Koz! Is that you?!"

CHAPTER FIFTEEN

Spilling the Wine

Symon sat in his temporary study, rubbing his eyes. It was scarcely past Sext, and he already felt as though a full day of diplomatic games and intrigue lay behind him.

Get a grip on yourself, old man, before someone sees you.

He reached for the decanter of red wine that stood within easy reach on a side table but then thought better of it. Not that he felt he didn't really need the drink. He was just sick of what the local vineyards had to offer.

Everything is so blasted sweet here, and you know you'll have to make countless toasts tonight using the swill. Find something else to fortify yourself before you go crazy and throw the decanter out the window.

Sighing heavily, Symon stood up and went over to the sideboard. He did have to admit, the residence the Astrikhon king had finally—and most likely grudgingly—provided Lianne and her entourage had come well provisioned. The foodstuffs were more than adequate for anyone who wouldn't be satiated by the evening banquets, and the liquor stores were quite abundant. He found what appeared to be a good starka and poured himself a couple fingers of liquid.

Perhaps the queen mother didn't care for the local wine, either.

He raised his glass to the deceased former owner of the mansion he was standing in and proceeded to gulp his drink down in quite an undiplomatic fashion. The warmth from the rye-based liquor immediately spread through his body, and he looked at the bottle again in newfound appreciation.

Jarek would love this. I must arrange to bring some home for him.

His partner had been on his mind ever since the night before when he had finally had time to read the note the princess had brought with her. It had reminded him why he had fallen in love with the younger man in the first place. Symon knew that Jarek's old soul would be quite at home in this study, sharing in the quiet moment and the good liquor.

Of course, he would want to hear all the gossip from the past several days. He has such a keen ear for picking out important pieces of information from the maelstrom of rubbish. I could certainly use his input on what has transpired since the princess got here.

Symon shook his head and poured himself another drink. This one was larger than the first, but he only sipped at it as he made his way back to the desk. He had found over the past year that the longer he stayed in Boloto, attempting to negotiate with the Astrikhon court, the more he was driven to combat the isolation he felt with inebriation. But the ongoing events were too important to lose what mental edge he could still command.

See it through to the end, my good man. You'll be home and in the arms of your loved one soon enough.

He sat down again at the desk and began to assemble his writing instruments. He needed to prepare some remarks for the evening's banquet in a few hours, as there was supposed to be the standard round of toasts between the attendees. But Mikhal had already informed him that the king would not be present tonight, which meant that there would probably be other dignitaries who would find an excuse not to attend.

After only a few moments, Symon gave up on his sad attempt at writing an accolade of sorts. All in all, the unofficial visit of Princess Lianne to Astrikhon was rapidly becoming a diplomatic disaster, and an eloquent tribute to an absent king was not going to turn things around.

Symon sat back in his chair and resignedly stared out the large window at the gardens that surrounded the mansion.

At least the damn treaty was signed this morning. If Elric wishes to replace me with Justinian or somebody else when I return home, so be it. Drinking starka with Jarek and debating what to grow in our own garden this coming spring sounds quite appealing at the moment.

Instead of worrying about high society one-upmanship, he turned his thoughts towards more worldly diplomatic concerns. The excuse given for why King Haldir would be absent from his own banquet was the preponderance of emergency council meetings being held due to the ongoing orc incursion to the northeast. Mikhal had been very apologetic about the situation, but he had also continued to be extremely vague about the actual incursion itself. This fit the frustrating pattern of the entire Perizidon delegation being provided with unhelpful updates. Nobody in their little party had been able to ascertain exactly what was going on at the border.

Even the princess, with her budding friendship with Prince Hadeon, hasn't gotten many details about what is transpiring. All we know is that their army is already shifting some interior forces to their northern border. But there still hasn't been a general alarm raised here in the capital, and the harbor traffic doesn't appear to have changed all that much. So, things can't be that dire just yet. Or so I would hope.

The uncertainty over internal Astrikhon affairs was nothing new for Symon. Even under the best circumstances, he knew it would be rash for someone on their royal council to share intimate details with a foreign diplomat. However, he also knew that King Haldir specifically thought of him as conceited and unmanageable, which led to all the king's advisors avoiding Symon whenever possible outside of formal meetings.

Since none of the council members would ever do or say anything meaningful without first consulting Haldir anyway, their avoidance of Symon outside of official functions didn't mean much from a diplomatic standpoint. Still, it had led him to scramble for any sort of relationship at the fringes of the royal court, and his access to local gossip was not as strong as he could usually muster.

So, not as much of the terrible local wine is being spilled in your presence as you would like. At least you don't have to waste time fraternizing with people you don't care a whit about. Stop feeling sorry for yourself and get to work.

He looked at the scribbles of half-written sentences and pithy statements on the piece of paper in front of him. Still nothing worth writing came to mind, so instead, he amused himself by sketching some caricatures of King Haldir and his court. Mikhal's prominent nose found itself being stuck up the king's backside before Symon crumpled up his work and threw it into the fireplace that was warming the room.

Despite his previous internal vow to not drink too much, he found himself finishing his drink and wandering back to the sideboard for yet another pour. His thoughts wandered to the princess, and he had to admit that she was proving to be more resilient than he would have thought, given the circumstances.

She is definitely willing to stand up to that sharp-tongued arse of a king, something he is not used to. Especially from a woman! But how can I serve and guide her appropriately while keeping the kingdom's overall interests in mind?

The two of them, and several others in the princess's entourage, had suffered through a long welcoming banquet the night before, and Symon's own tongue felt like it was nearly shorn in two because of how many times he had bitten it. Even in the welcoming toast, there had been a passive aggressive comment regarding Perizidon and the kingdom's relationship with the Orcish tribes. All night, conversations always seemed to return to the troubled past between the two human kingdoms. It was as if

Perizidon reaching a separate peace with the orcs almost a century ago was the source of all ills that had beset Astrikhon ever since.

Symon had heard similar complaints and, in his opinion, outright whinging about the Perizidon relations with the orcs from King Haldir and his court for some time now. He had attempted to warn the princess about how prickly the Astrikhon king could be, but he himself and not been prepared for the preponderance of grumbling they had both suffered through. He had certainly received an earful from Lianne about it at the end of the evening.

Her being able to keep her temper in check in public has been the best piece of diplomacy we have had, truth be told. But how much longer until the proverbial dam breaks? You know how her father can be if someone finally sends him over the edge. At least the dancing seemed to go well between her and the prince. Hadeon seems to be the only one interested in being cordial and friendly with any of us.

Even this morning, during the signing ceremony of the long-awaited treaty between the two kingdoms, there had been an unreasonable level of tension. Haldir had managed to slip in a snide remark about how all humans needed to remember that dogs were meant to be tamed rather than treated like family members. It was more amusing than insulting, even if it was a direct accusation that Perizidon treated orcs better than they deserved, but Symon thought it to be in poor taste.

Lianne had smiled, waited for the irritable monarch to say his piece and sign the two copies of the document, and then made her own remarks. Symon had written them for her, making sure that they were neutral in nature and not meant to insult even the thinnest of skins. She had, in fact, added only one sentence at the very end, and Symon afforded himself the luxury of laughing out loud now that he was alone as he thought about it.

"In closing, Your Majesty, the Kingdom of Perizidon is indeed grateful for this treaty between our people. This is more than an economic agreement; it is a bridge between cultures, a shared promise of prosperity, and a symbol of trust. Moreover, it provides security for *our* kingdom, allowing us to maintain peace along *all* our borders, a peace that *our* people so richly deserve. For that, I thank you."

Under any circumstance, the statement would have been a tweak of Haldir's nose. Given the current situation, with orcs apparently running amok within his northern territories, it was a veritable slap to his face. Lianne hadn't even finished signing the second document before Haldir had stood up, his visage a dark shade of purple, and had stormed out of his own council's chambers.

Mikhal, a petrified look on his face, had immediately rushed after his king, while the other council members had silently risen and left the room without bowing. Prince Hadeon had remained seated at the table for a long moment, staring at Lianne without speaking. She had looked directly back at him, and something seemed to pass between the two young heirs.

Finally, he stood, with her quickly mimicking his movements. They had respectively performed a deep bow and curtsy towards each other before he quietly left the room with one copy of the fully signed agreement.

I should be outraged at her, but how can I berate her when she says what I wish to but cannot? Perhaps we shall suffer on the morrow for what has been done today, but if nothing else, she has put Astrikhon on notice that she is not just a pretty face they can ignore.

But before he could ruminate further on what had occurred just a few hours before, there was a knock at the door.

Having left explicit instructions to his assistant that he was not to be bothered, Symon knew that either something urgent had arisen or the princess needed to see him. Assuming the latter, he quickly hid his glass behind some manuscripts on the desk and turned towards the entrance to the study.

"Yes, what is it?"

The door opened, and he was surprised not to see one of Lianne's ladies-in-waiting or his assistant but rather Major Bannik standing in the entrance. She immediately strode in without any additional ceremony, and the door closed quickly behind her. It was as if the soldier standing guard outside the room wanted no part in the conversation that was about to take place.

She made her way to his desk, performing the king's salute but then glowering down at him. "Dragoman Chumak, I must have words with you immediately!"

Symon sighed and retrieved his drink. "Of course, Major. Have you perhaps heard any more about the orc disturbance to the north?"

"No, my lord. But my recommendation remains the same, that we quit this place as quickly as possible. This is especially true now, given that the treaty was officially signed this morning."

Symon regarded the experienced soldier over the lip of his glass as he took a sip. He knew better than to offer her a drink, given that she would consider herself to be on duty.

Although, she has probably sworn a personal oath to not touch alcohol, or engage in any vice, until her royal ward is safely back within the confines of Velych. That is, if she has any vices to begin with.

He knew more than most about Dijana Bannik's almost fanatical devotion to Arina Kalchik, Lianne's mother. Everyone in the Perizidon court knew the story of when she had saved Arina from certain death several years ago. The queen consort had mistakenly put herself between a mother bear and her cub during a royal hunting expedition near Lake Sanguis, and her personal bodyguard had been mauled to death by the frenzied beast before anyone else knew what had happened.

At the time just a sergeant in charge of part of the hunt's security detail, Dijana had heard the screams and had been the first to arrive on the scene. She had skillfully defended Arina on her own against the mighty beast, maneuvering them both out of harm's way until the cub's bleating was enough for its mother to stop her attacks and tend to her own.

When he had arrived and been appraised of what had happened, a shaken Elric had kissed Dijana's hand and promoted her on the spot to replace the bodyguard who had fallen.

What most people didn't know was *why* Dijana had come to Arina's aid that fateful day. It was much more than steadfast dedication to the royal family that one could argue anyone serving in His Majesty's service should have. No, only Symon and a few others knew that Dijana's loyalty came from a much more personal connection with the queen consort.

You followed her into exile, accepting a position far beneath you just to remain close to her. You have personally killed for her and would do so again without hesitation. And now you are the surrogate mother bear guarding our queen's cub...

Symon knew better than to waste too much of the major's time. He put down his glass and faced her directly. "Major, I certainly know your position on wanting to sail for home immediately due to safety concerns for Her Highness. But I trust this is not the reason you have come to see me?"

The major continued to eye him stonily. "No, my lord, it is not. It is about Guard Oldenfeld."

Symon kept a stoic look on his face, but inwardly he cursed his younger sister's offspring.

I assumed as much. God's piss, boy, you will be the death of me. But let us see what the major says about your most recent gaff.

"And what of him?"

"We need to come to an understanding about his duties while he is here in Boloto."

He nodded his head slowly and tried to take a conciliatory

tone with her. "Well then, speak freely, Major. There is no one here but me who will hear you."

"Beg pardon, my lord, but am I speaking to the dragoman of Perizidon or to the uncle of one of my soldiers?"

Symon looked down at the desk for the briefest moment, quickly deciding who had the upper hand between Dijana and himself in political goodwill back home.

It is close, Symon...you probably don't want to test how close.

He looked back up at her with a slight smile. "Both, of course. I cannot pretend to divide myself in two with either half not knowing what the other does. But, Major, rest assured that *our* mission for *our* king and country will take precedence over *any* personal feelings."

She nodded at this, and her own pose became slightly less rigid. "Thank you, my lord. I will be straightforward with you then."

As if you know any other way, Major.

Symon nodded back and motioned for her to continue.

"Guard Oldenfeld is known to be skilled with the sword, perhaps in the top three in the whole of the Velych castle guard. At his core, he is a well-meaning lad. But he is not fit for any sort of duty that requires discipline and decorum. He should *not* have been assigned to this highly diplomatic mission."

A fair and reasonable opinion if you ever heard one, Symon. With some tact thrown in as well.

The soldier continued. "I shall be discussing how personnel are assigned to royal escort duty directly with my staff upon our return. It is, of course, my responsibility for not speaking up about this matter before we sailed. But it is also my responsibility to minimize any problems with my soldiers for as long as we remain here."

Symon looked at her for a long moment before responding. He knew all about the shortcomings of his nephew when it came to the spit-and-polish side of soldiering.

"I agree with you, Major, that Dane...I mean to say, Guard Oldenfeld, should not have been assigned to this mission. Honestly, I do. But he is here, and we need every soldier we have, do we not?"

His answer seemed to surprise her, although she was professional enough to keep any deep emotions off her face.

After a brief pause, she responded. "You are correct, my lord. I am not suggesting that he be thrown into the brig of one of our ships until we leave. But what I am saying is he will only be assigned duties that keep him out of the sight of our hosts for the remainder of our stay."

"I understand, Major." With a practiced sigh of resignation, he picked up his glass again. "I know, of course, about the incident from this morning. Your decision will certainly eliminate any future public breaches of etiquette by the boy."

"Yes, my lord." The major seemed to want to say something else but stopped herself.

No doubt she wants to know if I have heard any gossip about how our soldiers cannot even maintain a simple marching formation when on parade. Thank the Almighty that I have not.

Symon took another sip and then slowly shook his head. "And if you could teach him to not assault peasants while escorting our princess, it would certainly give me one less reason to drink so early in the day."

To her credit, only the smallest sign of exasperation crossed the major's face. "Of course, my lord. My apologies for not doing this sooner."

There was another knock at the door. Symon briefly thought about hiding his drink again but decided it wasn't worth the effort. "Enter!"

His assistant opened the door but did not come into the room. "My lord, Her Highness has sent word that she would speak with you now."

"Yes, yes. I shall leave momentarily." Symon waved her away, and the door closed again. He looked back at Dijana. "I do realize that, if this was any other solider under your command, Major, you would not have come to me over this matter. For that, I thank you. Dane's mother will no doubt thank you as well when she hears about it."

Symon decided to let the major decide for herself if there was any political threat behind his words. Not that she would care.

He placed his glass on the desk and stood up. "But if we are done, I must go consult with Her Highness about tonight's festivities. I will, of course, impress upon her again the concerns we share about leaving for home as soon as it is politically prudent."

"Thank you, my lord." The major saluted and then wheeled

to leave.

Symon watched her go before looking back down at his glass.

I suppose you and your brethren must wait a bit.

CHAPTER SIXTEEN

Hell Hath No Fury

Maryska Shoikos walked quickly towards her homestead carrying two full buckets back from the well, trying not to cry. Something had gone horribly wrong since yesterday afternoon, and Father Malachi was dying.

She quietly entered the house and immediately went to the fireplace to boil more water. The main room was deserted, as the other children were out helping their father with chores while their mother was busy nursing the priest in the other room. The baby was upstairs, but she didn't hear any mewling from him and assumed he was fine for the moment. Focusing, she set to building the fire back up as quickly as possible.

Once that was done, Maryska went back over towards the door where a large, covered pot had been placed temporarily. Looking inside it, she saw that some of the greyish clay the boys had collected yesterday had been scooped out. She reasoned that, while she had been out visiting the root cellar and collecting water, her mother must have come out of the bedroom to make another poultice in an attempt to draw out whatever infection had taken root in the priest's leg.

She glanced over at the countertop by the fireplace that had been transformed into an apothecary and noticed that the honey and another small pot stood open upon it. It was totally out of character for Hannah Shoikos to be untidy, and it only increased Maryska's worry.

Poor Mother, she must have been in quite a rush to get back to Father Malachi. Think, Mary, think! What will she need next?

Knowing she needed to wait for the water to boil to make any additional teas or potions, Maryska went to the chest that was being used as a clean bandage hamper of sorts. It was nearly empty of rags and strips of cloth, as she had suspected. Mother had been going through them at an alarming rate, as the blood, pus, and ichor seeping from Father Malachi's most grievous wounds could not be stopped completely. Most of the bandages they had used were still soaking in cold water outside or hanging up to dry in the weak early winter sun, not ready to be reused. If more were going to be required this morning, she would have to make them.

Running upstairs, she quietly looked in on the baby, keeping out of sight so he wouldn't see her and immediately demand attention. He appeared to be amusing himself by attempting to catch some dust motes floating in the sunlight, cooing and gurgling to himself. She left the content infant to his own devices and continued to the bedroom she shared with her sister.

At least someone in the household isn't affected by a feeling of desperation. Oh, Mother, what shall we do?

Entering her bedroom, she went to the large wooden trunk that held her clothes. The vast majority of her garments were made from homespun wool, with linen being reserved for her head coverings and her unmentionables. Almost everything else made from linen in the house had already been torn or cut into strips for use as bandages. However, she blushed at the mere thought of using anyone's undergarments, let alone hers, to wrap the priest's wounds. Maryska instead grabbed a wool blouse from the chest and hurried downstairs again to find the shears.

Father Malachi seemed to have been stabilizing yesterday morning, having awoken for the first time since the orc had brought him to the farm several days ago. True, his wounds were deep and terrible, and Maryska's father was still worried about the long-term effects of *skaz* settling into the priest's brain. But it appeared they might be able to save his leg, and he had been able to eat and drink a bit while Maryska and her mother had continued to tend to all the bite and claw wounds from the warg attack.

The priest had drifted back to sleep after a spell, and Maryska's father had persuaded her mother to go upstairs and lie down for a bit herself. But the family had been given false hope, as several hours later, Father Malachi's fever was back, and he could not be shaken from his slumber to take more medicine. Nothing had changed through the long night hours except that his breath grew ever shallower.

As she thought about the past day's events, Maryska located the shears and began cutting up her blouse. It wasn't one of her favorite ones, being dark green with no secondary color or trim, but it was relatively new and not a hand-me-down. She had to stop twice to wipe tears away, but the second time she made herself laugh by admitting she was being silly about her clothes.

I would happily dress in burlap and give all my blouses to the cause if it meant Father Malachi would recover. Perhaps even my linen chemises...I don't think he would see their use as an insult, so neither should I.

"Mary? Mary, are you out there?" Her mother's voice, muffled by the closed door, broke through her thoughts. It had a strident tone to it.

"Coming, Mother!" Maryska replied at once. She looked over at the large pot on the fire, but no steam was coming from it yet. She put down the shears and the remains of her blouse and walked quickly to the room the priest was in to see what her mother needed.

Her mother was applying yet another compress to the priest's forehead when Maryska opened the door, but she glanced up from her work to give Maryska a quick smile.

"Mary, do we have more bandages ready by chance?"

"I'm just making some new ones now, Mother. And there's water about to boil."

"Excellent, my dear. Bring the bandages as soon as they're ready. Is your father on hand, by chance?"

"No, Mother. The last I saw him, he was still over at the barn dealing with the animals."

"I suppose you mean the four-legged kind?" There was bitterness in her mother's voice, and it made Maryska nervous.

She hesitated in replying as she wasn't quite sure what was

meant by the question.

Her mother looked up at her again. "I'm sorry, my dear. Don't mind me, just...just fetch me the bandages, please."

"Yes, Mother."

Before she left the room, Maryska looked at the priest, and she could tell that his condition wasn't any better. His face was pale, and he lay motionless on the bed. The mattress was coated with dried fluids of various types, as was the floor. She knew that, despite their best efforts to keep the man and his surroundings clean, his bed clothes would have to be burned or buried when he was done with them.

She quickly finished making the new bandages, and she put another log on the fire before going back to her mother. She was thanked with a quick smile, and without being asked, she began collecting the detritus from the past several hours of treatment that had gathered around the bed. As Maryska worked, she gave additional thought to her mother's earlier comment. It hit her suddenly that her mother was being uncharacteristically impolite about the soldiers that had come from Stren.

I know Father admonished the boys for calling them all clueless city folk from the south, but their manners must be as bad as their handiness for Mother to look down upon them. Luckily for me, none of them except that commander of theirs have come into the house. And I'd rather not deal with her any more than I have to, so I can't imagine what the others might be like.

She shivered a bit as she thought about the large, brutish

woman.

***

Yesterday, after Kira stormed out of the house after briefly talking with Father Malachi, she had been gone for several hours. Maryska knew the soldiers' commander had ostensibly been investigating the scene of the warg attack, and that she had gone alone. She returned to the farm after dark, stalking out of the gloom unannounced and unopposed, despite her soldiers supposedly having a perimeter alarm set.

Father was told of her approach by one of the boys who ran ahead of her to the house, and he ordered all the children to get inside, as if he was expecting trouble. He met Kira just outside the homestead, and there were terse words when she was told that she couldn't see the priest.

"Sard it all, Mykola! Ya know I have ta talk with Father Malachi!"

"Kira, please! He's..." Maryska wasn't sure, as she was hiding behind the partially opened front door to the house so her father couldn't tell she was eavesdropping, but he must have looked around to see who might be listening before continuing in a low voice. "He's not doing well at all, Kira. He's been unconscious since right after you left. You can't talk to him right now, and it's best if he's not disturbed at all."

"Pfah! That's Hannah talkin' now, Myko! Ya doin' what she wants all tha time now, huh? Maybe I need ta talk ta tha real boss."

"She'd rather not speak with you, Kira, and you know that."

"Sure, Myko, sure!" There was an evil-sounding chuckle. "She usin' that old magic of hers ta box yer spindle up nice an' neat in her bedside table, is that it?"

"Kira..." Her father's voice dropped even lower so that Maryska couldn't hear him anymore. She could tell he was whispering something to the woman, and he went on for some time. For what it was worth, there weren't any more outbursts or insults from her.

"I know, *I know*!" Kira finally responded. "Fine, but if he comes to, I *have* ta be told, Myko. I don't care what time it is, ya get one of yer brats ta come find me."

"I promise, Kira. Thank you for understanding."

"I ain't understandin' nothin', 'cept that ya better know that I can force my way in there if I have ta. So, don't make me!"

"I...yes, Kira. I understand."

There was some rustling, as if something was being unbound.

Kira spoke again, although, this time, there was a softer edge to her voice. "An' here...even if he ain't conscious, maybe these will help tha old man."

"Thank you, Kira. I mean it...these will, indeed, help."

Maryska quickly moved to the side of the door before her father opened it fully to come back inside the house. He was carrying a chest and some rosary beads in his hands, and Maryska could see a crucifix stuck in his belt.

He frowned at her as he noticed her and where she was

standing. “How much did you hear, Mary?”

She looked down at her feet. “Maybe half of what was said, Father.”

He sighed. “It does not become you, child, to hide in the shadows and listen in on conversations you are not supposed to be part of. But since you did, do you know the gist of what must be done?”

“Yes, Father. I shouldn’t allow Mistress Toth in to see Father Malachi without the permission of you or Mother.”

“Very good, Mary. Now, if you could bar the door for me while I go and talk with your mother.” Still holding the chest and the rosary beads, which Maryska now recognized as the priest’s, he walked over to the spare bedroom and let himself in.

It was still early enough in the evening that her father’s request was an odd one, but she did it all the same. She closed the door and then, with some effort, lifted an iron bar into place across the back of it. The bar fell into place with a solid *thud*, a barrier to anyone or anything that might be lurking outside in the night air. It took all of her willpower to not eavesdrop on her parents’ conversation, as well, but she dutifully remained near the fireplace and busied herself with the final preparations for dinner instead.

Eventually, both of her parents came out to the main room, her mother calling the other children down from their bedrooms for the evening meal. Nothing more was said about the priest’s condition with Maryska’s younger siblings present, although the family’s evening prayers were full of entreaties on his behalf. Father held her back, however, when the others were sent back upstairs to prepare for bed.

"Mary, your mother has agreed to split tonight's vigil with you. I would ask that you take first watch and allow her to sleep as much as possible. Also, if Father Malachi happens to awaken, come get me and *not* one of your siblings to go and alert the soldiers."

"I understand, Father."

He hugged her close. "Thank you, Mary. I am afraid there will not be much good news tonight or on the morrow but remember that we do not bear our burdens alone."

She went into the priest's room and closed the door behind her. There had been no change in his status, although his rosary beads were now wrapped around his right wrist and both of his hands had been made to grip his crucifix on his chest. To Maryska, it made him look all the more like he was already dead, and she drew a shaky sigh as she sat down to begin her vigil.

The night passed as silently as the grave.

***

Maryska was shaken from her reverie by a gasp from her mother. She looked up from where she had just gathered the last of the bloodied rags from the floor to see that Father Malachi's eyes were open.

"Mary, get your father, *now*!"

Duty to her mother overcame her desire to stay and see if the priest would say something. Depositing her load near the front door, Maryska rushed out of the house to find her father. She thought he might still be in the barn and made straight for it, calling out for him as she went. But when she reached the main door, she didn't see anyone inside. She called out for him again in vain as the cows looked at her curiously.

"He's checkin' tha fence wit' yer younger brother," a deep voice behind her said. "Whaddya need 'im fer?"

Maryska whirled in place and found one of the bigger soldiers standing a couple of paces behind her. He was carrying what was meant to be firewood, although she could tell at a glance that the branches were too green.

"Urgent business at the house, sir. My mother needs him. Do you know which fence he's checking?"

The soldier looked at her blankly for a long moment, as if processing her words was difficult to do. He finally motioned towards the south with his load of wood. Maryska curtsied quickly and then took off at a run.

As she ran, she remembered what her father had said the night before, that he should be the one who told the soldiers about the priest if he regained consciousness. She resolved to try and find him without calling out again, potentially warning the soldiers that something was amiss at the house.

At least I stumbled across one of the addled ones at the barn! Hopefully, he doesn't think to tell his commander anything.

Fortunately, the southern border of the land the family claimed as theirs wasn't too far away, and she soon saw her father and her younger brother. They were working on an older section of the wattle fencing. As she approached, her brother saw her coming and tugged at the sleeve of their father. When he looked up and saw her, he dropped his mallet and immediately started towards her briskly.

"Father Malachi?" he asked as he came up to her, wiping his hands on his trousers.

"Yes...he's awake..." she replied, somewhat winded.

He nodded and continued his pace back in the direction she had come. Looking over his shoulder, he called out, "Leave the fence, Roland! Find your brother and come to the house as quick as you can."

Maryska did her best to keep up with her father's long strides. He had a grim look on his face as he looked all around them. "Mary, have you seen the soldiers' commander?"

"Not today, Father..."

Suddenly, he swore and took off at a run. Bewildered, she called out to him to no avail.

"Father, what is it? What's—?" She broke off as she saw what, no doubt, he had seen a moment earlier. Kira Toth was making her way towards their homestead, and she would handily beat them there.

As far as she could tell, her father didn't bother to call out to the soldier to try and stop her. Rather, he ran faster than she knew he could as he attempted to close the distance. Kira either didn't notice him or didn't care about him as she stepped inside the house, closing the door behind her. Maryska didn't see any of the other soldiers nearby, but she was worried all the same. Their commander had noticeably been wearing her sword.

Her father reached the house some twenty or thirty paces ahead of her and merely pushed the door aside as he entered.

As Maryska struggled to close the distance, she began to hear heated words from all three adults. Suddenly, there was a loud crashing sound, and a scream rang out.

Mother!

Maryska stumbled through the doorway, pitching forward in her exhaustion and landing on her hands and knees. Looking up, she was horrified to see that Kira had a dagger in her hand, facing away from her. Her father was leaning against the table, clutching his left arm in his right hand, a wicked cut across it turning crimson red.

"You *monster*! Leave this house immediately before the Almighty damns you fully!" Maryska's mother, her face filled with a dark rage, supported her husband as she spit at Kira.

"Bitch, I'm gonna see tha priest if I have ta gut ya both!" Kira said heatedly, and she slowly drew her long blade out of its sheath. "Move aside or die!"

"No!" Maryska called out from her position on the floor, startling Kira, who swung around to face her. "Please, no!"

"Maryska, get out of here!" her father shouted, as he righted himself. "Kira, you leave her out of this!"

Kira took a step towards Maryska, a wild look on her face. What she was thinking of doing was anyone's guess, but everyone froze as they heard a rasping cough coming from the other room.

The saints preserve us, it's Father Malachi!

Upon hearing the priest, Kira pivoted again. She stuck her dagger back in her belt, but she kept her sword point fixed on Maryska's father as she began walking towards the room where the priest was located. He looked at Maryska, as opposed to the weapon, as if confirming in his mind she was all right, and he did not make a move to stop the soldier. Maryska's mother put her hands to her face, as if she couldn't watch Kira any longer.

The door to the side room closed behind Kira, and Maryska staggered to her feet and immediately went to her parents. The three of them hugged, forgetting about Mykola's wound for a long moment.

Finally, he kissed Maryska on the top of her head and then gently separated himself from her and her mother. "I don't know what insanity has overtaken Kira, but please make yourselves scarce until she is done talking with the priest. I'll wait for her to come out and then demand that she and her escort leave our farm today."

Hannah visibly bristled. "I will certainly *not* abandon you or our home to that *woman*, Myko! I can't believe she attacked you like that! It's unconscionable, and both the mayor and the sheriff will hear of it!"

Maryska's mother went to the chest holding the bandages and took out the last few that remained. She returned and began to wrap her husband's arm. Maryska, unsure of what else to do, glanced over at the closed door to the other room. She could hear murmuring, as if Kira and the priest were having a conversation. She looked back at her parents as her mother cried out in frustration.

"Ah, Myko, the cut is too deep for just a bandage. You will need to apply pressure while I make a tourniquet."

"It will soon be over, my dear. Mary, can you look and see if your brothers are on their way to the—"

Kira's voice broke cut him off from the other room. "Someone get in here, *now*! He's coughin' up blood or somethin'!"

Maryska was closest to the door, and without thinking, she went to it. She heard her mother call out to her, but it was too late to stop her impetuous action as she threw open the door. She gasped as she saw Father Malachi sitting up in bed, a blackish goo emanating from his open mouth and trickling down his chin and on to his shirt. Kira was on the far side of the bed, stooped over the priest. She had dropped her sword on the ground and was attempting to wipe his mouth with a dirty rag.

"Mother, he's vomiting ichor! Mother?" Desperate, and not knowing what to do, Maryska turned back towards her parents to see that her mother was already moving towards the countertop that held the herbs and potions. Her father, his forearm still bleeding through his wrapping, came towards her.

"Child, grab a bowl or something to contain the spillage," he said calmly enough, although she could see fear and concern in his eyes.

They entered the room together and crouched down across

from Kira. Her father held Father Malachi's head upright while Maryska emptied the remains of a water jug onto the floor and then propped the vessel under the priest's twitching lips.

"No...must tell you..." Father Malachi reached out towards Kira, his eyes probing her face desperately.

Maryska heard her father draw in his breath, but he said nothing as Kira took the old man's hand in hers.

"I'm here, Father. I'm here..."

Is she crying?!

"Kira, my child...the Almighty does not forsake...the works of their hands... Remember this..."

"It's too late for me, Father. Look elsewhere ta give yer final blessin'," the jailer muttered, and now Maryska could clearly see the tears on Kira's cheeks.

"*No!*" The ferocity of the word filled the room, and it was if the priest had slapped all of them. "No...never too late...to ask the Almighty for forgiveness," he whispered. His head lolled to the side as he tried to look over at Maryska's father.

Maryska sensed that her mother had entered the room, but she did not approach the bed to try and administer any additional aid.

A spasm shook the priest's entire body, and he coughed yet more black fluid up on himself. Maryska was crying now, as well. She knew the end had come for Father Malachi, and there was nothing she or any of the others could do to make the passing more comfortable for him. She grasped his free hand, bowing over it and closing her eyes.

"I believe in God the Almighty, maker of heaven and earth, and in Iesu, Their only Son, our Lord, who was conceived by the Holy Spirit..." Her father began to recite the Apostle's Creed in a hushed voice, and she heard her mother join him as she wept.

Maryska opened her mouth, but she could only gasp for air.

It was all over soon enough.

***

Kira stood just outside the Shoikos farmstead, gazing out at their lands in the late afternoon sun. She would quit this place today if she could, and they would be happy to see her go. But, unfortunately for both parties, she would need to wait until tomorrow morning.

I wish I had cut that harpy's tongue 'stead of her man's arm. Sardin' bitch, always got ta be holier than everyone else in tha room. But I'm almost done with her. Ain't no way I'll let her come back ta town with me an' tha body.

She was fairly sure there would be an argument in the morning about who from the family would accompany the soldiers back to Stren with the priest's body. There was little doubt that Hannah would want to register a complaint with Yuri and the mayor, what little good it would do her. Kira also knew that neither Hannah nor Mykola would trust her to make a formal statement about her visit without at least one of them being present.

Whatever, let Myko come an' say whatever he wants. I didn't do nothin' wrong, an' Yuri will just tell him that he shouldn't interfere with tha kingdom's business. He'll be lucky if we don't throw him in a cell for a few days an' make him think 'bout what he did tryin' ta stop me.

Kira could, and would, argue that the Wilds were still unsafe to travel for normal folk, seeing as the wargs were still out there as far as anyone else was concerned. Also, while she would be taking the priest's body back with her, he wouldn't be receiving a proper burial for at least two months. An inquisitor would have to be requested from Velych, and that would take a while. The Shoikos family would have plenty of time to pay their final respects, even more than they were doing now.

She glanced up at the dark grey sky to the north. *On top of all that, there's a storm comin'. We'll have ta make haste back ta town, an' that's gonna be trouble enough with a corpse ta transport an' dealin' with all tha half-wits I got with me. Nah, there won't be time ta babysit anyone else.*

Kira looked down at the priest's ledger in her hands, which she had secured as quickly as possible. Its existence was yet one more reason she didn't want any extra people making the trip back to town with her. That was because she had no idea what Kozel was up to right now.

She wondered if he would be brazen enough to meet her in the Wilds, before she reached Stren. They hadn't made any formal arrangements about how and where he was going to look at the ledger and debrief her. When they had last seen each other, he hadn't really been in the mood for a long conversation. That, and she had been too shocked at him calling her out to fulfill the first part of her contract with him.

Tha contract…yeah…well, Koz, ya got what ya wanted, 'cause ya told me ya wanted tha priest dead. An' I'm gonna say that's what matters.

She whispered to herself, almost as if she couldn't believe her luck. "What matters is that Father Malachi's dead…an' I didn't have ta kill him…"

CHAPTER SEVENTEEN

Slow Boat to Stren

It had been quite some time since Moirne had felt this cold. She stamped her feet to keep the circulation in them going as she made her way carefully through the newly fallen snow and into the underbrush on the far side of the tow path. She had volunteered to look for firewood as a way of contributing to the daily chores, but she also wanted separation from Olek's crew so she could complete her toilet.

They're still treating me like some noble-born lady, so either I'm not supposed to shite at all, or my shite's not supposed to stink. Better off to keep the illusion for any future courtier stupid enough to ask for passage on a damn barge.

She sighed and admonished herself silently. It wasn't really the mannerisms of the crew or the closed-in feeling of the barge interior that had her on edge. It was the stinking river itself.

Riding next to water was never an issue for her, but riding *on* water was another matter altogether. Being aboard any type of sailing vessel, even in a relatively shallow setting and not at sea, had always made her uncomfortable. She had been reminded of this on a constant basis since departing Tuman, and even a temporary respite from her phobia was welcome.

Her one constant nightmare was that of drowning, brought on by nearly doing just that on a battlefield a very long time ago.

The helpless feeling of that instant, being crushed under a dead knight's weight while slowly sinking into a muddy, fetid pool, held her in its clutches even now. She would gladly ride twenty leagues out of the way than ford a river with the water level higher than her waist.

Ah, but, Dear Moirne, that day's desperate prayer brought you into the service of the Almighty, did it not? Are you disparaging your true calling and your service after all these years?

She pushed the inner voice aside and, after discretely evacuating herself, looked for some fallen branches to harvest as she reflected on her current situation.

The first several days of the passage north to Stren had been fine once the crew had gotten used to having a strange woman sleeping on board with them. Moirne had kept mainly to herself and her mare during the day, but she had done her share of boat-keeping duties without complaint. Olek treating her with respect from the start of the journey had helped, as it was obvious his crew was loyal to him and respected his opinion on all matters. Liberally sharing her pipe tobacco and being unafraid to take swigs from the community bottle of *horilka* after each evening meal had certainly helped as well.

One the second day, they had made it through the main area where the tow path had collapsed with relative ease. The burned-out barge that had been part of the tavern banter that brought Moirne and Olek together looked black and lifeless on the far shore as they passed it, but Olek was not in the mood to investigate the site.

"Won't be nothin' left of value, an' we're heavy for tha donkeys as it is. Treants, my arse. That's bandit work if I ever saw it." He spit into the river for emphasis.

Moirne hadn't protested his decision, even if she had been curious and had wanted a break from being on the water. At least someone had taken care of the bodies, as several fresh burial mounds could be seen near the edge of the woods farther up the bank. Two of Olek's crew made the sign of the cross as they passed the site, and she quietly followed suit.

She had seriously considered quitting the barge once they were past the last area where the tow path was impassable and making her own way to Stren on horseback. It certainly would have calmed her nerves to get off the river and would also have allowed her to gain a day, or even two, in her arrival time. But she was still attempting to not draw undue attention to herself, and she knew leaving the barge would create all sorts of stories up and down the river about the insane, noble-born woman who had skipped out on her fare to wander about the Wilds on her own. She had ultimately decided it was better to grit her teeth and bear the ride for just a few more days. As fate would have it, she made the right decision.

Olek had been right to worry about starting the journey so late in the season. The morning of their fourth day on the river had brought winds from the north and the threat of storms. The next day saw the winds grow to gale force that threatened to blow anyone on the tow path or topside on the barge into the choppy water.

The snow had started soon after, dropping visibility to only a few paces and making the donkey team pulling the barge more irritable than ever. Olek had called a halt to their pitifully slow progress shortly before None when they reached a protected bend in the river. It was soon impossible to move forward, either on land or on water.

When Moirne asked about the chances of being stranded on the river's edge for the foreseeable future, the captain just shrugged. "First storm of tha season usually don't last that long, an' we should be okay with ice for another couple of weeks. We're less than two days south of Stren if we catch a break in tha weather. Don't ya worry, Derya, I'll get ya there. But ya might be stranded in that stink hole for a long while, an' I think you'll come ta miss my barge an' my pleasant company!"

It had taken the balance of the day and into the next morning before the wind and snow stopped, but Moirne had to admit that Olek's prediction on the storm's short duration seemed to be correct. After looking at the clearing sky, he had announced they would attempt to push forward after an early midday meal. Preparations to move out were already under way.

All the better, but it's still going to be at least another two days on this blasted river.

It took some time, but Moirne was able to knock enough snow away from a clump of trees to collect a reasonable amount of kindling and small branches. As she made her way back to the barge, she could see that the donkey team was almost ready to go. Their breath and that of their driver mingled in the cold air as they mimicked her in stamping their feet.

Suddenly, there was a call from the crewmember standing by the rudder. “Somebody comin’ up behind us, boss!”

Everyone else stopped what they were doing to look, and sure enough another barge had just rounded the bend in the river several hundred paces behind them. Something seemed off about it, and it took a moment for Moirne to realize that it wasn’t being pulled by donkeys. It was being pulled by men!

Olek appeared from the bowels of the storage section of his vessel to take a look. He shook his head and softly chuckled. “Figures that he’d push on as soon as possible. Well, he can damn well pole ’round us or bide his time when he gets here.”

“Vasily?” Moirne asked, fairly confident in the answer she would receive.

“Yup,” was the simple response. Olek then raised his voice to address his crew, who were all still looking downstream. “Well, don’t stand there gawkin’ like ya never seen two-legged types pull a barge before, ’less ya want me ta do it, too! Let’s get movin’!”

It still took some time to make their barge ready, and the other craft slowly and steadily made its way towards them. Moirne could see the men pulling it had been placed in harnesses that appeared to be fitted for human use. As they came closer, she observed that they were wearing leather jerkins that were connected via a metal ring to a rope that extended out from behind the shoulder blades of each person. So long as the eight men kept the same cadence, both their ropes and their feet would remain untangled.

So, this prisoner exchange between towns happens on a regular enough basis that they've created an easy way to "employ" them en route. I wonder if Vasily's donkeys are on board enjoying their respite or if he brought along any at all.

Vasily himself was walking behind the laboring men, smoking a pipe and looking quite smug despite the extreme cold. He was taking care to stay within the confines of the disturbed snow that the prisoners were plowing through. A whip was coiled at his waist, and he was armed with a short sword as well.

The men in the harnesses were all sweating despite the temperature. Heads bowed, they strained against the weight of their load. When they were some twenty paces short of Olek's boat, Vasily called out to them to halt, and the dazed looks on their faces portrayed confusion more than relief.

Vasily continued walking forward, going around his contingent of prisoners and ignoring Moirne and the other crew members of Olek's barge. He made straight for the other captain, who was making a final check of the haul line to his donkey team. Once there, the two men shook hands and spoke quietly with each other, their conversation lost in the slight breeze that lingered from the remains of the storm.

When they were done talking, the two captains shook hands again, and Vasily began to make his way back towards his own barge. This time, he acknowledged Moirne's presence as he came up to her, giving her a quick nod. He then slowed his pace as if he meant to have a conversation with her as well.

"Good day, fair lady. I assume my old friend Olek has been treatin' ya well?"

"Well enough, good sir. I can't blame him for the weather, at least."

He snorted. "Yeah, tha Almighty sends rain on tha just an' on tha unjust, alike. Or snow, as tha case may be."

She feigned ignorance at his use of scripture and instead pointed at the men in the harnesses. "May I assume that sorry lot are the unjust?"

"Aye, prisoners on their way ta Stren. There are more in tha hold, waitin' their turn in tha rotation."

Moirne began to sense how Vasily had been able to make up so much ground on Olek, even with starting out a day or two behind him.

"Their turn? How often do you switch them out?"

He seemed to give her question some thought. "Well, usually each group will go for 'bout half a day. But this mornin' being such a rough struggle through tha snow, I should probably switch out now while we got a bit of delay. Whaddya ya think, m'lady? Should I provide rest ta those that labor an' are heavily laden?"

Vasily's scarcely veiled reference to a second line of scripture in the span of just a few moments was enough for Moirne to realize he must think he knew something of her real identity. But she certainly wasn't going to break character out in the open. Instead, she replied in kind, so he knew they were now playing the same game.

"If they're truly criminals, sir, then whatsoever they sow, so shall they reap. But I don't necessarily know if you are the one who gets to decide their ultimate fate here on Terra."

He snorted again as he studied her. "Fair enough, m'lady. I certainly don't need any, uh, inquiries into my own business."

Moirne wasn't sure if he had wanted to say *inquisitions* but had decided that was too on the nose. She merely smiled back at him.

He was looking at me strangely back at the tavern the other night, and the bartender said he isn't originally from Tuman. Maybe he recognizes me from the capital or elsewhere if he gets around. So, is he trying get paid for keeping his knowledge a secret, or is he trying to warn me that somebody else knows who I truly am? I suppose I should find out, but it won't change what I mean to do in Stren either way.

Vasily turned downstream and let out a shrill, short whistle. Two of his regular crew members came into view onboard the other barge and leaned out over the gunwales to see what he wanted. He raised his right hand and made a large circular motion with it, and they returned the signal. One crew member disappeared from view, while the second one leapt over the side onto the tow path and started making their way forward towards the stationary men.

The tall, lanky one that disappeared…I could swear he looks familiar…

Moirne racked her brain about anyone she might have seen lurking about in Tuman and came up empty, almost missing what Vasily was saying.

"Not good ta have 'em standin' there doin' nothin' in this cold, anyways, so we'll get 'em inside for a spell."

"No good to you dead?" Moirne had openly wondered about this, given how exhausted the current lot of men looked in their harnesses. Almost all of them were merely leaning forward as they waited, the ropes they were tied to the only thing keeping them from falling face-first into the snow.

"Not as good as they are ta me alive," Vasily said in a matter-of-fact tone. "One silver each for a successful delivery ta tha Stren dockmaster. Minus transportation costs an' burial fees, as required."

One silver each…no wonder he didn't want the oxen.

"Then you didn't want me or my steed on your barge in the first place."

"Oh, I don't know. At tha rate ya gave Olek, it woulda been worth it." He shrugged and then looked at her knowingly. "Plus, we woulda had a long time ta talk."

Here we go…

"Oh really? About what?"

"My past…yer past…business propositions…whatever came ta mind. Maybe we coulda exchanged our favorite lines of scripture." Vasily smirked.

"Well, that seems like a conversation that needs to take place somewhere more private than the topside of a barge. Perhaps I can buy you a drink when we reach Stren. That is, of course, if that won't be too late to listen to this business proposition of yours."

"It ain't really a business proposition, but yeah, I'm thinkin' that talkin' in Stren may indeed be too late, m'lady." He then leaned in and spoke in a low whisper. "Or rather, *Sister*."

After seeing no visible reaction from her, he straightened back up and continued. "But you're right, there's no place on tha barge ta discuss discreet matters. Why don't ya walk with me for a bit, once Olek gets started?"

She nodded silently, and he bowed to her before continuing back towards his vessel.

It was only a short time later that Moirne found herself walking next to Vasily along the tow path, some twenty paces or so behind Olek's barge. The donkeys were making slow but steady progress through the snow and were leaving a wide enough trail that they could walk side by side with relative ease.

Olek had merely shrugged when she told him she wanted to walk for a while. No doubt he had recognized her discomfort while embarked. "Stretchin' yer legs is fine by me, Derya. It's not like tha donkeys are gonna outpace ya in this snow. But if ya decide to change berths, I'm still keepin' your full fare."

"No worries there, Olek. I have no desire to join the masses on the other barge. I'm afraid Vasily's crew may lose count of all the heads over there and try and hook me up to a harness!"

Thinking of the prisoners, Moirne glanced back at the other barge, which was some distance behind her and Vasily. The other set of eight men had been strapped in and were now pressing forward. Overall, their job would be easier than those they had replaced, since they had the donkeys breaking up any snow drifts ahead of them. Still, Moirne knew their labor would be exhausting.

She gestured back at them as she turned towards Vasily. "Is that part of their sentencing?"

"In a way. They all have a certain amount of hard labor attached ta their term, an' tha days spent on tha river count towards their total requirement."

"What have they all done to warrant their sentences in the first place?" Moirne knew it was a longshot that Vasily would know this, but she asked in the hopes he might share some gossip. As it was, he merely shrugged.

"Don't know, an' don't really care. Tha sheriff sentenced them, an' tha mayor signed off on their fates. I'm just transportin' them."

"For a price."

He wagged a finger in her face. "For tha kingdom's standard rate, mind ya. Maybe next time I'll try an' stack 'em two deep an' get thirty pieces of silver 'stead of tha sixteen I'm gettin' this trip. Would that fit tha picture ya got of me better, *Sister*?"

Moirne scoffed. "I seriously doubt you betrayed the Son of

the Almighty and placed him on your boat, Vasily. If those men broke the laws of the kingdom and were justly sentenced for their crimes, so be it. Just be sure you are also not breaking the laws of kingdom for ill-gotten gain. You seem to know your scripture quite well, so you ought to remember that treasures of wickedness profit nothing."

Vasily was silent for a while, as if he was deciding how much ill-gotten gain to confess to, whether on this particular trip or in his lifetime. Moirne assumed he would arrive at "none" as his answer, and he didn't disappoint her. Instead, he changed the subject.

"So, it really is *Sister*? Ya admit that you're a priestess of tha one true faith?"

She regarded him cooly. "Of course. I am no Simon Peter. I will not deny who I follow."

"But ya hide yourself away an' don't announce yourself like most of yer sistren an' brethren in tha church."

"If you wish for me to proselytize for you, I can. Or perhaps I can baptize you in the waters of the river, here and now." Moirne smiled and gestured towards the Gruminus.

"Uh, no, Sister, that's not what I meant."

Moirne stopped walking and faced him, her hands on her hips. "Then what *do* you mean, Vasily? Are you part of the inquisition, sent to test my faith?"

"Er, what? No, Sister, that's not—"

"What, then? If you mean to accost me or accuse me, have done with it!"

Vasily shook his head in apparent frustration. “God’s bones, woman, you’re a suspicious one, aren’t ya? I’m merely tryin’ ta make sure ya are who we think ya are!”

“*We?*”

“Yeah, *we*. I’m meant ta give a message ta tha priestess of tha faith travelin’ under tha name of Derya Asken after makin’ sure it’s really you. Er, really who ya say ya are.”

Moirne was intrigued, but not enough to immediately drop her cover. She began walking again, mainly so the barge behind them didn’t get too close. It forced Vasily to match her pace.

“What’s wrong with my name? Must I present my travel documents as proof of who I am?”

Vasily chuckled at this. “Sister, with enough coin, anyone can make whatever travel documents they want. Nah, I don’t care ’bout yer name. I’m just supposed ta ask ya somethin’ that an imposter wouldn’t know.”

Moirne assumed that whomever the message was from was the one really asking the question, not Vasily himself. “Fine, ask the question.”

Vasily furrowed his brow, as if making sure he remembered the question correctly. “I’m supposed ta ask if ya believe tha abbot of Septimo will make it through tha gates of Florentine.”

Moirne threw back her head and laughed. She immediately knew who had sent Vasily, and she silently admonished herself for not spending just a bit more time in Tuman.

It took a bit for her to regain her composure, but eventually she replied with a question of her own. “Let me guess, Vasily. Is the message you carry from Bishop Nicholas?”

“It’s from his office, yeah.”

Moirne smiled. “Then the answer is no, the abbot will not make it through. For the last time Bishop Nicholas saw the gates of Florentine, they were under construction, and carts of hay could not pass through them.”

Vasily nodded his head, acknowledging she had answered correctly. “Well, I’m glad ya get tha meaning of tha question, ’cause I sure don’t.”

“It’s the bishop’s twist on a joke about gluttony, Vasily. I’m sure he will explain it to you if you ask him.” Her nose tingled, as she remembered the amount of ale that had gone through it when the bishop had first told her his unique punchline. If nothing else, he had impeccable timing.

“Sounds like a joke my father would tell, so I think I’ll just let it go,” Vasily said without humor. He reached into his cloak and drew forth a somewhat flattened scroll that was sealed with red wax. “Anyways, here’s tha message.”

When Moirne took the scroll from him, she could see that the mark of the bishop of Tuman had been made on the seal. She nodded and stowed the document within her own cloak, intending to read it when she had a bit of privacy back on Olek’s boat. “Is a response expected from me?”

“Didn’t say, so I assume not.”

“Very well. Is payment expected from me?”

He hesitated, then shook his head. "Nah, I got paid in full. Enough ta keep me mouth shut for quite a while, too."

A point for honesty, at least. No need to remind him about what the scriptures say about breaking oaths.

Moirne nodded again. "Very well. I thank you for your discretion, and I would be pleased to buy you a drink when we reach Stren."

Vasily shook his head. "We'll see, Sister. Er, m'lady. Tha way tha winter weather is settin' in, I aim ta get back south as soon as possible. If ya don't see me at tha Wild Boar while in Stren, maybe you'll catch me back in Tuman someday."

Moirne reasoned that neither of them had a great desire to break bread with the other in the future, but she smiled and shook hands with him all the same before they went their separate ways.

***

Greetings and Salutations, Sister Dreya:

Much time has passed since you have graced my presence, Sister. So much time, in fact, that I have apparently forgotten your name, or at least, I remember you by a different name than what you go by now. No matter, the woman I once knew and believe you to be is indeed one with the Almighty, whose omniscience surely outweighs what little I know or remember. But what I do recall is a certain young acolyte spewing ale all over me a long time ago in response to a farcical joke I had just told. If you have a similar recollection, then this letter will find its way into your hands, and you are, hopefully, in both good health and sound mind as you read it.

I am saddened that you did not have time to locate and greet this old man on your way through town, but I know someone in your position has many important matters to attend to. There are probably quite a few issues you are dealing with that I do not know about or understand, which is as it should be. However, I must warn you that there are others here in Tuman that do not take their ignorance of your reasons for traveling north as lightly as I do.

It is strange for a woman to travel alone in the Wilds, no matter the time of year and no matter her vocation. You were bound to attract attention here, although if I remember your mannerisms correctly, this does not concern you in the least. In any event, a number of inquiries were made about you around town, but to my knowledge, no one was able to ascertain your true calling.

This lack of understanding may actually make things worse for you in the short term, as most people underestimate what a single priest or priestess can do. The specific people I am thinking of in this case would have deemed you harmless if they knew you to be "just" one of the clergy. I suppose that it is my fault for not having enough homilies on the terrestrial reach of the church. Not that the people in question would have heard them anyway. No matter, I shall continue to castigate them in their absence every Sabbath.

While I have no doubt you have little interest in the petty crimes taking place in Tuman, the petty minds performing them cannot fathom that the appearance of anyone, or anything, out of the ordinary has nothing to do with them. To that end, my child, know that messages via homing pigeon have been sent north to warn the local authorities of your pending arrival.

I do not believe it will take much time for you to quickly clear matters up in Stren when you do arrive. However, the local priest, a certain Father Malachi Ghent, will be able to assist you in any way you see fit. He is a soul who is beyond reproach. I daresay the manner in which he professes his faith in both words and action puts me to shame. And he is even likable! A rare breed these days, an overly pious person who is also not overly judgmental or full of themselves.

Regarding Father Malachi, I do have one request to make of you. Recently, when I had the opportunity to correspond with him, he mentioned the fear of a growing darkness in the Wilds around Stren and Mount Iklo. I have forwarded various messages of his on this issue to Velych, where, hopefully, they have not been ignored or overlooked by our estimable archbishop. I would ask that you make an effort to speak with Father Malachi and inquire about any recent findings of his. He is not prone to spouting old wives' tales. Perhaps this is the actual reason for your travels, in which case I urge both speed and caution.

I will pray for your safe arrival and for success in whatever mission you find yourself embroiled upon. If your return south brings you through Tuman, I would welcome your face at my humble dinner table so that we may reminisce about old times and drink to each other's health. Perhaps, however, I shall sit just a bit farther away from you this time.

Yours in Iesu,

Bishop Nicholas Zaleski

***

Sitting on her bunk on Olek's barge, Moirne reread the letter, berating herself once more for not stopping to see the bishop on her way through Tuman. He obviously knew something about why she was traveling north, and she had simply bypassed him in her haste! And beyond that, she knew him to be an old friend.

There should always be time to see a friend. You went out of your way to see Aery and gather what information she had, didn't you?

Sighing to herself, she carefully folded up the document and stowed it away, deep in her bag next to her inquisitorial brooch. She smiled at the sight of the small piece of jewelry with its encircled crux decussata. While she still believed that discretion about her true identity had been the best course of action to take so far, there was a time coming in the very near future when the full weight of the inquisition would be required. She could feel it in her bones.

Barring another storm, the barge would dock in Stren on the morrow. She made a mental note of the exact position of her brooch and then closed the satchel.

CHAPTER EIGHTEEN
The Human Condition

It was well after Compline by the time Lianne and her entourage made it back to their temporary residence from the castle. Mikhal had decided to accompany them back from the banquet, much to her annoyance. Symon had been right about his counterpart's constant fawning over people in power, and it was getting tiresome after just two days. It had taken her resorting to feigning fatigue from the long day to make him retire without insisting on coming into the mansion to make sure everything was suitable.

"Doesn't he realize that he's too old for you?" Olesea muttered as she and Lianne stood close to each other, watching Mikhal's carriage make its way back towards the castle. Most of his security detail were going with him, but two soldiers had conspicuously stayed behind to stand guard at the entrance to the residence.

Symon had warned Lianne earlier in the day that Astrikhon soldiers would be posted around the property, and city patrols would be doubled in the surrounding area, ostensibly to protect her from any local public nuisance. Given that the streets were completely deserted, Lianne didn't need her dragoman to tell her the real reason for the increased security.

While there still had been no public declaration, there were plenty of rumors swirling about the ongoing border problem with one of the orc tribes. Quite a few of the courtiers present at tonight's banquet had been obviously nervous, and there had been some notable absences from those who had attended on the first night. And that, of course, included King Haldir himself!

What news the Perizidon delegation had of the orc incursion was secondhand at best, but what little news they *had* heard wasn't encouraging. Lianne rubbed her forehead, as she really did have the start of a headache.

It's not like everything else is going perfectly. I don't need Symon to tell me that, either.

After dismissing everyone but Olesea, she turned to walk for a spell in the cool, night air within the garden that surrounded the mansion on three sides. Several of her own soldiers were already patrolling the area immediately around the building, but they recognized her and gave them a wide berth.

"Did you hear what I said, m'lady? About that pandering old man?"

"Oh, Ole, he's not *that* old. Regardless, I do not believe Dragoman Balakiv wants to sard me personally. I get the feeling he's been told to try and sard all of us."

Lianne muttered the last sentence, but her companion heard it anyway.

"What?! M'lady, like any of us would find him appealing! Although perhaps Anichka would take him on."

"Ole!" Lianne immediately regretted her play on words, but

Olesea wasn't going to let her off easily.

She leaned in, grinning. "Well, she's used to dealing with small needles, isn't she?"

"Olesea, that is enough! You know that is *not* what I meant," Lianne said as she nudged her lady-in-waiting sharply, but she couldn't keep a smile off her own face.

Olesea glanced around to make sure they were truly alone. "Well, m'lady, I just wish the crown prince had escorted you back instead of that dragoman. I'd, for sure, throw myself in front of you to stop *his* sword."

"Olesea Rudenko!" Lianne looked at her companion with mocked shock.

"What?! He's witty, seems smart enough, and he's certainly easy on the eyes. Never mind that he's a prince. I think he's a perfect match for me. And I'm certainly better for him than those trollops that always seem to hang about him."

Lianne sniffed and ignored Olesea's attempt to draw her into a debate about Hadeon's potential matrimonial matches, even though she herself had definitely formed opinions about the three young women who were constantly vying for the prince's attention.

"Well, I shall be sure to tell the prince to be careful where he steps the next time you are near him, given the wet trail you'll be leaving on the ground."

Olesea laughed. "Guilty as charged, m'lady! I suppose it was just as well that you sent me away for a spell today, so I didn't embarrass myself in front of either of you."

Lianne stopped walking and turned to face the other young woman, instantly becoming serious. There had been no time earlier in the evening to privately ask Olesea whether she had been able to secure a meeting with the archbishop.

"And how did it go?"

"Quite well, m'lady. It took a bit of convincing to meet someone important at the cathedral. But that signet you gave me eventually got me into the archdeacon's office. He listened to your request and immediately agreed to arrange a personal audience between you and the archbishop."

"Wonderful! When can I see His Excellency?"

"It is set for later tonight, m'lady."

Lianne's eyes widened slightly at this pronouncement. "Tonight?!"

"Well, yes, m'lady, you told me the request was urgent. And what with the ball scheduled for tomorrow night, and then that wild boar hunt that we heard about today, and then the Sabbath, and then—"

"Yes, yes, I see." She hadn't told Olesea the real reason behind the urgent request, that Major Bannik was becoming more insistent by the hour that they leave for home as soon as possible. Still, Lianne was glad that her attendant had pressed for the meeting. "Are we already late?"

"No, m'lady. The archdeacon said he would be able to track when we retired back here for the night and would only expect us sometime after that. I was going to tell you as soon as we got inside your residence."

Lianne nodded. It was no surprise that the archbishop would have spies within the royal court. Even if clergy weren't physically present at all the various court proceedings, they would still be aware of the accompanying intrigue.

Hopefully, whatever spies the king has within the church administration haven't caught wind of this late-night appointment. Even if it has nothing to do with him or his kingdom, it could raise unnecessary suspicions.

"Very well. Do you know the route we will take? We apparently have more guards here, as well as additional city patrols, to contend with now."

"Yes, m'lady. There are several side entrances to the mansion that the servants normally use. While Major Bannik has sentries posted at each one, it does not appear that there are Astrikhon soldiers anywhere but the main entrances in the front and back. I'll have to confirm this before we leave, but one of these side doors should be our way out of the residence."

"Are they unlit?"

"They are, m'lady. One in particular has a rather overgrown hedge next to it, as well, so we'll scout that one first."

"*We*?"

Olesea shrugged. "It is always good to have friends among the common soldiery."

Lianne briefly wondered exactly how friendly Olesea might be getting with the common soldiery, but she set the thought aside as her pulse quickened with excitement about what could be a very interesting evening.

"Very well. What next?"

"Once outside, we can exit the property through these very gardens. We just need to take care not to be seen by any patrols. Once off the property, there are any number of back streets we can take to get to the abbey grounds that are behind the cathedral. The abbey is surrounded by a high wall, but I have been given the location of a gate on the western side, which they use for deliveries. Once inside the abbey, we will be led to the archbishop."

"Excellent. And what are your thoughts on who should go on this little quest?"

Her lady-in-waiting smiled. "In my opinion, m'lady, the smaller the group, the better."

"How small, then?"

"Well, I'm good with a dagger, at least good enough to hold off any random beggar we meet along the way. We certainly don't need any soldiers clanking around in armor, drawing attention to us. I wager just you and I can sneak out and back in again before anyone's the wiser."

Lianne chuckled. "You are a veritable spymaster, Ole! But I suppose you haven't discussed this plan with Dragoman Chumak yet? He, at least, will need to know what is going on."

Olesea grimaced, and she shuffled her feet a bit in the gloom. "Uh, no, m'lady. There hasn't been time. I, uh, have yet to inform the major of the overall plan either."

Lianne felt her head pound. Even under the best of circumstances, she knew that the commander of her security escort would not want her creeping around the dark alleyways of a strange city in the middle of the night. And that was before the added worry over what may or may not be happening elsewhere in the kingdom was added into the mix.

None of this meant that Olesea hadn't accomplished exactly what she had been tasked with, though, and Lianne smiled at her with real affection. "Well, Ole, you have done a masterful job in planning this escapade. It really should be me that bears responsibility for sharing the plan with the others, so let us retire inside, and I will do just that immediately. I feel as though we should leave rather soon, while the night is still young."

***

"Forgive me for being blunt, Your Highness, but this so-called plan of yours reeks of lunacy!" Major Bannik snapped, glowering at Lianne.

They were with Symon in his temporary study, and Lianne had just completed her description of the intended foray to the abbey.

"What if you are caught? What if the random patrol who seizes you doesn't believe who you are? Do you really want to be thrown into the gaol for Almighty knows how long until we can rescue you?"

Lianne was ready for the pushback. "I shall wear my royal signet and—"

"They would assume it is a stolen trinket, Your Highness."

"—and I shall have the documents to be delivered to the—"

"It is doubtful that their common soldiery can read, Your Highness."

"—to the archbishop, which I can use to prove the importance of my—"

"Your Highness would willingly give up private documents of the church to save your skin?"

Lianne's face grew hot at being interrupted several times over, and she literally stamped her foot. "Of course not, Major! All I am saying is that there are multiple ways to prove I am not a petty thief skulking about in the night!"

"Your Highness, I cannot condone this course of action!" The major's eyes flashed dangerously, and Lianne unconsciously took a step back as the soldier gestured first at the dragoman and then herself. "We have sworn an oath to protect you, Your Highness, and that includes protection *from yourself*. Even if we did not have a horde of greyskins marauding ever closer to the city, I cannot have you sneaking about in the dark! This is needlessly rash."

Lianne could feel her face grow even hotter. "You believe it rash to attempt stealth over brawn in this situation, Major?"

"Your Highness, might I—" Symon attempted to intervene only to be cut off by the major.

"Even if your entire plan wasn't completely ludicrous in nature, Your Highness requires more protection than your winter cloak and your handmaiden's dagger. Your mother *personally* ordered me to never let you go *anywhere* unescorted."

"Then you have failed your orders every time I have gone to the privy!" Lianne retorted in a raised voice. She slammed her fist down on the dragoman's desk, realizing that she likely looked like her father when he was enraged. "My mother may wish for me to have a nursemaid, but I am quite capable of wiping my own arse and making my own decisions on where I walk and who I walk with!"

"Your Highness, *please*!"

Symon had gasped at her outburst and now stepped forward to insert himself physically between her and Major Bannik, wringing his hands. The major had snapped to full attention at the start of Lianne's eruption and was now staring straight ahead at the wall.

An icy silence descended upon the group as Lianne looked back and forth between her advisors, both of her fists clenched. It was just the three of them in the room, but she was sure the guards outside the door had heard the commotion.

Lianne took a deep breath and folded her hands in front of her waist before addressing the other two. "As I have already said, I have a diplomatic matter to resolve with the church. Specifically, I must speak with the archbishop of Boloto. It is a simple mission, but it was entrusted to *me*, and to me *alone*, both by my father and the inquisition. I cannot merely send the documents with a courier, even someone trusted by all of us in this room."

Neither the dragoman nor the major spoke, so Lianne continued in what she hoped was a more conciliatory tone.

"I share your combined hesitancy in trusting King Haldir and the Astrikhon court, but even if they *could* be trusted, I do not believe this religious matter involves them. That is why I have arranged this meeting outside of normal channels. I did not realize until just a few moments ago that the meeting with the archbishop would be held tonight. Otherwise, I would have alerted both of you of my plans earlier. As it is, having the meeting tonight is fortuitous given the disturbance that is ongoing in this kingdom. With the treaty signed this morning, and this personal task resolved, we will be free to leave as early as tomorrow morning if the security risk warrants it."

Lianne knew she was stretching things a bit, but despite her previous outburst, she still tried to appease the major somewhat with her last statement. However, she knew it would be pointless to try and convince the older woman to go along with any version of her plan to see the archbishop.

Will she actually stop me from going? Where does her duty to my mother stop and her duty to me begin?

Lianne looked at Symon instead. "With a small group, we have the best chance to succeed. The abbey is not far from here, and there are numerous back streets we can use to avoid the city patrols. It is getting quite cold tonight, so there will be very few random people out. I shall not tarry."

The dragoman raised his own clenched fists to his forehead,

his eyes closed. He appeared to be thinking of a charitable response, and Lianne waited for him to make up his mind.

He finally looked at her, pleading with both his eyes and his tone. "You are your own woman, Your Highness, but I would beg that you trust those of us who would advise you on the best course of action to take. Know that our words are based upon our experience and our sworn fealty to both you and your parents. Please, remember that you are the future of our kingdom!" He glanced at the major, who remained motionless and silent, before continuing. "Your Highness, if you truly want to do this, at least take a soldier or two with you. Four would be preferred. We do not know these streets at all, and we are blind to what true risks there may be."

Lianne looked at him, annoyed. *Would you be saying this if I was a prince and not a princess? What if Lucas was my age and here instead of me?*

Symon must have sensed her mood, as he put his hands together as if in supplication. "Please, Your Highness. When have you ever seen your father walk about in his own city, in his own kingdom, unescorted? Better to have some protection against the unknown, and the unknowns are far greater here than back in Velych."

She swallowed at this and briefly reconsidered. *He is right of course. Father always has at least one guard with him. And Olesea may be trained in sword work, but not like the soldiers have been.*

After a moment, she made a short bow to Symon. "I see

your point, Dragoman. Thank you, as always, for your timely advice."

Symon coughed lightly. "Your Highness, I would also suggest that you pretend to be your own servant. What I mean is, it will still look odd for a foreign noble to dispatch messengers in the middle of the night to do their bidding, but it is not irregular. You should still be afforded some modicum of respect if a patrol catches you. But there will be less, uh, diplomatic fallout if they believe they have only caught a few ladies-in-waiting with an escort doing the bidding of their princess, as opposed to the princess herself."

Lianne thought this was a wonderful idea. "Very well, Symon. I will eschew any personal royal signet but will be sure to carry the mark of Perizidon upon my person."

As he bowed and took a step back, she turned towards Major Bannik and attempted to be as diplomatic as possible in her tone and demeanor.

"Major, I would have you pick two soldiers you believe to be best suited for this type of situation. They will accompany me and my personal guard as quickly and as quietly as possible to the abbey."

The major gave her a crisp king's salute but refused to look anywhere but straight ahead. "Your Highness, I will do as ordered. They will be waiting for you in the main hall." She turned and exited the room without another word.

***

A short time later, Lianne exited through one of the mansion's servant doors with Olesea and two soldiers. When she had met the soldiers before starting out, she had been pleased to see that one of them was Ivan Kushnir. Lianne knew that his calm demeanor would work well in any situation they might encounter and had greeted him with a warm smile and kind words. He had simply returned her salutation in his typical polite and professional way.

The other soldier, younger and shorter than Ivan, had given his name as Gideon. Lianne didn't know him other than by sight, but she assumed he was well-qualified. The major might not agree at all with what Lianne was doing, but she would never compromise the mission out of spite.

Lianne and Olesea had both changed into dark robes that covered hunting outfits and boots. Olesea carried the satchel that Lianna had received from Moirne, but neither had a lantern or torch. Both guards had changed out of their banded armor and helms in order to move more quietly. The women were armed with functional daggers, while the men had kept their short swords that were conveniently sheathed in dark scabbards.

The quartet exited the mansion's garden quietly, taking care not to be seen by the Astrikhon guards posted at the front and back of the property. The overcast night hid what moon there would have been, making their escape much easier. Turning south, away from the main avenue, they were quickly lost in the shadows that shrouded the back streets of Boloto.

The journey was relatively short and uneventful. The market district was in the opposite direction they were traveling, so there were no taverns or wayward drunks to avoid. Only one city patrol passed them, and they were loud enough to give fair warning of their approach to allow Lianne and her escort time to scurry down a side alleyway and remain out of sight.

The wall surrounding the abbey was soon before them, imposing and monolithic in the dim light. Olesea motioned them to go right, and they made their way to the delivery gate. It was a wide double gate, meant to allow for horse-drawn wagons to be led through it, but there was a wicket door to one side that the group approached. The whole gate was set into the wall, giving them some cover as Olesea quietly rapped on the sturdy wooden structure.

After a wait that was long enough for Lianne to become anxious that another patrol would stumble upon them, the small door opened a crack and a cowled figure peered out at them, a shaded lantern in hand. The quartet was quickly beckoned inside the wall, and the door was shut and bolted quietly behind them.

Without any salutation, the hooded figure led them down a cobblestone drive before turning to the left and disappearing between two storage buildings. Not wanting to be left behind, Lianne and the others hurried forward and, after a few more steps, found themselves in a small garden courtyard.

They were immediately confronted by four people, with the three newcomers also wearing long, hooded cloaks. The one who had granted them entry still held their lantern, but the others were brandishing maces as if expecting trouble.

Olesea immediately maneuvered herself between them and Lianne. She slowly extended her hands, palms facing outward, to show she held no weapon. Ivan moved to stand next to Lianne, hand on his sword hilt, while the other soldier closed up to protect her from the rear. She saw Ivan tense, no doubt readying himself for the worst.

"What is going on here? Are we not expected?" Lianne called out sharply, her skin tingling.

The shade on the lantern was opened fully, casting its light directly on her. She winced slightly in the brightness as she was studied carefully for a moment before both the lantern and maces were lowered.

"My apologies, Your Highness," came a voice from the shadows behind the hooded figures, and a fifth robed person moved forward into the now slightly diminished circle of light. The newcomer was an older man with greying hair. His robe was similar to the others but with the hood down so Lianne could see his weathered face. He bowed low to her.

"I am Archdeacon Theodore Malin. Again, my apologies for the discourteous reception. We had to be sure it was you."

Lianne had partially recovered her poise. She realized that she was a stranger to them, no matter what Olesea had told the archdeacon earlier in the day. She gave a slight curtsy, even though her station did not require such a response, but she also couldn't help but tweak their collective religious noses.

"Thank you, Archdeacon. I would have hoped your men

would pack extra oil for their lamps as opposed to weapons while they waited for an expected guest, but no harm has been done."

The slightest flicker of emotion crossed the archdeacon's face, but he simply matched her theological wit. "I doubt there will be a wedding feast tonight, Your Highness. But as the Almighty's parable instructs us, we do remain ever vigilant for the coming of the bridegroom. Please, allow me to escort you to the archbishop."

The courtyard turned out to be an antechamber of sorts, leading into a much larger garden area filled with various trees and other plantings. The overall space was dimly lit, enough for the small party to make their way without fear of tripping over unseen landscaping. After a dozen paces or so, they reached a narrow flagstone pathway which led towards several buildings.

The cathedral loomed in the distance, marking the very front of the large, enclosed space Lianne and her escorts found themselves in. It became quickly apparent that was not where they were being led, as the archdeacon turned to the right to head towards what appeared to be a barracks of sorts. It was a long, single-storied building made from roughly hewn stone, with large wooden doors in the center of it.

Two more hooded figures stood outside the doors, and one of them pulled open one-half of the double door for the group as they approached. Only the archdeacon entered the building with Lianne and the rest of her group, and the door closed behind them with a solid *thud* to accentuate their isolation from the outside world.

They had entered a good-sized room with a series of wooden tables in it, laid out for serving perhaps two score of people at a time. A large fireplace was opposite the doors they had entered, and a small but bright fire was burning in it. Several lit lanterns were spread around the room on some of the tables, creating a cacophony of shadows across the ceiling and walls. Lianne could make out a small form sitting at one of the tables closest to the fire, facing the flames.

The archdeacon turned and bowed to the group again.

He addressed Lianne directly. "Your Highness, the archbishop awaits you by the fire. He felt this arrangement would provide a bit more privacy than the cathedral."

Lianne smiled. "A man after my own heart, Archdeacon. Thank you for guiding us here."

He nodded, then gestured at her escorts. "As you can see, the archbishop is alone, and I promise you that he is armed only with his sharp wit and tongue. I would request that your companions remain with me."

"Of course, Archdeacon," Lianne said immediately, and she held out her hand for the satchel that Olesea had been carrying with her.

The other woman handed it over and, bowing to her, wordlessly turned with the two soldiers and followed the elderly man to a doorway on the left side of the large hall. Lianne turned and made her way slowly towards the fire, clutching the bag that the inquisitor had entrusted to her with both hands.

A simple delivery mission, perhaps, but hopefully, the rewards are more than a prayer of blessing.

The archbishop remained facing the fireplace as she approached, and she could see that he held a simple wooden walking stick in his hands. As she got within a pace or two of him, he stirred, turning slightly to look over his right shoulder to see who was there. He, too, was wearing the robes of a common monk, and as he slowly rose to greet her, he pulled back the hood to reveal his head. It was all Lianne could do to not grimace when she beheld his mottled, wrinkled face.

Oh my...I knew he was old, but he looks to be every bit of seventy! Let us hope he is more attuned to the ways of the world than Archbishop Dorjan.

Lianne quickly put the bag down on an adjacent table and performed a deep curtsy. "Princess Lianne Kalchik of Perizidon, Your Excellency. It is an honor to meet you."

"Ah, my dear princess. I am Archbishop Petr Venko, at your service. It is wonderful to finally make your acquaintance. I have heard about you for some time now."

This statement surprised Lianne. "Me, Your Excellency? I certainly have not done anything of note."

"*Yet*, Your Highness." Now that he was fully facing her, the archbishop managed to slowly perform a stately bow.

He was quite short, perhaps due to his advanced age, and Lianne had the odd sensation of having to look down at him, even when he straightened back up.

"You haven't done anything of note, *yet*. But based upon your lineage and your upbringing, there is much you could do for or against the church."

"Against the church?!" Lianne was aghast at his remark. "Your Excellency! Please forgive this wretched soul if I have given any indication to anyone that—"

He held up his hand for silence, and she broke off speaking, troubling thoughts immediately racing through her head.

What have I done? Did I fail some test of the inquisitor? Has his counterpart in Velych poisoned his opinion of me?

The archbishop reached out to put a trembling hand on her shoulder. "Forgive me, my child. I suspect that you know less of your precarious situation than I assumed. Please, come and sit with me. It appears we have much to discuss in a short amount of time."

His eyes had a kind look to them, and Lianne took a deep breath and nodded her head. Still, her mind raced with questions.

Already this interview has gone sideways. By "precarious situation," does he mean an invasion of Perizidon by the Rus? Or does he have news of what's going on here in Astrikhon? Or is this something altogether different?

The old man gestured towards the opposite side of the table he had been sitting at and went to sit down again. After retrieving her satchel, Lianne sat down opposite him on a sturdily made wooden bench.

"I also apologize for the rudimentary nature of this setting," the archbishop said, waving his hands at the room, "but it affords secrecy of a sort in that there is nowhere for someone to hide while they attempt to eavesdrop on us. Would you care for some wine?"

Lianne was still thinking about what possibly could be wrong with either her or her kingdom, and it took her a moment to respond. "Wine? Uh, yes, Your Excellency. Thank you."

Archbishop Venko made a signal with his right hand, and a few moments later, a hooded figure came walking quickly over from the side wall.

"A large jug of wine with two mugs, if you please, Brother Marius. Oh, and a lantern as well."

"At once, Your Excellency!" The monk bowed and scurried away.

"Well, Your Highness, we must wait until the lantern arrives before I can inspect the documents that Grand Inquisitor Koval deemed necessary to send me via quite an unorthodox messenger. Might I inquire as to why you sit in front of me instead of the inquisitor herself?"

What an odd little old man. Still, he seems lucid enough.

She answered him directly. "The grand inquisitor initially intended to travel with me, Your Excellency, but she had urgent matters to attend to in the north of my kingdom. She said you are aware of why she is traveling in Perizidon."

The archbishop's face didn't betray any emotion, at least in the dim setting. "Where exactly in your lovely kingdom is she headed?"

"The— Uh, Mount Iklo, Your Excellency."

"Ah, I see. That mountain is in a rather remote area, at least based upon the cartography we have here in Boloto."

"Quite remote, Your Excellency. I have never seen it in person."

"Oh my, what a pity! I assume you wish to rectify this when you ascend to your kingdom's throne?"

Lianne nodded her head, thinking about her long-held obsession with The Mountain. "I do indeed."

"Is this desire based on the premise that a wise ruler should know the ins and outs of their entire territory? Or, perhaps, is this desire based upon some other, more fantastical reason?"

Lianne looked at him sharply, trying to keep a neutral look on her face. *Why did he ask that specific question*?

The archbishop merely smiled. "Oh, never mind, Your Highness. As with most desires, it is surely a mixture of various reasons that do not really concern me. Instead, tell me how your stay in Boloto has been so far."

Lianne reflected on the question for a moment, wondering how political her response should be. She must have taken too long to answer, because the elderly man coughed and beckoned at her.

"Come now, Your Highness. Do not worry about any court intrigue or scheming with me. Pretend you are at confession, if you are concerned about your words reaching the wrong ears. I would like, at least, to hear your honest assessment about the royal court."

Lianne paused yet another moment before answering him carefully. "My honest assessment is not very flattering for the majority of the court, Your Excellency. That is the reason for my hesitation."

"Since when are true confessions flattering, Your Highness? Although a confession is supposed to be self-reflecting in nature. Are you perhaps afraid that you see part of yourself, or your family, or even your kingdom, reflected in what you have encountered here?"

It was all Lianne could do to not scoff at this. "Hardly, Your Excellency," she said dryly.

"Hmm, I see. So, perhaps it is neither wrath nor envy, but rather pride that you should confess to me?"

Lianne quickly bowed her head so the archbishop couldn't see the anger that flared across her face. *This old man is every bit as bad as the inquisitor at twisting my words. I suppose he will throw them back at me now as well.*

However, there was nothing but a protracted silence from the other side of the table.

When she finally raised her eyes, she saw the archbishop regarding her calmly, his hands folded on the table.

"Peace be with you, my child. The Almighty already knows what is in your heart of hearts, and they are the ultimate judge of us all. We may discuss less onerous topics if you wish as we wait."

"I…" Lianne swallowed hard, then held her head high as she resolved to answer the archbishop's question truthfully but in a more gracious manner than she had been thinking. "I am eternally grateful that I have my father's example on how to rule both a kingdom and its people. I still have much to learn from him, as well as others. Perhaps part of my lessons is to observe that which I do *not* wish to be."

Archbishop Venko nodded. "A wise response, and I would respectfully agree with you. You mention your father. I have only met him twice, but my counterpart in Velych, and many others, have often spoken of his true nature over the years. Most consider him to be fair and just. Although"—and here he smiled— "any friend of Moirne Koval is automatically a saint in my book."

Lianne smiled back at him at this remark, thinking back on her extended conversation with the inquisitor. "The grand inquisitor can certainly be...intimidating."

He laughed. "Well, that is the nature of all inquisitors! Or at least, it is supposed to be. But please do not misinterpret my quip as disrespect or contempt of Grand Inquisitor Koval. On the contrary, I am grateful to know her and to have learned much from her over the years. I hope and pray this decrepit physical body of mine holds out long enough for me to see her once more on this plane of existence."

Lianne was somewhat puzzled by what the old man had inferred about knowing Moirne for a long period of time. *He looks old enough to be her grandfather. Perhaps she grew up here in the city?*

"You have known the grand inquisitor for some time then, Your Excellency?"

"Oh, yes. For many years. Many, *many* years..."

Just how old is the inquisitor, anyway?!

The archbishop's voice trailed away, and his eyes became vacant. Before Lianne could think of a question to call him back to the present, the monk named Marius was back with wine and light. These were enough to rouse the elderly priest from his momentary reverie.

After making the monk pour some wine into the mugs he had also brought and then shooing him away, the archbishop looked back at Lianne.

"Tell me, Your Highness, did Moirne brief you on this urgent matter of hers that took precedence over joining us here?"

Lianne took a small leap of faith. "You mean her quest, Your Excellency?"

"Hmm, yes, that is a decent word for it. Her quest."

Lianne paused to collect her thoughts and then attempted to quickly summarize her conversation with Moirne from roughly a week prior. The apparent invasion plans of Rusgorod, the reports of increased unholy activity in the northern reaches of Perizidon, and the planned trip of the inquisitor to the area surrounding Mount Iklo in search of answers were laid out for the archbishop in short order. He listened intently as Lianne spoke, drumming his fingers on the side of his mug and not interrupting.

He remained quiet for a spell after Lianne had finished her monologue, taking a long pull from his mug and then pouring himself some more wine. Finally, he nodded as if to himself.

"The grand inquisitor has kept me well informed of her

comings and goings over the years, and I assume most of what you have told me is included in the documents you have brought." He nodded at the satchel that was now next to the lantern and wine jug. "However, it is always good to have an accounting from someone whose ears and mind *might* be sharper than mine." He winked at her and took another sip of wine, but then his face and voice grew serious. "Did she mention the potential timeframe for an invasion from your estranged relative, or is that still speculative?"

Lianne sighed. "She did not say, but afterwards, my father told me our spies believe it will be within the next two years. I assume that he and the grand inquisitor spoke on this matter before she left."

"I see. And the reports she received from Archbishop Dorjan, what do you make of them?"

"I do not know what to make of them, Your Excellency. I must admit I find it hard to believe that evil from the abyss could stalk our lands without a general alarm being raised. Even in the Wilds around The Mountain."

"The Mountain?"

Lianne blushed slightly at her slip. "My apologies. That is the colloquial name for Mount Iklo."

"Ah, I see. Well, let me see what you have brought me." Putting down his mug, the archbishop reached over and carefully pulled the satchel closer to him. "What did your father make of the reports coming from the Wilds?" he asked almost nonchalantly as he undid the bag's buckles.

"He did not comment on them other than to say he trusted the grand inquisitor to get to the heart of the matter. And that he would follow the advice of the church in dealing with anything of substance."

"Anything of substance..." The archbishop grunted at this, but his attention was drawn to the stack of papers that had been disgorged onto the table. "Make yourself comfortable, Your Highness. I shan't be long." He motioned at the mug closest to her and then went to work.

Lianne sipped her wine carefully while watching the elderly churchman's eyes dart back and forth with purpose. She guessed that either he had a familiarity with what he was reading or most of it was uninteresting to him, given the speed at which he went through the stack of papers. She wondered how much of the documentation was tied to either the terrestrial or the infernal plot against Perizidon.

Archbishop Venko only lingered on one document that seemed innocuous enough amidst the rest. It was only a single piece of paper, but he seemed to read it through at least twice. When he held it up toward the lantern to inspect it more closely, Lianne could tell that it was a handwritten note without any apparent artwork or embellishments.

He looked up at her, the light from the lantern reflecting in his eyes, and gestured at her with the piece of paper. "So, Your Highness, what do you think of the inquisitor's so-called quest? Is she out of her mind, or perhaps just out of her jurisdiction?"

Lianne swayed back in her seat, surprised at the archbishop's directness. But he still had a serious look on his face and appeared to be waiting for a serious answer. She answered slowly, attempting to choose her words carefully.

"Well, Your Excellency, Grand Inquisitor Koval's arguments and explanations certainly made sense in the moment. My father corroborated what she discussed with me regarding the Rus. As to the reports regarding agents of the abyss prowling our lands, I have not seen them, but I take her at her word. I assume either my father or I could obtain some version of the reports from Archbishop Dorjan if there was a need to do so."

"Bless my counterpart's heart, but I doubt he remembers where those reports are filed, Your Highness. If anyone is tardy in answering the Almighty's call to come home, it is Nazar Dorjan."

Archbishop Venko made the sign of the cross and took a deep drink from his mug while Lianne almost dropped her own mug in surprise. The archbishop looked at the document in his hand again, and then again at her. The look on his face was as somber as it had been all night.

"No, Your Highness, I was speaking more to Moirne's desire to find a connection between the two issues. We have called it a quest in our conversation tonight. There are some in the church hierarchy who call it a fanatical crusade and would have her stopped at all costs."

Lianne was thunderstruck. "Your Excellency! Do they think she is lying?!"

"Not consciously. However, they think she has been blinded by matters pertaining to her basic human emotions. That she is no longer a neutral party to the coming war between two kingdoms who are equals in the eyes of the church. That she will stretch the limits of reason to bring the weight of the Almighty onto the side of Perizidon, no matter the cost to herself or those around her.

"Specifically, that Grand Inquisitor Moirne Koval is blinded by the love she holds for your father and will do anything to protect him and his family."

EPILOGUE

Sending a Message

Sarl stood in the shadows between the shells of two burned-out cottages, looking out towards the deserted street. It was hard to make out much detail under the cloudy night sky, but he knew where he was all the same. It had been years since he had been here in person, and he had no intention of ever going back.

There was a rustling noise in the darkness behind him, but he already knew who it was and didn't bother to turn around. She had called him here, after all. The smell of lavender was there as she walked up to stand next to him, and his senses tingled. It was almost as if they were truly together.

"Why'd ya bring me back here, Sister? Ya know I can't stand this place. I don't even like ta think of it."

"Because no one would suspect we would meet here, Sarl. And I don't know how closely you're being watched now." Elise spoke calmly, and he assumed she was staring straight ahead at the street just like he was.

Our street. Our town. Our past...

"What, just 'cause that infernal can't take a shot ta tha gut, ya think tha unholy powers got it out for me now?"

He felt her shift, and he matched her movements so that they wound up facing each other. He could tell she was looking up at him, but he couldn't see what emotions might be playing across her face.

"I just don't know, Sarl. I have prayed on the matter, but the Almighty has not provided me with further insight."

"Huh, imagine that..." Sarl muttered, and instantly regretted saying it. "Uh, sorry, Sister."

She ignored his blasphemous comment and continued. "That infernal beast sensed me when I called out to you, Sarl. You guessed as much, even before I could warn you to break our connection, and I am indebted to you that you suffered so to protect my identity. But I am sure the Unholy One will not be easily deterred in trying to find out more about both of us, now that they know there are more artifacts from the old times still active. Even here, we shouldn't tarry for too long."

She's probably right. Ya know better than ta question her on anythin' that takes more than pure cunnin' ta figure out. Especially when it comes ta how these meetings work.

It had taken quite a bit of trial and error over the years, but Elise had somehow discerned how to use the sending stones they carried as talismans to communicate directly through their dreams. She could now even bring their spirits together at any location they had both experienced enough in the real world that there was a residual imprint in their minds. He had heard her call tonight and had been willingly led through the strands of their combined memories to meet her.

But he had been completely surprised when he arrived in the alleyway, as she had always picked a more pleasant place to meet. Usually, it was a lively tavern in Velych, where they could dance. A few times, it had been a grove of birch trees just outside Stina, where they could lie in a field of clover and watch the stars. It had never been here, never the place that had seen their fates change in an instant many years ago.

Sarl turned away from Elise, and they stood side by side again, looking out at the cobblestones. He could almost see the corpse lying where he had left it in the middle of the street, twisted and torn and waiting for the night patrol to find it. He tensed involuntarily. He wanted it to be there, so he could spit in the dead man's face again.

He found himself holding her hand, and he squeezed it. "I miss ya, Sister. But I'll never miss this place."

He felt her squeeze his hand back and lean her head against his shoulder. Even though they were but spirits in the immaterial world of dreams, it felt real enough.

"Would you still do it all again, Sarl? Knowing the pain and heartache your actions that night have brought you?"

It was a rhetorical question at this point, one he had answered many times before. He could see the body now, as well as the blood running in rivulets between the cobblestones. Its dead eyes silently tried to pierce his soul, but he shrugged off their effect and just stared back. He couldn't see the ragged scrap of paper that was stuck in the front pocket of the corpse's tunic, but he definitely remembered the words he had scrawled on it in Orcish.

Sometimes dogs bite back

At the time, he had thought it an ironic touch to leave the note on body of the bastard who had raped and killed his sister. He smiled in satisfaction even now.

So what if tha bastard was tha sheriff of Stina...

"'Course I would, Ellie. Ya know that."

She sighed and said nothing more on the matter. They had argued many times over the state of his soul, and seeing the scene of his cold-blooded murder wasn't going to change any feelings or beliefs for either of them.

Elise let go of his hand and instead looped her arm through his, remaining close to him. There was a slight breeze, but only the illusion of the cool night surrounded them. Eventually, time moved forward and she spoke again.

"Anyway, my dear, I wanted to warn you that we should probably limit our communication for the time being so that it is harder for others to track our respective locations. I do not want you to come to any more harm, especially if it can be avoided."

Sarl chuckled. "So, ya call out ta see me just ta tell me that we shouldn't see each other?"

"It's more than that, Sarl!" Her voice seemed strained, and for an instant, her body shifted slightly, as if she was tossing and turning in real life in her bed far from where they stood. "It's not just this formal type of meeting we need to be worried about. You already know that we can sense when one or the other is in danger or under a large amount of stress, right? Well, you should know that you were transmitting your emotions quite clearly the other night!"

"Whaddya mean, tha other night? I wasn't in any—" Sarl stopped talking, and he felt his face grow hot.

Elise turned towards him again, and she reached up to lightly rap his chin. "Not in any danger, my dear? Are you sure?"

Sarl managed to smile, but he kept his teeth hidden. "Guess I'm 'bout ta find out, huh?"

She rose up on her toes and kissed him gently on his cheek. "Oh, Sarl. We had our chance to be together, a very long time ago now. I have no right to deny you anything in this world, even if you might catch the great pox from your actions."

"Ouch, woman."

"Yes, the great pox would be quite painful, my dear. But all I am really trying to say is to be careful whenever you may find yourself in a highly emotional state, regardless of the emotion. Perhaps the next time you find yourself in such a state, you should remove your talisman. That way, the chance for any transmission of, uh, inner conflict, is eliminated. For both of us."

Elise added the last sentence as a throwaway, but Sarl still knew her better than most.

He kept his voice carefree, but he could feel his pulse quicken. "So...ya got some inner conflict goin' on 'bout me then?"

Elise shook her head slowly, and he swore he heard her sigh. "No more than I always do, my dear *Sirry Vovk*. But my vows remain in place, despite your best efforts to tear them asunder."

Sarl looked down at her. The shadows were deep enough

that it was still hard to read the look on her face, and the setting's dreamlike effect would have obscured any minute details anyway. "Ellie, I'm sorry. Ya know I don't ever want ta hurt ya."

"We swore our love to each other many moons ago, *Sirry Vovk*. But love can take many forms, and you are still dear to me for many reasons. And none of those reasons want you taking unnecessary risks."

Sarl decided not to ask if she meant the risks of sleeping with someone of questionable repute or taking on an infernal in hand-to-hand combat. And he certainly wasn't going to ask why she was using her old term of endearment for him.

But I guess that answers tha question 'bout whether passionate thoughts can be passed through tha stones, don't it.

He knew it would soon be time to go. He wished that the moon would break free from the clouds for just an instant so he could get a good look at her, but the night would remain dark. After all, it was how he had managed to elude the town guards and escape into the Wilds after cutting the sheriff open from head to toe.

Sarl was sure she wouldn't be able to see his face either, but he smirked all the same and tried to keep things light. "Well, you're dear ta me too, Yer Holiness. So, I'll try an' be careful. I promise."

She chuckled at his statement. "Don't make unkeepable promises, Sarl. I only ask that you be vigilant."

"Fair 'nough, Sister." He bowed to her and kissed her hand gently.

Elise stepped forward to hug him close for an instant before releasing him. They stood facing each other, and she didn't seem to know what to do with her hands. As the strands of their dreams began to unwind from each other, the image of her face cleared for a moment, and Sarl could see her smile at him before she blurred from view and was gone.

He called out to her anyway. "Goodbye...*Soloveyko*..."

The connection was broken, and the dreamworld shifted back into another reality. Only the barest whisper of what had transpired remained for someone, or something, to find. Old magic was funny that way, after all, as not even the masters of a bygone era ever learned exactly how it worked.

Thank you for reading my book!

Stay tuned for more adventures in Book Three, The Enemy Within.

www.ingramcontent.com/pod-product-compliance
Lightning Source LLC
Chambersburg PA
CBHW060552310726
48982CB00008B/1104/J

* 9 7 9 8 9 8 9 8 7 5 4 2 9 *